SONG OF DESOLATION

BALLADS OF MAE
BOOK ONE

Salem Cross
www.Salemcrossauthor.com
Copyright © 2020 Salem Cross
All Rights Reserved
ISBN 978-1-7353482-0-9

SONG OF DESOLATION

BALLADS OF MAE
BOOK ONE

SALEM CROSS

To my dad who has always been my biggest fan

*To my mom who is always there for me when I
need her the most*

*To my husband who has encouraged me to
follow my dreams*

*To my fifth-grade teacher who I hated so much
that she inspired me to start writing just so I
could plot her demise*

At first glance, you would assume nothing out of the ordinary about the girl who stared back at me. She was pretty, maybe she could even be beautiful if she put a little effort into it. Yeah, maybe she seemed a little tired. Her tawny-colored skin looked a little pale. Even those wild, thick curls that were twisted into a bird's nest could be gorgeous after a few rounds with some hair products.

But that was just your first glance at her.

It would take you a second glance to notice something was off. My eyes, usually brown, had become a striking glowing violet color. The glow was eerie. Moving from my eyes downwards, you could just make out that same eerie glow running through a few small veins in my neck. That glow ran through my chest, arms, and even in my legs. The violet hue was dim now. The thirty to forty minutes I allotted myself to sleep before an alarm woke me up allowed me to gain just a little control over the energy humming right under my skin.

Lately, I had noticed even allowing myself that much time between alarms was becoming increasingly dangerous. Several times I woke up to the bed rattling, or more commonly, the tiles vibrating against my cheek. It was terrifying. At any given minute, my power was on the verge of finding release. If, one night, I was too tired to notice the heavy vibration or the shaking of my bed, I could bring the entire apartment building down simply by accident. I used to think the nights were the worst times, never being able to completely fall asleep; it was horrible.

Now, I knew that daytime was worse. Way worse. During the day there was the constant mental strain to hold back any leakage. Any extreme emotions, any time I got just a little bit too tired, or if I got a little too lost in my work, my mental hold on my power would slip and the world would quake around me. Windows and mirrors shattered; fire hydrants exploded; the roads cracked. It was a nightmare trying to keep on top of it. What was worse was that I knew my power was growing. The

Chapter One

The grimy, slightly damp, cold bathroom tile against my cheek would have once grossed me out. No matter how much I scrubbed with some of the toughest chemicals on the market, the black mold had permanently etched itself into the grout lines. The yellowish hue stubbornly clung to the tiles around the toilet. Even in college when I got shitfaced every weekend, I would have never put my face against something so filthy… but that was two years ago. Things had changed for me. Apparently, change meant my standards had dropped to an astonishing low.

In the other room (the only other room in the apartment), I could hear the eighth alarm on my phone go off. I listened to the beautiful crescendo of flutes and birds chirping, wishing it would just shut up. The moment the sound stopped I took a deep breath and pushed myself off the floor. In the downward dog pose, the room spun, and my stomach heaved. Luckily, I hadn't eaten in a full twenty-four hours or I would have thrown it up there on the bathroom floor. Once the nausea ceased, I reached up and used the counter to pull myself upright.

The only reason I looked in the mirror every day was to fix my wild curls, cover up the dark circles under my eyes, and to brush the bile off my tongue. The monster I found there was too terrifying to see for long. I took a deep breath, gritted my teeth, and pulled my gaze off the filthy sink. My eyes locked onto the creature I hated so much.

stronger it got, the harder it was to keep it at bay. Luckily, I had found something that helped.

I opened the small drawer under the counter and pulled out two gold roped cuffs. They were old. I'd found the antique cuffs at a pawn shop to use for the spell. There was nothing special about them. They were a bit bulky, but they did the job. Several months ago, I had summoned the spellbook that had appeared in my bedroom mirror when my power first emerged. After over a year of struggling, I prayed for a spell that would kill me. Instead, I found a binding spell. It was almost perfect. With this spell, I was able to go about my day without the threat of accidentally killing someone hanging over me. On top of preventing me from becoming a killer, with these bracelets on, the violet glow under my skin and in my eyes vanished.

Going through the motions as I did every Monday through Friday, I took a quick shower and applied just a little bit of makeup to cover up the lack of sleep. As I left the bathroom, I picked up the gold bracelets, and then I walked over to the small closet, grabbed clothes for work, and got dressed.

The studio apartment stunk. I could smell the mold in the walls. Mice scurried across the floor at night leaving their droppings in their wake. The walls were paper thin. I knew when my neighbors were home, when they were having sex, or when they were watching TV. With the state of the entire apartment complex like this, I was surprised my volatile power hadn't yet crumbled the building to the ground. Despite the less than stellar appearance and sketchy structural integrity of the building, it was better than sleeping in a tent, which was what I'd done for the past year. The rent was dirt cheap, which was rare in the city of Chicago and a godsend for someone who was trying to get back on their feet.

With a sigh, I slapped the bracelets onto my wrists. The searing pain that accompanied putting them on always caused my eyes to water. Immediately, my skin felt like it was shrinking.

An invisible noose slipped around my neck; my breathing came out as short gasps. My heart rate picked up and my bones felt brittle.

I hated these bracelets.

The anger I felt at the cards I had been dealt surged through me. Usually, feeling any strong emotion caused my power to leak out which, in turn, caused damage to things around me. When I wore these bracelets, my power was stopped short. Being unable to expel that pent-up energy caused a fiery pain to shoot through my body. I shuddered violently and found it harder to breathe.

Good. The bracelets still worked.

After I had regained my breath and the pain had subsided, I attempted to eat a power bar but choked on half of it. Frustrated, I threw the rest of it away. On my way out, I checked my camping gear sitting over by the front door. Every weekend, I escaped the heart of Chicago, opting to head to one of the many campsites on the outskirts of the city. At first, it was just for something to do, but for the past month my camping trips had been mandatory. My power was growing so fast that the build-up from lack of use during the weekday had become too intense, too painful, and too hard to keep at bay even with the spelled bracelets. Out there I could release some of the power that had built up which kept me sane enough to tackle the following week.

I left my apartment relieved it was Friday. Instead of heading straight to the office, I stopped at my boss's favorite café to pick up her coffee. It was the same drink made by the same barista every day, and every day Sharon spit it out and complained about the drink. But heaven forbid I went anywhere else and ordered the same drink…

From the café, I walked the eight blocks to the office building Sharon ran her real estate company out of. The city of Chicago was already bustling. People were always in a hurry. They brushed past me with their eyes plastered to their phone screens. Around me, cars honked, slammed on their brakes, and weaved through traffic. It was so loud here.

I hated the city.

Not just because of how busy the streets were, or how stale the city smelled, nor was it the self-centered assholes who had their faces buried in their phones. No, I simply hated the city because I knew that if I wasn't wearing these bracelets, I could bring down every building and kill everyone. That was enough to snuff out any fun I could have in a place like this.

Six months ago, I was walking the Appalachian Trail, alone and as content as someone could be who had no control over her body. I had walked the Trail for a year. Now I was here. Where I wanted to be was back in my house in Maryland, but there was nothing there for me anymore. My parents had died suddenly in a car accident, and I had dropped out of school due to the lack of control over my new ability. My closest friend, Rebecca Dewey, had ditched me the moment she found out I had power. Before I could hurt any of my other friends, I severed all contact and left.

No, there was nothing back home.

I approached my office building in a foul mood. My head was pounding. I should have been used to it by now since the headaches were a side effect of the bracelets. One of the glass doors opened, and someone walked out. I took the opportunity to slip inside the office building. As I did, my cell phone rang. Suppressing a sigh, I reached into my purse knowing who it was without having to check the caller ID. When I couldn't find it right away, I looked down, still rummaging through my purse with one hand while I held Sharon's coffee in the other. Blindly I walked forward towards the elevator.

My fingertips finally contacted my vibrating phone. Just as I pulled it out, I slammed into someone. I would have fallen backward if it weren't for a pair of strong hands that kept me standing. I gasped as the discomfort from my bracelets evaporated at the contact. I looked up and found myself staring into a pair of brown eyes.

The man had dark skin, short hair, and a salt and pepper goatee. He was tall, and his shoulders and chest were broad. Even in his expensive tailored suit, I could tell his arms were roped with muscle. I would have pegged him to be in his late forties or early fifties. The surprised expression on his face mirrored how I was feeling.

Where was the pain that came with wearing the bracelets?

How was it suddenly gone?

"Excuse me, I wasn't paying attention to where I was going," I said breathlessly.

The gentleman let go of me, and immediately I felt the effects of the bracelets again. I winced at the unexpected surge of pressure in my body. His expression changed from surprised to confused, and then to wary. His eyes narrowed, and I could have sworn he just took a deep breath as if to smell me. His gaze swept over me but paused when he caught a glimpse of the bracelets on my wrists.

A deep voice behind me asked, "Arthur, everything alright?"

The man I had bumped into, Arthur, did not answer his friend right away, but his gaze moved away from the bracelets to look behind me. I glanced over my shoulder to see another rather large man directly behind me. I watched as his whole body shook hard once as if he had been splashed with cold water. When he glanced in my direction, the newcomer's mouth popped open while his brows shot upwards. His hazel eyes looked down at me in wonder. This man was just as tall as Arthur, though he had sun kissed skin, jet black hair that was slicked back, a thick black beard, and appeared slightly leaner in stature.

"Who—what—" he stammered. The man closed his mouth but opened it as if to say something more, but nothing came out. He shut his mouth again. His expression shifted from surprise to suspicious, just as Arthur's had. This man's brows came together, and his lips turned downwards.

"I'm sorry, I've got to get going…" I was suddenly uncomfortable under their oddly piercing stares. I turned and scooted around Arthur.

Arthur turned with me. His brown eyes drifted over my face and the hairs on my neck rose. What creeps… Just a few feet away the elevator door dinged, and the doors opened. A single individual stepped out. Relieved that I had a chance to escape this bizarre encounter, I bolted.

As I hopped into the elevator, I sighed. I turned around as the elevator doors began to close. My stomach dropped as the bearded man stuck his arm in the closing the elevator doors, effectively stopping my escape. He stepped into the elevator and pushed the button that shut the doors. He turned to me and gave me a warm, albeit slightly bewildered, smile.

"Good morning. I apologize for making you uncomfortable back there. You took me by surprise, which on any other day, would be almost impossible to do."

Suspicious of his motives, I turned my body forward to face the metal doors.

"I wanted to check to see if you needed any help," the man continued as if I weren't ignoring him. I glanced over at him and found his attention pinned to the bracelets on my wrists. His eyes rose, and I met his gaze. His brows came together, and the corner of his lips turned downwards. "I usually get a pretty good read on people, and I can sense that you are a good person. The spell that coats your accessories… it was not intended for someone like you."

I jerked away from him as if he had slapped me. He *knew* about the bracelets and what they were doing. He knew about spells. I stared at him, stunned. I hadn't ever crossed anyone else like me… someone with extra abilities. My mind spun with a thousand questions, but which one to ask first?

"Whatever crime you have committed, it does not justify that type of punishment," the man told me. He reached into his suit pocket and pulled out a sleek yet simple business card. The elevator dinged as it alerted us that it had arrived on my floor, and the doors opened. "If you would like someone to look into your situation, please do not hesitate to contact me."

Still stunned, I reached out and took the card he handed me. As I stepped out of the elevator, trying to collect my thoughts but failing miserably, I was able to stupidly ask:

"Who are you?"

My voice came out strangled. The man smiled. As I inspected his face, I could see genuine concern for me.

"Zein Abad, a Guardian at your service, should you need it."

Zein bowed his head just as the elevator doors shut. Immediately I panicked, realizing I may have missed my only opportunity to talk to someone who had any type of information about what I was or how to control my power. Just as I reached out to push the button to call the elevator back, my phone began to vibrate again in my hand, pulling me out of my panic. I looked down to see Sharon's name on the caller ID.

Seeing her name and knowing the wrath I was about to endure snapped me out of my shock, and I hurried over to my desk. I answered it only to find she had already hung up. Oh boy, I was in for a huge lecture when she got in. Being her only administrative assistant, I got the worst of her ire. Karla quit the moment she had walked me through everything. Little did I know why she was so excited to leave.

Once I dropped my purse on my chair, I immediately listened to Sharon's furious voicemail. This took the same amount of time as it did to turn my computer on and load all one hundred and fifty-eight emails. I printed out Sharon's to-do list that she'd sent. On my way to the printer, I placed the coffee on Sharon's desk. When I attempted to call my boss back, she did not answer.

By the time Sharon walked into the office twenty minutes later, I had completed a handful of tasks she had marked as important on the to-do list. Her drawn-on brows were pulled together in a permanent scowl, and her pursed lips emphasized the wrinkles around her mouth. Her piercing gaze told me she was out for more blood than usual today. I braced myself for a rough day ahead of me.

By the time four o'clock rolled around, I was nauseous from the pounding in my head and from lack of food. I stood in front of Sharon, who sat in her rolling chair behind her desk. She stood and leaned forward, bracing her hands on her desk.

"Why are you so incompetent?" she demanded. "I told you to call Sheryl Stone and tell her that I need to reschedule my listing appointment. Why did Sheryl just call me asking where I was? Huh? Why don't you listen?!"

"Sharon, you told me to call her back last week when you realized you did have time. Here is the email you sent telling me this," I said and handed it to her.

She didn't even bother looking at it. Instead she took it from my hands, ripped it up and threw it on the floor.

"Pick it up and throw it away," she commanded me, her pupils narrowing. "Can you at least do something as simple as that?"

Sharon's cruelness was relentless. Every day it was the same thing. Constant haranguing, unreasonable demands, heavy workloads… Inside me, something snapped. What was I doing here? When I had been accepted for this job, I had been excited to start. As an employee under Sharon's prestigious realty firm, I knew the position would open doors for me. I could make connections with her high-end clients, and once I finished school, I had planned to use those connections to find a better job.

But just because I was desperate to jump back into the real world after a year of self-isolation, that didn't mean I had to suffer this horrible woman's abuse. Without another word, I turned and left Sharon's office. She shouted something about coming back, but her voice was muffled by a ringing in my ears. My body trembled, and I could feel the rush of my power surging just beneath my skin. I clenched my teeth in pain as my bracelets kept my power from leaking out. The pain was intense, but my rage was greater – at least for now.

I collected my few belongings from my desk and then shut down the computer. I could hear Sharon's chair roll against the plastic mat she had under her desk. She would be coming down that short hallway any second to berate me. As if on cue, I heard her footsteps storming towards me. I walked over to the elevator and pressed the down arrow.

"Where do you think you're going? If you don't get back to work this instant you're fired," Sharon said as she charged towards me. The elevator doors slid open. I stepped inside and pushed the button for the lobby. I turned and watched my now former boss.

"Good riddance!" she yelled just as the doors closed.

My adrenaline slowed, and the anger I felt suddenly did not outweigh the pain pulsing under my skin. The noose that always hung around my neck when I wore these stupid bracelets tightened the same time my skin felt like it went up in flames. I doubled over as my vision swirled. If I didn't get my anger under control, I was going to faint.

With several long deep breaths, I forced myself to calm down. I would not have to deal with that bitch again. This wouldn't be the only job in the city. I would find another. Until then I could take a nice long camping trip until I figured out what to do next. In just two weeks I would be starting school again, and then I could focus solely on that. For now, I would relax and take some time for myself.

By the time the elevator doors opened, the pain had subsided. I still felt slightly ill, but at least I could stand up straight and walk out into the lobby without looking like a drunkard. I left the building and headed home. With a deep breath, I tried to think positively. My vacation could start now. The sun was shining, the temperature was comfortable despite the constant wind that plagued the city, and there was still time to get out before the traffic became terrible.

I didn't make it far from the office before the hairs on the back of my neck stood on end. The uneasiness that crept down my spine was unnerving. With a nervous glance over my shoulder, I quickened my pace. I rounded the corner and almost ran into someone in my attempt to hurry home. I mumbled an apology to the elderly woman and scooted around her.

I glanced back over my shoulder, and my stomach dropped. Strolling confidently a few feet behind me was the gentleman I had run into this morning. Not Zein, but the other guy. The quiet one. There was no doubt his attention was solely focused on me. His expression was unreadable. What the hell? Was he *following* me?

Years of Mixed Martial Arts training flashed through my head. Unfortunately, that was when I had been thirty pounds heavier with muscles to show for it. Now I was almost skeletal since I couldn't keep a damn thing down. I picked up the pace. Instead of heading towards my apartment complex, I crossed the street and headed towards Lake Michigan. That area was populated and had a nicer crowd. Nothing sketchy happened on that side of town.

Three blocks later, I looked back over my shoulder. Damn; he was still right behind me, still watching me. I made random turns, hoping to throw him off my trail. My heart slammed in my chest; each time I looked over my shoulder he was just a little bit closer. His expression remained blank. Part of me wanted to call 911, but something in my gut told me they wouldn't be able to help me.

He was getting closer. I could almost feel him breathing down my back. I reached down and touched my bracelets and wondered if I needed to remove them to defend myself. Immediately I balked at the idea. If I took them off, I could crumble the city in a moment of panic. Just thinking about using my power caused it to surge forward. I hissed in pain and stumbled as my muscles cramped up. I took a deep breath trying to force my power to recede.

I turned another corner and then another. The next corner I turned down, I glanced over my shoulder to make sure I was being stealthy as I tried to ditch this guy. When I didn't see him right away, I grinned. Feeling good that I had shaken my stalker, I turned to see where I was going. I skidded to a stop when I realized it was a dead end.

I turned and ran out back onto the main sidewalk. Before I had time to decide to bolt across the street or continue in the same direction I had been going, a hand with a vice-like grip wrapped itself around my bicep, and I was yanked sideways. I yelped as I was thrown into the back of a black SUV. I tumbled onto the floor, and before I could scramble to get myself upright the man who had been following me slid into the back with me. The slamming of the door sent a shiver down my spine. The SUV lurched away from the sidewalk before I could get a grip on the handle.

I scrambled up onto the seat and pressed my back against the opposite door while glaring at the man who had just kidnapped me. He was watching me with narrow eyes, his mouth pressed into a thin line. He was an imposing figure. Oh, God, what was happening?

"Mae White, it is a pleasure to meet you," he said, conversationally.

Carefully, he removed his tie from around his neck, folded it, and then placed it in the inside of his jacket pocket. The gesture seemed menacing. I tried to push down my fear; it was causing my power to rush forward, and the pain was making my body shake like a leaf. The man looked over me, probably thinking my shaking came strictly from fear. His gaze landed on my wrists.

"My name is Arthur House, and I am a Guardian. Do you know what that is?"

The man from earlier had said he was a Guardian as well. If Zein was anything like this guy, both of them could go to hell.

"Tell your driver to pull over," I demanded through gritted teeth. "Whatever the fuck is going on, I don't want to be a part of it."

"My job is to make sure the supernatural world is protected and kept hidden from humans as well as keeping humans safe from unhinged supernatural creatures," Arthur continued as if I hadn't spoken. "When we ran into each other this morning, I did not immediately recognize your scent. Then I noticed your power is bound, which, as you must understand, is concerning. It is my duty to investigate what danger you may present to those around you. So I am inviting you to my private quarters to discuss what role you play in both worlds."

"I want to be let out of this car, *now*," I snapped.

My power surged forward harder than ever. I cried out in pain as fear and anger collided. My whole body shuddered hard. When my body finally relaxed, I looked over to Arthur who was stroking his goatee thoughtfully as he watched me struggle.

"Just let me go." I tried to keep the whine out of my voice. "This is crazy."

"I cannot do that until I am certain you are not a threat to either species," Arthur said, his tone sounding almost bored. "Besides, I know someone who will be pleased to meet you."

The SUV came to a sudden stop outside of a building in a nice part of the city. I tensed, ready to make a run for it.

As if reading my thoughts, Arthur commanded, "You will walk into this building with me without making a scene."

I said nothing, already waiting for the cars to pass on my side of the SUV before I opened the door. If I was going to make a run for it, I had to make sure I didn't get hit by a car in the process. Just as an opening between cars would allow me to make an escape, Arthur's hand wrapped around my upper arm. I didn't look at him; I threw my door open and tried to throw myself out of the SUV into the road. Arthur yanked me back, and I spun around to stare into a pair of blazing red eyes.

I opened my mouth to scream, but my power surged forward in reaction to my fear and pain ricocheted throughout my body. I convulsed painfully in my seat. Arthur took my inability to fight him as his opportunity to snatch me out of the SUV. He threw me over his shoulder, and he headed for the door of the building. Fear at being incapacitated and vulnerable made my power continue to fight against the binding spell. Tears ran down my cheeks as my body continued to convulse.

A security guard waited next to the door of a swanky building. He didn't bother to check Arthur's ID. He opened the door for Arthur and didn't spare me a glance despite my obvious distress. My fear escalated as we walked into the dark space. Instead of taking the door on the left where jazz music could be heard, we headed up a flight of stairs.

I reached for my bracelets. If I could just remove them, I could stop the pain. Yes, the whole building could crumble down, but whatever was about to happen couldn't be good. He knew my name, he knew about the bracelets, but I knew nothing about him. Unfortunately, my body continued to shake, and I couldn't get a grip on the bracelets.

We made it up the stairs, and at the top, another security guard was standing in front of a leather-padded door. I choked out a scream, but the security guard didn't blink. He opened the door for Arthur and didn't look back at me as I was carried inside. The door shut as we entered the room, and my heart sank. Was I about to be murdered? Raped? Tortured?

Arthur dropped me onto a suede couch and continued to walk over to the bar on the other side of the room. I scrambled to my feet, trying to take a deep breath to push down the pain and fear so I could function properly. Whatever Arthur was, he was definitely not human, which made all the human-like kidnapping scenarios I had created in my head obsolete. New, horrific, scenarios replaced the old ones, and they made the situation worse.

We were inside a small, private bar with several lounge chairs and couches. The carpet was red, and the walls were painted a dark navy blue. There were pictures of abstract art hanging in fancy frames, unique pieces of artwork on small stands under protective glass, and the jazz music that played downstairs in the main bar drifted through the speakers in the ceiling above us. This was probably where drug deals and scandalous activity happened.

I rushed over to the door and tried to open it only to find it locked. I choked back the rising fear that was threatening to consume me. I whirled around and found Arthur leaning up against the bar counter watching me, sipping what appeared to be whiskey from a glass. His eyes were no longer glowing red. What type of creature lurked under the surface of that flawless skin? Whatever it was, I didn't want to find out. I was not going to be a victim. I reached up and yanked off both of my bracelets. The instant relief of removing them was tremendous. I could breathe, my skin fit better, and my stomach loosened its knots.

"Ah, so you can remove them. I wondered if someone had made it so you could not take them off," Arthur mused out loud. "Please, take a seat. I mean you no harm."

"Tell your guard to open the door," I snapped.

"Not quite yet," Arthur said. "I have a few questions for you first. Then, you can leave."

"Do you think I'm stupid? In what movie has the villain ever let the good guy go after they chat?"

Arthur chuckled but the sound was cut off immediately. An odd expression crossed his features. Confusion? Wonder? He tilted his head sideways and continued to stare at me.

"Amazing… absolutely *amazing*," he muttered. He pushed himself away from the counter and walked over to a chair and sat down. "Please, Mae, I truly mean you no harm. I am fascinated by you and would like to learn more. As I said, I need to make sure you are not a threat."

"And if I am?"

"Then you will be dealt with accordingly," Arthur said with a one-shoulder shrug. "Your situation seems to be oddly unique, so termination will be put on the back burner for the time being."

His nonchalant attitude made me sick with dread. Termination? Dealt with accordingly? It was as if he was disciplining an employee, not talking about harming another person. What sick plans did Arthur House have in mind for me?

"What do you mean unique? No, you know what? I don't want to know. If you don't open this door, I'm going to—" I stumbled over my threat. What would I do? Have the whole building crash down over our heads?

Arthur read my hesitation and smiled knowingly. The smile cut off quickly, and his brows came together. He shook his head and asked, "What *can* you do, Mae? I am curious as to why you are spellbound. That type of spell is not used on the innocent."

I glared at him. Fuck, he had me. I couldn't jeopardize the lives of others, not even to save myself. It was why I had cast the spell on the bracelets in the first place. The only way to function as a normal human being without destroying everything or accidentally killing innocent people was to bind the power within me.

"How about a drink to settle your nerves? I am aware this is an uncomfortable situation you have found yourself in. Not many people run into Guardians, and when they do, usually we pay them no mind if they are not a threat."

"What the fuck is a Guardian? No, wait, stop, I don't want to hear it. I don't care!"

I turned around and let out the loudest scream possible. Maybe someone would come running in, and I could escape once the door was open.

"Scream all you like. The room is soundproofed," Arthur said with a sigh. He must say that to every kidnapped victim he brought here.

I screamed again, this time in frustration. Of course a room that was, I assumed, used to conduct illegal activity would be soundproofed. I slammed both palms against the door, and this time my anger caused my power to surge forward. The moment my palms contacted the solid surface the entire room shook. *Hard.* One of the abstract paintings fell off the wall. I turned around and glared at Arthur. He wanted to know what I could do? There, he had gotten just a taste.

"Look, Mae, maybe I can help you. What if I can find a solution so you do not have to wear those bracelets? Just tell me about yourself."

I balled my fists at my side. "You can't help me, and even if you could, I wouldn't accept the help. I don't know you; I don't know what the hell you are, and you *kidnapped me*! It's not like you've given me a great first impression."

"If I tell you about myself, would you share something with me?" he asked.

"No, because I. Don't. Care. I want nothing to do with you. I don't want to get to know you. What are you not getting about that?"

"If you do not comply willingly, I will force you to tell me," Arthur said, his voice dropping an octave. I watched in horror as his eyes changed from brown to a blazing red. My fear caused the room to shake again.

"Force me how?"

"Guardians have certain abilities… One of them is the ability to compel others. Would you prefer it that way?"

"Compel? Do you mean hypnotize?" My voice came out as a squeak.

Arthur shrugged one shoulder. "Call it what you wish. It means the same thing."

He could *hypnotize* me? I stared into those red eyes, and all my bravado disappeared as I realized he could be telling the truth. The room shook again as my fear mounted. Another piece of artwork smashed to the ground.

"Don't you dare," I said.

"Then, I suggest you take a seat and tell me what I want to know."

I warred with myself. If I walked over to where he sat, he could still try something on me. If I did not cooperate, I was positive he would attempt to compel me. The thought of being unable to control what I thought and said was horrifying. I would do anything to not be in that position. If he could hypnotize me, what could he make me do? The sick images in my head popped up like a crashing computer from the early 2000s.

My feet felt heavy as I forced them forward, towards Arthur. The room vibrated as I walked. It took every ounce of willpower to keep my mental barrier in place so the room wouldn't implode. I sat down in the suede chair farthest from him, on the edge of the room, and clenched my jaw tight. Arthur's eyes changed back to brown, and he gave me a reassuring smile. The smile disappeared almost as quickly as it appeared, and he shook his head. What was his problem?

"You truly are safe, Mae."

Then why did I feel like I was trapped in a room with a viper?

As Arthur opened his mouth to speak again, the door to the room opened behind me. This was my chance! The room shook hard and one of the art pieces that sat on its little podium under the protection of glass toppled over and shattered. The lights flickered and a bottle somewhere behind the small bar exploded. I leaped to my feet and whirled around but then froze where I stood.

Standing there in the doorway was a man I could only assume was the fallen angel Lucifer in his most sinful form. The man was tall, easily over six feet. His short wavy blond hair was pushed back so I could see the harsh lines of his angelic face. His nose was straight and true; his jawline looked like it could cut through diamonds. His shoulders were broad and his chest wide, tapering down to a lean waist.

Despite freezing at the sight of him, my whole body went up in flames. My heart took off like it was in a race for its life. My breathing came in small gasps, and the room shook again but this time it wasn't in fear or anger. My mouth suddenly went dry. Holy shit, I was ready to die and go straight to hell right now if I knew he would be waiting there for me.

Chapter Two

The newcomer shut the door behind him without taking his eyes off me. His expression was unreadable as he approached us with long, confident strides. When he was only a few feet away, his stride faltered and his whole body shuddered as though the room had become chilly. He blinked several times and then glanced from me to Arthur, a frown marring his handsome features.

"Ah, Rylan, thanks for coming on such short notice," Arthur said. Out of the corner of my eye, I could see him rise from his seat. Realizing that I was sandwiched between Arthur and his incredibly, drop-dead gorgeous friend, I took a wary step back so I could see both of them. "I want you to meet my new friend, Mae White. Mae, this is Rylan Wellington."

Rylan turned his attention back to me and gave me a full once over. I almost melted under his gaze. The incredible urge to reach out to touch him, to see if this angel was real, was hard to resist. Rylan stepped closer to me, his gaze travelling over my face. His features softened as he studied me. As he took another step towards me, Rylan lifted his nose, and I watched him take a deep breath. Wait, was he… *smelling* me?

"What is this?" Rylan hissed, his thick blond brows coming together. "Her scent is… peculiar."

"Mae was just about to tell me a little about herself. Let us all take a seat."

Instead of listening to Arthur, Rylan continued to stare at me. With him standing this close to me, I could admire his gorgeous teal eyes. His expression shifted so much I couldn't tell what he was thinking. For a moment I thought he was in awe, before suspicion masked it. He reached out as if to touch me only to let his hand drop. With a shake of his head, he moved away from me.

I glanced warily at Arthur, who had sat back down and now leaned comfortably back in his seat. I stole a glance at Rylan, who moved around me to a nearby chair. I took a deep shaky breath to settle my nerves then shot a glance towards the door. Had the door locked behind Rylan?

"Mae." The warning in Arthur's voice made me grimace.

Stiffly, I sat back down on the edge of the suede couch and glared at Arthur.

"Now, Mae, Rylan has led me to my first question: What exactly are you?" Arthur asked as he slung an arm over the back of his chair.

I clenched my jaw. What was I? Hell, if I knew. If I knew, I'd probably have more answers on how to control my power. I shrugged.

"Mae, if you do not answer with words, I will be forced to compel them from you," Arthur scolded.

The room shook hard again as anger and fear mingled.

"I don't know," I mumbled. Arthur rose his eyebrows as if he didn't believe me. "Really, I don't. Where is your other friend? He wasn't as terrible to deal with. I'll talk to him."

Arthur rolled his eyes, and Rylan shot him a questioning look.

"Zein decided to offer his services to Mae this morning," Arthur answered the unspoken question. Rylan scowled deeply but Arthur continued. "Unfortunately for you, Mae, Zein left shortly after your encounter to return home. Now, where were we? Ah, yes... Mae, what were your parents?"

I shrugged again but quickly added when Arthur leaned forward in his seat, "I don't know, I- I was adopted when I was a baby."

"When you use your power, do any markings appear? Do you need to do an incantation? Do you have to make a sacrifice?"

The image of the pentagram on the back of my hand appeared in my head. The little research I had done had confirmed the pentagram was a vital symbol within the witch community. With that research and with the spellbook I could summon, I had surmised I had to be some type of witch. But the spellbook was basically empty, and the one or two spells I had tried were hit or miss. The spellbinding that I had cast over my bracelets was the only spell that had actually worked.

What if I told them I was a witch? Would they try to burn me at the stake? Would that put me in danger? Well, more danger than I was already in. Where were these questions leading? I bit my lip and glared at Arthur.

As if reading my mind Arthur said, "I told you, Mae, you are safe."

"Yeah, for now, while I answer your questions," I snapped at him. The room shook again. Arthur said nothing for a moment, but his eyes narrowed.

"You will not be harmed. *Ever*," Rylan assured me as Arthur and I glared at each other. I glanced over at Rylan suspiciously. Gazing at him caused my heart to flutter wildly in my chest. My face flushed, and I looked away from him.

Arthur glanced over to his friend, and his thoughtful expression turned amused. Suddenly, there was a soft buzzing in my head. It was like listening to bees buzzing around their hive. The sensation didn't hurt, but it wasn't necessarily pleasant either. Abruptly the buzzing stopped.

Arthur looked back at me. "As Rylan promised, no harm will come to you. I promise."

"Your promises are shit," I snapped. "Maybe if you hadn't kidnapped me, I would trust you."

"You kidnapped her?" Rylan's voice dropped an octave.

Arthur glanced over at him and that soft buzzing started back up in my head. I made a face. Where was that coming from? To my amazement, Rylan bared his teeth at Arthur and scowled at him. The buzzing continued for a moment longer before Rylan's expression shifted back to curious. Rylan turned his attention back to me. Arthur sighed and did the same.

"I apologize for kidnapping you. You will be free to walk out of here, unharmed, and I will never bother you again as long as you cooperate."

I looked between the two men. Rylan was watching my face intently, his body motionless. He reminded me of a coiled snake about to strike. Arthur was waiting expectantly for an answer. Despite my anger and fear of the man sitting across from me, I knew I needed to start playing by his rules. If I could just get him to open the door for me at the end of this, I would disappear, leave Chicago forever, and he wouldn't be able to find me ever again. Stiffly, I scooted back further onto the seat and nodded. Fine. Let's get this over with.

Arthur read my body language and smiled. This time the smile lingered longer than the last two had before disappearing.

"Good. Now, as I was saying; markings? Incantations?"

"Yes," I grumbled. "A pentagram appears on my hand when I summon my spellbook."

"A spellbook? You are a witch then," Arthur said with a frown.

I shrugged. Yeah, maybe.

"Her scent is not fully witch. It does not match her aura," Rylan said, more to himself than to either of us. "Her power feels different… It radiates off her in a most unusual way. It was what we were warned to look for when detecting a god."

Arthur nodded in agreement. "Perhaps a quasi-deity? From a strong heritage?"

Completely taken back by the turn of the conversation I laughed in disbelief.

"A god?" I looked at both men in incredulity. "You think I could be some type of god? What is this? Some sort of joke?"

"No, it is not," Arthur said gravely, "The aura of a god-like power clings to you, although which god you are linked to I have no idea. Someone must have been concerned about your heritage to have gone through the effort to create those bracelets you wear. Who gave them to you, and why do you willingly wear those things?"

Rylan frowned in confusion.

"She has been wearing spellbound bracelets all day," Arthur explained. Rylan whipped his head back to me. Those gorgeous, drown-in-their-depths teal eyes suddenly changed to red. Even with red eyes his beauty was immeasurable and undeniable. Despite their beauty, I cringed away from the predator that was glaring at me.

"Answer the question," Rylan demanded through clenched teeth. "Who has bound you?"

"I created them," I said quickly. "My power is… difficult to control, so to be a normal person I made them."

Rylan rose from his seat like a king rising from his throne. He took a menacing step towards me. I leaned away from him, afraid of the violence in his eyes. As scared as I was of this handsome stranger, I couldn't tear my eyes away from him.

"You wear cursed jewelry," he growled, "*intentionally?* Give them to me."

I stared up at him as he bent over me, fury radiating from him. Part of me almost reached for the bracelets and handed them over without a fight. How could I deny this angry angel anything? Next to me, Arthur shifted. The movement caused me to snap back to reality. This was a man who didn't seem bothered that his friend had kidnapped me. He was no better than Arthur. How could I possibly find him so attractive? Disgusted with myself, I scowled up at him.

"No."

"If you do not give me the bracelets, I will forcibly take them from you," Rylan snarled. Before I could respond Arthur chuckled. Rylan turned to his friend, "Is this funny to you…?" Rylan's fury disappeared from his face and disbelief colored his features. His red eyes changed back to a lovely teal. "Arthur… You are laughing."

Arthur rose from his seat with a wide grin across his face. He walked over and placed a hand on Rylan's shoulder.

"Yes, I am *laughing.*"

"How is that possible? You are not her mate."

"No, she is most definitely your mate, Rylan, but still, all of my emotions have returned. I can feel frustration, anger, annoyance, and yes, amusement. It is in the presence of Mae that they return in full force. They disappear again when she gets too far away."

Both men stared at each other in awe. What in the hell was all of this about? Mates? Emotions? Why were they so surprised right now?

"What are you saying? That I gave you back the ability to feel *emotions?* You can't feel anything?" I asked.

Both men blinked, remembered I was in the room, and turned, as one, towards me.

It was Rylan who answered, "Many millennia ago, the gods cursed the Guardians. This curse took away our ability to feel any emotions, and only when we find our mates do they return."

I stared at him. These two were obviously not in their right minds. That was becoming quite clear. But how far gone were they in their insanity? There was no way Rylan could believe a thing he was saying. Could he? The solemnity in his expression worried me. Maybe he did believe a little of it. Or at least, he *wanted* me to believe he believed it. How the hell had I gotten wrapped up in this?

"I don't get it. I don't get any of this, but this all sounds insane. I'm not part god, I didn't do anything to you or your emotions, and I'm not a mate."

"Apparently, you do not need to do anything for me to regain my emotions," Arthur said with a wide smile. "When we ran into each other, I regained everything I lost. It was overwhelming and delightful. But when you walked into that elevator everything was sucked out of me once more. When we crossed paths again during your break, I felt the stirrings of my emotions, but you were too far away. It was only when I approached you on the sidewalk that my emotions returned."

I stared at Arthur. This man was utterly insane. All of this was insane. Why was I still sitting here talking to these men when they were obviously out of their minds? I shook my head, and I rose from my seat. I raised my hands in surrender.

"Look, if you don't have any more questions for me, I want to go."

Arthur turned his attention back to Rylan, ignoring me. "Rylan, she could be the one to lift the curse on all of us. She may be your mate, but she may be our savior."

"You've said that twice now, what are you talking about? What is a mate?" I asked exasperated.

Rylan pulled his gaze away from Arthur's face and turned to me.

Suddenly, the temperature in the room spiked. Those red eyes had simmered back to that stunning teal, and my breath hitched in my throat as he stared down at me. Rylan pulled himself to his full height and stepped closer to me. I bit my bottom lip and tensed.

"After the Guardians were cursed by the gods, our people went to the witches for help. They were able to take half of our souls, cleanse that half of the curse, and threw our halves into the cosmic universe. We were promised that one day our souls would return to Earth inside of our mates. Once we found our mate, we found the other half of our soul; thus, breaking the curse on that individual Guardian. We would know when we found our mate because our mark would be imprinted onto our mate, and our emotions would come back permanently. There would be no doubt," he said. His voice dropped, "I can feel everything and you wear my mark now."

Wait, what?

"A mark? I don't have your mark on me," I said as I struggled to understand.

"It is on the back of your neck," Rylan assured me. His eyes turned smoldering, and his voice dropped another octave, "You are most certainly my mate."

The suspiciousness and doubt that had marred his handsome features since he entered the room disappeared. In their place, a sweet serenity brightened his gorgeous eyes and softened his mouth. The smile that tugged a corner of his mouth upwards was breathtaking.

My heart skipped a beat. I reached up to touch the back of my neck knowing exactly what was there. The night I first realized I had gained power a tattoo appeared on the back of my neck. The symbol was of a thin crescent moon. Cut downwards through the moon was a sword. The mark had terrified me when it appeared, but now I hardly thought of it. Before I could say anything, the door opened behind me. The sound of it opening clicked common sense into me.

The heated moment between Rylan and I vanished. This could be the only opportunity to get out of this room, and there was no way I was going to miss it. I jumped to my feet and let my power go, slightly sending out a prayer to whatever god would listen that I wouldn't bring the whole building down. Rylan and Arthur were thrown backward in different directions across the room. The room shook so violently that the rest of the paintings fell, the furniture toppled over, and the ceiling above us cracked.

I was across the room before either Guardian hit the ground. The server stumbled out of my way, trying to find his footing as the room continued to shake. Outside, the guard held onto the railing for dear life. He attempted to grab me, but I twisted out of his grasp and was down the stairs before he could try again. I busted through the glass door that led outside and throat-punched the startled security guard who had turned to see who was leaving.

I sprinted down the street, moving as fast as I could. As I ran, the ground beneath me rolled and alarms from nearby parked cars began to go off. People cried out in alarm and confusion. The pentagram on the back on my hand began to glow, and my body shook with fatigue as I tried to rein in my power. *You are the Spirit within me, you are the Wind in my hair, you are the Earth beneath my feet, and you are Water that flows through me, and you are the Fire that drives me,* I chanted in my head as I ran. Underneath my feet, the ground stopped shaking.

Thank God.

I didn't bother to flag down a taxi. It would take longer to drive than to run now that it was past five o'clock. I headed northbound. I wove in and out of the pedestrians who were in my way and crossed streets without pausing to see if a car was coming or not. Let them hit me; death would be preferable over the crazy hell I was living with these days. A few times I circled, made unnecessary twists and turns down random streets, just in case I was being followed.

When I got close to my apartment complex, I slid on the first bracelet. Just like every time I put them on, pain ensued. I stumbled and cried out but I kept moving. Once the pain had subsided enough to put the other one on I did. This time my vision blurred, and I gagged. Thank God I hadn't been able to keep anything down for lunch. Taking deep breaths, I rushed into my apartment complex.

Before the door to my apartment had a chance to close, I was already stripping out of my work attire. I changed into jeans and tee shirt in the bathroom, only pausing to note the new dark bruises that marred my arms, chest, and back. Another lovely side effect of the bracelets. That was the price of trying to keep my power at bay.

I ordered an Uber as I shoved extra clothes into the duffle bag sitting with the camping gear by the front door. Who knew when I would come back, now that I didn't have a job to return to and there were two crazy men after me? Impatient for my driver, I checked the refrigerator for dinner. The only thing inside was a yogurt that was soon to expire. My stomach twisted uncomfortably at the thought of eating anything. When was the last time I had something to eat? Half a protein bar this morning? Urgh, I needed to eat more. I grabbed the yogurt and forced myself to eat a few bites.

Just as I tossed the empty yogurt cup into the trash, I got the alert my driver had arrived. Perfect timing. I grabbed my purse off the console table and the rest of my stuff by the door and then left my apartment. I didn't take the elevator in case Arthur or Rylan were waiting for me in the lobby. Instead, I took the ten flights of stairs down to where I exited out the side of the building. Outside, my driver was waiting for me next to his car. Or at least I thought he was there for me. Had I ordered an SUV by mistake? I was about to pull out my phone to double-check when an older driver walked up to me with a warm smile.

"Miss White?" he said.

Oh, I must have ordered this upgrade by accident. Well, he was here, and I needed to go, so I'd pay the extra. Whatever it took to get out of here as quickly as possible. I nodded, and he opened the back door for me. I handed him my large backpack full of my camping gear and duffle bag but kept my purse with me. I climbed in and relaxed against the leather seats. As the driver walked around the car to get into the driver's seat, I turned around in my seat to check the sidewalks. Were they nearby? Had they followed me?

No, I was sure I would have noticed. I was in the clear.

"The KOA south of the city, Miss White?" the driver asked me, confirming the location.

"Yes, that's right."

The man nodded and pulled away from the sidewalk. It would take about an hour to get there. I had time to relax. I leaned my head back and closed my eyes; the excitement from the day was catching up to me. I felt drained. On top of the emotional baggage of walking out of my job, being kidnapped, and the lack of sleep I had gotten the night before; the pain in my head was stifling. Between keeping my power at bay all week and the unexpected surges of power from today's ordeal, both my head and body throbbed. The bruises on my body were just one indication of the pain it caused to hold back my power. Usually, by the end of the week my head felt like a cracked egg.

I was certain my power was killing me. One morning I wouldn't wake up from my short nightly naps. There was a cost to having power, and I knew my body was paying for it. Tears threatened to leak through my closed eyelids, but I fought them. Now wasn't the time to cry. Now was the time to be relieved I had just survived being kidnapped. I replayed the conversation with Arthur and Rylan in my head and wondered how crazy people like them were able to function so well in society.

For the past two years, camping had been my salvation. Knowing I couldn't harm anyone eased the tension I carried in my heart. After today the woods would be my haven once again. The Guardians wouldn't be able to find me any time soon. I used cash to pay for all my camping trips and cash for anything I did outside the city. I was safe until I could figure out where to go next.

Eventually, I was able to doze off. My eyes opened when my car came to a halt and the engine was turned off. I blinked as I tried to remember where I was. After a moment, everything came rushing back, and I sighed in relief knowing I was about to sleep under the stars for the night. Just as I scooted over to the door, my hand reaching for the handle, I froze.

The SUV was parked outside of a large brick colonial home. A glance at the driveway told me the house was tucked way back off any main road. There were no other houses in any direction, just trees. Alarm bells went off in my head. Something was very wrong. Had my driver just gone rogue and now he was kidnapping me? I had heard about these situations on online blogs warning women of the dangers of these driving apps.

This could not be happening.

I grabbed my purse and threw the door open. Part of me half expected it to be locked. I leaped from the car and ran around the back, hoping to race down the driveway back to the main road. Unfortunately, as I rounded the back of the SUV, I slammed right into Rylan. It was like I had run into a cement wall. He didn't budge at the contact, but the force of hitting him sent me toppling backward. Rylan caught me before I landed on my butt.

Rylan stared down at me with a look that spelled the end to any ideas of fleeing. Not because I wouldn't be able to escape. No, this look was one that promised a delicious type of punishment, one I would beg for; I knew I would. This was the look of a man who had starved for hundreds of years and was finally granted a delicious feast. The hunger that burned there in the depths of those teal eyes caused my whole body to shudder. The lust that rushed through my veins was terrifying. I should want to stomp out the burning in my body, but suddenly I wanted him to touch me, to devour me like the hungry man he was.

I was speechless, staring up at him.

"Thank you, Wilbur. Please place Mae's belonging in the guesthouse, and then you are free for the evening," Rylan said, pulling his teal gaze away from me.

I forced myself to glance over my shoulder. The driver had gotten out of the vehicle and was standing near the back of the SUV, waiting for his orders. Seeing him brought the severity of the situation flooding back to me, and I pulled myself out of Rylan's embrace.

"No, wait!" I called after him, but Wilbur ignored me. I turned my whole body to run after the man, but Rylan held onto me with a grip gentle enough not to leave marks but strong enough that I couldn't escape. I turned to Rylan and tried to pull free. I shrieked my outrage. "What the hell is this? I got kidnapped *again*?"

"Would you have come if we had shown up at your doorstep and asked for more of your time?" Rylan asked with a raised brow and a smug smirk. Reading the answer on my face he continued: "So, you see, I had to take the necessary measures to ensure a private conversation. Please, come inside."

"No," I snapped and stepped out of his grasp. He let me go. "Are you insane? You want me to just walk into that house okay with all of this? No, no, no!"

In my ire, my foot stomped without thinking. Shit, how childish could I be right now? Rylan's smirk grew as if he was amused by the gesture. Seeing his amusement only pissed me off more. My anger grew; I wanted nothing but to slug him in the cheek. My rage triggered my power. I choked on a cry of pain as my body absorbed the impact of what could have been a devastating blast. My body violently shuddered as the pain radiated outwards and then back within me.

"Take those damn bracelets off," Rylan snarled, his blond brows crashing together in anger. He reached for my wrist, but I was able to stumble out of his grasp as the pain subsided.

"No," I said through gritted teeth.

When he reached for me, a wave of fear crashed over me which caused my power to react again. The impact of my power charging through my veins felt like I'd been hit by a bus. It stole my breath, and my legs almost gave out. Rylan grabbed my forearm, whether it was to steady me or to make a grab for the bracelets, I wasn't sure, but the moment his skin contacted mine the pain vanished. The sudden loss of pain was a shock. I gasped in surprise.

"It is insane to wear those things," Rylan snapped while he pulled me towards him.

"How'd you do that?" I whispered in awe as I stumbled towards him. I looked from his angry gaze down to his hand that was wrapped around me.

"Do what?"

"Stop the pain…" I whispered, my voice trailing off. I shook my head, "It's never just stopped like that before." Except when Arthur had touched me this morning. Interesting.

"I did nothing, but you would not have any pain if you did not wear these things in the first place."

"It is to protect everyone."

I sighed, suddenly exhausted. All I wanted to do was collapse into my sleeping bag. Too bad that didn't look like it was going to happen anytime soon this evening.

"We can tell that you do not have a strong grasp on your power," Rylan said, still scowling at me. "Because of that, we chose not to pursue you while you were still in the city. It is much safer for everyone if you lose control here. Now you can remove them."

I hadn't thought about that. Of course, they would see I was out of control and would back off until they could guarantee the safety of others. According to Arthur, it was their job to protect the supernatural and human world. With me running through the city causing an earthquake, I would have brought unwanted attention to the supernatural world, and I could have caused a lot of injuries.

While I understood his thought process, that didn't mean I wanted to be held against my will. I was at my wit's end. My head felt like a balloon was expanding inside of it, and I knew that last surge had just caused some real internal damage. I needed to be alone in the woods to take off these bracelets and let my power go. It was the only way to make the coming days more bearable.

"Look, Rylan." I took a deep breath and tried to sound reasonable. "I'm not taking them off here, but I do need to remove them. When I take them off, I have to be far away so no one in the nearby vicinity gets hurt. I don't know anything about your world, and I don't want to get involved in crazy shenanigans. So, please, just let me go."

Rylan took a deep breath. As he let it out, his expression changed from anger to one of patience.

"I understand you are confused and apprehensive. You have much to learn, as do we. We would just like to talk to you to figure out where your place is in our world. Once we are all sated with information, should you wish to leave here you can go, as promised, without harm."

I clenched my jaw and bit back an angry retort. I wasn't going to win this fight. I glanced past him at the long driveway that fed into the woods and then back at the house. There was no way I could outrun him. Even if I dove into the woods, I wouldn't make it far. I was far too tired and too weak to run another marathon trying to escape him. The best bet would be to conserve energy for the next few hours and hope to slip away tonight. I couldn't see another way out of this.

My shoulders sagged in defeat. Rylan's victorious smirk made me curl my hands into fists. The urge to punch him in the face was strong. It took every ounce of discipline not to do it. As if he could sense my irritation with him, his smile disappeared. His facial features smoothed out, and a small frown tugged the corner of his mouth.

"There is much you do not know, but what is important for you to understand is that, as your mate, I am your protector. I will not allow anything to happen to you."

The gentleness in his voice caused my defenses to slip. The softness in his expression caused my heart to beat frantically in my chest. Embarrassed and annoyed by my ability to be swayed by the guy who was about to hold me hostage, I turned away from him. I eyed the large house in front of me. Nothing seemed too menacing about it. I wasn't sure if I should feel better that it didn't look like the house from the Addams Family or if I should be even more concerned that the house seemed so inconspicuous.

Unconsciously, I rubbed my arms but winced and stopped. I looked down and noted the new bruises forming. Mentally, I shook myself. If I could control my stupid power, I wouldn't have to use these bracelets, and these bruises would just disappear.

Rylan came up to stand next to me.

"Maybe I can help you," he added softly.

I looked up at him suspiciously. Help me? Help me how? He reached out and took my hand. My instincts told me to jerk away from the contact, but my hand fit so perfectly in his. My whole body quivered at the gentle contact. If Rylan noticed, he didn't say anything. Instead, he brought my hand up to his lips and kissed the back of it. My body quivered harder, and my heart rate spiked. *That* he had to have noticed.

"If my touch can ease your suffering, maybe I can do something more."

From the way my pulse was racing and how my skin felt like it was on fire under his contact, I was sure his touch could do a *lot* more. Annoyed at my train of thought, I pulled my hand out of his.

"I can leave after we're done talking?" I asked warily. I tried to keep my mind on more pressing issues rather than the lust causing my mouth to dry and my toes to curl. "*Tonight?*"

"Yes, you may leave tonight."

"Alright, let's do this then."

He nodded and began walking towards the house. I looked over my shoulder at the driveway wishing it were plausible to run away. But it wasn't. I had to hope that Rylan and Arthur were men of their word. With a deep breath, I forced myself to follow Rylan towards the house. He opened the front door and stepped to the side to let me enter first. I stepped into the house, into the foyer, and looked around while Rylan entered and shut the door behind us. Inside, the décor was very traditional. There were gold framed pictures of nature, fancy wallpaper, a colorful runner that led down the hallway to what, I assumed, was the main living area. On either side of us were two sets of doors.

"This way." Rylan directed me to the doors to our left.

One door was already slightly ajar, and Rylan pushed it open further. I followed him inside; my heart pounded wildly and my hands trembled. What was going to happen now? When I entered, I half expected the room to look like a dungeon. After being kidnapped for a second time, I was sure this would be worse than the first. They had to be more than a little pissed that I had broken most of their stuff during my departure.

I was pleasantly surprised to see the room was a reading den and home office. There was a small fire lit in the fireplace across the room which gave the space a cozy feel. Four chairs faced each other in a circle on one side of the room, and at the other end sat a large, ornate desk with tall bookshelves crammed with books behind it.

Standing next to the fireplace was Arthur, who looked up from the flames as we entered. I immediately took note that his eyes were warm brown, not red. He nodded his greeting and even gave me an unexpectedly warm smile when our eyes met. When

Rylan shut the door behind us, my anxiety spiked. It took more willpower than normal to keep my power at bay so I wouldn't turn into a convulsing wreck in front of these two men. Rylan ventured further into the room, but I stayed close to the door. I hadn't heard it lock, which was reassuring.

Arthur straightened and took a step towards me.

"Mae, I apologize for snatching you off the street today. I should have handled the situation differently. I hope you can forgive my recklessness and allow me to start over?" His apology sounded genuinely sincere. When he paused, I awkwardly nodded for him to continue. "Mae White, my name is Arthur House, a Guardian and a protector for both humans and non-humans in this world. In all my time on this Earth, I have not run across another like you. I wish to learn more about you, will you do me the honors of telling me about yourself?"

His worldly way of speaking would have come off condescending if it had been anyone else, but from Arthur, it somehow seemed appropriate. Maybe even a little expected.

"What do you want to know?" I asked, wary of their motive.

It was Rylan that answered. "You seem fairly new with your power. The lack of control is a red flag to us and is concerning. Binding yourself is not something done for those who wish to control their power. When did you begin learning how to use your power? Who is your teacher?"

As Rylan talked, Arthur moved. Suspiciously, I watched as he made his way over to the desk, pulled out a decanter full of dark liquid, and then took three glasses from a drawer in the desk. I watched as he poured the dark liquid, plugged the decanter back up and then put it back under the desk. Once he had completed that task, he grabbed all three glasses and walked into the middle of the room. He handed a glass to Rylan, who took it and then made his way over to me. I tensed as he approached. When Arthur handed me a glass, I hesitated. What was in this? Could he have drugged it?

Arthur waited patiently while I weighed the pros and cons of not taking the glass. Finally, I clenched my teeth as my manners overrode my fear and accepted the drink. Rylan took a sip of his. Was it to put me at ease? I realized they were waiting for me to say something, and I found myself a little embarrassed by their attention.

"Um... My power *is* new. At the end of my sophomore year of college, it emerged, and I've been struggling with it ever since," I said slowly, looking from Arthur to Rylan. "I don't have a teacher. I've been trying to figure this out on my own."

Rylan scowled.

"On your own?" he repeated. "Every non-human has a teacher. Wizards have schooled mages, witches have their coven, elves have their Alpha, and so on. It is dangerous to not have any guidance."

I shrugged. Whether that was how things were done or not, it didn't change the fact that I didn't have someone to guide me through this.

"It is odd for your power to emerge so late in your life. There must have been some type of trigger," Arthur said, stroking his goatee thoughtfully. "I wonder where your power derives from..."

"I have no idea," I admitted, my voice barely more than a whisper. I hated that I didn't know what information I should or should not be sharing. What would be turned against me at the end of this meeting? "Like I said before, I assume I am a witch. I could just be a late bloomer."

Arthur frowned.

"Yes, your witch blood is certainly evident but a late bloomer? I am not so sure of that."

"You are not a full-blooded witch," Rylan added.

"How can you know that?" I asked him.

"Because we are Guardians. We have certain abilities, and one of them is to distinguish humans from non-humans," Rylan explained. He stepped away from the fireplace and walked over to Arthur and me. "Please, sit down and make yourself comfortable."

I looked at both men and then towards one of the leather chairs. To sit or not to sit… Sitting made me more vulnerable to an attack. On the other hand, I was already quite vulnerable. My body was beginning to shake from fatigue. Had Rylan noticed?

Arthur walked over to one of the chairs, and begrudgingly, I followed him. Rylan sat down on one side of me while Arthur sat down on the other. I glanced back towards the door before sinking into my chair. Nervously, I fingered the rim of my untouched glass.

"So, if you can differentiate between species, why don't you tell me what I am?" I asked, turning my attention to Rylan. Rylan ran his fingers through his blond hair as he thought about his response.

I wanted to repeat the action with my own fingers.

"Arthur and I have been discussing this since your departure. You do not have a specific scent. The gods do not have a specific scent either, which makes it harder to differentiate them from each other, but it is their immense power that tells us they are more than supernatural. Their power lingers in the air long after they are gone. Much like yours does. It is a… *sensation* you leave in your wake that tells us you are more than meets the eye."

I nodded as if I understood when, in fact, that was the farthest from the truth.

"Are there more like you, Mae?" Arthur asked.

I shrugged.

"No… Well, maybe. I don't know," I said, exasperated. "I didn't know there were other people with power until I met you. I wouldn't have thought you were anything other than human until your eyes changed color."

Arthur flashed me a toothy grin.

"Believe me, I can do more than change the color of my eyes."

I did believe him. I, wholeheartedly, believed that there was much more lurking just beneath that handsome façade. I shuddered as fear tightened its grasp around my heart. Rylan looked over at Arthur and scowled. Arthur smirked at him. He was *enjoying* making me nervous.

Arthur turned his attention back to me and he asked, "If you do not know of anyone else with your power and you have no living family, then why did you—"

"How do you know I don't have any family?" I interrupted.

"A background check of course," Arthur said as if it was obvious. "How else do you think I knew your name?"

A background check? Arthur had done a *background* check on me?

"If you have all this information on me already, why bothering asking these questions?" I snapped. What an invasion of privacy!

"Because what we are looking for is not in your file."

I gritted my teeth. So, they were trying to get to know *everything* about me. Why? So, they could make sure no one came looking for me if they murdered me or whisked me away somewhere that I wouldn't be found? I gripped the glass in my hand hard, debating if I should chuck it at his head and storm out. Why was I cooperating again?

"Like I was saying, without family or anyone who could help you, why would you move to Chicago? Where were you for the past year?"

Of course, they wouldn't know about the Appalachian Trail. I used cash for everything, I had a trail name, and even when I needed more money, I picked up waitressing jobs at random dive bars that required nothing but a pair of boobs and the knowledge of how to work a register. There was no identification required in those places. To the rest of the world, it would have looked like I had just disappeared off the face of the Earth.

"I wanted to be around people again, so I picked a big city and went there. I visited New York enough on the weekends in college, so I was over that city, and I'm not a beach girl, so L.A. was out. I went with the next biggest city. In a big city, I knew I could find a decent job quickly, and I could blend in easily enough while I tried to balance being normal and dealing with my power."

"Where were you before Chicago?" Rylan asked again. I looked over at him but looked away immediately when I found him staring at me intently.

"I was hiking the Appalachian Trail. I was on the trail for a year."

"With whom?"

"It was just me."

"Why walk the trail?" Arthur asked.

I clenched my jaw. If I told them, according to their duties as Guardians, they would kill me. This was it. I had to decide if I trusted them enough to tell them everything. Did I trust them? I looked down into my glass. The smell of bourdon wafted up into my face, and my mouth watered. When was the last time I had a drink? I was too afraid of what would happen if I got tipsy. I never wanted to take the risk of hurting anyone.

Maybe I needed to tell them. Maybe it was for the best if they did kill me. It wasn't as if I hadn't tried to off myself a few times already. If they decided I was a danger to both the supernatural and human world, this would be the end of the conversation, but maybe it was time to face the facts. This needed to end. My power was only growing stronger, and I was literally killing myself trying to contain it. Maybe the end would be swift.

"I left because I almost killed someone," I said, my voice so soft I wouldn't have even called it a whisper. "I was at a gas station pumping gas one night. Someone tapped me on the shoulder to get my attention, and it startled me." I swallowed hard as I continued to stare at the bourbon. "My power… I didn't get a chance to stop it. The pump next to us exploded. I was able to get out of the way, but the guy… He was burned badly. I can still remember the smell of burning flesh."

I looked up at Arthur, unwilling to meet Rylan's teal gaze. The shame of the damage I had done was so strong it choked me. The blood rushed from my face as I recalled the events of that night. The screams still haunted me.

"The next day I packed up my things, called a company to rent out my family's house where I had been staying, bought camping gear, and took off. I didn't trust myself around others. I have absolutely no control over whatever this is inside of me, and it grows stronger daily. I don't trust myself not to hurt anyone; it's why I wear these bracelets. But then certain events on the trail the last few months had me rethink the decision to stay hidden. So—"

"What events?" Rylan interrupted.

"These *things*," I struggled to describe them. "They were these huge, eyeless, inky black, large toothed monsters… The noises they made were terrifying. The first one found me while I was sleeping. The second one attacked me a few weeks later while I was hiking. Both times I barely escaped with my life."

The noise Rylan made sounded like a choked growl. His jaw clenched tight and his hands closed into fists.

I hurried on. "That was my turning point. I couldn't hide in the mountains for the rest of my life, though, so I made a plan. I found the binding spell in my spellbook and decided that I would try to live life how it is supposed to be lived. If life in a new city didn't work out…" My voice trailed off.

"What would you do if Chicago did not work out?" Arthur pressed. He leaned forward, and we stared at each other.

"I'd try to kill myself again."

Both men were on their feet at the same time. I flinched as the glass in Rylan's hand shattered. He didn't seem to notice. His eyes changed to red, and he pinned me with a look so engulfed in fury I could feel the flickers of heat from where I sat.

"*No!*" he snapped.

"Rylan, calm yourself," Arthur said, putting a hand on his friend's shoulder. Rylan slapped the hand away and continued to glare at me.

"Why are you upset?" I watched them in confusion. "I… I don't get it. I thought it was your job to terminate a threat. That's what you said." I turned to Arthur. "Who cares if the threat takes care of itself?"

"I also said you are unique," Arthur reminded me, but his attention was directed at his friend. Rylan was seething, his shoulders heaved up and down and his whole body shook. "Rylan, I know it is new to be upset, but it does us no good. Settle yourself. We will all work through this together."

Rylan stormed away from the two of us, glass cracking under his footsteps. I rose from my chair but didn't turn to look where he was going. I wasn't about to turn my back to Arthur. Out of the two of them, for some unexplainable reason, I trusted Rylan not to kill me. With Arthur… I wasn't quite sure where he stood on that topic.

"Why is he so upset?" I asked.

Arthur ignored my question, but his scowl disappeared. Rylan walked back over to us; his red gaze burned with the rage inside of him, but his expression gained a semblance of indifference. Even as pissed off as Rylan was, it only enhanced his devilishly handsome looks. The fire that had ignited in his gaze sent butterflies fluttering in my stomach.

Despite his friend's ire, Arthur suddenly smiled.

"It is a strange sensation to become angry after several lifetimes of being unable to, is it not?" he asked Rylan. Rylan turned his piercing glare towards Arthur. They stared at each other for a moment, a soft, tinny noise cutting through the silence. What was that? Just like back at Arthur's club, it felt like I was listening to bees buzzing.

Rylan turned his head to look back at me. His eyes had reverted to normal, and I was suddenly sinking into them. My breath caught in my throat as he took a step towards me.

"Please excuse my behavior, Mae. It was unacceptable," he said, his voice soft.

I said nothing. I was ensnared by the intensity of those teal eyes. I should have looked away or taken a step back, but I was unable to think clearly. The need to step closer, to close the space between us, was overwhelming. I licked my suddenly dry lips, and his impossibly vibrant eyes turned their attention to the motion. I could feel the heat rise in my cheeks.

Arthur cleared his throat. I was snapped out of the thrall immediately. I turned away from Rylan and tried to look anywhere else but at him. Oh, God, what was wrong with me?

To try to get back on topic, I asked, "So, now what? You got your answers, so what are you going to do with me now?"

Arthur and Rylan exchanged glances. That soft buzzing started up in my head again. Wait a minute... Were they communicating telepathically right now? No way. Impossible. Or... was it? No, I was crazy. The buzzing stopped as abruptly as it had begun. Arthur turned his attention back to me.

"What happens next is up to you," he said, his tone grave. His lips turned downwards into a frown.

"What do you mean? I can leave now?" I asked suspiciously. Was this some sort of trick?

Arthur nodded.

"You can leave, if that is what you wish," he said. "Or you can stay here with us for a while."

I barked out a laugh in disbelief. "Why would I do that?"

"Mae," Arthur started, "While, usually, this would end quite differently for most people in your situation, your circumstance is very unique. Your very presence is life-altering for both myself and Rylan. You are his mate, a gift not bestowed upon us very often. To me, and for our species, you have answered a prayer we long thought had been ignored."

That was not what I expected him to say. Arthur frowned and stepped closer to me. A sound rumbled through Rylan's chest. A growl? No, people didn't growl. Arthur looked over at Rylan. With a sigh, Arthur stood to one side of me instead of directly in front of me. The sound of rumbling from Rylan stopped, but he pinned Arthur with a steely look. Arthur turned his attention back to me.

"A Guardian's life is lived without emotions. Everything we feel is strictly a primitive need. Hunger, exhaustion, physical pain; we can feel that. We are unable, however, to feel joy, happiness, love, sorrow, or admiration. Imagine not being able to feel sad at a friend's funeral or elated at the sight of a new life. It is a terrible curse. When someone walks into your life and gives you that ability to feel, you never want to go back to a life without emotions. You have given me the ability to feel *hope* that maybe this curse can be lifted. Mae, if you leave this room you take with you the ability for me to hope."

"Arthur," Rylan snapped. "It is not Mae's responsibility to worry about the curse."

Arthur did not turn to look at his friend. Instead, he kept his gaze pinned to me while scowling at his friend's words.

"It is easy for you to say, Rylan. You will walk out with her when she leaves," Arthur said, his voice sad. "Besides, she needs to know. She will be a part of our world through you. Mae, our species is a dying breed. Many of us cannot handle the dark world that we were unfairly cursed with. After living centuries, millennia, our people are killing themselves, unable to wait for their mates anymore. But you see, when a Guardian leaves this world without his mate, without the other half of their soul, they cease to exist. There are no Golden Gates for them to pass through. We were forced into this existence. Forced into servitude. Then we were cursed by our creators when we fought for our freedom. After what we have been through, our people do not deserve that type of ending. You could somehow be the key to ending this harsh existence. I am asking you to stay and help the Guardians survive."

Chapter Three

I stared at Arthur stunned. He was being serious. He truly thought I could be the answer to their problems. I could see the need for me to understand burning there in his brown eyes. There was also fear. Deep down, where he thought I wouldn't notice, I could see Arthur was *scared*. He did not want to go back to a world void of feeling. Arthur was trying not to panic, and his earnest plea for me to stay suddenly didn't seem so absurd when he explained to me why I was so important. My legs felt weak. Slowly, I sank back into my chair.

"Arthur… I'm sorry but, I'm not *doing* anything to bring back your emotions," I said softly. I could feel myself getting sucked into this craziness. "My power is destructive; it doesn't mend things or lift curses."

"The power surging through your body is immense, Mae. You may not realize you are doing anything, but I am certainly affected by you and the power radiating from you. Just being around you, in the same room with you; it is a breath of fresh air after wading through a dark, stale pit of despair," Arthur replied. His face twisted in pain.

"Enough, Arthur," Rylan said his tone firm, but he put a comforting hand on his friend's shoulder. "You have said what you needed. Do not push, Mae."

I looked at Rylan, who was frowning at his friend with a grim glean in his eyes. Rylan could not only empathize, but he could sympathize with his friend. Whatever curse the Guardians had hanging over them, Rylan had suffered just as greatly as Arthur had.

What was I supposed to say? What did they expect me to do? I felt incredibly inadequate and out of place. This wasn't my world, and yet suddenly I was thrown into it with high expectations. I couldn't control my power, let alone figure out how to lift a species-wide curse. On top of all of this, they expected me to be a *mate* for Rylan. As this thought hit me, I felt the blood drain from my face, and my throat tightened.

This was too much to deal with.

"Mae, breathe," Rylan said, his voice rough.

Unable to sit still anymore, I stood up quickly and paced over by the fireplace. How could I be stuck in such a mess? Why would these men look to me for help when I was so obviously out of my depth? I had no idea what to do to help them. With an exasperated sigh, I turned around to pace back to the chair. I found Rylan and Arthur standing in front of the door to the room, shoulder to shoulder. I stopped mid-stride.

"What the hell is this? Did you think I was leaving?" I demanded.

My surprise turned to anger when I realized they had no intention of keeping their promise. They were not going to let me leave. I had been under the impression they were offering me a choice at a life where curses and Guardians were real or I could go back to my almost normal life. In reality, I was going to be forced into this mess. How could I have been such an idiot? Why would I have put myself in such danger? I should have tried to run for it. I began to see red as my body tensed, and my hands curled to fists.

The flood of anger that coursed through my body triggered my power. The pain flared up through every nerve in my body. The invisible noose that always hung around my neck tightened, and the muscles in my body spasmed. I choked on a cry as my legs gave out from under me, and I crumbled to the ground. Tremors wracked my body as wave after wave of pain travel throughout each limb. My stomach churned so intensely that I was sure I was going to vomit all over the expensive carpet. My mind went blank as the pain increased. I tried to breathe through it, but it was impossible while I was so infuriated with the Guardians.

Suddenly there was a pair of hands helping me. One came around my back, and the other took my hand to help me up. The moment those hands connected with my skin the pain receded. I was able to breathe again, and the tremors stopped. A tear rolled down my cheek as I gasped for air. My relief was almost tangible.

Rylan helped me to my feet with a deep scowl on his face.

"Take these awful things off," he growled.

Before I could stop him, he grabbed both of my wrists in one hand and pulled off each bracelet. Rylan stared at the thick scarring from the burn marks the bracelets had left behind. His eyes began to glow so brightly I could have sworn I was looking into the sun.

"I need those!"

I tried to reach for the bracelets, but my body was exhausted and the attempt to yank them back was halfhearted at most. Rylan shoved them into his back pocket, ignoring my attempt to struggle in his grasp. Then, he let go of both of my wrists to grab one of my arms. Rylan stared down at the dark bruises; disgust caused his upper lip to pull upwards. The bruises appeared even darker in the fire light.

"You are hurting yourself by wearing these," he snapped.

"Better me than anyone else," I countered. "Now give me those back."

"You cannot hurt us as easily as you could a human," Arthur said, walking over to me and Rylan.

"For now, you will not wear these," Rylan told me with finality.

I stared at them in incredulity. Did they not see what I could do back at Arthur's establishment? I was an uncontrollable monster, and they *wanted* the destruction that came with my presence? They were crazy. They had to be.

"Why does it bother you that I'm wearing them?"

"Because you are harming yourself for no reason!" Rylan snarled and leaned over me. His eyes blazed red as he glowered. "I promised you would not be harmed while I am around, and I vow to keep that promise, even if that means I have to protect you from yourself. Do you know that spell is used specifically to torture people? The spell was not created to be used as carelessly as you have been using it."

Oh… The blood drained from my face. Torture? The spell I had cast upon these antique bracelets was used to *torture* people? Rylan was right. I didn't know the back story about the spell I had cast, and now that I knew, it made me feel sick. But that didn't mean that I would stop wearing the bracelets. If I had to torture myself to prevent others from getting hurt, then so be it.

"Rylan, you have to give them back to me, and you have to let me put them on. You got a taste of what I can do back in Chicago. I could accidentally crumble this house with just a thought."

"What if… What if we could help you learn how to use and control your power?" Arthur asked thoughtfully. "You would not need to wear those anymore."

The room went silent. Rylan glared at Arthur while I tried to process what he had just offered. How many times had I wished for help? Wished for control? No, this had to be a trick. It would be another broken promise. I started to shake my head, but Arthur continued, "Think of it, you would be able to do whatever it is you pleased without ever having to worry about hurting someone. To help you, we will have to determine what exactly you are but once we know, we will find someone knowledgeable enough to teach you how to control what gifts you have been given."

I pulled my arm from Rylan's grip, but the fight in me had disappeared. Hope blossomed in my chest. It was asinine to believe him. Arthur had said it himself that he had never run across someone like me before. How would we figure out what I was? And if we did find an answer, what guarantee was there that we could find someone to help me? What if I was so different from everyone else there would be no one who could help me?

But I had been wishing for this opportunity for two years. As much as I tried to squash it, the hope in my chest was growing stronger. Could I just let this opportunity slip away on the chance that it could be a trick? There had to be a catch.

"In return for what?" I asked suspiciously, looking from Arthur to Rylan then back to Arthur.

Arthur stared at me with his warm brown eyes and said, "In return, we ask that you stay with us and help us find a way to lift this curse."

I took a step back from both men. I knew it. I had been kidnapped, and while I was not necessarily physically restrained, I now knew how they could keep me here. The need to control my power was monumental. There was no doubt within a year that I would be too powerful to ever take off those bracelets again, and if I accidentally had a power surge, at that point, I would kill myself. It was an inevitable, painful fate. I needed to get a handle on my power.

But at what cost? My freedom?

The silence that followed his offer stretched out. I stood there as I weighed my options. There weren't many choices, but the two that I went back and forth on were important enough to give heavy consideration. I could leave and die within a year by my own hand or stay with these two men and hope that we could help each other. What if there were ulterior motives here that I wasn't seeing?

"You do not have to take the offer, Mae," Rylan said, breaking the silence. Arthur shot an angry look at him, but Rylan ignored it and stepped towards me. "You do not have to do anything you do not wish to do. If you wish to leave, you can. Before... that was a knee jerk reaction. I admit we panicked. It is a new emotion for us, and we did not respond to you hurrying away from us very well. I sincerely apologize. As promised, you can walk through those doors. The Guardians are not your responsibility."

He frowned and reached out to take my hand. He brought it up to his lips and kissed my knuckles. The unexpected touch caused me to tense as a wave of heat coursed through me. My breath was trapped in my throat, and my body trembled as roiling desire unfolded inside of me.

"But if you leave, know that I am coming with you."

"Ah, what?" I stammered, trying to focus on him and not the sudden yearning in my body. Why was I so drawn to him? I should be scared; I should be fleeing the room while screaming. These Guardians had just abducted me. Where was my common sense?

Apparently long gone because all I could think about were those lips.

"You do not have to give us an answer now. How about you spend the night here?" Arthur suggested.

I pulled my gaze from Rylan and freed my hand of his. The insane reaction my body was having towards this man was going to make me do something incredibly stupid if I didn't put space between us now. I stepped back.

"I can't stay here. I have to go to the campgrounds," I told them. Rylan frowned, confusion washing over his handsome, perfect features.

"Why there?"

"Because all of my power builds up throughout the week. If I don't release all of this pent-up energy, it finds its way out in a more destructive manner," I admitted. God, I hated feeling so out of control. "Every weekend I head out to find somewhere secluded and let go a little bit. It makes the next week more bearable."

"It is late now; I am sure the welcome desk will no longer be open. Why not use the woods behind the house?" Arthur suggested quickly. "There are no neighbors nearby, and once you are done you can stay in the guesthouse. You will find some privacy there."

Rylan looked over at Arthur; his face became unreadable. That soft buzzing began back up in my head. I was torn between curiosity and annoyance. Were they plotting something nefarious for me? This time I had to ask, "What are you two talking about?"

Arthur and Rylan both exchanged a look of surprise. Rylan frowned.

"You know we are communicating?"

"I guessed that was what you were doing. I don't know how to explain it, but I can *feel* your communication," I said, hoping they would understand.

"Interesting," Arthur said as he reached up to stroke his goatee.

I felt the buzzing again, but this time instead of feeling it around me, it felt directed at me.

"Did you just try to talk to me telepathically?" I asked him in surprise. There was no way to contain the sudden excitement and awe that flooded me when I realized that I might be able to talk to someone with my mind. The skin around Arthur's eyes crinkled, and the corner of his lips turned upwards.

"Yes," he confirmed. I couldn't stop a brief grin. "It is interesting you cannot hear me, but you can sense the touch of another's mind. This may be something we can explore later on. For now, why not call it a night? Rylan can show you to the guesthouse where you will find your belongings. Once settled, feel free to explore the grounds."

Was I okay with this? Was I going to put my trust in these two strangers? At this point, what was there to lose? I had lost my job, my lease for my apartment was up at the end of the month, and my classes could be taken online, so I could do them from anywhere. They were offering to help me find answers. They also didn't seem afraid of me. I looked at Arthur and then at Rylan; both were waiting patiently for my response.

If what they were saying was true, that the Guardian species was dying out and I could be the answer, they had to be sitting on the edge of their seats. But there they stood, patiently waiting for my response. I wasn't sure I would be so calm if the situation were reversed. What could be the harm in spending the night?

"Alright, I'll stay tonight."

Arthur closed his eyes, and when he opened them, his brown eyes sparkled with relief and hope. The grin that spread across his face spoke volumes. He turned slightly to look at Rylan and slapped him on the back. Rylan studied my face, his expression unreadable before looking over at Arthur.

"Wonderful!" Arthur said, his white teeth shining as he grinned at me. "Rylan, would you show Mae to the guesthouse?"

Rylan nodded and walked over to the double doors we had entered through. I followed behind him while Arthur lingered in the room. As I turned to shut the door behind me, I caught a glimpse of fear and despair in Arthur's eyes as he watched me leave the room. He had said the emotions he felt while I was around were sucked from him when I wasn't close enough. Was he feeling that effect now? The idea was unsettling. Rylan took the lead and led me deep into the interior of the house. The colonial house was set up traditionally; every room had its own designated space. Everything in the house was extraordinarily clean and tidy.

I followed him to the back of the house. We walked out a glass door and onto a wooden deck that looked out onto the back of the property. There must have been a half a mile of grass between the deck and the woods. Good, I didn't want to be too close to others once I was out there. I followed Rylan down the wooden steps. Off to the left of the house was a cozy cottage with the lights already turned on. We walked in silence over to the small building. Rylan stopped and turned to face me when we reached the door to the guesthouse.

"Everything you need to make yourself comfortable should be inside, but the door to the main house will remain unlocked should you need anything else," he said.

Suspiciously, I looked from him to the door. I didn't see any external locks that could keep me inside. I hoped this wasn't a trap. I looked back at him.

"Thanks," I said lamely, feeling browbeaten into this situation. Hadn't he told his driver when we had gotten here to put my stuff inside the guesthouse? Had the two Guardians been so sure I wasn't leaving tonight? He opened his mouth to say something but closed it. His brows came together, and he frowned.

"What is it?"

"Be safe out in the woods tonight," he said, his voice rough.

I was taken aback by his concern. This coming from the guy who kidnapped me. I scoffed and rolled my eyes when his brows rose in surprise. The only reason he was concerned about my well-being was he thought I could save his species. I didn't need his concern. I would be fine.

"Will do," I said sardonically and crossed my arms over my chest.

I wasn't walking into the guesthouse until he left. As if reading my mind, Rylan bowed his head and left me standing alone outside the cottage. I watched him walk back up to the deck, cross it, and head back inside before turning my attention to the little guesthouse.

I walked inside and immediately shut the door behind me so no one could come bursting out from the darkness and attack me from behind. The guesthouse was a little bit bigger than the size of my studio apartment. From a quick walkthrough, I found my camping backpack, duffle bag, and even my purse in the small bedroom. There were fluffy white towels and new toiletries in the bathroom. A glance in the refrigerator revealed a variety of beverages.

I shut all the blinds and turned out all the lights that were not needed. I kept a light on in the kitchen and one on in the bedroom so I could see where I was going when I returned. I debated hiding my purse but then let the idea go. If they had wanted to go through my things, they probably would have already. A quick check inside of it told me my credit and debit cards were still there, and the handful of cash I kept on hand – even my phone was still sitting in the pocket I normally kept it in. Huh; I guess they thought I wouldn't call for help.

I stood in the middle of the small guesthouse and debated if it was worth making the trek towards the woods. Logically, I knew I needed to go and let off some steam. If I was going to entertain the idea of being around these two Guardians longer than just tomorrow, I would need to let out the power coursing through me. But I felt spent, emotionally and physically. My limbs felt heavy, and my eyelids drooped. I needed to sleep. The large queen bed with the thick down comforter was waiting for me just down the small hallway. No. I couldn't sleep. Not yet at least. I would go out tonight for just as long as it took to make myself more comfortable, and then I could go to sleep. With that thought in mind, I left the guesthouse and headed towards the woods.

The night sky was clear, which made it easy to maneuver through the trees. I could hear the bugs and nightlife sing their songs as I quietly walked through their natural habitat. I loved nature. Even before I had power, I loved exploring the woods, hiking trails, and camping with my family. When I was far enough that I could no longer see the house, I stopped. I scanned the area around me with a slow, deliberate turn. I didn't want anyone seeing me in my appalling state of chaos.

When I was sure I was alone, I relaxed. I closed my eyes, took a deep breath in, and as I exhaled, I allowed myself to let go of the shaky control I had over my power. The rush came hard and fast, but I was ready for it. It came out like an explosion of wind, and it went in every direction. Trees swayed violently around me and the ground rolled under my feet. Somewhere nearby, a large branch cracked and fell from a tree. I took another deep breath and let go of a little more control. A bush nearby exploded, ripping itself into pieces. The leaves got caught up in the blast of energy and carried off into the woods. I heard another explosion followed by another as more energy seeped out.

The heat rose in my cheeks as a sick excitement overtook me, the way it did every time I allowed this much power free. The built-up energy that made me sick, tired, and scared rushed out of me like a dam with a crack in it. The tension in my body eased significantly. Tears leaked down my cheeks in relief. My shoulders shook as I suppressed a sob.

How much longer could I take this? Could the two men back in the house help me? The desire to be fixed was overwhelming. If I could get a better handle on all of this, life wouldn't be too bad. I could deal with having some power as long as I could use it how I wanted.

Next to me a tree snapped in half and fell. Another one followed suit. Both times as the trees fell the ground shook. It was wild to think that this was just a fraction of power that I allowed out. What would it be like to let it all out? I stood there, mentally struggling to hold the flood of energy back. Letting it all out would probably tear the entire state of Illinois to pieces.

When my body began to shake with exhaustion, I knew it was time to stop. I struggled for a moment to get a grip on my power. I raised both of my hands in the air, palms facing out as I chanted:

"You are the Spirit within me, you are the Wind in my hair, you are the Earth beneath my feet, and you are the Water that flows through me, and you are the Fire that drives me."

I knew the chanting didn't draw back my power. In my spellbook, the chant was used to center oneself. By concentrating on the chant, I was able to focus on internalizing my power. It took me chanting the verse three times before I was able to seal the mental barrier in my head, halting the flow of power. The air around me stilled, and the night went silent.

I stood there swaying with fatigue and studying the damage I'd caused. It was like a bomb had blown up underneath my feet. The trees were bent away from me in every direction, shrubs had been ripped out of the ground, and fallen branches were everywhere. Hopefully, Arthur didn't have a favorite tree.

I turned and headed back to the guesthouse. The thought of climbing into a bed tonight instead of a sleeping bag had me quicken my steps. I was always tired, but tonight I was exhausted. The lack of sleep, the constant fear that I could hurt someone, the inability to keep food down… They were all starting to add up, and tonight I could really feel it. All I wanted to do was curl up and sleep forever.

When I got back to the guesthouse, I stripped down out of my dirty clothes and stepped into the shower. The warm water helped ease my sore body. My bruises were dark and ugly. I poked a few larger ones and winced. Hopefully, this wouldn't happen for a while if I wasn't going to wear those bracelets.

By the time I was done in the shower and dried off, I was stumbling blindly through the guesthouse to the bedroom. I turned off the light, checked to make sure my alarms were set on my phone, and collapsed onto the bed. The last thought I had before sleep stole over me was how my life couldn't possibly get any crazier.

Chapter Four

The next morning I stared at my reflection in the bathroom mirror after dressing. Due to the expulsion of power last night, I looked more like myself today. Instead of violet eyes and glowing veins, my brown eyes stared back at me. My skin appeared less pale, and even the dark circles under my eyes seemed lighter. If I could blow off a little more steam today, I could continue to look like this for another week, until the build-up became too much again.

Still staring at my reflection, I turned slightly and leaned my head forward, then tilted it to the side. There was that weird tattoo that had shown up one night just after my power had emerged. I had been scared then, wondering what it meant, but after doing some research online and coming up with nothing I had let my fear of the mark rescind; I had more important issues to worry about. Now, I was more concerned about the mark than ever. It obviously meant something to Arthur and Rylan; especially Rylan.

After leaving the bathroom, I left the guesthouse and made my way to the main house through the patio door. It was silent. Where was I supposed to meet Arthur and Rylan? Were they awake yet? Were they plotting something sinister right now? As I walked through the house, I made sure to step as quietly as possible, and I kept a lookout for anything that might be a part of some elaborate trap. Finally, I found the kitchen, where an older woman was scrambling some eggs. She looked up and smiled at me.

"Good morning, Miss White. I hope you slept well," the woman said. Her smile was warm, and she seemed friendly enough.

"Um, yes, thank you," I said. What should I do? Should I leave her alone? Should I sit down at the island?

"Please, have a seat. I can make you breakfast," the woman said and ushered me over to a barstool. Uncomfortable with someone making me food I offered, "Can I help you?"

The woman laughed.

"No, no, it's my job to make sure everyone here is taken care of. What would you like to eat?"

I thought about food. My stomach growled hungrily but then twisted uncomfortably. I needed to eat, but the thought of ingesting anything made me feel nauseous.

"Actually, I'm not hungry," I lied.

"Nonsense, Mary, she will eat an omelet," Rylan said strolling into the room.

I jumped at his sudden presence. He was even more attractive than I remembered. I could smell the perfume from his soap he'd used in the shower this morning. His hair was still damp, and his cheeks were pink from the warm water. My own cheeks warmed under his gaze as it swept over me.

"I just said I wasn't hungry."

"I can hear your stomach in the other room. You need to eat," Rylan said as he came to stand near me. He leaned against the counter and crossed his arms. He raised a brow expecting me to fight him on this. As I glared at him, I could see Mary look between us, smile, and go back to whisking the eggs in her bowl.

"It's a waste of food. I *can't* eat it," I said giving up the staring contest and turning to Mary.

"The food's not poisoned if that is what you are worried about," Rylan said.

I rolled my eyes. "This has been the oddest kidnapping experience. Taken to a nice house in the countryside, offered a cozy place to sleep, and now I'm being forced to eat a delicious breakfast? If I'd known being kidnapped would be this enjoyable, I would have tried to be taken a long time ago."

My stomach growled. I guess I could eat a few bites. Mary just smiled. Did she think I was joking?

A noise escaped Rylan, and I looked up at him curiously. He coughed and turned away from me. Gazing at his profile, I could see a smile tugged the corners of his mouth upwards. I studied him for a moment and found myself again admiring how incredibly attractive he was. My eyes trailed over his body. He wore a plain t-shirt and jeans. His shirt was snug against his body, and I could see his muscles under the fabric. It was such a simple outfit, but I could almost smell how expensive it was. What did he do for a living?

Rylan looked back at me, and I looked away, embarrassed to be caught ogling him.

"Do you like vegetables, Miss White?" Mary asked as she opened the refrigerator.

"Please make it however you want, Mary. I'm not picky," I muttered, feeling bad that I wouldn't be able to eat much of it.

I stared down at the counter with a frown. Absentmindedly, I touched the thick scarring around my wrists. God, they were ugly. Suddenly, Rylan reached over and gently took my wrist in his hand. I flinched in surprise, but I didn't pull away from him. Oddly enough, his touch seemed to ease the mental stress it took to hold back the force of power inside me. The feeling was calming, and the tightly coiled knots in my stomach eased up a little in response.

"Do these hurt?" Rylan asked, staring down at the thick scarring.

I shook my head. No, they were just humiliating to look at. They were a sign of my failure. He ran his thumb over the scars.

The gentle caress was oddly soothing. The thought of enjoying this man's touch unnerved me, and I pulled my hand away as a warmth began to burn in my cheeks.

"Ah, you are awake," Arthur said, walking into the kitchen.

He paused mid-stride, and I watched as his whole body shuddered hard. The corners of his mouth slowly turned upwards, and his face brightened. The smile seemed to surprise him. I realized that the few times I had seen emotion on his face were probably very new to him. I was sure he was feeling pleasantly surprised to find that the person he had helped kidnap had stayed the night and was sitting in his kitchen.

"I'm being forced to eat breakfast," I complained. Just as I said it, Mary placed a Spanish omelet in front of me along with a set of silverware. My stomach growled, but the blood ran out of my face as nausea followed. "Thank you."

"It's my pleasure, Miss White," Mary said beaming. She turned to the two men. "Can I get either of you something to eat?"

"No, thank you, Mary," Arthur said while Rylan shook his head. "You can leave us now."

Mary nodded and left the kitchen.

"Does she know about you two?" I asked curiously.

"No," Arthur said. "But I am sure she has an idea that we are different since she doesn't need to cook while we are here."

I looked at him curiously.

"Why is that?"

Arthur's smile returned as he shared a look with Rylan. Rylan's lips twitched upwards. The amusement on their faces made me uncomfortable. Okay, maybe I didn't want to know.

"We will tell you more about us later," Rylan said. "Now eat."

I looked down at the omelet and sighed. I picked up my fork and knife and started cutting into the egg.

"So, what's the plan for today?" I asked, uncomfortable under their scrutiny.

"We wanted to learn more about you. How does your power work? Was the onset gradual or immediate? Was there a trigger that caused it to arise after being dormant so long?" Arthur answered. I took a bite of egg and my mouth watered in enjoyment. I swallowed and took another bite. Mhmm, this was delicious.

"Who else knows about your power?" Rylan asked me.

I took a third bite before answering him. "My childhood best friend was around when I first realized I had power."

Rebecca wasn't around anymore. She hadn't been around to witness how horrible my power had gotten. Thank God for that. But these two didn't need to know about her. I wasn't about to pull her into this crazy life.

"Your childhood best friend? Has he or she told anyone else about you?" he pushed.

I was on my fourth bite of omelet when my stomach protested painfully. I put down my fork abruptly and tried not to gag. I guessed that was all my body was going to allow for the day. At least it had been delicious. Much better than the yogurts or the protein bars I was usually able to keep down. Nausea rolled through me. I leaned back and tried to focus on what Rylan had asked and not on the need to throw up.

"No."

"No? Are you sure?" Arthur pressed. "The more people who know about you, the more dangerous it is for them and you. We need to figure out who is closest to you, how much they know, and who they may have told."

Another wave of nausea rolled over me. Please don't be sick, please don't be sick, I chanted in my head. I pushed the plate away from me, hoping that being further away from the smell would stop the feeling of wanting to vomit. There was a brief silence as I took slow, deep breaths.

When I was certain I wouldn't heave all over the table, I answered, "This person is the only one who knows, and they won't say anything to anyone."

"Who is this person? We need to look into this," Arthur pushed. He looked down at my plate, "You need to eat. You need your strength."

"I can't eat anymore."

"You have barely eaten," Rylan pushed.

"I told you I can't eat it," I snapped and pushed my stool away from the island. Rylan and Arthur frowned. "Why are you so concerned about me eating breakfast?"

"Because you are wasting away in front of us," Rylan said calmly. "You've slept. Now you need to eat. You only ate yogurt for dinner last night; you must be starving."

I stared at him. How the hell did he know what I had for dinner when he hadn't even been there? I lived ten floors up; there was no way they could have seen into my windows. I could feel my anger rising. The plate on the counter trembled, and the unused knife clattered to the ground. Had they been spying on me since the moment I left Arthur's establishment? When would this become too much?

"*Excuse me?*"

"We had to see what you were up to," Arthur explained with a shrug, unperturbed by the vibrating plate. I took a deep breath and reined in my temper. It wouldn't do any good to shatter the plate and cause a mess.

"Wait," Rylan said and put a hand on my shoulder. The queasiness I was feeling stopped abruptly. Odd… "You said you *can't* eat. Not that you are not hungry."

I glared at him, not sure where he was going with this.

"Why can you not eat your food?" he pressed. "Do you have a specific… dietary restriction?"

I gritted my teeth in annoyance and debated whether I should answer truthfully or not. After a moment, I sighed and decided to go with the truth.

"It makes me sick to eat. It doesn't matter what is in front of me, but I just cannot eat without feeling like I need to vomit. When I have the bracelets on, I wouldn't have been able to eat what I just did. Without them, I have a little more wiggle room with how much I can stomach."

"Which still is not much," Rylan noted, glancing at the omelet.

"The stronger my power becomes, the less I can eat… and sleep," I added begrudgingly.

"What do you mean?" Rylan's pupils narrowed.

"I can't fall into a deep sleep. I lose all control of my power and horrible things happen. So, I put several alarms on throughout the night to wake me up so I can't fall into a deep sleep."

The thunderous look in Rylan's face threw me off guard. He exchanged glances with Arthur, and both fell silent. I pulled my arm free and grabbed for the plate. I guessed I could force another bite down. Just as I grabbed the plate, a thought hit me. I turned to look at Rylan curiously and then back at my breakfast. I grabbed the fork, cut off a small bite of the omelet, and plopped it into my mouth. Just as the egg landed on my tongue I reached out with my free hand and touched Rylan's arm. The feeling of nausea vanished. I let go of Rylan and dropped the fork. His brows came together in confusion.

"I don't feel sick when there is contact," I mused out loud. But why? I frowned. "When you touched me the other night, when I was in pain from my bracelets, the pain vanished, too."

When Arthur had thrown me over his shoulder during my first kidnapping, my pain had been there. But there had been no skin to skin contact then…What did this mean? Maybe fate brought us together for a reason. Maybe they really could help me and … maybe I could help them. I had yet to run into anything else that soothed the pain or made it virtually disappear as Rylan could.

Rylan placed his hand on my shoulder, startling me from my thoughts. I looked up and met his gaze.

"Eat," he commanded.

I opened my mouth to protest, but then I realized that he was purposely making contact so I could enjoy a full meal. Cautiously, I did as I was told. When was the last time I had been able to eat an entire meal? While I ate, the two Guardians remained silent. I couldn't even feel the soft buzzing that indicated they were communicating with each other. Maybe they were absorbed by their thoughts. By the time the plate was empty, I felt comfortably full. I put my hand over my stomach as I felt my lips turn upwards.

"That was…" I shook my head as my throat tightened. I was finally *full*. My eyes started to water. "Thank you." My voice came out as a whisper. I looked down and blinked back tears. I mentally chided myself for being so emotional. Rylan's hand that gripped my shoulder tightened before he released me.

"We will figure this out," he promised.

A knock at the front door caused me to jump. Arthur left the kitchen, and I went to the sink to take care of my dishes. A moment later, I could hear voices, but not what was being said. As I started to dry my plate Mary came back into the room and saw me at the sink.

"Oh no, Miss White! That's my job, please leave the rest to me," she said and hurried over.

"I don't mind."

"Let her take over. Come," Arthur said at the entrance to the kitchen.

A soft buzzing in my head told me the Guardians were speaking with one another. Part of me was annoyed they were keeping something from me. What was going on? Who had been at the door? I glanced at Mary who was oblivious to the telepathy happening around her.

I got up and followed Rylan and Arthur out of the room. We headed back to the den where we had convened the previous night. I shut the door behind us and turned towards the two Guardians.

"That was the police," Arthur said.

"I didn't call them."

"No, the neighbors called about the earthquake that happened last night. They wanted to make sure all the surrounding neighbors were doing alright," Arthur confirmed.

"No one got hurt, did they?"

Arthur shook his head, and I let out a sigh of relief.

"No, but this raises a concern. We will have to move to a more secluded area if we are going to work with you," Arthur said.

Immediately, red flags went up in my head. How much more seclusion could they ask for out here? The neighbors were already a good distance away. Could *more* distance help? Or was there a more menacing reason they wanted me further away from civilization?

"I have a house outside of Savannah with plenty of space," Rylan offered.

Arthur nodded as if he knew of the property Rylan was talking about. They spoke telepathically to each other for a moment, maybe discussing details about moving there. I stood there unsure what I wanted from all of this. Last night, Arthur and Rylan had offered to help me with my issues if, in return, I would help them. Was I ready to trust these two men with my life? It wasn't like I'd had much time to think about their offer. But did I need more time?

Did I know these men? No, but I could already see benefits from being around them. This morning I had my first full meal in almost six months. They had promised to help me find answers;

that was more than I could have hoped for in this situation. *And* even though I was annoyed I didn't have my bracelets, it was a relief that I wasn't in my normal state of pain. When was the last time I could say I wasn't in pain?

Selfish reasons aside, I might be able to help them with their problem. According to both men, they were unable to feel emotions; a curse placed upon them by gods. Around me, though, they could feel. I had already seen them both smile and even heard some chuckling. I'd seen curiosity and suspicion. Most noticeable, though, was the passion in Arthur's voice and the flare of hope when he talked about the idea of lifting the curse. They were hoping that I could do it. They looked to me as the answer to their problems. How could I walk away from such a horrible situation knowing that I could be the answer to helping lift the curse?

There was always a chance this was a trap of some sort. The past year had taught me that there were nefarious creatures out there. Twice on the trail I'd had run-ins with monsters… Luckily, I had escaped with my life. But were Arthur and Rylan evil? I would just have to keep an eye out for any suspicious behavior from both men.

Honestly, I had nothing to lose by helping them. With their help I could possibly have control over my power, meaning I had my freedom to gain. Was there any more incentive I needed to go with them? No, my freedom was enough for me to risk everything.

"Alright, when do we leave?" I asked, feeling confident in my decision.

Both Arthur and Rylan turned their attention back to me.

"Are you sure you want to do this?" Rylan asked, his brows coming together and a frown turning his mouth downward.

I nodded. "I want to grab my stuff from my apartment, but yes, I'm sure I want to do this. If we can help each other, then let's do it."

"Wonderful!" Arthur said, and a grin spread across his face. Rylan's smile was more subdued, but I could see those teal eyes warm as he looked at me. Arthur shook his head, still smiling, "You are a true blessing to all of us, Mae. Of course, we can get your belongings. We will head back to Chicago in an hour. I will call Phillip to ready everything."

"Phillip?"

"Our private pilot. We will take my private jet to get to Savannah," Rylan said.

The blood ran out of my face. Fly? They wanted to *fly* to Georgia. What was wrong with a little road trip?

"What's wrong?" Rylan asked frowning.

I shook my head, trying to keep the panic down. "Do you have my bracelets?"

Rylan scowled, "You do not need those around us."

"You don't understand," I said, trying to remain calm. "I don't want to panic if we hit some turbulence in the air and take the plane down by accident."

Rylan shook his head as I talked. "We will be right there with you. Our contact seems to help you keep a hold on your power. I will hold your hand if need be. You are not putting those things back on."

"Rylan's right," Arthur said, interrupting my argument. "We will be there with you. Use us as your aid to control yourself. The internal damage that you cause yourself when you use those bracelets is unnecessary."

They didn't understand. I was not afraid of flying, but knowing that I was a ticking time bomb stuck in a metal contraption high up in the air was a little daunting. I took a deep breath.

"Can we compromise? Can I have them nearby in case I need them? Please? I don't know how durable you two are, but if the plane explodes, I know I wouldn't be able to survive it."

Rylan's jaw clenched, and the teal swirled to maroon then shifted to red. Okay, he was not a fan of this plan, but he had to see the safety behind having the bracelets. The way he towered over me and the real anger on his face almost made me backtrack. He had to see the practicability of the bracelets.

I placed my hand on his arm and pushed a little more. "*Please?*"

He gave an exaggerated sigh and looked away from me. "Alright."

I relaxed and couldn't help but grin. Ha! Victory was mine! Arthur chuckled, and Rylan gave him a dark look. This caused Arthur's chuckle to turn into laughter.

"Go collect your things, and be ready to leave in an hour," Arthur told me with a half-smile.

With that Arthur strolled across the room, opened the door, and left without a backward glance. The moment the door shut, the air in the room became stifling. I turned my attention back to Rylan, who had closed the distance between us while my attention had been on the other Guardian.

Standing toe to toe with Rylan, I had to tilt my head back to look into his handsome face. His eyes had shifted back to that wonderfully cool teal. He towered over me, drowning me in his personal space. We stood so close together that his body heat resonated from him and warmed me. My whole body began to hum as lust unexpectedly made another appearance. His mouth was turned downwards into a frown, and his brows came together. His teal eyes began to change again, deepening in color, reflecting his own desire.

"You do not owe the Guardians anything. Not your presence, not your time, not your concern," he said, his voice low. It rumbled through me like a thunderstorm. I shuddered.

"I'm not doing it for them." *Or you.*

"I know," he said.

Had his head lowered just a little? If I just rose on my toes, our lips could brush together…

"But, all the same, by agreeing to help us, you are saving the lives of my brethren. Your graciousness will not be forgotten."

His breath skimmed across my face, and I was lost. My heart rate was too fast. Could he hear it? Could he see the flush in my face or the longing in my own eyes? His warm teal eyes shifted down from my eyes to my lips, and my breathing stopped.

Instead of leaning down and planting a kiss on my lips, he took a step back and lifted his arm, showing me the direction of the door. Sanity came roaring back, and shame colored my cheeks. How could I want this man so much? I was willing to kiss a man I'd just met, who had just kidnapped me, and then just coerced me into staying in the house they had brought me to.

"Come, we need to pack our belongings and get ready for our trip," Rylan said. Was his voice strained?

I followed him out of the room, keeping my gaze on my feet. Rylan walked me to the back of the house before leaving to gather his own things. I headed back out to the guesthouse and began shoving things back into my duffle bag. I grabbed my phone off the charger and noticed a missed call. It was the Chicago Police Department.

Frowning, I listened to the voicemail. According to the officer, someone had broken into my apartment around midnight. They were calling to make sure I was okay and had questions for me. Odd, why would someone break into my apartment? I had nothing of any real value. Once I finished listening to the voicemail, I called the officer back and assured them that, no, I was not harmed. No, I had not been home. No, I had no idea who would do this. Twenty minutes later, I hung up the phone and sat down on the edge of the bed.

When I got to the apartment, I would look through everything to see what had been taken. The apartment had come pretty much furnished, so whatever had been stolen probably hadn't been mine. Would that come out of my security deposit? Grumbling over the potential loss of my deposit, I grabbed my stuff and headed out to the main living space of the guesthouse. As I put everything down, there was a knock at the door. I opened the door, wondering if maybe I was holding everyone up, and found Wilbur waiting patiently for me on the front step.

"Good morning," he said with a warm smile.

How dare he smile after he helped kidnap me? For a moment I was angry with him, but my anger lasted all of five seconds before I relaxed. There was no need to be upset with this man when everything seemed to be working out.

"I'm here to take your things to the car. Are you almost ready?"

I nodded and stepped back into the house so he could come in.

"Very good. Mr. Wellington is waiting for you in the foyer of the main house," Wilbur informed me as he picked up my backpack and duffle bag off the floor. He left the guesthouse with my belongings in tow. I walked through the guesthouse one last time to make sure I'd gotten everything before I headed to the house.

Rylan was waiting exactly where Wilbur had promised he would be. He turned at the sound of my footsteps coming down the hall, and I couldn't help but feel breathless as I approached him. God, he was stunning. Those cool teal eyes pierced me with a focused stare, and a smile, which was slow in coming, warmed his stony features. I felt my heart flutter in my chest under his attention. Staring into his face I wondered how old he was. He looked to be somewhere in his thirties.

"Are you ready to head back into the city?" he asked as I came to stand close to him. I nodded. "Good. Arthur has already left to meet Phillip at the airport. We will see him in a few hours."

I nodded again, and we left the beautiful colonial house. Outside was the same black SUV that had kidnapped me the night before. I frowned but said nothing.

The ride back to my apartment was relatively silent. Rylan seemed lost in his thoughts. I wasn't quite sure what we could discuss with Wilbur within earshot, so I remained silent. Briefly, my mind went to the fall semester coming up in two weeks and I made a mental note that I needed to order my textbooks before September arrived. Hopefully, whoever had broken into my apartment hadn't stolen my laptop. I had forgotten to grab it in my haste. The thought of going back to school filled me with both excitement and dread. While most of my classes would have to be taken online due to my inability to control my power, I would soon be finishing the degree I had set out to get. The homework and studying would be hard, but it would be completely worth it in the end; I just knew it.

As we approached the city, I could feel my body change slightly. I could feel the tension grow in my muscles. Although I wasn't wearing the bracelets, I could feel the brewing of a new headache. City life had been a mistake. While I wasn't quite keen on being kidnapped and forced into a new situation, I was glad to be leaving Chicago.

As we ventured deeper into the city, my control slipped while I battled my headache and kept my power at bay. A few times the car or the road would vibrate just enough to notice. A few car alarms went off as we passed parked cars, and once a traffic light flickered as we passed under it. This was why I had to wear those horrible bracelets. I was always uncomfortable the day I came back from a camping trip. It was like my body didn't like to be around all the tall buildings and people. Watching the mild chaos follow us turned my mood sour. I was a monster, and I would never be able to hide from that fact; no matter how hard I tried.

I said nothing to Rylan about my discomfort as we began weaving through traffic, but he seemed to notice the change in my mood. Rylan turned his attention to me, coming back from wherever his mind had taken him. He unlocked my seatbelt and gently pulled me towards him. I stiffened in surprise. The instant he made contact with me the chaos ceased. The tension and my headache were still there, but muted, and my power settled down. He wrapped his arm around my shoulders and leaned down until his mouth was next to my ear.

"Are you alright?" he asked.

I sat there stunned at his boldness. Why would he think that dragging me over towards him so he could drape an arm over my shoulders was acceptable? Part of me was outraged and the other part of me… Well, I was relieved.

"I am now," I said begrudgingly.

"Good."

Had he been worried that I was going to hurt us? I didn't blame him for feeling like that; I would be uncomfortable in his position, too. Instead of straightening, as I expected him to, Rylan moved his head even closer, and I could feel his nose brush against my hair. His arm around my shoulders tightened just slightly.

"Hm… You smell lovely."

I let out an awkward laugh at his unexpected compliment.

"That's nice to know," I said. He smirked and straightened in his seat.

After the almost hour-long car ride, we finally pulled up in front of my apartment complex. Two police officers were standing outside the doors talking to one another.

"Do you usually have security here?" Rylan asked, eyeing the officers as Wilbur came around to open my door.

"Not usually," I said as I slid over to exit the vehicle. "They're here because someone broke into my apartment last night."

I almost had my foot out the door of the SUV, my mind already thinking about what I should be packing, when Rylan's fingers snaked around my wrist and yanked me back towards him.

"*Excuse me?*" he snapped.

I turned back to look at him, surprised by his sudden change in demeanor. "What?"

"Someone broke into your apartment last night, and you chose not to share this information with me?" he asked with a deep scowl, his eyes burning red. I stared at him for a moment wondering where this anger was coming from. It wasn't like he had anything at the apartment that could be stolen.

"No, why would I?" I asked still baffled. Rylan's eyes glowed brighter as his scowl deepened. He leaned over me, and I recoiled instinctively at his fury.

"Because I am your mate and I need to make sure you are always safe. Your personal space has been violated by an intruder, which means your living quarters are not safe. I will be damned if I allow you to walk into a dangerous situation," Rylan explained angrily.

I rolled my eyes and opened my mouth to tell him the police had come and gone so there was no danger, but I didn't get a chance.

"Do you think this is a *joke?*" he snarled. I watched in a horrified fascination as his cheeks hollowed, his red eyes became slightly sunken, and his canines lengthened into fangs.

I stared at Rylan. My mouth hung slightly ajar, stunned by his transformation. My heart slammed in my chest, and my breath stuck in my throat. My body was paralyzed with fear; my mind went blank. Thank God Rylan still had his fingers wrapped around my wrist, or the entire street would have crumbled underneath us.

"Wilbur, shut the door and drive around the block," Rylan snapped.

Wilbur, seemingly unaware of the very angry Guardian in the back of the SUV, shut the door and walked back to the driver's seat without a word. Once he had gotten behind the wheel, we were pulling back into traffic. Rylan took a long, deep breath and closed his eyes. I watched as his face changed back to the human façade.

He opened his eyes as his face relaxed and said, "Mae, breathe."

Oh, yeah, breathing… I needed to do that. I took a shaky breath and tried to steady my rapidly beating heart.

"I am sorry I startled you," he said. "Are you alright?"

Was I *alright*? Had I just made a horrible decision to go with this man and Arthur to some unknown location in the hopes that they were going to help me and not murder me? The same moment the thought crossed my mind, I was flooded with unexpected guilt. How could I even consider that as a possibility now? Even furious, Rylan hadn't held my wrist any tighter or hurt me in any way. More importantly, he was mad that my *safety* had been jeopardized. How could I be afraid of someone concerned about my well-being?

I nodded. Yes, I was alright.

"Do not be afraid of me, Mae," Rylan said softly, staring down into my face with those mesmerizing teal eyes. "I swear, I will never hurt you."

I opened my mouth to say something but found my throat dry. I swallowed and tried again.

"Okay," I said, my voice barely more than a whisper as I tried to regain my composure. "I was just surprised. I wasn't expecting Vampire Rylan." I glanced nervously towards Wilbur who was studiously ignoring our soft voices. I looked back at Rylan, who gave me a half-smile.

"Not vampire, Guardian," he corrected. Huh; could have fooled me.

"Um… what's the difference? I saw fangs, red eyes… Do you burst into a thousand bats as a form of travel?"

"Vampires are creatures that thrive in the night and run on pure instinct. They do not have the power, nor do they have the strength of a Guardian."

"Any other surprises I should know about? Just so next time I can properly react to them?" I asked, trying to make light of the situation. It worked. Rylan chuckled.

"Too many to share now," he assured me. I gave him a weak smile, and he relaxed further. The SUV came to a stop, and I found that we were back in front of my apartment complex. "Come, let us collect your things."

Rylan was out of the SUV and opening my door before Wilbur was out of his seat. The moment Rylan let go of my wrist I gritted my teeth and held back the wave of power that crashed forward. I grimaced, but by the time Rylan opened my door, I was able to compose my facial features. He reached out, and I took his hand, grateful for the contact. We walked past the police officers, and I took Rylan over to the stairs, giving a skeptical glance to the old elevator.

I wondered if Rylan would complain about the number of stairs, but he said nothing. The moment I opened the door to my floor, he pulled me behind him as if to lead. What the hell did he think he was doing? He didn't know which apartment was mine. Oh, wait… Yes, he did. If he and Arthur knew what I had eaten for dinner the previous night, then they knew which apartment I lived in.

While I briefly rehashed my irritation at being spied on and kidnapped, I realized how tense Rylan was as we walked down the hallway. Was he really that worried someone would still be in my apartment? While the idea first seemed ludicrous, worry swelled up in my chest. I stopped walking. He turned around to see why I'd stopped, and I found his eyes were red and burning.

"I don't think there will be anyone in my apartment, but if there is, I don't want you to get hurt either," I said softly.

A corner of his mouth twitched upwards.

"It is hard to harm a Guardian," he assured me. I wasn't sure what that meant, but he seemed confident, so I resigned myself to believe him. I sighed and nodded, indicating that he keep going.

We walked the rest of the way down the hallway to my front door. Or rather, what was left of the front door. I gasped. This hadn't been a normal burglar who picked locks to enter places. My door was in shreds, hanging off two hinges. The caution tape was lamely placed in front to keep everyone out. A sound similar to a growl escaped from Rylan, but I couldn't see his expression.

He pushed the tape aside, and we walked in. Anything that had been sitting on a flat surface had been thrown around the room. The mattress was ripped to shreds; there were huge gouges in the wood floor. Any mirrors or glass décor was shattered into small pieces. All the kitchen flatware, pots and pans, and cutlery were broken or thrown around. My clothes were either ripped to mere shreds or in random piles on the floor.

"Who would do this?" I asked in horror, more to myself than to Rylan.

"Not who, *what*," Rylan said grimly scanning the room. "A spider demon was in here. The same creatures that attacked you on the trail."

A spider demon… The blood drained from my face and a ringing started in my ears. I stared around at my stuff realizing the danger everyone in the building had been in.

"Spider demons are incredibly dangerous, Mae. If they are willing to come into the city to find you, then you are in more danger than you realize. They are attracted to power and hunger for it."

The only time I had ever encountered them was when I had been alone and far away from people. Without thinking about it, I reached out and grabbed Rylan's wrist to steady my nerves as my power threatened to overwhelm me. The floor began to shake, and my eyesight blurred with tears. *Don't lose it, don't lose it,* I repeated in my head. Rylan pulled me under his shoulder, but I barely noticed the gesture as I fought down the pressure that was humming under the surface of my skin.

"Breathe, Mae," I heard him whisper somewhere far away.

I'm trying! I wanted to scream in frustration. All I really wanted to do was crumple onto the floor and cry. I didn't want any of this. I didn't want power; I didn't want to be attacked by spider demons; I didn't want to be fighting back normal reactions that occur when someone breaks into your house.

After another moment of struggling with my feelings, I finally got myself somewhat under control. I stepped out from under Rylan's arm and forced myself to look around the mess. I was starting to feel numb, which allowed me to step back and take a look around. Absentmindedly I touched my wrists. I frowned as I realized my bracelets were not there to help me.

"Do you have my bracelets?" I asked. My voice sounded odd to my ears.

"You are doing fine. You do not need them," Rylan growled.

His voice seemed so far away. I didn't fight him on this. He was right. I was okay now. I moved away from him and looked around the studio apartment, suddenly feeling indifferent. I walked over massive gouges in the floor. I began to walk away when something peeking from under the mattress caught my eye. I bent down and pulled out my laptop. If I weren't so numb, I would have been amazed to see that there was not a mark on it. Good, I didn't have to buy another one for school. I tucked it under my arm.

Rylan was studying the damage as I continued to check over my personal belongings. I moved some clothes with my foot to see if anything was salvageable, but there was nothing. I would have to buy a few new things. I moved away from the clothes and walked into the bathroom where I stopped to stare at where the mirror above the sink used to be. Now the mirror was in thousands of tiny pieces all over the counter, in the sink, and on the floor. Where the mirror used to hang was a massive hole that went through the drywall, the stud, and almost out into the hallway. I could almost see light coming through the thin drywall on the other side.

Out of all the damage in the apartment, this was probably the most interesting. This hole in the wall seemed deliberate. There were no other holes in the rest of the apartment, so why here?

"Excuse me, you can't be in here. This is a crime scene," a male voice said from the front door. I walked out of the bathroom to see an officer stepping past the tape.

"This is my apartment," I said stepping between Rylan and the officer.

"You're Miss White?" the officer asked skeptically.

"Yes, would you like to see some identification?"

The officer frowned and shook his head,

"No need. We spoke on the phone earlier, so you already know the details. If I can get you to sign the statement you gave, we can clean this up," he said. He shot a suspicious look over my head to Rylan. "Neighbors say that you're a loner. Who's this?"

"A friend."

"Where were you last night?" the officer asked Rylan as I took the pen and clipboard from his hands. Quickly, I signed my statement and handed it back.

"He was with me," I snapped. "Are we good here?"

"Yup; I'll call you if there's an update," he said. "Have a good day."

I nodded and watched as he left the apartment.

I turned and looked around the room one last time. There was nothing to save here. So now what? What did I do with all this stuff?

"I will hire a cleaning crew to come in and take care of this," Rylan said as if he was reading my mind.

"You don't need to do that," I said with a sigh. "I'll clean—"

"Nonsense," Rylan said cutting me off with a wave of his hand. "You do not have to do anything. It will be taken care of."

I stared up at him, boiling with conflicting emotions. Part of me was annoyed that he was so bossy. Who did he think he was? This wasn't his problem; it was mine, and he couldn't tell me what I did and did not have to do. If I wanted to clean my apartment, then I would clean my apartment. Another part of me was suspicious; what would he want in return if I let him take care of this? Was there an ulterior motive behind his offer? Then, a very small part of me was relieved that I didn't have to look at this mess anymore. A demon had snuck into my building to try to kill me. The evidence of the monstrosity surrounded the two of us. All I wanted to do was get far away from this room.

I hesitated a moment longer before caving to Rylan.

"Alright, thank you," I muttered. "I need to go drop my keys off with the office manager and let them know I'm leaving two weeks early," I told him.

I didn't wait for a response. I didn't need one. I tucked my laptop under my arm, pushed back the crime scene tape, and almost ran down the hallway to get away from that small hellhole. Rylan didn't say another word, but he followed closely behind. The conversation with the office manager was brief. No, I would not be getting my security deposit back, but lucky for me my renter's insurance would cover the damages to my apartment.

Wilbur was waiting for us, parked in the same spot that we had arrived in. He stood by the open back door and waited for both Rylan and me to climb in before shutting it and heading to the driver's seat. I placed my laptop on my lap and my purse on the floor of the car and turned my head to watch the city fly past us as we drove towards the airport. Rylan remained silent, and I was grateful for the space to collect myself after what I had just witnessed.

Chapter Five

By the time we got to the airport, the numbness was beginning to fade away. Wilbur pulled the car around to the back of the airport. We pulled up to two sliding glass doors, and Wilbur parked the car. Both Rylan and I exited, my laptop and purse in either hand, and we walked through the sliding glass doors to a lobby similar to one in a hotel. We approached a tall, black door. Rylan opened the door, and we stepped inside to a small private lounge where Arthur was waiting for us.

Arthur looked up as we entered and rose from his chair, placing the newspaper he was reading on the glass coffee table in front of him. He began to smile, but his smile slipped away when he read our expressions. He came over to us with his brows furrowed.

"Mae, you look… Are you alright?"

I wanted to heave a long, exaggerated sigh. No, I wasn't alright. On the trail, stumbling into a spider demon, two different times, could be considered simply a coincidence, but for them to come to my home to find me? They were after me. Already, I wished the day would end. On top of the stress from finding out demons had entered my apartment, I was still dreading the plane ride. With how emotional I was feeling right then, getting on a plane sounded like a terrible idea.

"Have a seat, Mae. I will fetch you some lunch while you relax," Rylan offered.

He looked over my head at Arthur. The soft buzzing in my head told me they were relaying information back and forth to each other. I'm sure Rylan was sharing all the details about my intruder to Arthur.

"I'm not hungry, but thanks," I said, ignoring their telepathy.

I walked over to the swanky bar across the room. The bartender walked over and greeted me, but I didn't smile. He poured me the glass of water I requested, and I nursed it. Thankfully, the two Guardians left me alone for a while. Starring down at my disfigured, scarred wrists, I felt proud that I hadn't needed the bracelets back at the apartment. Instead, I had emotionally shut down. That was better, right? Then I couldn't hurt anyone. I thought about Rylan and Arthur, and how neither could feel emotions when I wasn't around, and for a moment, I wished I could be like that. At least, sometimes.

Finally, Rylan and Arthur began to speak aloud, albeit in soft voices behind me. It was probably for me to feel included, and I found that I appreciated the gesture. I was feeling extremely… alone. I missed having someone to talk with. I had been keeping people at a distance since I found out about my power. But just because I had to keep people at an arm's length didn't mean I didn't *want* relationships.

I couldn't make connections with people without picturing their terror and disgust if they ever found out the truth about me. I wanted a relationship where I could be myself and not have to hide. I wanted to be around people who knew what I was and didn't cower in fear. Kind of like… how it was with the Guardians. The thought came unbidden. The Guardians were very comfortable in my presence. They didn't quake in fear when my power leaked out. They didn't give me odd looks or cringe away from me.

I stared down at my water as realization struck: We might not be friends, but maybe that could change? They were supernatural just like me. I didn't have to be alone anymore. So, what was I doing over here when I could be with them? Why was I being so distant with the very people who *wanted* to be around me? Because I was being an idiot. That was why. I sucked down the rest of my water and left my seat at the bar. I walked over to the two Guardians and then sat between them and attempted to relax. Their smiles were wide, warm, and welcoming. I was glad that at least two people could stand to be around me.

"Mae, we were just discussing what we should do when we get to Savannah. There is a wonderful restaurant we can go to for dinner before heading to the house," Arthur suggested. "We have staff at the house now preparing it for our arrival, but I do think it will be much more convenient to eat before we get there."

The image of Rylan's face in the car when he had gotten upset popped into my head. I looked over my shoulder to find the bartender had disappeared and then looked back at Arthur. I leaned forward so I didn't have to speak loudly.

"Do you guys eat food?" I glanced at Rylan. "I couldn't help but notice the long fangs earlier."

Arthur openly glared at Rylan, and I turned to find Rylan smirking at his old friend. Oh, was I not supposed to have seen them?

"I lost my temper," Rylan explained to Arthur with a shrug. "It appears it is difficult to remain indifferent now that my emotions have returned."

"I apologize for Rylan's behavior," Arthur said still staring at his friend. I heard buzzing in my head again.

"Are you reprimanding him?" I asked curiously.

Arthur turned his attention to me as Rylan chuckled.

"Yes, he was," Rylan answered with a grin. "I have not been lectured for a long time."

"I have not needed to," Arthur said sternly, but he couldn't hide the smile that played around the corners of his mouth. "But to answer your original question: We do not normally eat human food unless other humans are around. It cannot hurt us, but it provides us no sustenance." He paused, I assumed, to gauge my reaction. "We drink blood to survive."

I stared at him. Then I turned to stare at Rylan. Blood drinkers, huh?

"So... Guardians are vampires..."

Rylan shook his head, "No, but we have a similar diet."

"I just want to make this clear to both of you," I said slowly, choosing my words wisely. I clasped my hands together as if to restrain myself from doing anything rash. "If you try to drink me like a juice box, I'm going to lay hands on you."

Rylan threw back his head and laughed. The deep, throaty sound echoed throughout the room and struck a chord somewhere inside of me. I couldn't help but grin at the sound.

"Lay hands on us?" Arthur asked confused.

"She is saying she will fight us," Rylan clarified for his friend while trying to regain his composure but failing miserably.

"Ah, of course, we won't. Not without your permission," Arthur assured me, chuckling. That seemed to snap Rylan out of his amusement. He glared at Arthur.

My permission? I nearly snorted. Those fangs looked like they could cause some serious damage. Nope, no teeth in the neck for me.

"I'm not sure why you think it's funny that I would fight you. I *would* win, of course," I said playfully serious as I leaned back in my chair. "But anyway, we don't need to stop at this nice restaurant if you two aren't going to eat. Plus, just catching a glimpse into your lifestyle this past twenty-four hours, I have a feeling I wouldn't be able to afford a plate."

"Nonsense, you will pay for nothing when you are with us," Rylan said dismissively.

I looked at him and rolled my eyes. "You're letting me stay with you for only God knows how long. I can at least buy my food and whatever else I need."

"Truly, Mae, that is not necessary for you to do," Arthur said as Rylan's brows began to furrow. "Money means nothing to us. We have accumulated so much wealth in our lifetime that, were we to live another ten millennia without working, we could do so comfortably."

I looked at him in surprise. That's how wealthy they were? Well, even if that was the case, it felt strange for someone else to buy things for me when I could very well do it myself.

Before I could respond, Rylan spoke, "We will make sure you eat tonight. I understand that, after the ordeal at your apartment, you are not hungry now, but you need to eat regularly."

His tone told me this was not up for debate. Well, we'd see how I felt later. If I needed to fight him on this, I would. Truth be told, another full meal sounded wonderful, if I could keep it down.

Arthur pulled a cell phone out of his jacket pocket and said, "Phillip said the plane is ready. Mae, would you like to grab your things, and we can head out onto the runway?"

We all moved to stand up.

"Rylan, do you have my bracelets?"

"You did fine without them at the apartment. I am sure you will do just fine on the plane," Rylan said.

Before I could contain it, my anger rose swiftly from panic, and the room began to vibrate.

"You do not get to decide when I'll be fine, Rylan. Give me the goddamn bracelets," I snapped. Rylan said nothing and didn't make a move to retrieve the cursed jewelry. I clenched my fists at my side and continued, "I'm not leaving this airport without them, so you can give them to me, and we'll be on our merry way, or we can go our separate ways. I can always make new ones. The choice is yours."

"Mae, you will be next to one of us the entire time. Do you really think you will need them? Does flying cause you distress?" Arthur asked.

"This isn't up for negotiation," I said, ignoring him. "If it was just my life, I wouldn't bother with those stupid things, but it's not. I'm worried about killing both of you, the pilot, and everyone on the ground who might get hit with fiery shards of metal from the plane exploding because I got *nervous*. I cannot have that on my conscience."

I crossed my arms and waited for one of the Guardians to cave. They needed me just as badly as I needed them. If they wanted me to come with them, then they would need to just deal with the stupid bracelets. It wasn't as if they were pleasant to wear. They were ugly as sin, and it hurt like hell to wear them, but it wasn't about me. It was about everyone else now. I could suffer for a few hours until we got to Savannah and then I would take them off.

The soft buzzing around my head told me they were discussing this. Truly, was there anything to discuss? Rylan had promised that I would have my bracelets back for this flight, so he already knew this battle was over. He was just wasting time at this point. To make a point, and to be a little petty, I tapped my foot impatiently. The buzzing stopped, and I met Rylan's red eyes. My foot tapping stopped immediately when I realized there was no give in that gaze.

Shit.

Before I could say anything, Rylan moved. The motion was so quick, especially for his large frame, that I was not at all prepared for it. One minute I was standing, and the next I was thrown over Rylan's shoulder and heading out the lounge door.

For a moment, I was stunned into silence. What the hell just happened? It was a no-brainer! All he had to do was let me wear the bracelets for a few hours, and that was it. How could he not understand what was at stake? The shock dissipated; the second clarity cleared my head, I began to pound on his back. I kicked wildly as we passed the front desk staff who seemed to be trying hard to ignore us. The entire facility shook before I remembered to keep up my mental barrier.

It pissed me off that with Rylan touching me, it seemed like my power was easier to contain.

"Rylan, no! Put me *down*! This is insane; I can't get on that plane without those bracelets!" My voice cracked at the end in panic. "Please, Rylan, please don't do this. I'll kill people." Tears blurred my vision as I thought about all the horrible things that could go wrong once I stepped foot on that plane. "Please, Rylan." My last plea came out as a sob. I still tried to fight him, but his strength was immeasurable. My struggling didn't seem to faze him in the least.

We didn't have far to go. Just outside the sliding glass doors was a beautiful white jet standing by. A young man dressed in a nicely fitted captain's uniform stood at the bottom of the steps leading up into the cabin.

"Good to see you, Phillip," Rylan said to the young man as we approached.

"You too, Mr. Wellington. The weather is looking favorable during our flight, we should be there in about three hours," Phillip said.

"Wonderful," Rylan responded and took the steps up to the cabin. He didn't stop to put me down or even bother to introduce me. What a barbarian.

Once we were inside the cabin, he finally put me down, although he shackled my wrist with his fingers. I pushed at him the minute my feet touched the ground, but he didn't loosen his grip. I glared up at him with watery vision and scowled.

"Let go of me, *now*! You're kidnapping me *again*. I said I wasn't going without the bracelets." I was so mad.

Rylan's teal eyes stared down at me impassively for a long minute. What could he possibly be thinking right now? I had the biggest urge to reach up and just wring his neck. Rylan reached into his back pocket. He pulled out my bracelets and handed them to me. Instantly, all the fight left me, and my shoulders sagged in relief. I made a move to grab for them, but he moved his hand and held them just out of reach.

"I promised you that you could have these on the plane, not that I would allow you to wear them. I will be near you the entire trip. Hopefully, that will suffice. Only put these on if you truly need them, do you understand me?" he asked, his voice steely.

I nodded, eager to have them back. Whatever he said, if I had them nearby, I would concede to anything. He lowered the bracelets, and I snatched them out of his hand before he could change his mind. I slid them into my front pocket and stepped away from him, feeling a mixture of relief and anger. I moved further into the jet trying to calm myself down and wiped away the tears that had escaped during my struggle. I wanted to hate him, but hate required energy I did not have.

I walked to the furthest seat away from Rylan and sat down next to the window. Coming up behind Rylan, Arthur stepped into the cabin holding my purse and my laptop. He glanced between us, and his mouth curved upwards in an amused smile. Oh, did our fighting amuse him? Irritation simmered under my skin, but fear was overriding it. It was taking too much effort to keep my power back; my head, which had been aching since my return to Chicago, was pounding harder now. Arthur walked over and sat down in the seat across from me that faced my direction. He placed my stuff in the seat next to him and reclined in his seat.

"Why aren't you guys worried?"

If anyone else in the world knew about me, they would be just as terrified of my power as I was. Rylan walked over and sat down in the leather seat next to me. I glared at him but didn't pull my arm away when he grasped my wrist. Despite my annoyance with him, the pressure in my head lessened, and my shoulders slumped in relief. My heart fluttered, but I ignored the stupid, irrational response.

Before either could answer, Phillip stepped into the cabin and shut the door behind him. He nodded as he passed and walked into the cockpit. I hadn't realized there was someone else in there, but I could hear him talking to someone before shutting the door behind him.

When the door shut, Rylan looked at me and said, "There are two options: Allow you to put the bracelets on so that you suffer for hours or allow you to use me to buffer your power's effects without any pain. I choose the option where you suffer less. I trust you will work as hard as you can not to harm anyone here. You have been doing it for years; you will continue to do it now."

Wow, that was a lot of faith in someone he just kidnapped yesterday.

"I could blow up this plane," I said, desperately needing them to understand why this was dangerous. I was not overreacting.

"We would survive," Arthur assured me.

"Oh, you would survive a blast and the plummet to the ground?" I asked skeptically.

"We all would. We would just fly you out of here," Rylan said with a shrug.

I opened my mouth to refute his response, but I choked on the words as I processed what he said. I closed my mouth, then opened it again. I stared at Rylan in utter disbelief. His smug amusement did nothing to help me recover from my shock. Arthur chuckled.

"You can fly?" I asked, finally able to speak. Rylan nodded once. I looked at Arthur to see if this was some sort of joke.

"Yes," Arthur said and then laughed at my expression.

I leaned back in my seat, feeling overwhelmed again. I tried to picture these two men flying around but simply could not see it.

"Could I, you know, see that sometime?" I asked when I was done trying to wrap my head around what they were telling me. I looked at Rylan, whose smile widened. God, he was so handsome… My wayward thought almost distracted me from my initial question as my gaze went to his mouth.

"I can do better than that," Rylan said. "Sometime soon, we will fly together."

Okay, I couldn't stay mad at him when he offered to do something like that.

Chapter Six

The flight was long, but during it, I learned a lot about the two Guardians. Arthur and Rylan were the money source for several large financial, cybersecurity, and pharmaceutical companies throughout North America along with smaller companies all over the world. This was how they always had a continuous flow of cash. Apparently, most large corporations were run by supernatural creatures.

When I pressed them for more, I was bombarded with information about other creatures. Vampires were real. They were typically nomadic but occasionally banded together. Shapeshifters lived among humans, usually sticking to the Midwest where there was plenty of land to run free. Bigfoot was a hoax; I found myself sorely disappointed about that. When Arthur mentioned witches, I made a face. I already knew that witches were real, but I didn't know much about them. According to the Guardians, they lived in groups called covens where they quietly practiced magic. As we talked about witches, I was reminded of the large hole in my apartment's bathroom.

"The demon had to be after my spellbook," I told them with a frown.

Arthur and Rylan traded looks with one another. They didn't seem surprised by the information.

"It would make sense. It is said a spellbook itself is power," Arthur said with a shrug. "Mae, I am surprised you can conjure up one. I was under the impression only a Supreme could call upon a book so powerful, and Supremes are always full-blooded witches."

I shrugged. I didn't know how I produced the book; I only knew that I could.

"Why would you keep your book in the bathroom?" Rylan asked, curiously.

"I keep it hidden in mirrors," I told them both. "I usually pull it out of that one because it's easier to reach my hand in."

"May we see your spellbook?" Arthur asked.

I shrugged. "If you want to. I'll retrieve it later, but you won't learn much from it. Most of the pages are written so even I can't read them."

"You cannot read it? How did you come by this book?" Rylan asked.

"The night my power first started to emerge it appeared in my bedroom mirror. At first, I thought it was a journal since the pages were blank, but as I ran my hands over each page, I could feel the indentations of words. I checked the book almost every day for a month before the first spell became legible. Since then, a new spell or potion shows up every so often. But like I said, you can't see much of anything."

Both men were silent as they digested this information. After a long pause, Arthur continued with his questions. "Did your spellbook teach you how to spellbind your bracelets?"

I nodded and Rylan frowned. I rolled my eyes at him.

"I know you're not a fan of them."

"What other dark spells has the book shown you?" Rylan demanded with a scowl.

"I don't know about dark spells, but the few potions and spells I've read I wouldn't know what to use them for. They seem harmless enough, I guess. Honestly, I've tried to avoid reading any of them."

"Why?" Arthur asked curiously. I shifted uncomfortably under his gaze.

"Because I don't want to know any spells. I don't want any of this," I admitted. "I'll take a look to see if anything else has appeared since the last time I opened it."

Both men said nothing. When Arthur did speak again, it was to ask me about my life before magic. This was a topic I was comfortable with. I had been adopted straight from the hospital the day I was born. My parents had no information about my biological family; the paperwork had gotten lost in the system. I told them about the adventures on the many road trips we had taken, the theater plays we saw each holiday season, and the trips to the beach my family and I had gone on.

It hurt to talk about my parents, but talking about them was cathartic. There hadn't been much time to grieve their loss. Just a week after their death my power had emerged. Saddled with this new and scary burden, my focus had been to keep a low profile and stay as normal as possible.

I told the Guardians about my time in high school and college. I had enjoyed school and back then I had been an exceptional student. The summer after my sophomore year in high school I joined a Mixed Martial Arts group where I propelled quickly through the ranks. I had loved being fit and strong. The thrill of being in a ring had never dimmed, and I missed it. A lot.

The conversation died the last hour of the flight. By then my head was throbbing. I visualized the barrier in my head. I pictured it holding back the power, pulsing aggressively in the same tempo as the throbbing. Despite Rylan's hand on my wrist, I was struggling to keep my power under control. By the time we landed, my body had started to tremble. We waited while our belongings under the plane were placed in our next mode of transportation. Rylan let go of my wrist to exit the plane first. The moment the connection ended, the rush of power that he was helping hold back came crashing down. I stumbled as I followed him, and it was Arthur who steadied me.

"Are you alright?" he asked in my ear.

I nodded.

It was too hard to talk now since most of my attention was directed toward calming the raging rush of power. I gripped my bracelets harder. They wouldn't help now. The buildup was too strong, and the backlash would hurt too much if my precarious mental control slipped. Outside of the plane, we had another SUV waiting for us. Rylan climbed into the driver's seat after he helped me into the back. I pressed my forehead against the window and enjoyed the feel of the cool glass against my skin. Arthur sat in the front seat, and we were off.

According to Arthur, it was about twenty minutes from the airport to the restaurant, Havanna, which was in the heart of the city of Savannah. My stomach growled, eager for food. Another meal today? I smiled at the thought. I wasn't too keen on heading into the middle of the city while feeling on the verge of being out of control, but the prospect of food outweighed the concern I felt. I was *hungry.*

The Guardians spoke amongst themselves for a while. I tuned them out as I watched the city fly by. As summer came to an end, it was beginning to get darker out sooner. It was almost seven o'clock by the time we arrived at the restaurant, and the sun had set behind the tall buildings. As I climbed out of the car, I glanced at the clientele coming in and out of the restaurant. I was most definitely underdressed. The valet took the keys from Rylan, and we entered the foyer where a beautiful hostess stood waiting for us.

The young woman greeted us warmly and led us through the restaurant. It must have been my appearance that captured a few patrons' attention because conversations stopped, and heads turned as we strolled by. I could feel the heat in my cheeks rise. Oh, what I must look like with two large men, both dangerous and handsome, on either side of me. Watching them, I noted they walked with confidence and purpose. They radiated power. They also kept me close, almost as if they were bodyguards.

We were taken to the very back of the restaurant in a secluded spot. The table was intimate; with a warm flickering candle, a vase with a red rose, and rose petals scattered on top of the white tablecloth. From here, people would hardly be able to see us. Arthur held the chair out for me, and I awkwardly sat down. When was the last time I had been on the receiving end of manners like this? Immediately, a waitress came to our table and went over the different wines the restaurant offered for the night, along with the specials. Rylan ordered a bottle of wine for the table, and the waitress left to fetch our drinks while we mulled over dinner options.

"I can't drink alcohol," I said quietly, feeling my face warm. "It makes it too hard to—" I waved a hand. "—control myself."

"Do not worry. You do not have to drink it. The wait staff gets excited when you order the best wine on the menu. The service is quite nice once they realize you will spend an obscene amount of money," Rylan said with a half-hearted smile. I looked away from his smile, feeling my cheeks warm even more under his gaze.

I looked over the menu, and my stomach growled in anticipation. My head, on the other hand, felt like it was going to split in two. My face felt warm. I found myself having to blink several times as the words on the menu began to blur. Maybe some cool water on my face would help. I excused myself from the table and made my way to the restroom. As I walked, the floor felt like it was swaying. When I got to the ladies' room I had broken out in a sweat. Was it hot? I walked over to the sink and reached out to turn on the faucets. My hands were shaking hard now. My heart was thumping loudly in my chest. The ache in my head matched the beat of my heart, and it was making me feel sick.

I braced myself over the sink and closed my eyes as the bathroom began to spin. Something warm and wet touched my upper lip. I looked up into the mirror at my reflection and stared at the blood dripping from my nose. Crap! I grabbed some paper towels and held my head back to stop the bleeding. Great, I'm bleeding, and the two men waiting for me love the taste of blood.

As I stared up at the ceiling, I found the floor wasn't the only thing moving. The ceiling seemed to spin above me. I tried to ignore it. I took deep, slow breaths hoping the dizzy spell would subside. My heart twisted in fear as I realized I was in trouble. My legs felt shaky and slowly the ceiling seemed to get farther away until suddenly I couldn't see anything.

I opened my eyes slowly. The cool tile of the bathroom floor against my cheek gave me pause as I tried to remember what had happened. Had I fainted? I pushed myself off the floor and pulled myself up with the help of the bathroom counter. I stared at my reflection in horror. My bloody nose had smeared all over my face while I had been unconscious. It looked like I'd been through the wringer. I must not have been out for very long since no one was standing over me yet. There was no way someone would have seen me in this state and not have gone for help.

The faucet I had turned on was still running. Good. I washed my face until I was sure any trace of my blood was gone. I waited a moment to see if my nose was still bleeding, and when I was sure it wasn't, I headed back to my table.

I forced a smile at both gentlemen as I sat and grabbed the menu again. I was no longer hungry. Unfortunately, I was sure both men wouldn't take lightly to me not eating, so I forced myself to find something that wouldn't be too heavy. Before I could decide on what to eat, Rylan plucked the menu from my hands.

"What?" I looked at him in confusion.

He wasn't looking at my face. Instead, his gaze was staring down at my shirt.

"What happened?"

His voice was so deep, and he had spoken so quietly, that it came out like a growl. I followed his gaze and found a smear of blood at the very bottom of my shirt.

"Nothing," I said a little too quickly. I tried to take the menu back out of his hands, but he moved it further out of reach.

"What. Happened." His tone sent chills down my spine.

"I had a bloody nose while I was in the bathroom. No big deal."

His gaze rose to my face and pinned me with a look that should have scared me. Instead, I found myself warming under it. God, he was gorgeous, even when he was terrifying.

"How often does that happen?" he asked.

I thought about it. When was the last time I had a bloody nose?

"Not often," I admitted. "It's probably because I'm tired."

"You have a bruise coming in on your left cheek," Arthur said, just as quietly. Rylan's hard teal gaze turned red.

"I fainted. I'm sure it happened when I hit the floor," I said with an exaggerated sigh of frustration. When was the last time someone had been concerned for me? It was an odd and uncomfortable feeling, after all this time, to be someone important enough that people cared about. "I'm fine now. Can I have the menu back, *please*?"

Rylan shifted his seat to sit closer to me. He reached out and gently put his hand on my arm. Instantly, the touch of a Guardian eased the burden of keeping my power contained.

It must have been a visible relief because he leaned in and said, "You are in pain. We should leave."

"No, we're here. Let's eat," I said as firmly as possible.

The two men exchanged glances, and I could feel their wordless conversation flow between them. I was sure they were trying to figure out a way to force me to leave without causing a scene. Before they could decide on what to do, the waitress came over and took our order. Without having much time to decide I grabbed the menu from Rylan and picked the first thing I saw. With obvious displeasure, both men ordered their dinners.

As the waitress walked away, I leaned forward and said, "You don't get to decide what to do with me without my input. If I say I want to stay, then I am going to stay. But if you wish to leave, go right ahead. I'm not a child. I'm not a prisoner. I'm a human being with the freedom to do whatever I please. Do you both understand?"

I pulled my hand free of Rylan's grasp, annoyed with him and Arthur.

"Of course," Arthur said with a bow of his head.

I couldn't tell if he was placating me or not. I turned my attention to Rylan, whose jaw ticked in annoyance. His eyes were that surreal teal again, and they searched my face for a long moment. After a long pause, he gave me, with what looked to be a great deal of difficulty, a nod.

"As long as it is in your best interest," he said.

Um, no. What I thought was in my best interest could vary from what he thought. I opened my mouth to protest but he interrupted me.

"But I will try to be reasonable."

I clamped my mouth shut. At least he would try. Annoyed that the conversation hadn't gone my way, I turned away from him and leaned back in my chair.

Thoughtfully Rylan added, "You are being difficult. I almost think you enjoy suffering. First, the spellbound bracelets and now the insistence to stay when you are obviously suffering."

I gaped at him. How could he possibly say that? He had no idea what I could do and the reasons behind my actions. It had taken months, almost a year, to be able to build up the limited control I had now. Sitting in a restaurant full of people had seemed impossible a year ago. The struggle it took not to let go of the delicate control I held on to was exhausting. Not that he cared or understood the enormous effort it took to sit here. The thought was souring. I shut my mouth and turned away from him again.

To my surprise, Arthur came to my defense. "Enough Rylan. You are being narrow-minded. Has Mae not explained the ramifications that come with her abilities? Is the blood on her shirt, the bruises on her arms and now cheek not enough for you to see how hard she struggles to remain in control? If she wishes to feel human, to eat a full meal in a quiet atmosphere, then let her do so in peace."

I gave Arthur a grateful look. His face was void of any emotion, but his eyes were red, and his attention was on Rylan. The tension was high between the two of them, and a shiver went down my spine. Rylan's face shifted in shadows cast by the candlelight. His eyes sunk into his face, his cheeks hollowed, and then in a blink, his face reverted to normal. The muscles in his arms flexed. The glasses and flatware on the table shook as I fought down the rising fear. These were not normal men I was dealing with.

I could feel their conversation buzzing in the air. They exchanged scowls, and Rylan leaned forward as if he were going to leap over the table. I leaned back and watched their wordless communication in fascination. Finally, both men relaxed their stiff shoulders. Rylan leaned back in his chair; his expression looked like he'd swallowed something sour.

"You are right, Arthur. Mae, please forgive me," Rylan said.

"It's fine," I mumbled as I looked down into my lap.

I must have absentmindedly started rubbing my pounding temples because suddenly Rylan's hand was pulling mine away from my face. His contact slightly eased the pain in my head. Reluctantly, I looked up at him. He gripped my hand tightly.

"Truly, I am sorry," he said earnestly. His thumb skimmed the inside of my wrist. "It sickens me to see you in pain. Leaving here to get you somewhere to ease your suffering seems like the most obvious course of action to help you. For someone who has a shaky control on your power, you are doing quite well."

I sunk into the twin teal lagoons that were his eyes. His striking features seemed even more pronounced in this intimate lighting, and it swiftly stole my breath away. Before I could say anything, the waitress returned with our food. I pulled my hand away from Rylan and straightened as our food was placed in front of us. The eggplant parmesan I ordered smelled even better than it looked, which seemed nearly impossible since it looked delicious. My stomach growled in anticipation before it immediately tightened into a knot. My shoulders stiffened, and I took a deep breath.

I was going to force this dinner down even if it killed me; that's how good it looked. Both Guardians received their steaks and baked potatoes. I glanced at their plates curiously. The waitress left, and my hunger was momentarily forgotten as I watched both Guardians cut into their food. Rylan picked up his fork, stabbed a piece of very rare steak, and plopped it into his mouth.

"Does it taste… good?" I asked curiously. Rylan looked over at me and smirked, understanding what I was asking.

"It tastes like nothing."

I thought about that as I turned back to my dish. My stomach tightened painfully as I thought about taking a bite. I took my fork and knife and cut up my meal. I took a small bite, testing the waters. My throat tightened, and I almost choked on the most delicious tasting eggplant.

Immediately Arthur and Rylan's hands were patting my back. At their contact, my throat loosened, and I was able to swallow. As we ate, at least one Guardian always had his hand on my shoulder or arm. It wasn't as helpful as it had been this morning. My power was fighting me. I pictured that barrier I had built in my mind and focused on keeping it erect. It wouldn't last, but the mental image was helping for the time being. As I brought my last bite up to my mouth, the violet glow in the veins of my hands caught my attention. I dropped my fork and folded my shaking hands under the table where they would not be noticed.

When both men were done eating, we didn't wait for the bill. Arthur dropped some cash onto the table, and we left. In the car, we all remained silent, and I was grateful. My skin felt painfully tight. My body was shaking hard. My jaw clenched so tightly my gums ached.

I barely noticed Savannah as we cruised through the streets. The lights of the buildings, streetlamps, and signs flashed by causing a strobe effect. My head was imploding; I could feel it. Scared I would have another nosebleed, I had stolen the napkin off the table before we left. Now the cloth was balled up and being crushed in my fist.

We weren't in the city long. Once we'd left the main part of the city and the suburbs, it was all flat farmland. When I glanced out the window, I could see the stars twinkling brightly in the night sky. They were easy to concentrate on, and they were pretty to view. You couldn't see them in Chicago; even on the outskirts, in the campgrounds I visited they were hard to see.

We drove for an hour before it was beginning to be too much. My control was slipping in leaps and bounds now. Instead of a slight vibration of my seat or a flicker of the overhead light, the road began to crack and roll, causing our SUV to bump along. On the side of the road, a tree would split in half or crops moved like water rippling. I gritted my teeth and squeezed my eyes shut, praying I could hold out until we got to our destination.

More time passed. We drove through a small town. How were we not at our destination yet? Normally I would have enjoyed the fifties look of the town that flew by, but I was almost out of time. Maybe, if we were not too far away, I could come back and check it out during the day. Thankfully, it didn't take long to pass through. We were out of the town and passing a more wooded area. My stomach twisted, and I swallowed down bile. I closed my eyes and struggled to remain calm.

I wasn't sure how much more time passed, but sitting there in the darkness of the car with my eyes closed, I felt the break happen. My exhausted mind couldn't hold my power back any longer.

"Rylan, pull over," I choked.

I wasn't sure if it was the tone of my voice, or he happened to look in the review mirror and see I wasn't doing well, but he listened. The moment the car came to a stop my door was opened.

"Text me the address, I'll find you!" I choked out as I stumbled out of the car. I shouted my number as I raced for the woods. I had to get off the road, or I could throw the car and kill both men inside. I barely made the tree line when my mental barrier collapsed.

Around me, the woods exploded. The ground beneath my feet erupted, uprooting trees and bushes and throwing soil in every direction. The rush of power flowing out of me was unbearably painful. It burned. Oh, how it burned. The sensation was like having branding irons shoved through each limb of my body and into my chest. My skull felt like it had shattered into large fragments and the pieces were bouncing around in my head. My muscles clenched, making running hard.

But I kept moving. I had to. Chaos followed close behind, erupting all around me. Massive trees flew by, branches came crashing down, and the wind was whipping up small dirt tornados and carrying off debris. Rocks pelleted me, and vines tangled around my legs. The roaring of the wind was like a band of banshees.

I needed to scream. If I just opened my mouth and let it out, I was sure it would bring me relief. But I couldn't. I couldn't scream. I knew if screamed I wouldn't stop screaming. So, I just kept running. Further and further into the woods, praying that no one was nearby and would get hurt. A tree flew past me, missing me by inches.

Finally, I tried to slow down, take a deep breath and gain some semblance of control. Fate had another plan for me. A heavy branch slammed into my legs causing me to fall. I landed on my side. I rolled as a thick, gnarly bush flung past me. A small rock slammed into my back, and dirt flung up into my face. I sputtered and coughed as I choked on mud. A large crack overhead warned me of my impending doom. I turned slightly and stared in horror at a massive oak tree crashing down above me. Terror paralyzed me. I squeezed my eyes shut and braced myself to be crushed.

I was hit hard.

But not in the direction I thought it would come from. Instead, I was hit from the side. Something caught me under my arms and dragged me out of the way of the falling tree. Startled, my power raged harder. Around me, it was like land mines were going off. The loud explosions, the blast of dirt, and the horrible howl of the wind was a thing of nightmares. I was dragged to my feet and slammed against something hard. I didn't push away from the solid object I was pressed against. It was the only thing not moving in the storm around me. Instead, I squeezed my eyes shut tighter, waiting to be hit by rubble.

I wasn't sure how much time had passed, but finally, I could feel the strength of my power weaken. The moment I realized I could stop the chaos; I started my chant. I whispered it under my breath and screamed it internally. It took much longer than normal to regain control, but when I was able to build that mental barrier back up, I sighed with relief. My body sagged against the solid object I had been pinned to and I was grateful that it held my weight.

Around me, I could hear things settle down. The pain in my skull eased; fatigue weighed heavy on my body. My body's shaking slowed to a tremble, and all the tension in me loosened. Exhausted, aching, and sluggish, my mind felt like mush. I forced my eyes to open, and the task felt enormous. Feeling slightly dazed, I looked up, expecting to see an old tree or a stone. Instead, I found myself ensnared by a pair of blazing red eyes.

Rylan's face was in full Guardian mode. His eyes were sunken, his cheeks hollowed, and his fangs could be seen as he bared his teeth at me. His blond hair was a mess, and his face was covered in dirt.

Rylan? What was he doing here?

What was going on?

How had I ended up cradled in Rylan's arms? My hands were braced against his muscular chest. Surrounding us was a massive black shield; this must have been why I hadn't been hurt further from the chaos. Upon further inspection, I realized the "shield" around us was a pair of massive, black-feathered wings. They protruded from Rylan's back and had wrapped around both of us like a protective cocoon.

Rylan had saved me… From myself.

Chapter Seven

I stared up at him, my mind reeling. My body felt leaden, my thoughts sluggish. My heart was racing, and my skin was throbbing. I wanted to put my head against Rylan's chest and just allow the darkness hanging around the edges of my sight to engulf me.

But my wonder and awe at the man holding me momentarily won out over the exhaustion. With a slow, deliberate movement, I reached up and gently touched Rylan's hollowed cheek. He did not move or flinch away from me. Was he horrified? Disgusted? Did he regret promising not to hurt me? Would he tell Arthur, who might feel it necessary to kill me now that they knew what type of damage I could cause? Would Rylan do the honors of killing me himself?

Rylan's expression told me nothing. He could have been made of stone.

My heart sunk like a rock as he continued to say nothing. Well, if he was going to kill me, maybe it was for the best. I would never have to go through that ordeal again. I at least had to make sure he was alright before I died. The thought that he could be hurt because of me was sickening.

"Are you hurt?" My voice came out as a hoarse whisper.

Guilt beat at me. I prayed that he would say no; that he wasn't hurt. Hopefully, he had not taken the brunt of the punishing storm I had caused. He could have died, and for what? To save a monster?

He did not respond. Instead, he only stared down at me. Had saving me been a knee jerk reaction? Was he wondering how to kill me? If he had let the tree fall on me, he could call it an accident, and no one would be any the wiser.

"Rylan?" I tried again. "Are you okay?"

My hand traced down his cheek as it fell away, too heavy to hold up anymore. His whole body suddenly shuddered, and he closed his eyes as if in pain. Concerned, I tried to step away, so I could look over him. Instead of letting me go, his grip tightened. He opened his eyes slowly and stared at me again. His eyes had turned a terrifying shade of red.

"I am fine," he said, his voice more gruff than usual. "Are you injured?"

I let out a sigh of relief.

"No, I don't think so."

His body relaxed. The thick black wings wrapped around us shifted. A light shower of fine dirt rained down on us as his wings moved. They slowly rose, and I stared in awe as they folded neatly against Rylan's back. I pulled my attention away from the beautiful wings and looked around us. My heart nearly stopped as I stared at the destruction.

We were standing in the middle of a crater. Outside the crater, the trees had been cleared a hundred yards in every direction. All vegetation had disappeared, and large chunks of dirt were missing from the Earth around us. Even the stars were gone, replaced by a thin cloud of dirt that had not yet returned to its place on the ground.

I was a bomb that had detonated. I stared in horror at the devastation. I had done this. I hated being a monster. What if I'd done this in the city or around other people? I had lost all control, and there had been nothing I could do to stop it. Tears welled up, and I did nothing to stop them as they spilled down my cheeks.

I moved again to escape Rylan's grip, and this time he allowed me to move away. My legs wobbled under me, and for a moment,

I thought I was going to crumble to the ground. Using Rylan's outstretched arm, I was able to steady myself. Glancing around again, I studied the damage I'd caused, and my stomach twisted painfully. In the beginning, my power had come out in destructive blasts. Small, isolated incidents that continued to grow in size until I knew it was time to leave civilization and take to the woods where I couldn't hurt anyone. None of those previous incidents compared to the scene around me now. My trek through the Appalachian Trail had been one of misery as I struggled to adjust to the monster inside of me. Once I had learned to build a barrier within my mind, I gained some control. When I found the spell to bind my power, I thought I was prepared to enter society.

I had been naïve. How could I have thought this was something I could push aside and ignore? What had possessed me to believe that I could be normal again? That letting out a little power here and there on the weekends would suffice? I should have tried to kill myself again. I couldn't go around pretending I was normal, that I could control whatever this was inside me. God, I hoped Rylan was planning on killing me. I needed to be stopped before something horrible happened.

Except for the rise and fall of his chest and the way his eyes followed my every moment, Rylan remained still. Of course he was wary of me; I would be too if I were in his situation. I bet he wondered what else I was able to do. The answer to that was I didn't know. And I knew that made me even more dangerous. I had to be stopped before my power became too great. There was nothing that could be done to help me. I knew it in my bones. I had given myself false hope when both the Guardians had offered to find me a solution to help. This was a reminder of the destruction that followed in my wake when I wasn't careful. I didn't deserve a solution or a remedy. I needed to be stopped. I would make Rylan's hesitation easier for him.

"Do it, Rylan. I'm ready," I assured him. Rylan's brows came together in confusion. Oh, did he think I wouldn't guess his train of thought? "You can go ahead and kill me now. I know I need to be stopped. I'm okay with it. Just, please, make it fast."

Rylan's body went rigid. I braced myself for the killing blow. I forced my hands to drop to my sides, and closed my eyes as I prepared for the inevitable. A minute ticked by and nothing happened. As another passed, my acceptance of my death shifted to impatience. I opened my eyes and found Rylan's teal ones staring back at me. He took a step towards me, closing the small distance between us and took my face in his hands. The gentle touch was so unexpected that I shuddered.

"Mae, why do you want me to kill you?" he asked, genuine confusion bringing his brows together again.

"Look around you," I said. *Wasn't it obvious?* "Look what I can do. You must stop me before I hurt someone. It's your job as a Guardian. I'm a monster, Rylan."

For a moment, there was silence as turmoil darkened his teal gaze.

Finally, he spoke. "You are not a monster, Mae." His face relaxed, but his mouth turned downwards at the corners. "We will figure this out, I promise you." He paused as he looked around at the mess I'd created. To my utter amazement, he smiled. "Now I understand your *reservations* about the plane."

Was he *joking* right now? Tears rolled down my cheeks harder as frustration and fatigue collided. How could he be so nonchalant? What part of *monster* did he not understand? I was a danger to society. I was a danger to him. I was a danger to myself. It had to end for everyone's sake.

"Why aren't you getting this? I could *kill* someone because I can't control this. And it's getting worse. Every day my power grows a little stronger. I'm going to slip up, and I'm going to lose control and hurt people. I can't have that happen!" I sobbed. "Please, Rylan, please make this all stop. I know you can do it. Just kill me now. I would do it myself, but I already tried and I couldn't."

Rylan's frowned confused me. Why wasn't he scared of me? He shouldn't feel concerned over the feelings of a monster. What good was I to anyone? I was kidding myself thinking I could finish school, get a real job, make new friends, and just start life over again as if my power were just going to up and disappear as abruptly as it had appeared.

I was cursed to suffer for the rest of my life. The only things guaranteed were the constant pain and fear I would grapple with. I bowed my head in defeat as sobs wracked my body. Rylan wrapped his arms around me and pulled me close to his chest. I was wrapped up in his thick muscular arms, pressed against his hard chest in the warmest hug I had ever received. The sweet gesture was another unexpected response, and it undid me. I cried even harder against him.

I don't know how long I stood there in Rylan's arms and cried. I was surprised to find that it felt good to have someone truly know about me. Rebecca hadn't stuck around to see what happened after my power first appeared. From then on, I had kept to myself. It had been a lonely two years, but who would want to befriend someone who suffered from bouts of chaos? It was apparent Rylan wasn't afraid of me, and deep down, I was grateful.

Finally, I ran out of tears. When Rylan was sure I was done crying, he let go of me. He didn't step away though. Instead, we stood chest to chest. He tipped my chin up with one of his fingers.

"I vow to you, one day you will find peace with the power you have. I will search the world for answers and look to other worlds if this one does not hold the answers we seek. Until then, I will be at your side to keep you safe. Mae, you are my mate, and I will take care of you."

Who was this sweet and caring man? How could he appear so calm and promise me peace with such confidence despite the danger I posed to him and those around me? In the past twenty-four hours, I had seen angry Rylan, annoyed, frustrated, controlling, and amused Rylan. This was a whole other side of him. I found myself wanting to believe that this Guardian cared what happened to me. He was probably more concerned about his species and what would happen to them if I were to die, but, for the moment, I let myself believe he cared only about my well-being.

Sniffling, I nodded, not sure what to say.

Rylan searched my face for something. He must have found it because he nodded and said, "Let us head home."

"Is Arthur still waiting by the car?" I mumbled miserably, trying to figure out how long we had been out here.

"No, he left once I came after you—" He stopped talking. He scowled, and I thought I was about to get a lecture from him. He must have thought better about it though because he relaxed and continued, "But we are not far from the house now."

Oh, we were going to walk. I thought about walking miles to the house and inwardly groaned. It was going to take forever.

"Ok, lead the way."

I stepped back and looked around us, trying to figure out how we would tell which direction we were facing. I had never been good telling north from south. Thank goodness I carried a map and a compass with me when I hiked the trails, or I'd have gone around in a circle for months. Hopefully Rylan had some idea where we were and which way to go. He gave me a half-smile.

"We are not walking," he said. "It would take much too long, and you are not up for that."

Then how were we getting to the house? It took me maybe a few moments too long to realize what he was saying. My eyes darted to his wings and then back at his face. There was no stopping the excitement that began to blossom.

"We're *flying?*" I whispered in hushed awe. Rylan grinned. If I had the energy, I would have leaped for joy. "I won't be too heavy for you?"

Rylan rolled his eyes as he chuckled. "No."

"We're really going to fly?" I needed the confirmation. This would be cruel if it turned out he was joking. He laughed.

"Yes, we will fly. Luckily, you decided to dart onto the edge of the property line. The house is about ten miles west of here." Rylan looked up to the sky. He looked back down at me, and I could see a twinkle in those cool teal eyes. He was just as excited as I was. "Are you feeling well enough to head home?"

As much as I wanted to immediately confirm that I was ready to fly, I hesitated. I did a mental check to make sure my power was under control. My barrier was erect but fragile. Most of the energy that usually pressed hard against it had escaped, though, so fragile would keep my power at bay for the time being. My mind felt foggy, and my arms and legs felt boneless, but I was sure I could handle the experience.

"Yes."

Rylan closed the distance between us.

"Wrap your arms around my neck."

Without hesitation, I did as I was told, and he scooped me up into his arms. His massive black wings stretched out behind him, and I stared at them in utter amazement. The feathers themselves looked soft and silky. Would Rylan let me touch them? Rylan crouched down slightly, and then suddenly, we shot up into the air.

My stomach dropped away, and a gasp was pulled from my lips. We were over the treetops, through the clouds, and soaring under the stars in the time it took to catch my breath. When I was able to, I giggled in absolute delight. I stared around us as I took in the night's beauty. The cool air slid over my skin; it was soothing and therapeutic. My worries and fears temporarily disappeared as elation bubbled up and spilled out as squeals of breathless laughter. I turned my face to stare at Rylan, who was grinning. His eyes glowed red, and his wild curls were blowing in the wind. He seemed wild and free. I looked away from his face as my body warmed under his gaze.

The flight didn't last long.

Below us, I could make out a white house with lights on. While the immediate property around the house had been cleared, surrounding the house, trees went for miles in every direction. Rylan had been right; it was secluded here. Our descent was gradual. Rylan circled the house twice before he landed near a cluster of trees. Once we were on the ground, he carefully placed me on my feet. I stepped back to give him space, but I couldn't feel my legs and instead crumpled to the ground.

"Are you alright?" Rylan asked, crouching down next to me with a frown. I must have been beyond exhausted because I giggled.

"Oops." I shook my head with a smile and tried to stand up, but my legs just wouldn't cooperate. "Just give me a minute. I'm too tired to move."

"Of course."

He stood up and took a deep breath. Behind him, Rylan's wings stretched out far above his head. He closed his eyes, and I watched as a ghostly smile teased his lips. His wings lowered, and I watched in amazement as they retracted into his back. Now that his wings were gone, I was able to admire the rest of his physique. His chiseled abs and thick chest rippled with muscle when he moved. His arms were bands of steel. With all of that going for him, added to that gorgeous face and his gentleness from earlier, I found my body going from warm to hot. The junction between my legs burned the hottest.

I must be losing my mind.

Rylan took a deep breath and suddenly opened his eyes. He caught me admiring his body, and my cheeks burned with embarrassment. I glanced away from his sudden smirk. To distract myself, I pushed myself off the ground. I wobbled at first but was finally able to find my footing. Had I ever been this tired? The joy of flying wore off quickly as I thought back to the destruction I had caused and all the dirt I would have to wash off my body before I could climb into bed.

"Thank you," I said turning to look at him again. "That was easily the most amazing thing I have ever experienced. And thank you for not… freaking out back there." I waved my hand in the general direction we came from. "I'm sorry if I scared you."

Rylan said nothing. His face became unreadable. His teal eyes darkened as whatever thoughts crossed his mind weighed on him. Was he wondering what to do with me now? Was he debating how to broach the topic with Arthur that they were harboring a monster? My mood soured at my dark thoughts.

"You did scare me," he said softly. Then his jaw clenched. "But not because of what you can do. You threw yourself into a dangerous situation, and had I not arrived when I did, you could have been lost to me. That… is unacceptable. I will not lose such a treasure bestowed upon me."

His words stunned me into silence. As we stood there staring at one another, he trailed his knuckles down my cheek. My heart stuttered in response, and my breath caught in my throat. The gesture was so intimate it caused bumps to raise on my arms.

"Let us head inside," Rylan said after a long pause.

I followed him out of the woods and across the massive lawn. As we approached the building, I realized it wasn't your typical house; it was a mansion. The property was enormous. The plantation-style house was two stories, with massive pillars and a grand stairway that led up to the front door. Rylan gripped my forearm as we walked up the stairs, probably because each time I lifted my feet my legs wobbled, threatening to collapse underneath me. When we got to the front door, Rylan pushed it open, and I gaped.

The foyer was two stories tall. In front of us was a short hallway, and on either side, there was a set of staircases that led up to the second floor. Above us was a mezzanine that looked over either side of the house. I could see that once we walked under the stairs, the house opened to an informal setting. On either side of us, like the house back in Chicago, there was a pair of double doors. Instead of going through either set of doors or into the main living area of the house, Rylan guided me over to the stairs. I almost groaned. More walking? Rylan must have had the same thought because without a word he scooped me up and carried me up to the second floor.

He carried me down the long, wide hallway to the left. I should have protested at Rylan carrying me; my body still felt a little too warm after gazing at him just moments ago. I had to admit, though, that it was nice not having to walk anymore. He carried me to the end of the hallway until he stopped at a set of double doors. He placed me on my feet and opened a door.

"This will be your room," he said, his voice quiet.

I didn't make a move to enter. I stood there with my mouth open trying to process how a room this size was even practical. The king-size bed sat in the middle of the room on a grand four-poster bedframe draped in gorgeous silks. The comforter on the bed was so fluffy, there must have been a mass murder of geese somewhere to have created it. There was a thick carpet under the bed, but the rest of the room was hardwood floors. There were four floor to ceiling windows on the right side of the room, and in the middle of them were French doors that lead out onto, I assumed, a balcony although it was too dark to tell now. In front of the windows were a pair of small cozy chairs, a coffee table, and against the wall was a small fireplace. On the other side of the room was another set of double doors. These were open and from where I stood, I could see they led to the bathroom.

"Rylan, this is too much," I choked when I finally found my voice. "I just need a bed and a dresser. This... I don't even know what to say. It's too nice for me. I'll accidentally destroy everything of value." I could hear the wistfulness in my voice as I spoke. I didn't deserve something this nice.

"The glass in this house is bulletproof," Rylan said. "It would take a lot to shatter it. Everything else is replaceable." I shot him a curious look. Who builds a house with bulletproof glass? Understanding my surprise, Rylan explained further, "This house was built to protect and house Guardians. The entire structure is made from steel beams, and there is even an underground bunker."

"What do Guardians do that you need all of this?"

"I will tell you another time. If I told you now, it would take all night. There should be toiletries in the bathroom for you. Your things have been hung in the closet. Do you need help bathing?"

His question threw me for a loop. All the heat in my body made a mad dash into my cheeks.

"Absolutely not!"

Even if I did need help, I certainly wouldn't want him to touch me. God, I would go up in flames… Rylan's half-smile told me he was amused with my quick response. I looked away trying to hide my mortification.

"As you wish. I will check on you in fifteen minutes to make sure you did not fall in the shower," Rylan said.

"You don't need to do that; I'll be fine," I said dismissively. That bed looked so good that I almost wanted to forego the shower.

"Fifteen minutes," he said firmly, his smile disappearing. With that, he turned and walked back down the hallway.

I walked into the bedroom and shut the door behind me. I walked over to the edge of the bed to find my purse and laptop on the nightstand. Someone, I assumed Arthur, had even put my phone on the charger. How considerate. I picked up my phone and turned on my eight, random alarms. I knew when I got out of the shower I would forget before passing out.

When I was done, I walked into the bathroom and stared at the luxurious jetted tub and separate shower. A shower would be quicker. I walked over to it and turned it on. As I waited a moment for the water to get hot, I eyed the jetted tub. If I rinsed off quickly, I could soak a moment before I headed to bed. My muscles felt spent and were already aching. Tomorrow I would be stiff. With that thought, I made up my mind. I was going to get into that tub. I walked over to it and turned on the warm water. Grabbing the bottle of bubbles sitting on the edge, I poured a cap full in.

I stripped down and headed back to the shower. The water pressure and warmth were exactly what I needed. I placed my hands against the shower wall and let the water run over my body. As I stood there I looked down and grimaced. The self-inflicted bruises were splotches of purples and yellows all over my stomach and thighs. I was lucky that they hadn't spread to more noticeable places like my face and hands.

Disgusted with my appearance, I washed my hair and my body quickly. I turned off the water and grabbed a fluffy white towel hanging on the rack. Oh, the towel rack *warmed* the towels! I groaned in pleasure as I wrapped it around me. I walked over to the tub and turned off the water. After folding the towel, I climbed into the steaming water. Had I thought the shower was wonderful? This was better than anything I could have imagined. I slid under the water until it was up to my chin and closed my eyes.

Chapter Eight

I opened my eyes to find myself tucked into bed. I sat up and blinked. When had I gotten out of the tub and climbed into bed? I looked at my phone and saw that I had snoozed each alarm I'd set. So, I must have woken up and turned each of them off. But usually, I remembered doing so.

Frowning, I threw the covers off me. As I swung my legs out of the bed I paused. When had I changed into my pajamas? After a moment, fuzzy memories of climbing out of the tub and getting ready for bed eased the discomfort that had begun to build in my gut. That meant that I had turned off my alarms… or had I? Something about that didn't seem right. That wasn't something I normally did. I should have been concerned.

Instead, I felt… rested. My mind was alert and focused; my body didn't feel so weighed down. When was the last time I had slept through an entire night? At least a full year, maybe even longer. I glanced around the room, just to make sure my sound slumber hadn't triggered an earthquake or caused any devastation. Nothing appeared broken. But… how? If I hadn't woken up to any alarms, my power would have slipped out, and yet, there was no sign that had happened.

Strange.

I stood up and walked into the bathroom. On one of the two marble countertops sat my toothbrush, some fresh toothpaste, and floss. I stared at the items wondering if I should be annoyed, creeped out, or touched. I decided on indifference. I splashed some water on my face and brushed my teeth. I did a mental examination of my body as I got ready for the day. My body was sore, as I expected it would be. My mind and my mental barrier felt stronger than they had been for a long time. My stomach growled, another good sign.

Overall, I was feeling great.

Slowly, I brought my gaze up to stare at my reflection in the mirror. Instead of being ringed with dark circles, my eyes looked bright and alert. There was even a little bit of excitement in those brown irises as I looked forward to the day. Once I was done at the sink, I turned around. On the far side of the bathroom sat a door slightly ajar. Curious, I walked over, opened it, and then paused in wonder.

The closet was almost as big as the bathroom and full of clothes. In the middle sat a large tufted ottoman with my camping gear and duffle bag on top. I walked over to my belongings and found a small piece of paper folded on top of the duffle bag. I picked it up and unfolded it.

> *Miss White,*
> *Please enjoy the wardrobe Rylan has ordered*
> *for you. Should you require anything else,*
> *please let me know.*
> *-Laura Coleman, the housekeeper*

Of course Rylan had a housekeeper. I put down the note and looked around the closet, feeling lost. I wondered if I should wear some of the new clothes that had been bought for me. I decided against it. I would feel more comfortable in my own clothes. I pulled out a shirt and some shorts, along with fresh undergarments, and changed.

Feeling better than I had in a long time, I left the bathroom and the bedroom to explore my new home. Now that I was wide awake, I could admire the decorative wainscoting and coffered ceilings. I peeked into a few rooms as I passed by. Each room was considerably large for a guestroom, but none were nearly as large as the one I occupied. I would have to tell Rylan that I would be happy to move into one of these.

I walked across the balcony tethering the two grand staircases together and wondered if I could poke around on this side of the house. As I thought about exploring more of the house, the smell of greasy bacon wafted through the house. My stomach growled loudly. Okay, exploring the house would have to be put on hold for a while. I leaned over the other side of the balcony and stared down onto the main living area of the house.

Just the downstairs itself was larger than the house I grew up in. There was a family room with thick leather couches, a living room with a formal sitting arrangement, a dining room that could easily seat twelve people, and I could just barely see the lengthy marble countertop of a center island in the kitchen. On the far side of the house, a wall of glass looked out onto the property. The view was stunning. In the distance, I could make out a herd of deer grazing peacefully on the freshly cut grass.

I walked down the stairs and made my way into the kitchen where an older woman quietly hummed as she cooked breakfast. She looked up as I entered and smiled.

"Good morning, Miss White. How are you fairing this morning?" the woman asked.

"I'm fine, thank you," I said, feeling my cheeks warm at the attention. "Are you Ms. Coleman?"

"You can call me Laura," she said. "Please have a seat. I stopped by the butcher's this morning on my way in and couldn't resist buying some of this bacon. I have French toast cooking, and I'll pull out the fruit. Everything should be done in just a few minutes."

"Thank you. You didn't need to go to all this trouble," I said as I walked over to one of the many bar stools.

"Don't be silly. It's my job, and even if it wasn't, I love cooking and to be able to do that in *this* kitchen is wonderful!" Laura said with a laugh. "I don't get to cook often."

"Have you worked here long?" I asked her curiously.

"Oh, all my life!" she said cheerfully as she flipped the long strips of bacon in the pan. "And before me, it was my parents, and the time before that, it was my grandparents. My family has worked with the Wellingtons for many, many generations."

Oh! Did she know about Guardians? I wondered if I could ask her questions but hastily decided against it. What if she didn't know about them? Laura hummed and tapped her foot to some unheard music. She moved back and forth between two pans and then fluttered over to the industrial refrigerator and pulled out a small bowl of fruit.

"Thank you for ordering those clothes," I said as she placed the three slices of thick French toast onto a plate. My stomach roared with excitement.

"You don't have to thank me, Miss White," Laura said as she coated my breakfast with powdered sugar.

"You can call me Mae."

How did she know French toast was my favorite breakfast? She placed several strips of bacon on the plate and placed it in front of me. My stomach roared again, and I was sure she heard it this time. She handed me some silverware, and I picked up the fork. My stomach's growl this time was cut off as it twisted with nausea. Damn, I had been feeling so much better I almost forgot I couldn't eat much without a Guardian present. Maybe I could force a few bites down...

"Is something wrong?" Laura asked, concerned. I looked up and forced myself to smile.

"No, nothing is wrong! I was just thinking about how I was going to be able to eat all of this." Without help.

Laura laughed.

"You need to eat it all. You're about as thin as my pinky finger!" As she talked, she began cleaning up. "My little crew and I are here from five to ten in the morning and three to eight at night. If you need anything, let me know, and I'll make sure it gets done. If you have any preference for what to eat for dinner, let me know about that as well, along with any dietary restrictions, and I will work around those."

This was going to be weird, having someone around all the time. Would I ever get used to it? I forced a bite of French toast into my mouth. Oh! This was the best French toast *ever*. I tried to swallow it and was able to choke it down with a gulp of water that Laura had put in a glass for me. My stomach twisted painfully. Keep it down, I demanded of myself. My stomach rolled. I clenched my jaw together. As I began to wonder how to slide the rest of the breakfast into the trash without hurting Laura's feelings, Arthur strolled into the kitchen. His warm smile seemed wider this morning.

"Ah, good, you two have met," he said as he came around the island to stand next to me. He casually placed a hand on my shoulder and immediately the knot in my stomach loosened. I shot him a thankful look and took another bite of the sweet brioche bread. "I hope you found your room to your liking. Laura triple-checked that everything was properly prepared for you."

"The room is great," I said after trying the bacon. "But it's huge. I don't think I need all of that space."

"Enjoy it!" Laura said with a chuckle. "It's a dream suite for sure. My little Penelope is probably in there now wishing it was hers as she makes the bed."

Arthur chuckled and said, "We are sharing a home now. I'm sure you'll want to escape to your own space now and then for some privacy."

Privacy would be nice. But did I need *all* that space? I didn't argue. I just shoved another bite of French toast into my mouth.

"Laura, we will be having another guest coming to stay with us for a while. Jasmine will be arriving around supper and will be staying with us for an undetermined amount of time," Arthur told the housekeeper.

"I'll get her room prepared right away," Laura said as she dried the last pan. "Same accommodations as before?"

"Yes, thank you," Arthur said. Laura beamed at both of us and left the kitchen.

"She seems nice," I said with a mouthful of food. Arthur smiled and nodded.

"She is a good woman," he agreed.

"Who's Jasmine?" I asked curiously after a bite of bacon.

Arthur did not answer right away. Instead, he seemed to be listening for something. Footsteps?

"Jasmine Sing is one of the most learned Guardians when it comes to magic. We hope that she will be able to help you with your problem," Arthur said.

"Does she have any idea what I could be?"

Arthur shook his head.

"I told her nothing about you. All she knows is that Rylan has found his mate and there is an urgent need of her assistance," he said. "May I ask how you slept last night? You must have been tired after your ordeal."

I cringed. Ordeal? More like a nightmare. I put down my fork and looked at him,

"I'm sorry. I couldn't stop it from happening." I paused and shook my head. "I slept like the dead last night."

"Do not apologize for something you cannot control," Arthur scolded gently. "Rylan showed me what happened, and I cannot begin to imagine how hard it must have been to contain your power for as long as you did. We had no idea the extent of your discomfort. We will not downplay your suffering ever again, Mae."

"How would you know what's going on inside of me? It's not your fault," I muttered, still feeling embarrassed at my inadequacy.

"You tried to tell us all day about your power and its destructive nature, but we did not heed your warning. We could see the physical pain you were in, though you chose not to say anything to us, and we chose to ignore it to give you some privacy. We certainly will not turn a blind eye again," Arthur said firmly. I could see the resolve set in his facial features. "In any case, I am glad to hear you slept well."

I finished the last bite of bacon before pushing the plate away from me. With a full stomach, I felt almost as good as I had before gaining my power. Arthur removed his hand.

"Thank you."

Arthur shook his head. "We will do whatever we can to help you. You do not have to thank me."

"Well, I am thankful and because I was raised with manners, I'll tell you whenever I feel like it's necessary," I told him. I looked over my shoulder to see if Laura had come back. When I was sure Laura was not nearby, I leaned closer to Arthur and asked, "Did you get to fly last night? Rylan brought us back to the house that way, and it was the most incredible experience." I grinned at the memory.

"Unfortunately, no," Arthur said shaking his head. "Before Rylan left this morning, he said it was indescribable to experience flying again."

"You guys don't get to fly often?" I asked. My heart sank. Rylan left? Was he running away from the monster he witnessed last night? Maybe his kindness last night was only to keep me calm and to keep himself safe from another episode. "Where did Rylan go?"

"We fly whenever we get the chance, but we cannot feel the joy it used to bring. Having no emotions takes the pleasure of living away." Arthur stroked his goatee thoughtfully. "Rylan left to get a bite to eat. He will return shortly."

Oh. Arthur's words gave me pause.

"So, Guardians really can't feel anything?" I asked, trying to wrap my head around what that meant.

Arthur shook his head sadly. "Hopefully, that will change now that we've found you."

I made a face. The hope in his voice grew every time he mentioned this curse and me lifting it. I didn't want to let him down, but he needed to be more realistic.

"I don't know how I'm affecting you, Arthur," I admitted. I focused on the mental barrier I had erected and tried to feel if any power was leaking. If any power was seeping out, the leakage was so minuscule I was unable to detect it. "There has to be something more than just my power causing your emotions to return. It's in check right now. Even when I wear my bracelets, you can still feel emotions, and my power can't come out at all when I wear those."

"We will figure this out. I hope that Jasmine will have some answers or at least point us in the right direction. I took from Rylan's mind the image of what the area looked like after your ordeal in the woods. We both studied it in the hopes there would be some clues or maybe some sort of pattern in the destruction that may help us solve this riddle. Unfortunately, we were unable to discover anything of any importance. We are not sure what we are dealing with."

What we are dealing with.

Yes, of course, Rylan wanted to show Arthur the chaos created by the monster they were housing. I was sure it was a warning to the other Guardian to watch his back. I shook my head and made a face.

Another thought popped into my head: Rylan was going to drink someone's *blood* as his "bite to eat." The thought distracted me from my darker ones. Why was I morbidly curious to see what that would look like? I thought about his victims: Were they willing participants, or were they dragged into a dark alleyway? Did it hurt to be bitten? Did it leave a mark? I thought about

Rylan bending down to bite my neck. The thought should have frightened and repulsed me. Instead, I was instantly aroused. My cheeks warmed, and my breath quickened. I could just picture those red eyes coming closer, his mouth on my skin… Bumps rose on my arms as I pictured every moment leading up to that bite…

"Will you be alright on your own for a little while? I have some business to attend to," Arthur said, pulling me away from my sudden onslaught of erotic thoughts.

"Yeah," I assured him, mentally shaking myself. "I think I'll just poke around for a bit. I have to go into town to buy a car and look for a job at some point. Oh, that reminds me. Where exactly are we?" I probably should have asked that before we had left Illinois.

"We are outside of a town called Salisbury," Arthur said while he studied me curiously. "You don't need to work, and there are plenty of cars to choose in the garage. You can have your pick."

I snorted in amusement.

"I need to provide for myself. It feels… slimy expecting everything to be taken care of for me. And if I need to leave—" *Or escape.* "—I want to be able to do so in my own car."

"As you wish," Arthur said with a shrug. He pushed away from the island. "If you need anything, Laura will be around for a while. Her daughter Penelope is around somewhere, and her husband, Charlie, is outside tending to the grounds. They all will be happy to assist you with anything that you need."

I nodded and watched as he left. I popped up from the barstool and took my plate over to the sink. When I had washed it and found the correct places for everything, I began the rest of the tour around the house. There was a hallway beyond the dining room where I found a small movie theater that could seat eight people in large leather recliners, a full-size gym, a conference room with a large oval table, and a library with a cozy fireplace. The sheer size of this place was amazing. And Rylan said there was a bunker? Part of me wanted to see that. Another part wanted absolutely nothing to do with it.

I made my way back into the large open living area and walked out through a sliding glass door along the back wall onto the enclosed deck. I immediately began to sweat once I stepped outside. Luckily, in the enclosure, two fans were whirling to keep the hot air moving. I stared out onto the vast piece of property and, despite my situation, felt oddly at peace.

I couldn't imagine standing here feeling void of any emotions like Rylan or Arthur would have done countless times before. What would it be like to feel nothing? Rylan's image popped into my head, and I imagined him standing here wanting to feel something, anything. Without emotions, how could someone appreciate anything about life? Arthur had told me that there were Guardians who could not handle the nothingness. That Guardians took their lives despite knowing that there would be nothing waiting for them on the other side. Was ceasing to exist better than existing in a world where you couldn't appreciate anything?

My heart became heavy as I realized that was what Arthur and Rylan battled daily. The "is it worth it anymore" thoughts probably swirled around their heads all day. I could almost relate, except it was the overflow emotions I battled with, not the lack of them. It was the constant fear of losing control, hurting or killing someone, that made me question my existence. The difference between Arthur and Rylan and me was they still lived after many centuries of fighting themselves while I had tried to end my own life after only two years of this hell.

Shame washed over me, and I hung my head. If they could deal with their curse for as long as they had, I could continue to deal with my own burden. I walked across the enclosure to the door that led outside and stepped out. I wandered around to the side of the house. In the grass, I spotted a small lizard weaving through the green blades. How could these two men survive as long as they had when others decided they could no longer take it? For now, the three of us had each other. We could stay strong for one another now. We gave each other hope, and we could hang onto that.

It was more than what we had before, right?

I came around the corner of the house and found, nestled in the nearby trees, a large garage. I walked over to it, curious to see what type of vehicles Guardians drove around. I was mildly surprised to find the side door unlocked when I reached for it. I guessed out in the middle of nowhere like this they weren't expecting too much trouble.

Inside, there were seven cars lined up, shining under the harsh LED lighting. I didn't know much about cars, but from what little I did know, I could tell these cars were fast and expensive. I walked past each car, staring at the sleek-looking vehicles. I tried to imagine Rylan sitting behind the wheel of each of these cars, wanting to feel the rush of the speed or the excitement over the roar of the engine but being unable to. Frowning, I ran my hands over an especially nice looking red Porsche. As my fingers absentmindedly stroked the paint, my mind strayed to a new thought:

The image of Rylan's hands trailing up my arms. Those hands coming around from behind me and grabbing my breasts, squeezing them gently. One hand slips off my breast and pushes me in between my shoulder blades so I was leaning over the hood of the car. I could almost feel him push my legs further apart as I lay against the car. My breath came in rapid succession, and the arousal I felt was so sharp and immediate I knew it had been built up from the last twenty-four hours in close proximity with Rylan. I could feel myself become damp with need.

I blinked away the erotic images in my mind. I stopped caressing the car and took a deep breath, trying to control this sudden onslaught of arousal. My body hummed with a need that was so unfamiliar it was scary. I reached up and touched the back of my neck. Where the mark was. Somehow this mark was tied to Rylan. Now that he was in my life, was this tattoo causing these waves of lust? I was sure I had never felt this hot and bothered about anyone before. It took a few minutes of deep breathing before I was in control again.

I left the garage feeling shaky. Instead of heading back to the house, I walked across the grassy backyard and headed to the woods. The freedom to roam around the property was nice. It was beautiful, and I knew that if I lost a little bit of control of my power I would be alright here. Any other Sunday, I would have been scrambling to break down my tent and pack up my belongings to head back into the city. I would be dreading the long, painful, lonely week ahead of me.

I walked into the woods and instantly felt relief from the hot sun there in the shade. I could hear the cicadas singing and the birds chirping as I walked deeper into the woods. I caught sight of a deer before it took off. It was gorgeous here. How could anyone want to live in a crowded, stinky city? The peacefulness of nature was settling for my soul. Feeling good, I started a brisk jog. A good night's sleep and some food were doing wonders for my body. I felt stronger than I had in a long time, and I quietly sent up thanks. I needed this. I didn't jog long; I wasn't in the proper attire for a run, but I started planning a workout regimen in my head.

Up ahead there was a break in the trees. As I stepped out of the tree line, I found a small pond glistening in the sunshine. Stunned at the absolute tranquility of the scenery before me, I stood there simply staring at it. Small ripples from bugs moved the water, causing it to sparkle in the sunlight. I walked over to the very edge of the water and sat down. The sound of nature and the soft lapping of the water was hypnotizing.

Time slipped by. I lay on the ground, staring up at the sky, enjoying the silence. Occasionally, I hummed to myself. For a while, I forced all depressing thoughts aside. I would enjoy the moment. After last night, practically begging Rylan to kill me, I knew I needed to recoup emotionally.

Rylan was another topic I tried to avoid. The desire that I was feeling for this strange man was disturbing and terrifying. Despite how hard I fought it, occasionally I wondered about him. What was he doing now? Had he eaten? Was he having second thoughts about having me around after last night's episode? Would his hands feel as good as I imagined?

Eventually, it got to be too hot despite the shade that the trees provided. Just as I sat up, a cold chill ran down my spine. The hairs on the back of my neck and my arms rose. I turned, looking around at my surroundings trying to find the cause, but there was nothing there. I stood up and brushed off the dirt. As I turned around to head back to the house, a scream pierced the silence.

I froze in place as terror rippled through me. It caused my mental barrier to slip, and in turn, the ground beneath my feet shifted. I checked myself, stopping the leakage of power, and then I took off towards the sound. The scream never stopped. It was a horrible gut-wrenching scream that could only mean someone was in a lot of pain. A strong feeling of dread oozed down my spine.

I burst onto the scene and almost crashed right into my worst nightmare.

Chapter Nine

Standing just a few yards away from me was a black, inky creature with no eyes and a large mouth full of sharp teeth. The thing was larger than an elephant but much more agile with its eight long legs that helped it scurry across the ground like a spider. The three talons on each long leg were sharp and coated in a greyish powder.

Rylan called these things spider demons. I called what I was staring at a monster.

The demon leaned over an older looking gentleman and shrieked as it bent its head to kill its prey. The sound was like a banshee underwater: high pitched but slightly gurgled. The creature paused just inches from the man's head and turned its eyeless head towards me as I stumbled towards it. I was not exactly sure what I planned to do, but I knew I had to do something. I stared at it with my mouth hanging open.

Without warning, the creature leaped towards me. It covered the distance between us in a single bound. I threw myself to one side as it tried to strike me with a leg. The creature shrieked and tried to crush me with another leg. I attempted to take off into the woods, hoping the large trees and thick vegetation would slow it down. It didn't. The demon flew over me and landed directly in front of me before I had gotten very far. I ran back towards the man on the ground.

Off in the distance, I heard another shriek.

My stomach sunk in despair as I realized there was more than one. While my stomach felt weighed down, my heart had taken flight; it beat faster than a hummingbird's wings. I let my mental barrier drop. My power unleashed was just as dangerous to myself and this man as the demon was to us, but despite the danger, if we wanted a chance at surviving, we needed an edge. My power had saved me the past two times I had run into these things; hopefully, it would help me again. The ground around us began to ripple. The demon stumbled as it charged towards us, which gave me time to throw myself on top of the man. I had to protect him.

Unable to stay upright, the demon climbed a nearby tree and turned to face me. It let out another shriek and tried another attack. I screamed in terror as the demon threw itself from the branch it clung to. Before I could react, the demon slammed into me, throwing me a few feet backward. I rolled another few feet before I skidded to a stop. The ground exploded around me as I lost control of my power. As the demon leaped again to pin me down, the ground erupted underneath me and we both were flung upwards, into the air, and then came crashing down along with dirt and rocks.

The demon didn't pause. A large leg arched over me and shot downwards. One of the demon's talons slammed into my upper thigh. I screamed again, this time in pain. The demon let out a guttural shriek in return, which was answered by the other demons who sounded much closer now. It dragged me towards it, its talon sinking deeper and deeper into my leg, I couldn't help but scream again. Energy whipped around me, and the ground exploded again. The demon was thrown off me, and I was tossed to the side. Without hesitating, I rolled onto my knees and started towards the man, who had not moved. The pain in my leg caused my vision to blur. The amount of blood pumping out of the hole in my leg was alarming.

Just as I got to the unconscious man, I heard the demon coming up behind me. This time my power reacted before it could get me. The energy billowing around me began to pick up and circle me. I covered the man's body with my own to protect him from debris and watched as my power twisted upwards, causing a cyclone to form with us in the center. Dirt, rocks, fallen branches, and shrubbery got caught up in the cyclone, causing an effective barrier between me and the demon that was just on the other side.

The demon circled us, waiting for its opportunity to leap into the center. I knew I had to get this cyclone of energy under control, but while fighting back pain and panic, the feat seemed near impossible. The man under me groaned in pain, but he didn't move, and when I glanced down his eyes were closed. The longer we were stuck in this cyclone, the higher the risk we would be hurt by the debris.

The demon must have seen an opportunity because suddenly it jumped towards me. I braced myself for contact but a massive branch from a nearby tree was ripped off the trunk, flung around, and hit the demon, throwing it backward.

A shriek behind me and to my left warned me of more visitors. Internally, I screamed over and over at the nightmare that I was witnessing as three more spider demons, much larger, emerged from the woods around us. They appeared to pause as they studied the cyclone of chaos surrounding myself and the man on the ground. A tree fell close to one of the newcomers. It jumped out of the way and took the opportunity to rush forward. The ground erupted once more, and the force threw the creature backward. A massive rock missed my head by inches.

The other three took the opportunity to attack as one. I closed my eyes as they descended upon us, waiting for the attack. Nothing happened. Instead, there was a horrible screech followed by what sounded like an angry gurgle. There was another scream. The ground rolled, and there was another explosion as I flinched from the noise. There were more angry shrieks, but nothing hit me from any direction.

I looked up and a strangled cry of relief slipped past my lips. The Guardians had arrived, and they were in full warrior mode. Rylan and Arthur stood in the midst of the chaos. Rylan held a sword, and Arthur held a flail; both used their weapons with deadly accuracy. Their wings acted as a shield from any offensive attack, and they used them to knock back demons as they got closer. The demons tried to defend themselves, using their long talon-like claws and those razor sharp teeth, but it was to no avail. Neither Guardian seemed phased by the danger they were in. I watched in awe as their weapons cut through the spider demons like butter, removing limbs and skewering their victims with ease.

Despite the raging storm around them, the Guardians fought as if it was only the spider demons they had to worry about. They were able to move around the flying debris. The spider demons, on the other hand, kept getting hit by rocks, dirt, and branches. Unable to defend themselves from the Guardians and the debris at the same time, the demons did not last long. The moment the last creature collapsed in a heap on the ground, Rylan turned, and our eyes met. His blazing red eyes were bright with the excitement of the fight.

"Mae, it is over," he said loud enough for me to hear over the destruction my power was causing. "I am coming to you."

Shit, he was going to get hurt. I had to pull back the wild energy.

"No! Wait," I shouted as I choked back fear.

Rylan tensed.

I took a deep breath and tried to control it. I chanted, and chanted, and chanted, but it wasn't helping. I took another deep breath, trying to concentrate. Another minute ticked by, but the cyclone of debris wasn't slowing down. It was taking much longer this time to rein back my power. Was it because I was well rested and fed? If my body was stronger, was my power stronger too?

Finally, the cyclone slowed and debris began to fall around us. Both Arthur and Rylan had to dodge several falling rocks and large branches to keep from being hit. A small tree slammed into the ground just inches behind me and the unconscious man. I flinched in surprise, and the ground rumbled.

Before everything had settled Rylan was there crouching down beside me. He took his sword and shoved the tip into his abdomen. As he pushed in the sword, it *vanished.* I gasped in astonishment. Once the hilt of the sword had disappeared into his abs, a mark appeared. It was a crescent moon with a sword cutting through it from top to bottom. Just like the symbol on my neck. I stared at the mark then back up at Rylan's face in awe.

Before Rylan could say anything, I pulled myself off the unconscious man, panicked that I was hurting him, and looked down. He was missing an arm. I choked back a scream. My breathing came in short gasps. Uncertain of what to do, I tried to put my hands over the stump to stop the bleeding, but the action did nothing to help. Instead, it coated my hands with thick, warm blood.

"He will be okay, Mae," Rylan said, pulling my hands away from the ragged stump. "Leave him."

"We can't leave him, Rylan! He stopped moving a few minutes ago. He's probably dying of blood loss or… or something," I said. My voice was high-pitched and breathless.

"You are going to die of blood loss if I do not get you back to the house," Rylan growled and suddenly I found myself in his arms. I hissed in pain as he jostled my bad leg. I glanced down at the hole and found blood was still gushing profusely. I covered it with my bloodied hands and tried to apply pressure. I winced.

"We can't leave him!" I shrieked as Rylan began to turn towards the house. We couldn't leave this poor man here to die all alone.

"We will not leave him to die, I promise you. Arthur—"

"I will get him help, Mae. Go with Rylan." Arthur approached us and crouched down next to the older gentleman.

Rylan didn't wait for any other objection from me. He shot upwards into the air at lightning speed. My stomach dropped. I quickly wrapped my arms around his neck as we flew towards the house. We were there much faster than I expected. Rylan landed in front of the house. His wings retracted into his back as he strolled up the steps and kicked open the front door.

"Laura!" he yelled as we entered the house. Rylan walked under the mezzanine and through the main area of the house. Behind us, I heard soft footsteps coming towards us.

"Oh my God, what happened?" Laura asked staring at my leg. Blood dripped onto the floor, leaving a nasty trail as we walked.

"Laura, go to the hospital. Arthur will meet you there. There was an accident and Charlie's hurt," Rylan said without stopping. He didn't even spare her a glance. I watched as Laura's face went deathly pale.

"Oh!" Laura said with a gasp. She turned, and I heard her run through the house. "Penelope!"

"Where are we going?" My words sounded slurred, and my head felt cloudy.

"To the bunker."

We approached the locked door. To my surprise, a small camera scanned his iris, and the door slid open. I gasped. How had I not noticed the camera before? We walked down a flight of stairs, and at the bottom, I found myself in a stark white hallway with several doors on either side. Rylan opened the first door on the left. Inside was set up like a surgical room with a hospital bed, a surgical cabinet full of tools, stark fluorescent lighting, and a sink. Rylan set me gently on the bed and walked over to the sink. I laid back on the thin, padded bed and closed my eyes as the room began to spin.

The smell of blood was revolting. I wrapped my arms around my waist hoping I wouldn't throw up. My body shook. Why was it so cold in this room? Behind my eyelids, I could see the older man and his missing arm. I groaned from a mixture of terror and pain.

"Mae!" Rylan snapped. "Keep your eyes open."

His no-nonsense tone scared me enough to obey. I lifted my hands and stared at all the blood that had dried on them. I made a face and dropped my hands to the table. Demons had done this. Real, honest- to-God demons. The first two times I had been attacked I had gotten lucky. This time, if it hadn't been for Rylan and Arthur, I would be dead. What were they doing here? Did we have to leave? How many more were out there? Deep inside my mind, I screamed in terror.

The throbbing in my leg was horrible. Blood pumped from the wound. The dark liquid soaked my shorts and spilled onto the table. Anytime I moved, I couldn't stop a hiss of pain from escaping. I vaguely wondered if I was going to lose my leg. The thought drifted in a fog of pain and shock.

I needed to get my mind off the pain. I turned my head and watched Rylan as he moved around the room. He walked over to the medicine cabinet where he pulled out a small bottle and cotton swabs. My body shook as I replayed what had happened outside. I could hear those horrible shrieks echoing in my head. Those eyeless faces would haunt me for years.

Once Rylan had pulled the items he needed out of the medicine cabinet, he placed them on a stainless steel tray and came over to me. He pulled up a small rolling table and placed his tray down on it. There were cotton swabs, a needle, thread, a dark unlabeled bottle full of liquid, and bandages. I stared at the items suspiciously and then glanced up at his face.

"Take your shorts off," he commanded.

What? I stared at him as if he had grown three heads.

"Do it, or I'll do it for you."

"No!" I said affronted.

I sat up to glare at him. The wound was just a few inches lower than my hips. If I removed my clothes, I would be very exposed to a very attractive, albeit extremely angry, Guardian. Rylan's jaw ticked. It was the only warning I got. He reached forward, and before I could stop him, he used both hands to tear my shorts completely off.

"Rylan!"

My outraged shriek was ignored as Rylan looked down at the gaping hole in my leg. I looked down at it too and gasped. Not only was it larger than I had thought, but from what I could see black streaks were forming and spreading underneath my skin. My heart started pounding faster as I realized that this wasn't just a wound. I had been poisoned. My shaking intensified as fear began to mount. Way in the back of my mind I noticed that despite the horror and fear I was feeling, nothing in the room was shaking or breaking.

Rylan dragged his red gaze from my wound and looked up at me. His face was unreadable. I wasn't sure if that was scarier than being poisoned by demons or not. He reached up and cupped my cheek, and his gentleness took me by surprise.

"I am going to clean your wound and stitch you up. You will be alright," he assured me. His voice seemed calm. Maybe it wasn't as bad as I thought. I stared into those red eyes, and I had to admit I was glad he was here with me right now.

I nodded.

"Lie down," he commanded.

I did as I was told and laid back down. Rylan leaned down and stroked my cheek with his thumb. The intimate gesture was sweet and sent butterflies fluttering in my gut. Unexplainably my heart skipped a beat. He let his hand drop away. Heat blossomed in my cheeks.

Rylan started working quickly. With the amount of blood flowing, I was surprised I was still conscious. I prayed that it wasn't an artery that had been severed. Rylan opened the dark bottle on the counter and poured the liquid onto a cotton swab. He glanced at my face; his expression suddenly grim.

"This bottle is filled with fairy tears."

Fairy *what?*

"They can eliminate most poisons from the body if the poison is detected early enough. This will be uncomfortable," he warned.

Before I could ask Rylan what he was talking about, his shoulders tensed, and he dabbed the tears onto my leg. A horrible, agonizing pain flared up from the wound. This wasn't hydrogen-peroxide or even rubbing alcohol. This was something completely different, and the pain was unbearable. I screamed, and then screamed again as he dabbed the wound, but the sound seemed far away. The room dimmed and then disappeared. From a great distance, I could hear my name being called. As I tried to focus on the voice, a searing pain pushed me back down into darkness. I tried to fight the heavy weight lying on my consciousness. It took an incredible amount of energy, but finally, I could see the bright lights of the surgical room.

"Rylan?" I asked out loud, afraid to find myself alone in the stark room. The ceiling came into focus first, and as I took another deep breath, my vision cleared completely.

"I am here," he said, his voice deeper than normal.

I felt a nauseating tugging on my leg. It took a moment to realize that he was stitching me up. How odd; a sword-wielding, angel-winged, blood-sucking warrior was carefully stitching me back together. I drifted between conscious and unconsciousness while Rylan continued his stitching.

How many times had he done this before? Curious and probably in shock I asked him, "Did you ever study to be a doctor, or am I your first patient?"

My voice sounded far away and slightly slurred. The tugging stopped for half a breath before Rylan continued. The silence between us dragged, and I wondered if I had overstepped some unknown boundary.

"The last time I administered first aid was back during the Civil War," Rylan answered. "Science and medicine have come a long way since then. I do not believe that I would be able to keep up with all the changes that happen in the medical field."

The Civil War? My head spun, and I wasn't sure if it was because of the blood loss, pain, or simply the shock from the information he shared. How did someone accept this type of information without feeling crazy? Was I supposed to nod and pretend like that wasn't incredible? I said nothing as I tried to picture Rylan in a Civil War uniform.

"Does that information bother you?" Rylan asked, breaking the silence.

"Um… no," I said, my answer lacking confidence. "I'm just thinking how grateful I am that you didn't just saw off my leg and get me addicted to opium, like most doctors back then would have."

Rylan paused his ministrations, threw his head back, and laughed. I shifted my elbows under me to prop myself up and stared at his face in awe. For the moment, his face was relaxed and carefree. Gone was the solemn warrior, and in his place was a man whose laughter seemed to stop time and replace fear with joy. My breath caught in my throat as desire unraveled within me. He was stunning. Warmth spread through my veins, and my heart fluttered as I watched the amusement twinkle in those red eyes.

"No, you are safe from that," Rylan assured me as his laughter died down. A warm smile remained on his lips, and I found myself staring at it. "I was not a doctor back then, but a few truly good men deserved saving."

"What side of the war were you on?" I asked curiously. This should be interesting…

Rylan's smile wavered. "Guardians do not participate in human wars."

"Why not?"

"Humans cannot learn about the supernatural world. It would be hard to hide our wings when we flew across a battlefield. We need to remain inconspicuous, which means staying out of their affairs when possible."

I tried to picture Rylan flying over a battlefield littered with Union and Confederate soldiers, wielding his sword and cutting down the enemy.

"I thought it was awesome how you fought those—" I couldn't say the word *demon*. "—*creatures*. Since we might be spending a lot of time together, would you teach me how to fight, too?"

Rylan's smile disappeared immediately and was replaced with a deep scowl. "Absolutely not."

It was my turn to frown.

"But you were incredible the way you moved! You took them out like it was nothing. I need to learn how to defend myself just like that."

Rylan's face relaxed but his frown remained.

"You should never have to worry about defending yourself. I should have been there sooner, and you would not have gotten hurt," he said.

I snorted in amusement. My head felt fuzzy, so I laid back down. I closed my eyes and said, "You can't be everywhere I am all the time. I need to learn how to defend myself." A thought popped into my head. I opened my eyes and sat back up. "You stuck a sword into your torso and instead of turning yourself into a kabob *it disappeared* and became your tattoo. I have the same mark on my neck now. Can I pull a sword out of my *neck*? That was… that was awesome. I mean, at the time I was terrified, but now looking back…" I shook my head in awe.

Rylan's frown turned upwards.

"No, you will not be able to conjure a sword. Only Guardians can produce their weapons in such manner," he told me. I felt the last tug of the string. "You are done with stitches."

"Thank God," I mumbled.

I stared at Rylan's handsome face as he placed the needle on the stainless-steel tray. I noticed the bloody rags in a pile next to the tray on the table. He must have cleaned up my leg while I fainted.

"I will remove them in just a moment," he continued.

I looked at him, confused. "I haven't had stitches in a long time, but if I remember correctly, they have to stay in for at least a week or so, right?"

"For others, yes," Rylan said, turning his gaze towards my face. His red eyes were suddenly blazing.

"Rylan…?"

"Hold still," he commanded quietly.

I watched in fascination as his fangs lengthened. My heart slammed against my ribs with both fear and excitement. What was he about to do? With very deliberate slowness, he bent down over my leg, his eyes watching my face. When he was just inches over my stitched-up wound, he turned his head and ran his tongue over my skin.

Rylan might as well have lit a fuse running straight to my libido. Every single nerve in my body went mad. The blood under my skin boiled, my skin tightened, and my breathing turned into panting. The pleasure that rocked me straight to my core caused me to throw back my head and an involuntary moan escaped past my lips. I should have been mortified; tongues carried all sorts of bacteria, but I couldn't concentrate on anything but the incredible sensation humming throughout my body. I could feel my exposed panties dampen, and my nipples hardened. What sorcery was this? Why did his tongue feel so damn fantastic as he slid it over my skin?

After a few long, slow strokes, Rylan raised his head and looked at me. His eyes were brighter than I had ever seen them. His cheeks had hollowed, and his fangs were even longer now. His gaze studied my expression. Did he think I was frightened? Was he expecting some reprimand? I should have been terrified. I should have screamed and pushed away from him. Instead, I sat up slowly, mesmerized by the man in front of me. Rylan watched me, unmoving. As I sat up, I was just inches away from his face. In a move so uncharacteristic of me, I tentatively leaned forward and brushed my lips against his.

Had I thought his tongue against my skin had been hot? His lips were heaven. I planted another light, sweet kiss on his lips before pulling away to study his face. Was he feeling this too, or was I suffering some side effect of the demon's poison that was causing me to react weirdly? Rylan's jaw clenched, and I watched a shudder run down his body. He reached up and touched my face with one hand.

"Mae," his voice came out as a strained whisper. "Are you sure you want this?"

What was he talking about? His kiss? His touch? I didn't think I could be any more certain that was what I wanted. Ever since I had laid eyes on this man, I had been drawn to him. Yes, I nodded, I wanted this.

Rylan groaned, "Mae, you are my mate. Created for me. I have been fighting every fiber in my body over the urge to touch you until you understood what that means. If I give in, I will not be able to fight Joining with you for much longer. The emotions I felt seeing you in trouble…" He shook his head as another shudder ran through him. "I already do not know if I could live in a world without you in it."

Was he warning me about something? Because all I was hearing was his need for me as well.

"Rylan," I said and placed a hand on his bare chest.

It was like touching a bronze statue. There was no give to his muscles. Oh, how I wanted to slide my hand down his chest to explore the rest of him, but I had to focus on what I was saying, "All I know is that I've been thinking about you since I laid eyes on you. Please, just kiss me."

I watched the change in Rylan's face. Gone was the indecisive Guardian, and in his place was a hungry one. A hunger I completely understood. His hand slid from my cheek to the back of my neck. He leaned down, and his lips crashed against mine. Oh! This is what I needed! My body went up in flames. Everything scary, wrong, and horrible in my world vanished in that instant. I reached up and ran my fingers through his tousled blond hair. I pulled and tugged at the golden strands, wishing that he would come closer.

Rylan's tongue slipped passed my lips, and I welcomed its arrival. I moaned in pleasure as he explored my mouth. He tasted like heaven, and I wanted more. I leaned forward, into him, and our chests pressed together. He pulled away from my mouth and leaned down to trail kisses across my jaw. His teeth gently scraped against my earlobe, and I shuddered. Had I said I didn't want him to bite me? As he trailed kisses down my neck, I trembled. What would it feel like to have those fangs sink in there, at the hollow of my throat? The thought turned my overheated body up another notch.

My hands left Rylan's hair, and I pressed both against his chest. The heat radiating off his body matched mine. The contact with his skin was divine. My hands slowly slid down his chest on their own accord. My hands would always remember every hard groove, the smooth skin, the warmth. My heart pounded harder as my fingers caressed the trail of fine hair just underneath his navel. A growl, deep within his chest, reverberated through his body, and I could feel it in my fingertips. His mouth came down on mine and once more our tongues clashed together. My fingers reached the first button of Rylan's pants. My hands shook as I began to unbutton the clasp.

Suddenly, a vibration in his pocket caused both of us to pause. Our heavy breathing sounded loud in the quiet room. Rylan pulled away first. My hands dropped from his waistband, and he reached into his pocket, taking a step back as he did. I took in a deep steadying breath and brought a shaking hand up to run it through my mass of curls. As I did so, I realized my hands were still caked in blood.

"Arthur," Rylan answered.

My body cooled rapidly as I stared at the blood. How could I have gotten so carried away after what just happened? I looked down at my leg where my wound was and was astonished to see there was no longer a wound there. Just the stitches.

"Good. Yes. I will take care of it. What time? Good," Rylan said. "Alright." He hung up the phone.

I ran my bloodstained hands over the stitches in awe. How was that possible? How did Rylan have the power to do this? How little I knew about him and yet… I had just thrown myself at this Guardian. Where had my sanity gone?

"I'll remove those," Rylan said grabbing the scissors from the tray. I moved my hands out of the way and watched as he carefully clipped each string. I made a face as he cautiously pulled out each string from my skin.

"How did you do this?" I stared at the spot where blood had been spewing out just minutes ago.

"My saliva has healing properties," Rylan explained. "I can heal smaller injuries. Unfortunately, the hole in your leg would not have healed without stitching you up first."

Oh.

"Thank you."

My mind reeled. The power to heal. Is this what Rylan meant when he had mentioned administering first aid to a man back during the Civil War? Despite the evidence of his powers, my mind couldn't grasp what it was seeing.

I let the conversation go and asked, "Is Charlie going to be okay?"

I was unable to look Rylan in the face. Our intimate moment was still burning at the forefront of my mind. Why was I acting so… irrational?

"Yes, he will survive," Rylan assured me. "Mae."

I felt the blood rush to my cheeks.

"Are you alright?"

I forced myself to look up into his teal eyes and gave him a rueful smile. "I'm alright thanks to you. I'm glad Charlie is going to be okay. Where is Arthur now?"

"He is going to head to the airport and wait for Jasmine's plane to arrive," Rylan said with a sigh. "I need to scan the rest of the property to make sure it is safe. I would like to get you upstairs and comfortable before I leave."

My heart rate spiked. Panic caused my throat to squeeze shut. Rylan wanted to go out there by himself to make sure the area was safe? There could be more of those creatures lurking about. I couldn't let him go by himself.

"I'm going with you," I told him and hopped off the bed. I stumbled and almost went down as the room spun. Rylan grabbed my arm to steady me. I put a little bit of weight on my healed leg, testing how it felt. I was relieved to find I was able to stand on it without pain.

"No."

"Then you can't go," I told him with a scowl. I blinked away the spots dancing along the side of my vision. "What if there are more out there? You don't have backup. You could get hurt."

Rylan raised a brow. "You consider yourself backup? You can hardly stand."

"I just need a minute, and I'll be ready to go."

"I will be fine. I came upon Arthur destroying a pack of demons before we knew you were in trouble. They do not usually run in large packs, so I doubt there are more, but I will not make the mistake of letting my guard down again," Rylan said bleakly.

A pack of demons was roaming the property. I leaned up against the hospital bed as dread trickled down my spine.

"Where are they coming from? I thought 'The Devil Went Down to Georgia' was just a song. I didn't realize he and his minions actually hung out here!" I said, my voice raising a pitch as I realized we could be surrounded as we spoke.

"Mae, calm down," Rylan said in a tone used for toddlers throwing a tantrum. "I will keep you safe, but I have to make sure the property is secure to do that."

Without warning, he scooped me up and carried me out of the surgical room. I felt like I was about to shatter. My emotions were everywhere. One moment I was hot and bothered, and now I was terrified that Rylan was about to go out and get himself killed. Where was all of this coming from?

"Rylan, I can walk. I'm fine," I told him. He ignored me. "Please don't go out there by yourself," I pleaded as he carried me up the stairs. We reached the top, and I watched as Rylan had to scan his eye again for the door to slide open. He carried me down the hallway and over to the kitchen.

Rylan sat me down on a stool, walked over to a cabinet, and opened it. He grabbed a glass and headed over to the refrigerator and pulled out a container of orange juice. He poured me a glass before placing the carton back in the refrigerator.

"Drink this," he said and placed the glass in front of me. I ignored the glass and stared at him.

"Look, I know you could probably handle this on your own, but you don't have to. I can come with you and at least be a lookout while you search," I offered.

Rylan stared back at me without any expression on his face. When he looked so detached like this, it made me want to cringe under his gaze. I saw how efficiently he could kill these demons. He was a killing machine. What would he do to me if I ever upset him? So far he had been kind to me, but would that change if I didn't do what he wanted?

"I appreciate your offer, Mae." He paused and clenched his jaw. He took a deep breath and continued, "You are dizzy from blood loss. You will be too tired to be any help. You need to drink something and rest."

"I won't be able to rest while you're out there," I snapped. "What if the situation was reversed? What if I told you to sit and wait while I went on patrol? You wouldn't let it happen."

"Your life is more important than mine," he said gravely. "You hold a piece of my soul within you. You are a treasure to me, Mae. You may also carry the answer we seek to lift the curse on our species. You are too important to perish. Should something happen to me… the world will continue to go on."

Not for me.

The thought popped into my mind, and while completely absurd, my heart twisted in agreement. What was going on with me?

"Everyone's life is equally important, Rylan," I told him with a scowl. "And you and Arthur are just hoping I can help. Who knows if I can do anything for the Guardians? What if my power is to destroy you and your race? What then? So, for now, let's not talk about whose life is really worth saving because, in the end, it will probably be yours if I'm the monster I think I am." Rylan's deep scowl and the tick in his jaw told me I had hit a nerve. Oh well, he needed to get over it. "Please, let me go with you or just wait for Arthur to come back if you're so against my presence."

Rylan's scowled deepened. Instead of responding, he came around the counter and walked past me. I turned around in my seat and watched as he strolled over to the sliding patio door, opened it, and left the house. I watched as he crossed the enclosed space and stepped out into the open. His wings grew out from his back, and suddenly, he was gone.

Chapter Ten

My mouth dropped open. How could he have just left like that? We were still talking! The floor shook as I struggled to rein in my temper. Stupid Guardian! I turned around to face the orange juice he had placed in front of me. I had the urge to throw the glass across the room. The only reason I didn't was that I knew I would have to clean it up. Instead, I stood up from the stool, intending to follow Rylan. Unfortunately, my head spun, and I had to brace myself against the island to keep from falling.

Okay, maybe I wouldn't have been much help, but I'd be damned if I would admit that to him now. I took a few deep breaths until the room stilled. Reluctantly, I grabbed the glass of juice and sipped it. My stomach churned at the liquid. Without a Guardian around, I was unable to keep much down. I slammed my fist down on the counter in frustration, and the room vibrated. Somewhere in the house, something fell and shattered.

Good. I hoped it was valuable.

I walked over to the sink and turned on the hot water. As it warmed, I placed my bloody hands under the current. With soap, I began to scrub my hands. I watched the blood turn the soapy water pink as it drained down the sink. When my hands were clean, I turned off the water and dried them. I glanced at the clock on the oven and was surprised to see it was already five o'clock. Where had the day gone?

Briefly, I thought about lying down.

And give Rylan the satisfaction that he was right? Absolutely not. If Rylan thought I couldn't be helpful, he was about to be sorely mistaken. With a deep, steadying breath, I cautiously began my trek up to my room. I had to brace myself against the wall, grab the banister, and sometimes just sit down as I made my way. By the time I had made it back to the bedroom, I was exhausted.

Damn his correct assessment of my condition.

I stripped off the few articles of clothing I had left on and made my way into the bathroom. The shower I took was long. Most of it was spent on the floor, simply absorbing the warmth of the water. My extremities were pruned by the time I got out. I wrapped myself in a thick soft towel and walked over to the mirror. Gone was the refreshed looking young woman I had been this morning. Back was the tired and fearful monster I was used to seeing.

Instead of staring at the monster in the mirror, I decided to be more productive. I raised my hand and a violet pentagram began to glow on the back.

"Book, come to me," I whispered.

My reflection rippled in the mirror and was replaced with the familiar leather-bound book. I reached forward, and my hand sunk into the mirror. Wrapping my fingers around the item on the other side, I pulled it from its hiding place. I did not open it right away but instead carried it into the closet with me. I changed into clean clothes, and once I was dressed, I walked into the bedroom with the book in tow. I sat down on the edge of my bed and stared down at the book in my lap. Hesitantly, I opened it and began to read.

A knock on my door caused me to jump and look up. I blinked several times to clear my head. How long had I been reading? I had gone through spells, potions, curses, and hexes but found nothing to stop demons, nothing that would help me gain control over my power, or how to lift the curse on the Guardians. There was no information about marks appearing on the skin either. I guess I was stuck with Rylan's mark on my neck for the time being.

I glared at the closed door, wondering if I should just ignore it. I was not over being angry with Rylan, though I knew my anger was unjust. He had been right (at least partially); I was not fit to go out searching for demons. With a sigh, I climbed out of bed and glanced at the time on my phone: 9:30 pm. How had hours passed without me noticing? I walked over to the door and opened it, expecting Rylan. To my surprise, it was Arthur standing on the other side of the door.

"Good evening, did I wake you?" he asked with a frown.

"Oh, hey, Arthur. No, I was doing some reading. Come in," I said and stepped aside for him. He hesitated before he stepped into the room. "I pulled out my book to show you once you got back and decided to pay it some attention for once. While I didn't find anything helpful, some of this stuff is cool."

"Oh? Like what?" Arthur asked curiously, following me over to the bed where I left the book. I opened it up to the page I had stopped on. He leaned over my shoulder and glanced at the page.

"There are spells that could help a whole crop flourish or destroy it. There are ones that can cause the weather to be beautiful or create storms. I've read potions that can cure ailments or fix broken bones. There are even potions that can turn someone into a cat for a short period," I said shaking my head in amazement.

How had I been afraid of this?

"You can read this?" he asked softly after a moment. He then looked from the book to me. Baffled by his question, I looked down at the page we were on. The handwriting was a little rough, more of a scribble than scripture, but it was certainly legible.

"Yes, can't you?"

"To me, this is a blank page."

"Really?"

I stared down at the book. The page was filled from the top to bottom with a spell that would remove dust from a room.

"I can see indentions as if something had been written there but I cannot make out the words. May I?" he asked, indicating he wanted to hold the book. I shrugged and pushed the book towards him.

"Sure."

Arthur reached down to grab the book. Before his fingers made contact, Arthur was thrown clear through the wall into the bedroom next door. The room shook with the force of impact. I yelped in surprise as Rylan stood before me in all his Guardian warrior glory. His wings were outstretched; his muscles were tense. His bare chest heaved up and down in anger. Pieces of his shirt littered the floor from when his wings ripped through it. He let out a deep loud roar. I recoiled from him in alarm. Rage radiated off his body in waves. The murderous look he had as he took a step towards Arthur made me grabbed his wrist, fearful for his friend.

"Rylan!"

Arthur stepped through the hole in the wall, his eyes blazing red. I could see shame and humiliation on his face.

"Arthur, are you alright?" I asked him, worried.

I tried to move around Rylan, but Rylan snarled a warning and brought his wing down to stop me, completely blocking my view of Arthur.

"Yes, I—"

"*Leave. Now!*" Rylan bellowed.

"Forgive me, Mae," I heard Arthur say.

I felt a soft buzz in my head letting me know they were communicating. Rylan shifted his stance, and I could see Arthur. Arthur bowed his head, turned, and left the room. Rylan maintained his fighting stance. His shoulders heaved up and down, and I could hear his heavy breathing. His wings shifted and retracted into his bare back. His body shuddered. He turned to me with a deep scowl and flared nostrils.

"*Never* allow another male into your sleeping quarters. *Ever*," he hissed at me. He was mad that Arthur had been in my room?

"Why? I invited him in to look at my spellbook," I asked, trying to understand Rylan's anger.

"Because you are *my* mate," he said sharply.

What? What did that have anything to do with Arthur being in my room?

"I'm not allowed to have people in my room because you think I am your piece of *property*?" I asked incredulously. My anger flared. "Is that what you're trying to say?"

"We have not Joined yet," Rylan snapped. "Which means someone could still lay claim to you despite my mark on you."

"*Claim* me?" I repeated. My anger boiled under my skin. The room shook. I could hear the mirror in the bathroom shatter. "No one *owns* me. Not now or ever. I can do what I like, whenever I like. If I want Arthur to come into my room, he's allowed in here."

"How many times in my lifetime have I heard similar arguments between a man and a woman?" a woman's voice said from the doorway. I jumped in surprise. Rylan did not appear startled. He didn't bother to turn towards the woman.

"Not now, Jasmine," he snarled at her while continuing to glare at me.

"Hm…" Jasmine continued as if she hadn't heard him. "If anything is to be learned by past events, it is not wise to lay down the law for a woman. There is this thing called a woman's scorn that should not be tested."

I watched as Rylan's features softened, and his shoulders relaxed. He turned away from me to greet our newcomer. I stepped around Rylan to see the most beautiful woman I had ever laid eyes on. Her long, jet black hair hung down past her hips. Her skin was porcelain white, flawless, and timeless. She was tall, lean, and every bit as intimidating as Rylan and Arthur despite her feminine features. Her eyes were dark, and her perfect red lips were turned upwards in a small smile.

"A joke, Jasmine?" Rylan said, his tone changing from cold to warm. "It sounds like you have a sense of humor all of a sudden."

Although Rylan still stood in front of me, I could almost hear the smile he was wearing. For the briefest moment a stark, ugly emotion twisted in my gut. Who was this woman that could make Rylan forget being angry and cause him to smile? Jasmine stepped into the bedroom and walked over to us. Her attention was solely on Rylan.

"How is it that it feels good to see you after all this time?" she asked in awe as she stared up at him.

She embraced him in a warm hug. Jealousy darkened my mood further as I watched Rylan return the hug. Why was I so possessive? Was it because we had just shared the most passionate kiss I had ever experienced? That had to be it. There was no other rational explanation for my mood.

Jasmine stepped back, still smiling, and turned her attention to me.

Rylan turned with her and said, "Jasmine, this is my mate: Mae White. She is the reason behind the return of your sense of humor and goodwill."

To my surprise, Jasmine stepped forward and caressed my cheek. Not expecting the contact, I jerked back in surprise. Jasmine giggled, and then stopped mid-giggle, a look of confusion crossing over her beautiful facial features. She giggled again.

"Ah, so, this was the emergency Arthur insisted I drop everything for," she said. "He warned me that I would know what our situation was once I walked through the door, but I never, in a thousand years, would have guessed that I would be seeing the answer to all of our problems standing before me. Oh my… How odd it is to *feel* again after all this time," she muttered, more to herself than to me.

Jasmine beamed. She looked over at Rylan, and I could feel a soft buzz of conversation between them before Jasmine turned her attention back to me. I scowled.

"What are you two talking about?" I asked her.

Jasmine's brows rose in surprise. Rylan chuckled.

"You can intercept our conversation?" she asked, again shooting Rylan a glance as if for confirmation.

"I don't know what you're saying. I just know you're doing it," I explained, impatience coating my tone. "You must be Jasmine; Arthur was singing your praises earlier."

"Hm…" Jasmine brought her index finger to touch her red lips thoughtfully. "Any other time, I would know you were exaggerating as that would mean Arthur would have to feel affection to sing praise for anyone. Now, I am pleased to know that your statement may be true. You are correct, Mae. I am Jasmine Sing. It is a *pleasure* to meet you."

"Jasmine, would you mind giving Mae and me a moment? We can all reconvene shortly," Rylan said.

"Of course, I will have Arthur catch me up while we wait for the two of you," Jasmine said with a laugh that sounded almost sing-song. She beamed at me before she departed the room.

I shook my head. How had it gone from calm to chaos in just a few minutes? I had completely forgotten about Jasmine's arrival while I had been submerged in my reading. Rylan turned around to face me. I braced myself for a fight. While exhaustion beat at me, I was not backing down on this. He was not going to push me around or give me ridiculous rules to follow if I was going to live here.

As Rylan gazed down at me, his anger seemed to have disappeared. I didn't trust him; I kept my guard up. I crossed my arms over my chest and raised a brow. He said nothing for a moment as he studied my face. His eyes were still red, but the rest of his face had returned to normal. Even his breathing had relaxed.

"You look tired," he said softly. He reached up to touch me, but I stepped back, bumping into the bed.

"Gee, thanks."

He sighed. I wasn't sure from exasperation or his own fatigue.

"I am sorry for my behavior, Mae. I should not have snapped at you like that," he said. Was he placating me, or did he mean that? He looked genuine enough... "Guardians are more animal than human. We are possessive and territorial when it comes to what belongs to us. You are my mate, but we have not gone through the Joining yet. Whether you understand it or not, you are mine."

I opened my mouth to protest when Rylan raised his hand to stop me.

"Let me explain, as I should have when we first met. You carry my mark which assures to me, and everyone else, that you are my mate. That and the return of a Guardian's emotions are the guarantee that mates have met. As a Guardian's mate, you carry the other half to my soul. Once Joined, my soul will be merged with the half you possess, and we will be able to be together as one in the next life.

"While uncommon for a Guardian to Join with someone else's mate, it is not unheard of. If you Joined with another Guardian while in possession of my soul, it would allow that Guardian to feel emotions again, and they would be able to move onto the next life instead of blink out of existence when their time came. A desperate Guardian may do anything to feel again. With your ability to produce emotions within us, you may trigger someone to do something stupid to maintain the ability to feel again. Another male could force you to Join with him just to keep from not feeling anything at all.

"The threat of having a mate stolen is a fear among all Guardians. There is honor among us Guardians; we know to keep a respectful distance between mates who have not Joined. Arthur knew it was unacceptable to come into your personal quarters."

He paused to allow me to digest all this information. I stared at him in shock as I realized what he was saying. The *importance* of what he was saying. I carried his entire existence within me. If we didn't Join, whatever that meant, when he died, he would be no more. There would be no afterlife for him. Someone could use me to steal Rylan's soul to use for their own. It made sense why he wouldn't want any other male in my bedroom. He was doing this to protect me and himself.

"I must remind myself how new everything is for you," Rylan continued after a moment. "You have no understanding of what a Guardian's mate is or what role you play. You were thrown into our world only a few days ago. We have placed our hopes and our burden on your shoulders. We have moved you from your home, you have had limited privacy, and you are feeling the effects of being a mate. You must be overwhelmed.

"But being a Guardian's mate is an honor. While you might not get a choice about who your mate is, trust me, a mate is sacred in our species. You are the flame to my dark existence, and I will kindle that flame for all eternity by trying to make you happy. Your happiness, well-being, and safety will always be my top priority. You are the only woman I can see, the only one I need or want. You were created specifically for me; you are a gift I will cherish for as long as I live. You will have everything your heart desires."

When he reached for me, I did not move away. He took my hand and brought my knuckles up to his lips. My heart fluttered at the contact, and my whole body warmed. Just like that all my anger dissipated. All the lust I had felt earlier, in the garage, on the surgical table, and from the first time I had laid eyes on him, it all bubbled up, and my body trembled.

"I wanted to keep a distance between us until I was able to explain to you what it means to be a mate. But it is my duty and my desire to care for you. I could not bear it to see your tears last night when we were out in the woods. Today, when I found you, surrounded by demons, my world stopped. Your laughter is music to my ears. Your smile steals my breath away. How can I stay away from you when you are the only thing that has any importance in my life? You are mine, Mae White, but I am also all yours. Forever."

I stood there, stunned. What could I say? Everything fell away around me. All the chaos in my life, all the questions, and angst. It disappeared. In their place was Rylan Wellington. Despite not knowing anything about me, he had just pledged his life to me. His vulnerability was raw and undiluted. A sane person would have tried to run; this was all too surreal. But apparently, I was not sane. His words touched me on a level that I hadn't known existed. His words sent warm tremors scurrying through every vein in my body. That warmth reached and filled my heart causing it to swell.

How could I tell him that his words were a soothing balm to all the pandemonium in my world? Anything I said now would come out lame and inferior to the emotions I was feeling. Instead of using words, I leaned forward on my tiptoes and kissed him softly. The moment our lips touched the spark between us erupted into an atomic heat, causing my soft kiss to turn ravenous. Rylan returned the kiss with equal passion. The desire that struck me was electrifying and coursed through my body. I wanted to wrap my arms around his neck and lean against his hard chest. To lose myself in him. Instead, I forced myself to pull away. I looked up into Rylan's red eyes and shuddered under the onslaught of desire and concern for the man standing before me.

"I understand now," I told him, my voice a whisper.

Rylan took a shaky breath and sighed. As he did, he raised his hand and ran his knuckles down my cheek.

"Are you feeling up to talking with Jasmine this evening? We can always reconvene tomorrow."

Fatigue and curiosity warred within me; I did not want to go downstairs to talk with the others, but maybe Jasmine had the answers to the questions I had been asking for the past two years. If I was this close to getting them, I didn't want to wait any longer. I nodded.

"Alright but first let me feed you," Rylan said. He glanced over to the open spellbook on the bed. "Did you find anything in there?"

I shook my head.

"Nothing that would help us. Let me put it away before we go downstairs."

Knowing that the mirror in the bathroom wouldn't be any use now that it was broken, I grabbed my purse, pulled the compact mirror out and raised my palm. The reflection in the mirror rippled, and my image disappeared. Thanks to magic, my book sank into the mirror with ease. Rylan raised a brow in surprise but remained silent.

Rylan wrapped his arm around my shoulders and guided me from the bedroom. On the way out, I stared at the large hole in the wall where Arthur had crashed through. Rylan had flung a full-size adult clear across the room without any trouble. He was so impossibly strong… How was I not afraid of him? I shook my head in incredulity.

We made our way downstairs and into the kitchen. The house was quiet. Were Arthur and Jasmine nearby? I walked over to the refrigerator and opened it. It was well stocked. I should have been hungry, but the thought of eating anything made my insides twist. I knew, though, that if I didn't grab something it would start a fight with Rylan.

I grabbed a Tupperware container and opened it. It was soup. The scent wafted upwards towards me, and I froze. I stared down at the contents in disbelief. I could see chunks of potato, tomato, carrots, onions, beans, celery, and crabmeat. There was a ton of crabmeat. The Old Bay seasoning wafted up, and immediately my heart stuttered. I looked over to Rylan who was watching me.

"Who made this?" I asked quietly as I struggled to hold back the painful emotions threatening to overwhelm me.

"Laura," Rylan responded. "It was pulled from a recipe book found in your storage unit in Maryland. It is your favorite, is it not? It was starred in the book." When I looked at him, stunned, he continued, "I told you, I will do anything for your happiness. Since our first encounter, I have had my people research your likes and dislikes."

I opened my mouth to say something, but no words came out

"I'm curious, why do you keep the house? Paying the taxes and having people come to maintain the property is draining your inheritance despite the rent you collect from it."

"You know about my finances?" I asked although by now I was not really surprised.

"I know almost everything about you. With my connections, all I need to do is make a phone call and the information is at my fingertips," Rylan said with a shrug.

I glanced up at him, not sure how to feel about that. After what he'd just told me upstairs, I could see why he would want to collect information on his mate. Still, it seemed like a violation of privacy. Instead of responding, I took the soup over to the microwave and warmed it up. I turned to face Rylan.

"This *is* my favorite soup. Thank you," I said softly. "And I keep the house because if I sell the house I grew up in, my heart would break. I'm not ready to let go yet."

Rylan nodded, understanding my desire to hold on to my past.

The microwave dinged, alerting me that my dinner was ready. I pulled it out, grabbed a spoon from a drawer, and sat down on a stool at the island. Rylan came over and gently cupped the back of my neck with his hand. The moment his hand connected with my skin, the tension in my body loosened. The knot in my stomach unraveled; I would be able to eat now.

"Did you find any more of those creatures – I mean, spider demons, during your search earlier?" I asked as I took the first bite. Oh! I closed my eyes to savor the moment. God, I missed my mom so much. The soup was exactly how she made it; always with a ton of Old Bay and large chunks of crabmeat, just the way I loved it. I opened my eyes after I swallowed the bite and looked up at Rylan, waiting for his response. He was watching my face carefully. He smiled when our eyes met. Feeling uncomfortable under his attention I turned my gaze back to the soup.

"There were two more. I destroyed them and made sure to thoroughly mark my territory so nothing else will trespass onto my lands."

"Marked your territory?" I asked, confused. "Do you pee on trees like dogs?"

Rylan chuckled. "No."

"How did they know to find me here?" I asked.

I took a few more bites of soup. Rylan did not respond right away. The silence stretched as I ate. I was hungrier than I had thought. The portion of soup in the container probably could have been two meals, but I was quickly making a dent in it.

"Demons are creatures who feed on individuals with powers. I believe after you let your power out last night that you sent out powerful waves in every direction, and any demons in the nearby area felt it. They could not resist the pull. Since I have not been here for decades, they must have thought I abandoned the area and risked coming for you," he finally admitted.

Despite Rylan's hand on my neck, I suddenly found myself no longer hungry. I put my spoon down and pushed the bowl away. I thought about the two other times I had been attacked when I was on the Appalachian Trail. Both had happened right after I had let my power run free.

"What about the one who destroyed my apartment?" I asked. "I always made sure to bind myself when I came back into the city."

Rylan scowled, but I raised my hand to stop him from getting angry.

"You have seen why I do it," I said firmly. "I have not put them back on since we left Chicago, so it's not something we need to argue about now."

Rylan's jaw ticked in annoyance, but he nodded.

"That one must have been older, wiser, and stronger. They do not like to go into cities. They are too crowded and loud for them. That demon must have been determined to have you," he said. His eyes brightened in anger. This was upsetting to him. I frowned and looked away from Rylan, staring at the soup in front of me.

"I have to, you know, blow off steam or the buildup becomes too painful. Can I still do that here or should I find somewhere else to go so no one else gets hurt if demons decide to ignore your markings?" I asked quietly. I knew nothing about the area we were in. I would have to do some research about nearby parks.

"You are safe here," Rylan assured me immediately. "They will not dare to cross onto my territory again."

He let go of my neck to bring his fingers under my chin. He tilted my head upwards, so I was forced to look into his eyes.

"I hope that Jasmine will be able to help you somehow so you will not have to struggle with your power any longer. Are you ready to go speak with the others?"

I pulled my face from his hand and stood up. I placed the remaining soup back into the refrigerator and grabbed a bottle of water. Rylan and I headed to the other side of the house and stopped outside of the office doors. I looked up at Rylan, and he looked down at me.

"Ready?" he asked.

For answers? Hell, yes. I nodded, and Rylan opened the doors into the office.

Chapter Eleven

Inside, Arthur and Jasmine were waiting. In contrast to the rest of the house, this room was painted jet black. There was a gorgeous wood desk on the far side of the room, a modern chandelier hung from the tall ceiling, and the light leather couch and matching chairs were uniquely distressed.

Jasmine was seated in one chair, and Arthur stood just next to her. Both looked up as Rylan and I entered. Rylan shut the door behind me as we walked in. As I walked over to the two Guardians who were watching the two of us, Arthur made a move to come towards me. Rylan hissed a warning and stepped in front of me. Arthur paused. I placed a hand on Rylan's arm but kept my gaze on Arthur.

"Arthur, I'm sorry. I didn't realize it was a faux pas to allow you into my room," I told him sincerely. I didn't want there to be tension between the two men.

"I should have known better," Arthur told me, immediately brushing off my apology. "Curiosity got the better of me." He turned his attention to Rylan and said, "Rylan, forgive me. I have no desire for Mae to be my mate."

With my hand on his arm, I could feel the tension in Rylan. Would he forgive Arthur? There was a moment of silence as the two men eyed each other up. I glanced at Jasmine who was watching with interest. After a long pause, I could feel the tension ease from Rylan's body. Rylan nodded and stepped to the side of me. I let go of the breath I didn't realize I was holding onto.

"I, too, have no desire to mate with Mae," Jasmine added.

I thought she was joking, but the solemn look on her face told me that she was not. Rylan acknowledged her with a nod. Rylan put his hand on the small of my back and guided me over to the couch. I sat down and put my water at my feet. Rylan moved to stand by the unoccupied chair but did not sit. He crossed his arms over his bare chest. It took more will power than I was willing to admit to pull my gaze from his body.

"My, what a stir you have caused," Jasmine said, looking from both male Guardians before returning her attention to me. "I am torn between amusement and concern. Both feelings are so foreign..." She shook her head, frowning as she did so. "Let us start from the beginning. Mae, how did you stumble upon these fine warriors?"

How did I end up here with Rylan and Arthur? My mind whirled as I tried to think back to the past few days. I snorted in amusement,

"I ran into Arthur on my way into work on Friday and then he kidnapped me. I met Rylan at Arthur's establishment—" I started.

Jasmine held up her hand to stop me from talking. She turned her attention to Arthur, "Did you know she was Rylan's mate?"

Arthur nodded his head once. "Yes, as she walked away, I saw the mark on her neck. I called Rylan and told him I had a surprise for him."

"Hm..." Jasmine turned her attention back to me. "Please continue."

"I was able to escape and ran back to my apartment to grab my things to leave for the weekend, but then Rylan kidnapped me and took me to his house in the suburbs."

"Arthur owns the house. It was a temporary place to reside until we could figure out exactly what it was we were dealing with," Rylan interrupted with an amused smile.

"In any case, Arthur and Rylan propositioned me by offering to help me find a way to control my power as long as I was willing to help them break the curse the gods have over the Guardians. So, here I am."

"Ah," Jasmine nodded thoughtfully. "You believe that I may have a theory about her ability to break the curse over us." She turned her attention to Rylan.

"It is my hope you will be able to help her control her power," Rylan explained. "Mae's power right now is raw energy that builds up until it becomes too great to contain. It escapes her when she is feeling strong emotions or when she is too tired to hold it back. To live among humans, she has been binding herself."

Jasmine's hiss of disgust interrupted Rylan. She looked to me, and her dark eyes turned red. "You would bind yourself willingly?"

"*Yes*," I told her defensively. I turned to Rylan and said, "And *I'm* a human. So it makes sense I want to be surrounded by *other humans*."

I frowned as I thought back to the last year and how lonely it had been. Yes, I had been willing to suffer to make some type of connection with other people.

"You are not human," Jasmine said with a sniff of disdain. She used the word human as if it was derogatory. "And while you may have access to that spellbook of yours, you are not a witch either. Who are your parents?"

"Wilfred and Mary White adopted me when I was an infant," I told her quietly. My heart twisted as I thought about them again. "They died two years ago. I don't know who my biological parents are."

Jasmine turned to Rylan with a brow raised.

"I have had my people look into the adoption. The adoption agency seems to have been created solely to hold Mae until she was adopted out. What little information there is on the organization is false, and anyone who worked with the company has vanished or died," he told her.

I stared at Rylan, shocked.

How had he been able to find that information out in such a short amount of time? Once I found out I had power, I attempted to find my biological parents in the hopes that they would have some answers. From my search, I knew the organization had only been around a year or so before I had been given to them. Coincidentally, it had closed months after my adoption. But I hadn't realized the organization was made up. The employees no longer existed? Why would someone go through all that trouble?

"You have had your power all your life?" Jasmine questioned me. I shook my head.

"No, they started about a week or so after my parents died," I told her. All three Guardians exchanged looks with one another and the buzzing in my head immediately started up. "No, stop. I want to know what you are saying," I said firmly.

It was Rylan who spoke. His jaw clenched then relaxed. His gaze settled on me.

"The police report mentioned brake failure. I had my people do some digging and upon further inspection my team found the brakes had been cut."

Arthur sighed and turned to me. "Mae, it cannot be coincidence your power emerged right after their deaths. Someone knew that you had power within you that was not being utilized, and they needed to change that."

"Most species that have powers show signs of them from early on. Regular shifters can shift months after being born. Fae children can make plants grow or speak with the trees. Even witches can move objects short distances by the time they are seven," Jasmine informed me. "There are some species that need something to set off their powers. A female shifter cannot shift until the first full moon of her sixteenth birthday. A newly turned vampire may not know they are a vampire until they smell fresh blood for the first time and the change occurs. Many times, strong emotions can light the fuse of power within someone. Whoever was behind your parent's death knew that the extreme emotions following the death of someone close to you might cause your power to emerge."

My world stopped. My parents had been *murdered*.

The room vibrated as my heart broke. I looked down into my lap as my eyes watered. The room shook harder. Suddenly, Rylan was there. He sat down so close to me that our legs pressed together. His arm wrapped around my shoulders as tears rolled down my face.

"We will find out who is behind this, I promise," Rylan promised me softly in my ear.

With an extraordinary amount of effort, I forced my power to stop leaking out. The room stilled, and my tears stopped. I would cry later.

"Who else knows about your power, Mae?" Jasmine asked after a long silence. I didn't look up from my lap as I warred with my emotions.

"The three of you and an old friend."

"We are the only Guardians that know?" Jasmine asked. Her tone caused me to look up. She looked from Rylan to Arthur in disbelief. "How could you keep her from the rest of us?" she snapped, coming to her feet. Her cheeks hollowed, and her blazing red eyes became sunken. As she bared her teeth at both men, I could see her fangs descending from her canines. She was stunning. And terrifying.

"We must keep her presence a secret," Arthur said calmly.

"How can you say that? Our species needs her," Jasmine hissed. "Imagine the lives you could save right now if only the others knew!"

"Jasmine, we cannot tell the others," Rylan told her dismissively.

"Why not? Because she is your mate but you have yet to Join with her? That is a ridiculous reason not to save our species," Jasmine snarled. Her brows furrowed, and her body shook from anger. A deep growl reverberated throughout Rylan's body in response.

"Yes, that is one reason but there are others. Do you know what will happen when word gets out that Mae can invoke feelings within Guardians or that she could lift our curse? Our enemies would love to get their hands on her," he snapped back at her.

Alarmed by this new information I whipped my head around to look at Rylan. His gaze pinned Jasmine with a look that could wither flowers. The thought had never crossed my mind that there were any issues outside of my own. Rylan hadn't just been marking his territory because of the demons; it was to warn *everyone* to stay away. How narrow minded I had been. I leaned back in my seat wondering what type of enemies the Guardians had.

"We can protect her," Jasmine said flippantly.

"Can you protect her from the gods, Jazz?" Arthur asked her quietly, unperturbed by her anger. "If she does manage to lift the curse, the gods will know immediately. They would renew any effort to get back to this realm to wreak havoc. They will annihilate the planet in the hopes it would cause someone to come forth to tell them who and where Mae is. They will kill her, or worse, take her back with them. The fewer people that know of her, the less chance Mae could be betrayed."

Jasmine stilled.

"The gods *would* come back," she whispered in horror.

Her anger disappeared, and as it did, her cheeks filled and the darkness around her eyes disappeared. The Guardians fell silent. Arthur and Rylan had spoken about the gods before but, honestly, what could they do to us? What did they have to do with me?

"Which god cursed you? Do you know why you were cursed?" I asked.

Jasmine glanced at Rylan in disbelief.

"Have you not told her anything?" Jasmine asked in astonishment.

"It has been a hectic few days," Rylan said with a sigh. "I have not told her much."

Jasmine shook her head and very slowly took her seat. Her dark eyes searched my face. Deliberately she crossed her legs and clasped her hands together. She straightened her back and lifted her chin; she looked like royalty.

"I will tell you the story of the Guardians," she assured me. "This story goes way back before recorded time. The world was much different then. Humans and supernatural creatures coexisted peacefully. Back then, the demi-gods lived amongst us. They resided in temples and demanded to be worshipped by all. They loved the attention, and they loved to be feared. They were greedy, cunning, selfish, and easily offended. While they enjoyed the attention of the beings here on Earth, they did not enjoy sharing the Earth with each other.

"At times, the demi-gods would war amongst themselves. They vied for the attention of the Greater Gods, wanting to be noticed by them. The fighting became so intense the demi-gods created Guardians. Created to be able to fight a god or to defend one, the Guardians came in the form of what humans consider to be angels. We were born warriors. The Guardians were used to fight on behalf of every demi-god. The Guardians would fight amongst themselves in horrible, bloody battles that would last days, weeks, months, or years.

"When the Guardians were not battling each other, they were slaves to every whim of their masters. Their bodies were used and tossed aside. Duties ranged from torturing the innocent to starting wars between human regions so that the gods would be called upon for help. Guardians were puppets. They existed only to serve the gods.

"As the population on Earth grew and new regions began to form, the demi-gods decided they no longer wanted the attention of the Greater Gods. They wanted to *be* them. So, they began to plant the seed of doubt about the Greater Gods in the heads of humans and supernatural creatures. That doubt spread like the plague and soon the Greater Gods were all but forgotten. Each demi-god began to take up the role of a Greater God. They started performing miracles, answering prayers, and demanding sacrifices; just as the Greater Gods had once done. For a time, pretending to be the Greater Gods kept the demi-gods busy. They were uninterested in battling each other; instead, they were busy collecting believers.

"But peace between the demi-gods could not last. Narcissistic and greedy, the demi-gods did not want to share the humans. A war to end all wars broke out. The Guardians killed one another for their gods. They also killed humans and supernatural creatures who did not believe in their god. While the Guardians fought, the demi-gods showered down plagues, floods, droughts, and famine among the lands. Humans and non-humans joined together to fight back, trying to preserve the life they once knew.

"Millions of lives were lost. Generations, villages, cities, species, were all wiped out. The destruction was immeasurable. One day the Greater Gods looked down upon the Earth and saw what was happening. Angry at the demi-gods for trying to replace them, the Greater Gods gave the Guardians free will and a soul. Free from the chains of servitude, the Guardians turned on their masters. The Guardians pushed the demi-gods through the gate into the Realm of Divinity where the Greater Gods waited to sentence a punishment on their lesser halves. Furious that the Guardians had turned on them, just before the demi-gods were forced into the next realm, they cursed the Guardians by stripping them of their emotions: To be unable to enjoy the freedom or the joys life had to offer.

"When the war with the demi-gods ended, the Guardians spread out across the lands and helped humans and non-humans alike to get back on their feet in an attempt to make amends for their wrongdoings. Guardians took up the role of protectors to all species.

"As a thank you, the witches offered to try to break the Guardian's curse. The intention was to take the soul of the Guardian out, cleanse it, and then return it into the body of the Guardian. Unfortunately, the witches were not powerful enough to do this. Instead, they were able to rip half of the soul of each Guardian out, cleanse it, and throw it into the universe in the hopes it would come back within the body of another. Once the other half of the soul was found and Joined, the Guardian would become whole and free of the curse."

When Jasmine finished; the room fell silent.

My mind spun. Demi-gods? Greater Gods? Curses? Wars? The story was… a fairytale. It couldn't be real. But as much as I wanted it to be just that, a fairytale, a glance around at each Guardian's solemn expression told me the story was very real. I tried to picture a time when demi-gods roamed the land and the chaos they would have caused. I tried to envision these three Guardians, soulless and under the control of a demi-god. Seeing how Rylan and Arthur were with their weapons, the strength Rylan had displayed earlier by throwing Arthur through a wall with ease, and how fast they could fly… They would be a force to be reckoned with. Unstoppable.

"What role do you think Mae plays in all of this?" Arthur asked after we sat in silence for several minutes. Jasmine frowned.

"She could be placed here, as you believe, to lift the Guardian's curse. That seems likely, as we are all able to feel emotions right now due to her presence in the room. Or," Jasmine paused, looking at Rylan, "she could be here as a Trojan horse. Disguised as a gift, she could be another curse for the Guardians."

Rylan growled. I mimicked Arthur's frown.

Jasmine shrugged a shoulder. "It is just a thought, Rylan. She could simply be your mate with an amazing extra ability."

"Jasmine, when I first came across Mae, I thought she could have been a demi-god," Arthur said. "Her power radiates off her so greatly, even with the spellbinding bracelets. Her scent is quite unusual, too. Do you have an idea of what she could be?"

"Her scent is unfamiliar but utterly delicious," Jasmine said with a slow, almost seductive smile as she turned to look at me. I squirmed uncomfortably in my seat. "I do get a slight hint of witch, but it is very faint." Jasmine directed her comments to Rylan. "Surely you have tasted her blood? I'm sure you have some theories."

The thought of Rylan's teeth on my neck caused my body to warm instantly. I had been too quick to tell him that biting me was off the table. Had I thought about it more, like I had recently, maybe I would have privately broached the conversation with him. Maybe a little nibble? Rylan's thumb skimmed the top of the hand he held, and I shivered with desire under his touch. How quickly I went from scared to alert and needy.

"No," Rylan responded with a tone that said he didn't want to talk about it.

Jasmine frowned.

"No, you haven't tasted her blood, or no, the blood gave you no insight as to what your mate could be?" The room became tense. The heavy silence seemed to be her answer because she turned to me with a pretty scowl on her face and asked, "You do not want to feed your mate?"

"Enough," Rylan snapped at Jasmine. The soft buzzing in my head told me they were having a quick, heated debate.

"Tell me what you two are talking about," I snapped. My nerves were frayed, and my emotions were erratic. I was not going to be kept in the dark. "I want to know everything."

Jasmine raised a brow and gave Rylan a small, smug smile.

In return, Rylan heaved an exasperated sigh before he answered, "Several things happen when a Guardian finds their mate. The first thing is the physical attraction to their partner begins to override common sense. The need to Join takes priority over most things. The second is the Guardian will no longer be able to drink from another to survive. This is what Jasmine is talking about."

I looked at him in surprise. Was he feeling the desire, too? Maybe these intense feelings of desire and constant thoughts of the Guardian sitting next to me were normal. I thought about what Rylan had told me upstairs. He mentioned that I may be feeling the effects of being his mate. I was almost relieved that there was an explanation for my unusual behavior. But what about this feeding-your-mate thing?

"Arthur told me this morning that you had gone into town to get something to eat," I said confused. Rylan looked at me. His facial expression was blank.

"I was unable to do so," he told me. "But do not worry. You have laid down the law, and I will not break it."

"It would not matter if Rylan did drink from someone this morning," Jasmine said with a dismissive wave of her hand. "While drinking from someone other than their mate may temporarily ease the discomfort of hunger, once a Guardian has found their other half, it becomes necessary to feed on the blood of their mate to survive."

I stared at Jasmine, and then back at Rylan. My throat tightened until I couldn't breathe. So not only was I supposed to lift a curse on an entire species, but now I was supposed to be a constant source of food for someone else to survive? A walking blood bank. I needed space. I was done tonight. I stood up abruptly and walked out of the room.

The minute I shut the door, maybe a bit too hard, I ran for the front door. Without a thought, I darted out into the night. I expected the air to calm me, but it was hot and humid. The air clung to me like another layer of skin, which only made me feel more smothered. I jogged down the driveway to distance myself from the house and everyone inside. Once the building was out of sight, I stopped and tried to take deep breaths.

The ground trembled under my feet, and the leaves overhead shook. Quickly, I pulled my power back as I remembered spider demons were attracted to power. I lifted my head towards the sky and closed my eyes. Attacked by demons, saved from them, fighting off intense and unexpected arousal for a man I hardly knew, learning my parents had been murdered, that I could either save an entire race I didn't know existed or be the reason it ended, and to know that I had to be a food source for the man I couldn't seem to control myself around… I had dealt with too much today.

My deep breaths turned to soft gasps as tears trickled down my face. I squeezed my eyes shut, trying to stop the tears, but they kept coming. My heart pounded painfully in my chest. Why couldn't life be simple? Why wasn't I just this normal woman whose only problems were finding a nice guy to date or choosing what bar I was going to get shit-faced at on Friday night?

"Mae."

Rylan's detached voice in the darkness caused me to jump. I turned around to see him standing several feet away from me. At some point between when I left the house and now, he had kicked off his shoes. He had his hands shoved into the pockets of his pants, now the only article of clothing left covering his body. The shadows cast upon him made him look more handsome than ever.

"Please, Rylan, just let me be."

Instead of listening to me, he strolled forward with purpose. I was envious of the confidence in his gait. Oh, how I longed to feel confident and good about myself again. In the first two years of college, I used to be a strong, confident young woman. I had been in the best shape of my life, I was doing well in my classes, and I had my best friend by my side. Now I felt like a shell of that woman, and it was disheartening.

Rylan didn't stop until our chests almost touched. His closeness caused me to have to look up at him to see his face. The warmth radiating off his body should have been uncomfortable alongside the heat of the night, but instead, I found it nice. I wanted more of it. So, despite my request for him to leave, I found myself leaning forward to place my cheek on his bare chest and closing my eyes. He smelled like fresh air and freedom.

Rylan wrapped his arms around me, cocooning me in a warm embrace. In his arms, I felt safe and shielded from the world. We were strangers, and I had been thrown knee-deep into his world filled with curses, creatures, and mates. Staying emotionally detached and distant would be the safest thing for me. But here, in the darkness, in his embrace, I quietly admitted to myself that I was glad Rylan was here with me. I slowly brought my arms up and wrapped them around his waist. His body trembled once. Something brushed the top of my head. His lips?

Desire flooded my body instantly. I had been feeling alone this entire time, but I didn't have to anymore. We were mates, right? He had insinuated that he felt the desire just as much as I did. I turned my head and placed a soft kiss in the middle of his chest. The second my lips touched him another tremble shook Rylan. I did it again, placing this kiss next to the first. Rylan's arms tightened around me. I placed another kiss on the other side. Another tremor ran through his body.

I looked up to see his expression. He gazed down at me with those red eyes, which were bright and focused on my face. Tentatively, I rose on my tiptoes, tilted my head back ever so slightly, and pressed my lips to his. It was meant to be a light kiss, but the moment our lips connected my body heat skyrocketed. My breath came in short gasps as longing coursed through my veins. My breasts felt fuller, my cheeks ran hot, and the junction between my legs became damp with desire. There was no hesitation from Rylan. He answered my kiss with his own, demanding and passionate.

I opened my mouth, an invitation for him, and his tongue entered and clashed with mine. A small noise escaped me. I brought my arms up and wrapped them around his neck. I pressed my body against him, and I could feel the rigid outline of his hardness through his pants pressed against my belly. Excitement bubbled up through me, and I shuddered with need.

Disappointment immediately replaced the excitement as Rylan pulled his mouth away from mine. He cupped my face in his hands and stared down at me. I could see the struggle there in his eyes. He did want me just as much as I wanted him, but something was stopping him. He leaned down and softly kissed my forehead.

"It has been a long day for you," he said, his voice rough. "Let me take you to your room… *to rest*," he added when I smiled seductively. The smile disappeared when I realized he had no intention to resume this.

I stepped back, out of his grasp, turned and walked away from him. I needed to pull myself together. I stopped a few feet away. Rejection cooled my body temperature instantly. I ran my fingers through my mass of curls and took a long, deep breath.

When I knew my voice would not waver, I told him, "I'll go back when I'm ready."

"Mae, you are tired and overwhelmed—"

"Don't tell me what I am feeling," I snapped, still not bothering to look at him. "You are more than welcome to go back inside."

I didn't hear him approach, but suddenly he was there, taking my hand and turning me around to face him. I ruefully looked up at him to find his handsome mouth turned downwards. He brought my hand up to his lips, and he kissed each of my knuckles. To my annoyance, I felt desire rise again, although this time a little slower as logic reminded me that he had just rejected my advances.

After kissing the last knuckle, he said, "Let's fly."

I wanted to be angry with him. I wanted to blame him for everything wrong in my life, and I wanted to shove him backward, away from me. The urge to scream and fight was there, but instead of allowing bitterness to consume me, I let my anger go. None of this was his fault. He was right; I was exhausted. The emotional roller coaster I had been on all day was tiring. Letting him take me up into the sky far from the house, above the thin trail of scattered clouds where it was quiet, sounded wonderful.

I nodded.

Rylan pulled me close to him. I expected him to scoop me up, but instead, he leaned down and planted a kiss on my lips. When he pulled away, I was breathless.

"I want you with every fiber of my being, Mae," he admitted. "But you have been through so much today and the past few days. Once we come together as man and woman, it will set our Joining in motion. I will not be able to stop it any more than you could. While we cannot fight what is meant to be, I do not want us to come together while your judgement is clouded by your desolation."

As much as I hated to admit it, Rylan was right. I was desperate to feel anything other than scared or trapped. I would have welcomed his intimate touch tonight, but what about tomorrow when reality crashed over me? With a sigh, I nodded.

"Ok, I'll stop trying to jump your bones," I assured him with a half-smile. His answering smile, while brief, was warm and amused.

"The next time I may not be able to stop."

"Good, it's annoying when you do," I said as I rolled my eyes. Rylan chuckled warmly. This time when he leaned forward, he scooped me up into his arms. I watched as his wings emerged from his back. "Does it hurt?"

"No, it is as natural as breathing and just as easy," he said as he walked out from underneath the trees.

"Did you always know how to fly or is that taught to you when you are young?" I asked as I stared at the massive black wings stretching out behind him. I wrapped my arms around his neck.

"We must learn how to use them. Most Guardians cannot use their wings until they have fully matured."

We lurched upwards into the air, and I squealed in delight. Pressed so snugly against him, I felt more than heard Rylan's chuckle. We went straight up for what seemed like forever. He slowly spun us around as we approached the stars. The clouds coated our skin in dew as we flew through them. The cool air that brushed against our wet bodies felt amazing. We stopped ascending and for a moment we hung suspended in the air. I looked down and could no longer make out the shape of the house.

"Arthur mentioned you would like to go into town tomorrow," Rylan said, his voice low. "I will take you to explore."

I turned my attention to him.

"Thank you."

Rylan twisted carefully, and we took off aimlessly through the sky. As we flew, I bravely unclasped my hands from around his neck, and while still holding on to him with one arm, I reached out with the other to feel the air rush over my palm. It was amazing how, up here, all my worries disappeared with him. They fell away, leaving me to enjoy the night with Rylan. Several times I glanced at his face. Catching him with his eyes twinkling with joy and seeing the small smile tugging at the corner of his lips was even more delightful than flying. His smile widened as he caught me staring at him, and my heart did a cartwheel.

With a deliberate slowness, I reached up and brushed a strand of blond hair out of his face. Our eyes met. Time seemed to slow as we gaze at one another. I was so used to seeing such restraint and indifference in him that it was new and wonderful to see him so relaxed. He leaned his head down and pressed his forehead against mine. I brought my hands up and cupped his face. I tilted my head up slightly and pressed my lips softly against his. He returned the kiss with a soft moan. I broke away before it got too heated.

While we flew through the cool air, we barely spoke, but it was a companionable silence. We were both lost in our thoughts. Free from the worry and fear, exhausted by the day's events, I could feel my weariness pulling me under. I place my head in the crook of Rylan's neck and stared out into the sky, letting my eyelids drift downwards. I awoke briefly when we landed on the balcony outside my bedroom door. Instead of putting me down, he simply opened the door while balancing me in one arm and then carried me over to the bed.

Once he placed me on the mattress, I reached for my phone to set my alarms. Without lights, I had to blindly feel for the nightstand. I wouldn't be able to get away with two nights in a row without alarms. Suddenly, he was there pulling my hand away from my cell phone.

"I need to set—"

"You need a full night's sleep," he interrupted.

I opened my mouth to protest, but suddenly my words were stuck in my throat as there was a dip in the mattress next to me. I turned onto my side to see he had climbed into bed. Despite the desire that blossomed under my skin, I stiffened. What was he thinking? He lifted the covers for me to scoot under. I stared at him in surprise.

"I have found that you can sleep when we touch."

"Were you here last night?" I asked. My voice sounded slurred as I fought the sleep that was already pulling me under.

"Yes."

"Creeper."

Rylan chuckled but did not make a move to leave the bed. This must have been how I had been able to sleep so well last night; he had been laying here with me. I wasn't sure how to feel about this. I should have been outraged that he had snuck into my bedroom, climbed into the bed, and cozied up next to me. But it felt good to sleep through the night uninterrupted. I remembered how great I had felt this morning, and I wanted it again. I stared at Rylan while having an internal debate about what I should do. Kick him out or allow him to stay? He waited patiently; to him it was obvious he was staying.

Finally, I decided that it wasn't worth the fight. If he was willing to sleep here with me, why not accept the help? I scooted under the covers and allowed Rylan to tuck me in like a child. I turned toward him and placed my head on his chest. He wrapped his arms around me, and I breathed in his scent. It didn't take me long before my exhaustion pulled me into unconsciousness.

I jerked awake a few hours later. My whole body was shaking along with the rest of the room. A scream was lodged in my throat, but I covered my mouth to muffle it.

"What is it?" Rylan's sharp voice came out of the darkness.

I looked around the dark room as I came out of my nightmare. The screams of agony and the sight of soulless Guardians fighting each other and killing innocent people in the name of their gods began to fade. It took me a moment to stop the room from shaking as I tried to calm myself down.

"Mae, are you alright?"

"Yeah, just a nightmare... Did I break anything?" I muttered, placing my head back on his chest. He said something to me, but already I was back to sleep.

Chapter Twelve

When I awoke, my body was on fire. My nipples were hard, and the space between my legs felt moist. I slowly opened my eyes as the daylight warmed my face, and my body's needs became too demanding to ignore. I moaned as I stretched. Had I ever awoken this aroused before? As I stretched, I realized I had wrapped half my body around something very warm and solid. I blinked a few times and glanced at the object I was cuddling with.

"Good morning," a deep voice said.

I sat straight up, feeling disoriented. I looked at Rylan who had his hands behind his head, lying next to me bare-chested, and staring at me with amusement. How was it possible to look that good in the morning? It wasn't fair. I couldn't help but feast my eyes on his body. My own body hungered, and it wasn't food it was looking for. After a good long, unabashed look at his chest and abs, my eyes went back to his face. The amusement was gone, and he stared intensely at me.

"Do not look at me like that," he said firmly, and I knew I needed to listen to him, but I couldn't help it. I felt rebellious.

I looked back down at his chest. His pink nipples looked so delicious; my mouth watered. Without any warning, I leaned down and licked the nearest one. His whole body stiffened, and I smiled. I did it again, and this time I took his nipple in my mouth and let my tongue tease it. A growl vibrated through Rylan's chest, and I smiled in excitement. As I played with his nipple with my mouth, I took my hand and ran my fingertips over the thick, tight muscles of his chest and stomach. He growled again, and I could feel myself growing even more aroused. I let go of his nipple and planted kisses across his chest as I made my way over to the other one.

Before I got to the second nipple, Rylan grabbed a handful of my curls and gently tugged on them, pulling me upwards. He glared at me, his mouth set in a grim line. Instead of being discouraged, I smiled mischievously. Before he could tell me to stop, I planted a playful kiss on those lips. I leaned my hips into his body, and with the way my legs were wrapped around him, I found that his hip could apply just enough pressure in between my legs to be enjoyable. I moaned in pleasure.

Suddenly, Rylan moved. I found myself pinned under his body, my arms locked in his grasp above my head. Breathlessly, I stared up at him. How the hell did he just do that? He looked down at me with a warm twinkle in his eyes, and I grinned. He leaned down and kissed me. My heart somersaulted as our lips met. I opened my mouth, and he took the invitation without hesitation.

I wanted more than just his kiss. The desire coursing through my veins was demanding and needed to be sated. While my arms were pinned, my legs were free. I took my legs and wrapped them around Rylan's waist and was beyond pleased to find him harder than steel. I needed friction. I attempted to grind my hips against his. At the same time, I tried to tug my hands free, needing to touch him, but his grip was like steel.

"Rylan," I whined. He pulled inches away from my lips and stared down at me with those cool teal eyes.

"If I let you touch me, I will not be able to stop what happens," he said, his face serious.

"Then don't," I said, pouting. His grim expression turned amused.

"We talked about this last night," he reminded me.

I sighed and stopped struggling. I dropped my legs back to the mattress.

"Fine, leave then," I said with a scowl. "I have to take care of some urgent needs, and I'd like some privacy if you aren't going to participate."

His eyes turned red, and I watched as his fangs began to lengthen in his mouth. His brows furrowed together, and his face became sunken. Minus the wings, he was in full Guardian mode now. Was this reaction supposed to frighten me? If it was, it was having the opposite reaction.

"I am supposed to take care of your every need," he hissed.

I stared at him in amazement. Was he *angry* with me? My brows raised in surprise.

"Well, you don't seem very willing at the moment," I snapped. "God, I don't think I've ever felt this…" I struggled for a word to describe how my body felt.

Out of control? No, that wasn't quite right. My power was out of control. This crazy desire I was feeling was so intense and so demanding… My cheeks warmed in embarrassment. Why was I throwing myself at someone who was giving me a clear and concise *no*? Getting rejected once had been bad enough, but getting rejected twice in less than twelve hours? That was horrible. I turned my head away from him.

"Mae, listen to me," Rylan said, his tone softer than before. I didn't turn to look at him. Instead of cooling off from the rejection, my body was burning even hotter now. I just wanted some relief! His nose skimmed my jawline, and I shuddered. "If we do this, it will be the first step in our Joining. Our souls will begin to merge. It is more final and permanent than the human equivalent: marriage."

"According to you and Jasmine, our souls are supposed to join. It's fate or whatnot," I muttered. I sighed and turned my head to look at him. "And I checked my spellbook last night, and there is nothing in it on how to get rid of this mark on my neck. So, it appears we're stuck together."

The loud, deep, and angry snarl that erupted from Rylan's throat was abrupt and terrifying. I cringed into the mattress as his fangs came close to my face.

"You dare try to destroy our souls?" he roared.

I looked at him in surprise. What? No! I had just been looking at ways to cut ties with him. I had been hoping it would stop this need I felt for him.

"Um… At that time I wasn't sure what the mark meant. I wouldn't have done it intentionally," I floundered.

Rylan snarled again and tightened his grip on my wrists. I winced. He noticed and immediately loosened his hold on me.

"The witches have given us a chance at truly living in this world and the opportunity to move on into the afterlife, and you would seek to destroy that?" Rylan was shaking with anger now. I could feel the vibration of his body; his anger was almost tangible.

"Rylan, I'm sorry," I said. "I just wanted a break from my body's demands. I'm not usually like this. I have a very normal libido, so this lust is out of the realm of usual for me. I'm not in control of my power, and now I'm not in control of my body. I was just looking for answers so I could have some influence over something in my life. I'm sorry! Like I said, there was nothing in the book anyway."

Rylan's jaw ticked, but his body relaxed some. He took several deep breaths, and I watched as his face changed back to its human façade. He let go of my wrists and moved to sit beside me. I sat up and rubbed my wrists.

Rylan sighed and said, "This is my fault. I should have explained to you at the very beginning about what is between us."

I said nothing. I was struggling to calm my overheated body.

"What you are feeling is normal," Rylan explained. "It is believed that when mates find each other, the physical attraction is immediate and intense because it will cause the Joining to happen quickly. The pressing desire you feel will become normal; it will be there forever as it will be for me.

"Trust me, I feel it too, Mae. Maybe even stronger than you feel it as desire is so new to me. I have not felt lust or physical attraction to anyone. Last night as I watched you sleep in my arms, I thought of all the different surfaces in this house I wanted to make love to you on. I am hard whenever I think of you or see you. You are right; our Joining is inevitable, but I want to make sure you understand, in its entirety what it will mean for you. For us."

I remained silent. This would be *normal*? This heady feeling would be something I got used to? I wanted to groan out loud. My frustration was eased some knowing that at least Rylan was feeling it too. I imagined Rylan's hands on me in various places in the house, and my body shuddered with excitement.

"Tell me what you are thinking," Rylan asked, studying my face with a frown.

"I'm just processing everything you're saying," I said with a shrug. And picturing you naked on the kitchen island… I tried to pull my mind away from the erotic image. "What do you mean desire is new to you? You haven't had sex before?"

Rylan frowned.

"Desire is an emotion, and, as you know, we cannot feel emotions. While I could not feel desire, I would feel… discomfort if I did not meet the demands my body made," Rylan said slowly, trying to explain as simply as possible. "In any case, whether I wanted to or not I would go through the motions to please my wives."

Wives. My overheating body immediately chilled. Of course, he had been married. He was practically as old as time. So why was I so shocked? How many wives had he had? When he wasn't married and his needs needed to be met, how many women had he slept with? I was sure sex eventually became stale once you'd done it for thousands of years. That was probably the true reason he wasn't so keen on doing it now. It was probably a good thing anyway; with my lack of experience, I was sure I couldn't compete. I would be embarrassing myself.

I moved off the bed then, feeling oddly detached. I didn't look at him. My mind was too busy trying to wrap my head around how many wives Rylan could have had in his lifetime. Who were these women? When was the last time he had gotten married? The thought made my stomach roll. Learning about his wives would keep my body cooled for quite a while.

"I'm going to take a shower and get ready for the day. I'll meet you downstairs," I muttered. I walked into the bathroom and shut the door, not waiting to see if he took the hint. I needed some time alone. I turned on the water in the shower and stripped down out of the clothes I had worn the previous night.

Under the warm stream of water, my body relaxed. I braced my hands against the shower wall, closed my eyes and stood there soaking in the heat. Despite yesterday being a whirlwind of activities and emotions, I found myself feeling well-rested. It felt good to feel strong and alert, and it was all because of Rylan. He had been right again. His presence, his contact, had made it safe for me to sleep without alarms.

Regardless of how good I was feeling, I knew I couldn't let Rylan sleep in my bed again. I couldn't keep waking up feeling hot and bothered. Nor should I rely solely on him to eat and sleep properly. I needed to gain back control of my life. This morning I would keep my bracelets on me in case I needed them, and I would force myself to eat on my own. If I couldn't keep it down, then I couldn't. I had handled it before, and I could do it again.

A blast of cool air against my skin made me flinch. I opened my eyes and turned to find Rylan, stark naked, stepping into the shower with me. I stared at him, speechless. The Greeks and Romans had gotten it all wrong. They had created statues of the ideal body, but they obviously hadn't had Rylan as their model.

While I had gotten a great view of his upper half just moments ago as he laid in my bed, now I was treated to the full package. There was not a place on his body that wasn't packed with muscle. His wide, muscular chest tapered down to perfectly sculpted abs, a narrow waist, and thighs thicker than tree trunks. And sweet Jesus, he was thick, long, and happy to see me. The sheer size of it was intimidating. So why did my mouth start to water?

Had I thought I had been turned off by the mention of his wives? My body roared to life in the time it took me to give him an appreciative, long, up and down look. When my eyes rose to his face, I was greeted with a smug smile at my open appreciation of his body. My face flushed in embarrassment, but I was too excited to feel coy.

"How can I leave my mate when she has a need for me?" he growled. His nostrils flared, and his gaze roamed over my body. When his eyes returned to meet mine, his voice dropped an octave, "I cannot resist your siren's call any longer, Mae. Are you sure about this? Do you understand that, should we do this, the Joining will begin?"

As my answer, I simply nodded and stepped back to give him room in the shower. He stepped under the water with me and shut the door behind him. I looked up at him, my eyes devouring every inch of him. Without a word, he leaned down and kissed me. My body shuddered with arousal. I placed both of my hands on his chest and leaned into this kiss. His hands grabbed me at my hips, and suddenly I was lifted upwards so I was eye level with him. He pressed me against the shower wall. I gasped in delight against his lips and happily wrapped my legs around his waist. He stepped closer to me, so his body was pressed against mine. His manhood pressed comfortably against my stomach. Rylan pulled his mouth away from mine and stared into my eyes with his blazing red ones.

He growled and leaned forward to trail kisses down my neck. My nipples hardened, and my hands shook with desire as they raked through his hair and skimmed over his chest. Touching him sent electrical pulses racing through me, heightening my arousal. He paused where the curve of my neck met my shoulder, and momentarily, I thought he was going to bite me. My core clenched in anticipation, and my breath quickened. Instead, he continued his kisses. He only stopped to admire my petite breasts before continuing his trail of kisses down to my navel.

Before I knew what he was doing, Rylan lowered me to my feet and knelt before me. I looked at him, confused, almost delirious from the lust coursing through my body. Those red eyes locked with mine for just a moment before one corner of his lips turned upwards in a knowing smirk. Before I could ask him what he was up to, he leaned forward and plunged his tongue straight into my intimate folds. My strangled cry echoed around us. I spread my legs wider for him.

My hands went to his hair and grabbed a handful of blond strands. I cried out again as his tongue circled my bud. *Fuck*. His mouth was so warm; his tongue was so talented. The building pleasure was quick and overwhelming. My breathing came in heavy pants mixed with moans. Then, he lowered his head, and his tongue entered me. I screamed as my world shattered and pleasure rippled through me like electricity.

In the midst of the orgasm, which was taking its time rolling through me, I heard a hiss from Rylan. As my body came down from its high, I glanced down at Rylan and saw violet streaks of my power running through his face, arms, and neck. The bliss I felt vanished in a heartbeat as I realized I was killing him.

"Rylan!" I screamed. I tried to step back, but there was nowhere to move since my back was already against the wall. I yanked his head back with a fist full of his hair at the same time Rylan leaned back on his heels. "Rylan, I'm so sorry. Oh, God, what's going on? How can I help?" My power surged through him hard, his body was almost glowing violet now. A strong tremor wracked his body. His eyes were squeezed shut. "Rylan, talk to me!" His brows were smashed together, and he was using my hips to brace himself. He took several deep breaths, and after a few seconds had passed, I watched as the glow of my power dimmed before it slowly vanished. "Rylan!"

He opened his eyes slowly. At first, those red eyes seemed unfocused, but he blinked several times, and they cleared. As I stared into his eyes, I could see flecks of violet in his irises. Without thinking, I dropped to my knees in front of him and took his face in my hands. My heart raced in fear, and tears spilled down my cheeks. How could I have been so careless? I could have killed him. Rylan took one hand off my hip and used his thumb to wipe away a tear.

"I am alright," he said, his voice rough.

"I can't believe I lost control. I'm so sorry. You could have been killed! Are you hurt? Where are you hurting? Should I get the others?" I asked, panicking. What if there was internal damage? He could be hemorrhaging and not even know it. Could he have an aneurysm? A heart attack? A stroke? I felt like I was going to be sick. Please don't die, please don't die! A sob tore through me and more tears slipped down my cheeks.

"Mae, calm yourself," Rylan said. "I am unharmed. I am ..." His voice trailed off as his eyes went unfocused again.

He stood slowly, pulling me up with him. Rylan lifted his head to let the water of the shower run over his face. After a moment, he looked back down at me, and I saw the awe on his face as if he was seeing me for the first time.

"You have gifted me, Mae, with something incredible. I could feel your body come undone as if it was my own and now, I feel..."

I watched as he struggled for words.

"Stronger than ever before." As if to test the theory, his whole body flexed causing his muscles to ripple.

"You don't feel sick or in pain?" I asked in disbelief.

Rylan's answering grin was confident and excited. "I have never felt better in my entire existence."

My facial expression must have appeared skeptical because he bent down and kissed me wholeheartedly. I could taste myself on his mouth. Instead of being disgusted, I found it oddly erotic and my body started to warm again. No, wait, I couldn't get swept up in him again. I'd almost killed him. I pressed my hands against his chest and tried to gently push myself away.

Rylan pulled back and said, "You did not hurt me, Mae. It was unexpected, but I look forward to the experience again."

He stepped closer to me. His hard body pressed against me, sandwiching me between himself and the wall. He ran his hands over my breasts, and my traitorous body shuddered and came to life. He leaned down and kissed away the tears still lingering on my cheeks. When they were gone, Rylan's lips met mine once more, and this time the kiss was more demanding. I still hesitated, afraid to succumb to the desire again. Afraid to hurt Rylan. My lips tried to blunt the intensity of the kiss.

Rylan reached up and grabbed a handful of my hair, tugging my head back gently. He leaned down and kissed my neck. "Touch me, Mae. Place your hands on me."

His hands went to my breasts and massaged them. I could feel the fight leave my body. I sighed and gave in to the heat bubbling up under my skin. I reached up tentatively, afraid to hurt him, and placed my hands on his arms. My hands shook as I fought back my fear. My fingertips skimmed up his arms, across his chest and down his stomach. A low growl rumbled from his throat. That growl vibrated against my neck as he continued kissing and suckling on my skin. Knowing his teeth were so close made the heat between my legs burn hotter.

"Rylan... Bite me," I whispered. Rylan paused and lifted his head to study my face. "Do it," I encouraged when I saw the flare of excitement in his eyes. I watched as his face shifted, and his fangs grew. I licked my lips in anticipation, and my breathing quickened. I leaned my head back to provide him better access. Another growl rumbled through his chest as he leaned forward.

There was a pause. When he didn't move any closer, and I held my breath. The throb between my legs was unbearable, and the anticipation only made it worse. I craved his touch. I needed this. Before I knew what happened, Rylan moved, sinking his teeth deep into the vein in my neck. There was pain, lightning hot heat, followed by a tidal wave of pleasure. I cried out, pressing my naked body harder against his, needing to be even closer to him. As he fed on me, I could feel my body tightened. I was going to come undone with only his fangs inside me. The thought brought me even closer to the edge.

I wanted him to feel this. I wanted him to know how excited and alive my body was. I reached for his cock. My fingers wrapped around him, and I stroked down the length of him once, slowly and deliberately. Rylan's whole body shook, and I could hear his deep moan against my neck. I stroked him again, feeling every vein, following their trail with my thumb. I brought my hand up and down, faster now. My pleasure was building, and I wanted him to match mine. Rylan moaned again, his teeth still deep in my neck... I could feel his body stiffen, his cock hardening in my hand.

Suddenly, he pulled away from my neck. His tongue quickly lapped at the area where his teeth had been. Rylan reached down to grab my hand that was wrapped around him and stared down into my eyes. The violet in his irises was even more pronounced now. Was that because he had drunk my blood or because I had lost control earlier?

"I need to be in you," he said, his voice so deep and rough that my feminine lips clenched in response. "I need you to understand the importance if we do this—"

"Oh, *please*," I begged. "I *do*. I do understand."

He didn't hesitate. He lifted me up, but instead of pressing me against the wall, he held my weight without any effort. I wrapped my legs around his waist and positioned myself over him. I wasn't sure he would fit. He was massive; his length and girth were too big for my petite frame. But I needed this more than anything, so by God, I was going to die trying.

Slowly, he lowered me onto him. I was so wet and ready that the tip slipped in without any trouble. But as he entered me, I could feel the stretch and the protest from my body. I gasped as he filled me. He paused, his breathing heavy.

"Are you alright?" he asked through gritted teeth. I panted as I tried to focus on relaxing around him. Oh, it hurt, but as much as it hurt there was double the pleasure.

"Yes," I hissed as my body adjusted to the intrusion. "Just go slow."

He gave me another moment to acclimate to him before slowly continuing to lower me onto him. Finally, my body fully engulfed him.

"I have found my heaven," he whispered into my ear.

He planted a kiss on my lips, and I returned it passionately. I needed friction. I needed him so much I thought I was going to burst. I tried to grind against him, and he took the cue. He began to move, in and out. We groaned in unison at the pleasure. I felt so full that I was certain I would be ripped apart with each stroke, but instead I only found more pleasure. It built quickly. I moved more urgently against him, and he met every thrust with one of his own. My vision blurred as I choked on the intense feelings boiling up inside of me. "Lean forward and taste me," I heard Rylan's voice as if it was far away.

I didn't question where the wound came from nor did I wonder at his command. Without hesitation, I leaned forward and lapped at the large bleeding cut across his chest. His blood was hot and sweet. The taste was heady and addictive. My tongue repeatedly ran across the wound until my body could no longer hang on to the pleasure that was rocking its world. My body clamped down around Rylan. I threw my head back and screamed as my second orgasm rippled through me.

This one was much different than the first. Every nerve in my body was quaking. My vision turned white, and every molecule in my body seemed to separate then bounce back together. My world shattered, and I was loving every second of it. I could feel something inside me shift and connect with something… familiar. The connection was fulfilling and made the bliss of my orgasm even more intense. On another level, I could feel Rylan's answering orgasm, and I groaned as I felt his release inside of me.

Slowly, my orgasm subsided. My vision cleared, and reality slowly crept back in. My whole body was trembling, and my breathing was heavy. I looked at Rylan concerned that I had lost control of my power during our throws of pleasure. While Rylan was panting as he came down from his high, I could see that my power had, indeed, leaked out again. Around the creases of his eyes, I could see my power glowing under his skin. A few veins in his neck, chest, and arms glowed, too. I frowned and looked back into his eyes.

"I'm so sorry, Rylan. Are you alright?" I asked as I touched his face in alarm.

"I am more than alright," he growled as he lifted me off him and placed my feet on the ground. "What is that old saying? 'I can die a happy man' now."

I giggled, relieved that he was alright. I reached up on my tiptoes and kissed his jaw. He swooped down and kissed me on the lips. I placed my hands on his chest to steady myself and mentally noted the bloody wound on his chest had vanished. Curiously, I reached up and touched my neck, but I couldn't feel where his teeth had pierced my skin.

"Are you still hungry?" I asked him. "You can take more if you need it. I feel good today… Well, more than good now." I gave him a smirk, and he grinned.

"My hunger has been sated. Come, let us get out of here before the water gets cold," he said.

He turned off the shower and stepped out to grab a towel for each of us. Rylan left the bathroom as I walked into the closet to find some clothes. My steps felt lighter, and I couldn't keep the smile off my face. I grabbed a new shirt off the hanger and a new pair of shorts that were folded and placed in one of the custom shelving units. I changed into my clothes, left the closet, and brushed my teeth. The mirror was completely shattered, so I had to be mindful where I stepped as I stood by the sink. Mentally I made a note to replace it.

Once I was done in the bathroom, I stepped back into the bedroom and found Rylan waiting for me all dressed in casual, albeit expensive, clothes. How had he gotten dressed so quickly? He came over to me and took my face in his hands. He leaned down and kissed me gently before pulling back to stare down at me.

"Are you alright?" he asked solemnly. I blinked. Alright? I felt utterly amazing. Buoyant even. My body was still humming with joy.

I grinned. "Better than alright."

He gave me a half-smile, but his eyes remained worried.

Concerned, I asked, "What about you? Are you sure you are okay? I could see my power in you." While there were no remnants of my power lingering under his skin now, I was still anxious.

"I am quite well," he scoffed. His expression turned solemn, "I am more concerned that you will run away screaming since we have started the Joining process. We have had our first blood exchange and our bodies came together."

Oh... We did exchange blood, didn't we? Looking back, it seemed absurd that I would have done such a thing, but, at the time, it had seemed so natural and right. I reached up to touch my lips in wonder. I had drunk blood without hesitation.

"Mae?" Rylan's voice pulled me from my thoughts. I blinked and looked back up at him.

"I was a willing participant, Rylan. You told me our Joining would start if we had sex. I didn't realize we would be drinking each other's blood…" I hesitated. "I've never done that before."

"It is how our souls connect," Rylan explained with a warm smile. "Did you feel it? The spiritual Joining as our souls touched for the first time. It was exquisite. We are meant to be together, Mae, and our souls rejoiced."

I couldn't help but smile at the sheer bliss on Rylan's face. How young and carefree he looked at that moment. He stole my breath away. My heart pounded wildly in my chest. Any reservations I had about drinking his blood vanished.

Rylan grabbed my hand, and we left my bedroom. Downstairs, we found Jasmine who stood as still as a statue, staring out into the backyard. She turned towards us as we entered the kitchen. I could see her shudder as my presence temporarily lifted the curse that hung over her. She was stunning in her white, flowy dress. Her dark hair was braided down her back, and the way she stood she appeared regal, like a queen about to address her servants.

"Jasmine." Rylan greeted her with a nod in her direction.

"Rylan. Mae," she said as she walked over to us. "Mae, I hope you are feeling better this morning?"

"Yeah, thanks," I said. "I'm sorry I left like that last night."

Jasmine waved my apology away. "It was a lot of information at one time after, what I hear, was a long day. Last night I started to do some digging through my notes to find out how to help you with your power. What we need to know, first, is what you are. Depending on what species you are, your power may work differently. Elves use their blood to make things happen. Witches have chants that, combined with their aura, create spells, potions, and curses. Wizards have wands to help direct their magic."

"You chant when you use your power," Rylan said, looking at me.

I nodded as I pulled out a yogurt from the refrigerator and grabbed a spoon from a drawer. I leaned against the counter and stirred the yogurt in its cup.

"What is it that you chant?" Jasmine asked.

"At the beginning of my spellbook, it says to invoke the elements of witchcraft to center your power, so I call upon the spirit, wind, earth, water, and fire."

"And it helps you control your power?"

"I… I don't think so," I admitted. "I think it is more to help me focus so I don't panic."

With a frown, Jasmine crossed her arms over her chest. She turned her head away from me, lost in thought.

Rylan walked over to stand next to me and placed a hand on my shoulder. I gave him a distracted smile and began eating. Jasmine turned her attention back to us, and I saw her eyes narrow.

"I can't seem to keep food down without help," I mumbled, suddenly embarrassed.

"What did you do before you met Arthur and Rylan?"

I shrugged. "I ate what I could."

"Which was not much," Rylan added grimly. "She cannot sleep without contact either. She sets alarms that will keep her from falling too deeply asleep."

"That I can explain," Jasmine said. "Magic senses magic and will naturally ebb and flow between magical sources. Your power naturally flows between us as our power does with yours. Unfortunately, Mae, your power is so great the trickle of magic between us isn't enough to alleviate the distress within you. Your body is focusing so much on holding back your power that it cannot function properly. Physical contact allows more of your power to flow out of you, in a controlled manner, which in turn allows your body to focus on properly functioning.

"From what little information I have learned about you, your power is growing exponentially. In just two short years, your power has hindered your health significantly. I am concerned that as your power grows, eventually, the contact will not help. All that energy will become destructive to its host."

"What are you saying, Jasmine?" Rylan asked with a scowl.

"She will die, Rylan. A slow and quite painful death. With how strong you are now and how much you are struggling, your power will begin to eat you alive, Mae."

The silence that befell us was heavy with solemnity. Dread was like a cold, wet blanket draped over my shoulders. I looked down at my empty yogurt cup, grateful I had been able to eat it before the news of my impending death. With deliberate slowness, Jasmine walked around the island and approached me. A frown marred her beautiful face. She raised her hand and cupped my cheek.

"You do not look surprised."

I wasn't.

"I will do everything I can for this not to happen," she assured me. She turned her attention to Rylan and said, "Your mate is a great treasure, Rylan. I promise we will save Mae, and by saving her, I hope we can save our race."

"Mae, Rylan, Jasmine," Arthur said striding into the room. We all turned to watch as he approached. He paused as he assessed the tension in the room. "What is going on?"

"I told Mae and Rylan of my assessment of her situation as it currently stands," Jasmine said.

"Ah, have you shared with them what you believe should be the next step now that you have done some research?"

Jasmine shook her head before she turned to me and gave me an appraising look.

"What I would like to do is go inside your mind and your body to study you. Once while you are passive, and once while you use your power. I will be able to see the internal workings of your mind and how your body works."

I frowned as I struggled to understand this. "How?"

"As you join our world, you will learn that Guardians have amazing gifts," Jasmine said, a small smile tugging the corners of her mouth upwards. "I can see the electrical impulses in your mind. I can study your anatomy, the breakdown of your cells… It is quite fascinating. Imagine that I am a coroner, and you are my newest cadaver. Or think of being studied through an MRI or CAT machine. I will be inside your body to study how your magic works and search for similarities within other species. If I can figure out what species you are at a molecular level and understand how your power works, then I may be able to figure out how you can use it appropriately without it hurting yourself or others around you."

At some point, my jaw must have dropped because I realized my mouth was hanging open. I closed it quickly and looked up Rylan in disbelief. This strange woman wanted to somehow climb into my body to study me? The idea of being magically dissected sounded repulsive, and I recoiled at her offer.

"A coroner, Jasmine, really?" Rylan snapped, obviously just as appalled as I was with the analogy. Rylan ran his fingers through his blond strands frustrated with his fellow Guardian.

Jasmine simply shrugged.

Rylan sighed and looked down at me. "It is a good idea, Mae. It is non-invasive, and we will be able to gather information about your genetic make-up. It will help us determine what you are."

I looked away from him and the others as a shiver of fear and disgust trickled down my spine. I did not want anyone, especially these strangers, rummaging around through my head. I knew nothing about them, and yet they wanted to know *everything* about me. The idea of being so vulnerable to a group of strangers who had a strong interest in what I was seemed awfully trusting and ignorant.

"If Guardians have this ability, why wasn't it suggested before?" My voice came out harsher than intended. I could feel my guard going up.

"I could do it," Rylan said as he wrapped his arm around my shoulders. "But Jasmine knows exactly what to look for. She has studied the make-up of many different species."

"It is the most effective and fastest way to get answers, Mae," Arthur added.

"I will in no way violate your most personal thoughts," Jasmine added as if that had even been a concern up until this point. "I will not access your thoughts or memories at all. I will only study how your mind is working."

Access my thoughts and memories? Like mind reading? As if being studied under a magical microscope wasn't already repulsive enough, now I was completely turned off by the idea.

Unfortunately, as much as I wanted to recoil from Jasmine's plan, I knew it had merit. The plan would help find the answers to the questions I had been asking myself for the past two years. I had prayed and begged for these answers. Now I had the ability for them to be answered, and I was balking at it. Had I thought it would be easy? As complicated as my power was, getting the answers would be just as difficult. The room trembled as I fought back panic. As much as I did not want Jasmine to rummage through me like someone finding an old trunk in an attic, her plan might work. I bit my lip hard and forced my power to heel.

"Fine," I mumbled, looking down at my feet.

"I will be with you the entire time," Rylan assured me.

His assurance did not help ease any of the discomfort I was feeling.

Chapter Thirteen

Jasmine had asked for an hour before she wanted to dive into my body, so I escaped upstairs to hide in my room for a while. I paced back and forth, the room trembling occasionally as I accidentally lost control while I tried not to freak out. When the knock on the door broke my train of anxious thoughts, I jumped, which caused a hard jolt throughout the house.

I squared my shoulders, walked over to the door and opened it. Rylan waited on the other side; his warm smile caught me off guard. There were dimples in his cheek, and those teal eyes twinkled with joy. How could someone be this impossibly attractive? He reached out, took my hand, and brought it to his lips. When his lips connected with my skin, goosebumps rose on my arms, and butterflies took flight in my stomach.

"My beautiful mate," he muttered softly.

His affection and the genuine warmth radiating from him caused me to temporarily forget my fear of Jasmine's probing. He tugged at my hand, pulling me towards him. I pressed my free hand against his hard chest and looked up at him. He leaned down, and when our lips touched my thoughts turned to mush. I moaned as a flash of white-hot desire rippled through my body. My moan was involuntary and caused Rylan to smile against my lips. He pulled his mouth away but pressed his forehead against mine.

"Are you ready to meet with Jasmine?"

His words were like a switch to my libido. Immediately, my body cooled. Was I ready to be violated? No. Was I ready for some answers? Yes. I stepped around him,

"I guess so, let's get this over with."

"Mae, look at me."

I moved past him and started the journey down the hallway. I didn't hear him join me, but Rylan was there by my side. He grabbed my hand and stopped, causing me to stop, too.

"I promise you, I would never let anything happen to you. If I thought this could hurt you in any way, I would not entertain the idea. Trust me, Mae, you will be fine."

"I don't think it will hurt," I snapped, yanking my hand away from him. My anxiety was coming off as irritability. "I don't like the idea of being probed like I've been abducted by aliens. It feels so… violating. I don't know Jasmine, but she wants to get *inside* of me, and I'm supposed to trust her? How well do you know her, Rylan?"

"I have known Jasmine most of my life," Rylan answered quickly. "I trust her completely."

"You have known logical, emotion-free Jasmine," I corrected him. "What about this new Jasmine where emotions can rule her thoughts? Can you say you are the same person you were before you met me? That you look at everything the same way as you did before?"

Rylan frowned as he realized the truth behind my words.

I continued, "You don't know her now, Rylan. Emotions are what drive us as individuals to make certain decisions. What if she decides to plant thoughts in my head or tries to control me somehow, because let's face it: If she can get into my head, she can influence me in some way, can't she? That's what scares me! I don't know any of you, and you are asking for a lot of trust," I told him. "And, on top of all of this, to know that *you* can get into my mind and influence me in some way… You haven't done that, have you?"

Rylan bared his teeth in a snarl, and his eyes changed to red. I cringed away from the sudden anger.

"You do not know much about Guardians or the honor that we hold sacred within our race, so I will give you the benefit of the doubt that you do not know what you are insinuating. I would never implant a suggestion or compel you to do anything. As my mate, you are my equal. Altering anything within you would diminish our equality. It would destroy the trust between us," he said through gritted teeth.

Rylan took a deep breath. His deep scowl smoothed out, and his eyes slowly changed back to teal. "Jasmine is bound by honor; she will not do anything untoward to you. I trust her with my life and more importantly, with yours. She will do as she has promised; she will not touch your memories or thoughts. I can and will be right alongside her within you if that is what you wish."

I studied him for a moment. His anger at my accusation was genuine. It was comforting to know how much it repulsed him to want to get into my head. It settled some of my nerves, so I decided to trust him.

"Alright, I believe you. And if you trust Jasmine, then I will too," I grumbled. "Let's get this over with."

"You will see. Everything will be alright. Afterwards, we can go into town," Rylan promised.

Outside, Jasmine had set up a lounge chair for me and brought out another chair for herself. She was talking with Arthur as we approached. Both Guardians shuddered as I came close. Did it hurt when the curse lifted from them, or was it just a sudden onslaught of emotions that they had to adjust to? Jasmine did not wait until I came over to them. Instead, she broke off her conversation with Arthur and strolled over to me with an air of purpose.

She came right up to me, took my hand, and pulled me back towards Arthur. Immediately, I felt a soft buzzing in my head. I couldn't tell who was talking, but my attention was focused on what was about to occur. Was Rylan following? Panicked, I looked over my shoulder and found him pinning Jasmine with sharp glare. Rylan pulled his dark gaze off Jasmine's back to look at me. He visibly relaxed, a smile tugged up one side of his mouth, and the coldness in his eyes thawed. The genuine affection in his gaze shook me. My skin warmed and that desire that had been turned off flickered back to life. How did I land the most handsome man in the entire world? Without realizing it, I returned his smile.

Jasmine sat me down in the lounge chair, and my nerves returned. She sat down in the chair next to me and pulled a journal and pencil from under it. She placed her items on her lap and looked up at me with a polite but emotionally detached expression on her face. Arthur came and stood behind her.

"Mae," Jasmine started. "This will not take long. I want to first explore your body at a molecular level while you are lying here. I will take notes after I am done. Then, I want to see how your body works while you are using your power. That is why I wanted to do this outside. I'd rather not destroy Rylan's home."

"Yeah, me neither," I mumbled bitterly.

"As mentioned before, you will not feel a thing," she assured me. She glanced over her shoulder at Arthur. There was a soft buzz in my head before Arthur nodded. Jasmine turned her attention back to me and said, "Arthur is here because, while Rylan has marked his territory thoroughly, we had to destroy several spider demons lurking around town last night. They feel your presence, and while I work, I would hate for them to interrupt us. Arthur will be ready to defend us while I work. Rylan has said he will monitor my work to ensure I uphold my promise not to touch your memories or influence you in any way."

While neither her expression nor her tone gave away her displeasure, I could almost feel the irritation emanating off her. I almost felt guilty enough to tell Rylan to allow Jasmine to do her thing without hovering. Unfortunately for her, my fear of her rummaging around through my body outweighed my desire to make sure she didn't feel insulted.

"Are you ready to begin?" she asked with the raise of one perfect brow. I clenched my teeth but nodded. "Good. Now, look into my eyes, and please remain silent while I complete my exploration. You may lie down after a few minutes if you wish."

The ground rumbled under us, a sign of my discomfort. Embarrassed, I pulled my power back and mumbled an apology. With a deep breath, I looked into Jasmine's eyes. Anxiety was a rolling boil in my gut, and as I looked into her dark brown eyes, they started to change to red, and my heart began to race.

Suddenly, a large familiar hand gripped my shoulder. The moment Rylan's hand touched my shoulder my anxiousness eased. While not a hundred percent confident about what I was about to do, I didn't feel so alone in it anymore. I looked up at him and gave him a grateful smile. His answering grin made my toes curl. My mood changed back to desire as I stared up at him. What I wouldn't do to have a repeat of this morning's escapade instead of this…

"Mae, snap out of it," Jasmine interrupted my wayward thoughts. I flinched at her tone and turned to face her again. "I can smell your arousal. While I understand the intensity of the bond between mates, please try to control yourself."

My cheeks burned in mortification while Arthur chuckled. Jasmine's professional detachment suddenly cracked; an amused smile split her face. She bit her bottom lip but a chuckle escaped. The sound seemed to surprise her. She cleared her throat and said, "Do not be embarrassed. It is quite normal to desire your mate. But now is not the time."

I threw my hands up in the air with exasperation. "Let's just do this!"

My embarrassment was full-blown, and mixed with my anxiety, it was making it hard to keep my power at bay. The faster we got this done the better. Jasmine's smile faded, although it did not completely disappear, and she straightened in her chair. I forced myself to stare into her now red eyes.

"Mae." She spoke my name barely louder than a whisper. She leaned forward and said softly, "I laughed, Mae. I did not think I would remember how, but it came so naturally. I laughed because of you. I know you are nervous, I can hear your heart fluttering, but I want you to know that you are a treasure that I will cherish. I will do nothing that will cause you harm, and I will do everything in my power to help you. I never want to go back to feeling nothing."

The earnestness in her voice humbled me. Any lingering embarrassment disappeared. Even my nervousness eased as I realized by allowing Jasmine to meddle around inside of me, we could be one step closer to lifting a curse over an entire species. This wasn't just about me; whatever secrets she may uncover could help all of them.

"Let us begin," Jasmine said.

Jasmine had promised that her invasion wouldn't hurt, and she was right. It didn't. However, it was certainly unpleasant. The feeling of icy cold water trickling just under my skin was repulsive, and I flinched. Jasmine blinked, and the sensation stopped. Her brows came together.

"Why did you flinch?"

I shrugged. "It's nothing."

Jasmine leaned forward with a frown.

"Can you sense my presence?"

"Yeah, but it doesn't hurt. Just continue before I freak myself out too much," I mumbled, frustrated this wasn't over yet.

Jasmine did not wait. Her eyes glowed, and that cold sensation returned. I couldn't repress a shudder at the invasion, but I forced myself to sit still. Time moved slowly as she did her internal examination. Eventually, I got used to the cold sensation and laid back in the lounge chair. What was she finding? Anything helpful? Noteworthy? Would she find answers right away, or would she have to refer to her notes that she had accrued over the past... well, however long she had been alive?

I wasn't sure how much time had passed, but finally, the cold disappeared, and Jasmine leaned back in her seat. She picked up her journal, opened it, and began writing. I tried to be patient. Jasmine wrote page after page of notes, but from where I sat, I couldn't read what it said. Trying to be patient, I looked away from her journal up to Rylan, who was watching her with a grim expression. Then, I looked over to Arthur, who was reading over Jasmine's shoulder.

Finally, after a few minutes, my patience wore out. I sat up and sighed. "Okay, give it to me straight. What type of monster am I?"

Jasmine paused her note-taking and looked up at me.

Before she could respond, Rylan interrupted, "You are not a monster, Mae."

I looked over at him and rolled my eyes before I turned my attention back to Jasmine.

"Rylan is right; you are no monster, Mae," Jasmine said with certainty. She smiled and said, "Your DNA shows you are a witch. There are some slight differences in your chromosomes, but we knew there would be slight variances. If there were not any anomalies, we would not be sitting here. Now I just need to figure out what those abnormalities do to make you who you are."

Part of me wanted to accept Jasmine's assessment of me: that I wasn't a monster. She would have seen it in me, right? So why didn't I feel any better? Why couldn't I relax and breathe deeply knowing I was just a simple witch with a little bit of messed up DNA?

But she hadn't seen me at my worst.

Rylan had seen me at my lowest two nights ago. After what he'd witnessed, I wasn't sure how he was so convinced I wasn't a monster. He had to be blinded by this mate thing. Deep down I knew there was more to this than just some funky DNA glitch in my system.

"Are you ready to continue?" Jasmine interrupted my dark thoughts. "I would like to assess how your body processes this power that runs through you."

I looked away from her face and down into my hands that were folded in my lap.

"I can't control it." Shame colored my voice. "I can let out a little bit, but I can't hold it for long. I have to stop, or I lose too much control, and it will get worse."

"That is all right. If you need to stop, please do so. I will gather as much information as I can each time you call upon your power," Jasmine said pleasantly. I looked up at her, over to Arthur who was still reading Jasmine's notes over her shoulder, and then at Rylan who gave me a nod of reassurance.

I looked back at Jasmine and nodded. "Okay, let's do this."

I stared directly into Jasmine's glowing red eyes and let down my mental barrier. Warmth rushed through my body, and my skin tingled as my power rushed outwards. The ground began to ripple. The chairs Jasmine and I sat on rolled with the ground. The men shifted slightly to keep their balance. Through my peripheral vision, I could see Arthur's attention was back on me. I gritted my teeth as my power tried to fight my control. I tried to focus on Jasmine's face rather than the panic trying to well up as I fought back against the pressure in my head. She leaned forward, her eyes glowing brighter than before.

Then, I felt her presence again, and I knew immediately we had both made a grave mistake.

Her presence felt like an ice pick had slammed down into my skull, pierced my brain, came down through my mouth, and out through my jaw. The pain was startling and unbelievable. Before I could react, my vision changed to a violet hue while my consciousness seemed to slip away into the vast purple haze. My control slipped; I could feel that. What I couldn't feel was anything else except the extraordinary pain that was thundering through the rest of my body. I was surrounded by a violet fog. There was a ringing in my ears that muffled all other sounds.

Just as suddenly as it started, the pain vanished. I felt an odd sensation of mentally being tugged in one direction. I gasped in relief, and my legs gave out from underneath me. Wait… my legs? Hadn't I been sitting? I landed on my back, and the air I had drawn in was forced back out. I blinked away the violet haze that had blanketed my vision. Slowly, I pushed myself up onto my elbows.

As my vision cleared and I was able to see again, I froze in horror at the scene before me. I was in the center of a crater, larger than the one I had caused my first night in Salisbury, Georgia. Pieces of both chairs were scattered around me. A hundred yards in front of me, Jasmine and Arthur were braced for a fight, in full Guardian mode. I could see their chests heaving. Their black feathered wings spread wide, and even from where I stood, I could see the intensity of those glowing red eyes.

As the ringing in my ears began to fade, I could hear someone calling my name. Rylan suddenly crouched down in front of me. His eyes were blazing red, his wings came down around me, protectively, shielding me from the others. He was saying something. I could see the urgency in his face. His blond brows were pulled together. His fangs began to retract as he continued to talk to me. I stared at his lips, trying to focus on his words,

"—hear me? Focus on my voice. Focus, Mae!"

He took my face in his hand and leaned close enough that I could feel his hot breath as he called my name again. I closed my eyes and tried to center myself. After a moment of collecting my bearings, the ringing and the last of the violet haze disappeared. When I opened my eyes and looked into Rylan's, I felt grounded.

"What happened?" My voice sounded breathless.

Rylan's scowl deepened. "You tell me."

I wasn't sure what was scarier; the fact that I couldn't remember doing the damage before me or the anger on Rylan's face. Tears blurred my vision.

"I don't know," I whispered in horror. "I- I don't know what happened. I can't remember anything. Is everyone okay?" The thought of hurting someone caused my heart to skip a beat. A sob tore through my chest as I whispered, "I told you, Rylan. I told you I was a monster."

Tears spilled over, and I sobbed harder. How could I not remember doing all of this? There was so much damage! Why were the Guardians braced for battle? I had to have done something horrible. If it was at all possible, Rylan's scowl deepened. His upper lip pulled upward into a fearsome snarl. Without a word, he scooped me up, and his wings folded neatly behind him as he turned with me in his arms. Just behind him, Jasmine and Arthur had gathered nearby. When had they closed the distance between us?

I covered my face with my hands as I cried. I couldn't stomach looking at them. They must be rethinking helping me now. Guardians had to make sure that the supernatural world could not be compromised. They had to see how I was the very threat they kept an eye out for. A deep snarl rumbled through Rylan. I peeked through my fingers to see that Jasmine had taken a step towards us, but she froze at Rylan's warning.

"Mae, are you alright?" Jasmine asked, her face shifting from Guardian back to her human façade. Her wings retracted into her back, and she tried to take another step forward. Rylan snarled again, and this time Arthur put a hand on Jasmine's shoulder.

"Rylan, take Mae inside. Make sure she is well. I sense demons approaching from the south. Jazz and I will take care of them and then clean up out here," Arthur said. He looked at me with a frown.

Rylan did not respond. Instead, he turned swiftly, and we were sky bound. The flight didn't last long. He covered the distance between the crater and the door to the enclosed deck in a heartbeat. Without any effort, he yanked opened the door, walked through the patio, and slid the glass door open into the main house. While he carried me through the house, I could feel a continuous growl rumbling through his chest. I knew it was from anger, the murderous expression on his face confirmed that. I also knew that I was the cause of it. He must be repulsed. Our passionate moment this morning was probably haunting him. The thought of him being disgusted by me only made me cry harder.

We headed over to a couch where Rylan gently sat me down. He knelt in front of me and stared into my face, searching for something. Even in anger, he was stunning. My sobs subsided as I stared into this angel's face.

"How are you feeling?" he asked after a moment of silence.

Grimly, I did a mental assessment of my body. "Drained."

Rylan looked away from me, his jaw ticked. Feeling slightly dazed, I focused on that chiseled jawline. When he turned his attention back to me, his anger had lessened.

"Mae, none of us realized what it would do to you once your power became active and Jasmine tried to examine you. I promised you would not be harmed," he said. His expression turned bleak. "If I told you that I was sorry… it would not describe the depth of how terrible I feel. Please, Mae, forgive me."

My mind spun. Rylan was upset because I somehow had gotten hurt? I shook my head, confused and frightened. I looked down at my arms and only noticed the fading bruises from my spell bracelets. I was covered in dirt, but I didn't notice any scratches or bumps.

"Rylan, please just tell me what happened."

Rylan sighed and closed his eyes. There were worry lines etched into his forehead. Vaguely aware of what I was doing, I reached up and ran my fingertips over them. They disappeared under my touch. Rylan's eyes opened, and I found myself falling into those twin teal seas.

"Jasmine must have triggered a self-defense switch when she entered your body. Your power reacted to her presence by attacking."

I gasped. Tears trickled down my cheeks.

"Rylan, I didn't mean to—"

"Shh, I know," Rylan assured me. He reached up and wiped away my tears. "No one was hurt, Mae. The ground erupted around us, pushing us back, and you spoke to us in an ancient language. Then you collapsed."

I stared at him as if he had grown another head. I had spoken another language? An *ancient* language? Impossible. I barely passed Spanish in high school. This was too much. I covered my face with my hands and moaned.

"You do not recall *anything*?" Rylan asked. I pulled my hands away from my face and stared at him miserably.

"No. I felt pain and then nothing. Oh." I paused, thinking back to the moment I began to regain consciousness. "I felt, I don't know, like a tugging sensation. Like my power was being pulled in one general direction, but it was so brief, and I was so distracted by everything else, that didn't really pay it any attention."

Rylan searched my face again while his expression went blank. Wait a minute, that tugging sensation was important. I could see the wheels turning in Rylan's head as he mulled over what I'd told him.

I leaned forward and asked, "What is it? What's wrong?"

"Nothing," he said and gracefully rose from his crouch.

He walked into the kitchen, and I heard him rummage around. I sat there wondering what was going through Rylan's head. Something was wrong, but he wasn't willing to share it with me. But why? Did he not want me to react? Was it that bad? I bit my lip as I contemplated what could be wrong. Maybe someone *had* gotten hurt. Maybe I had threatened them in that other language.

I didn't hear him, but suddenly, Rylan came to crouch down in front of me again. In his hand was a glass of orange juice. Grateful, I gave him a shaky smile and took the juice.

"Was Jasmine able to get anything before…?"

"We will ask her when they return."

My stomach clenched painfully as I realized that they were out there killing demons that were toeing the line of Rylan's property. I sent up a prayer that both Arthur and Jasmine were alright. My shoulders sagged; they would be safe if I weren't here and giving off so much power.

"How are you not freaking out right now?" I asked Rylan. His grim expression shifted slightly. He gave me a half-smile, and he reached up to stroke my cheek.

"Guardians do not *freak out.* It would be very undignified."

"I'm freaking out," I admitted ruefully.

"You are safe, Mae," Rylan said, his smile fading. "If you are feeling up to it, I think it will do you good to go into town."

I stared at him in disbelief.

"You want to do *what?*" I shook my head. "No, I can't go."

"It will do you good for you to be around familiar things and clear your mind," Rylan assured me. "Let me give you a…" He struggled for the right word. Suddenly, he smiled and continued, "Let me give you a *normal* afternoon. A *human* afternoon. It will allow you to relax and escape your worries for a little while."

"Aren't you supposed to protect humans from abominations like me?" I mumbled.

Rylan scowled. His beautiful teal eyes shifted to red and he leaned forward menacingly.

"You are not an abomination," he snapped. "The only threat in this room is the self-doubt you continuously feed yourself. Self-loathing will hinder any progress we make. You will not talk about yourself in such an appalling manner, do you understand me?"

Surprised by his outburst, I simply nodded.

"Good," he said as he took a deep breath. He rose and offered me his hand. I took it, and Rylan gently pulled me to my feet. He grabbed my chin in his hand and stared down at me. "You are the most beautiful mystery this world has to offer, Mae. Your fear of hurting others and the lengths you have gone to ensure that does not happen shows how pure of heart you are. No monster would care enough to spellbind themselves to protect those around them. No monster concerns themselves to ask if anyone has gotten hurt, and that was the first thing you asked when you came back to me."

Rylan leaned down and gently kissed my swollen lips. I sighed into the sweetness of it and wrapped my arms around his neck. His free arm wrapped around my waist and pulled me closer to him. Pressed against his hard solid form, I found myself calming down. His presence, his confidence, his affection steadied me. I was still scared, but Rylan was still here, ready to weather the storm that was inside of me, *with* me. I wasn't alone, and the person who stood by my side believed in me. What more could I ask for?

Just as I let go of his neck to run my hands down his chest, he pulled away. He looked down at me with a warm smile.

"Let us get you some lunch."

Chapter Fourteen

I stood and headed towards the stairs. As I left the living room, I looked over my shoulder to see if Rylan was following. Instead, I found him staring out the wall of glass to the destroyed backyard. In the reflection of the glass, I could see his face was a mask of indifference. The way he stood there, so still and deep in thought, he could have passed for a statue. Was he secretly worried about the monster he'd been tethered to? Had the sweet words he had just uttered to me simply been meant to calm me down?

No.

I shook my head and hurried through the house. Rylan was right, the self-doubt I fed myself would hurt any progress I made. I needed to trust him. Upstairs I took the quickest shower and then changed into clean clothes. I applied a little eyeliner and mascara using the compact mirror in my purse. Just that simple application made me feel a little bit more normal. More human.

I grabbed my purse off the nightstand and checked to make sure my phone and bracelets were inside. I frowned; my phone was there but where were the bracelets? I checked the nightstand, under the bed, the pockets of my pants from the previous day but the bracelets weren't there.

I stood there in the middle of my room, baffled. How could I have been so careless? There was never a time that I didn't know where they were. After what had transpired outside, I certainly needed to put them on if I was going to go anywhere. As I double checked all over the room, I tried not to panic. I *needed* my bracelets.

As I stood in the middle of my room trying to hold back a wave of power struggling to break through as I panicked; it suddenly clicked. Hadn't Rylan been staying in my room for the past few nights? Rylan, who was so vehemently against me using the bracelets? My panic subsided just enough for anger to rise. I grabbed my purse and stormed out of my room. Rylan was waiting for me by the front door. He stood there, his hands clasped behind his back, watching me descend.

"Where are my bracelets?" I demanded, storming straight up to him. I stopped when my chest pressed against his. I wanted to come off intimidating but Rylan's much larger frame allowed him to tower over me and thwarted my plan. I turned my head upwards to glare at him.

"Destroyed," Rylan said, unfazed by my anger.

What? The blood drained from my face. I recoiled from Rylan as if he had hit me. He knew how important it was for me to have those bracelets. Whether he liked the idea of me wearing them or not, the fact of the matter was they kept everyone around me safe. He had destroyed the one surefire way for me to feel confident and comfortable enough to be around others. The walls around me felt like they were slowly moving towards me. Was there enough air in here? I couldn't breathe…

Rylan reached up and placed his hands on my shoulders.

"You do not need them," he said with a lot more confidence than was sensible.

How *dare* he tell me what I needed to feel safe and secure? I stepped out of his grasp and turned to head back up the stairs. My bottom lip trembled, a warning sign angry tears were going to start. I bit it, hoping to prevent a scene. Rylan grabbed my wrist and turned me around.

"Mae, you do not need them," he assured me again. "I promise you. Let us leave, and I will tell you why in the car."

"I can't *leave*," I snapped. "I'm not going anywhere now. You have taken away the one thing that would guarantee everyone's safety."

"We are leaving," Rylan said, his teal eyes slowly turning red. His voice dropped an octave, and despite my anger with him, desire began to simmer under my skin.

"*No.*"

I tried to pull my wrist out of his grasp, but it was useless. Rylan's pupils narrowed. It was the only warning I received. Before I knew what happened, I was tossed over Rylan's shoulder like a potato sack. The entire house shook hard as my vision turned red. I hit him in his back and attempted to flail around on his shoulder as he carried me out the front door. My efforts didn't seem to faze him in the slightest. He strolled down the front steps and headed over to one of the cars I had seen in the garage the day before. The ground under the car shifted, and Rylan paused.

"Knock it off, Mae," he warned as he set me on my feet.

I tried stepping away from him, but he didn't relinquish his hold on me. Instead, he guided me over to the passenger side, opened the door, and pushed me inside. He shut the door and was in the driver's seat with a speed I didn't know was physically possible. I hadn't even had a chance to grab the door handle before he was already pulling away.

"Why are you doing this?" I demanded as we headed up the beautiful driveway.

I hadn't gotten a chance the first night to see the entrance to the property, but beautiful confederate oaks lined either side of the driveway. Spanish moss draped the branches and hung down, casting a shadow on the paved drive. If I weren't so panicked and angry, I would have taken a moment to appreciate the scenery.

"We need to go into town to get away from the others for a while."

His response slowed my rising temper but did nothing to ease my panic. Okay, there was more to this trip than for me just to feel normal. I settled in my seat and clenched my jaw. I clasped my shaking hands together before I turned my attention out the window. I tried to use the pretty surroundings to distract myself from the impending doom that would occur when we arrived in town.

We drove for ten minutes in silence. Rylan was in his head, and I was too busy staring at the shaking trees and noticing the bumps we were hitting on the smooth, paved road. My power was not settling down, not when I was feeling so overwhelmed. Suddenly, Rylan pulled the car over on the side of the empty two-lane road and killed the engine. I turned to him, hopeful that he was changing his mind about going to town.

"Mae, you need to calm yourself," Rylan said with a sigh.

Ha! Easier said than done, that was for sure. I turned to stare out the window again, studiously ignoring him.

"Listen to me. You need to know something that is not for the others to hear, and it must be kept between you and me for now," he warned me. "Something has happened to me. Something changed after our time together this morning, Mae."

His voice was quiet, but I could hear the urgency. I turned to him, alarmed. As he stared at me with his cool teal eyes, I could see streaks of my violet power beginning to emerge. What anger I was holding onto disappeared. Concern took its place as I gave him a good once over. Physically, he looked perfect.

"When you came apart for me, I could feel your power racing through me, both times. It was almost like a charge, enhancing my abilities. I could feel myself grow stronger; I knew I was faster. Guardians have much better senses than most, but this morning after what happened… It was more than that. I could hear the heartbeats of animals from miles away. I could smell the rotting carcass of a fox at the edge of my property."

He paused and looked away from me. My mind reeled with this information. I had somehow enhanced him, but how was that possible? What did this mean?

"Then, I bit you," Rylan said, his deep voice growing soft. He turned his attention back to me, his eyes slowly changed color to red. "And it was like tasting the blood of a god." My face must have reflected the confusion I felt because he explained, "There is a rumor that when you taste the blood of a god, you feel invincible. It is said a god's blood causes euphoria, makes the drinker believe that they gained powers beyond belief. It incites a dark, irrevocable, and insatiable addiction for more of that blood."

A small gasp sucked through my lips as his eyes began to glow. His brows came together as his eyes became sunken, and his face hollowed.

"Mae, if you had not been my mate, I would have killed you right there in the shower. I have never tasted anything more potent and delicious than your blood." His gaze searched my face, his expression disgusted. Was he disgusted in himself because he thought I tasted good? Because he had been close to killing me? If only he knew what those teeth did to me, he would know that there would be no better way to go.

"Your blood tastes of pure sin. I had to fight the urge to continue to drink every drop from your veins. I have never felt a rush like that in all my life. And, unlike the rumors of what it is like to taste the blood of the gods, your blood, Mae, *did* give me power. *Your* power. I can feel your power coursing through my body as we speak. I could feel it back at the house when Jasmine attempted to see how your body processes the power you have. The magnitude of that blast… I felt it leave your body as if that energy had come from within *me*.

"Even now, your power is leaking out around you. I can feel that seepage through my pores as if it is my own. The power I absorbed from you this morning is calling out to be with you again. I feel it wanting to connect. The feeling is not as strong as it was initially, but it is still there."

He paused. His grim face suddenly shifted, and the corner of one side of his mouth twitched upwards.

"Look out your window to the tree you are causing to move right beside us."

He wanted me to do what?

I turned my attention to the tree outside my window afraid to see what would happen. It was shaking hard. The leaves were falling off it, a small branch snapped off and fell to the ground. I was the cause of the distressed tree.

"Watch," Rylan said, his voice so soft it was barely more than a whisper.

I did watch.

The tree shook harder for a moment before it suddenly stilled. Inside my body, I felt a shift. One minute my power was seeping out in every direction, despite my attempt to keep it back, and the next minute it was being pulled in one direction, towards Rylan. I turned to look at Rylan in amazement, but as I did, something shifted within me. The power that Rylan was pulling into himself started to flow back into me. As I absorbed it back into my body, I noticed it returned in a calmer state, less frantic and more controlled than when it had left. I shuddered at the feeling.

I stared at Rylan. He was watching me, his eyes glowing violet as he used his new ability. A stunned silence hung between us. How was this possible? What did it mean? How long could this last? Around us, the world stilled as Rylan recycled my power through himself and returned it to me. The sensation was like getting fluid from an IV. I sat there shocked as I realized the magnitude of what he was capable of.

Rylan could control the chaos.

I didn't need the bracelets; he could redirect the energy back to me without it hurting anyone. Everyone around me would be safe. The thought almost made me smile in relief. Almost.

"Does it hurt you?" I asked, my voice tight.

I reached out and touched his arm, needing the physical connection. His gaze dropped to my hand on his bicep. He reached up with his other hand and covered my hand with his. His hand engulfed mine. The warmth that radiated from him seeped into my soul.

When he looked back up into my eyes, he grinned. "It does not cause me any pain."

The relief I felt was liberating. A weight lifted off my shoulders, and I could truly breathe for the first time in a long time. Excitement and relief over this new development was overwhelming. So much so that tears welled up and spilled over. The chaos could be controlled! I laughed, and it sounded hysterical.

"You can control it!" I said breathlessly. "And I can absorb it back into me. This is amazing! Wait, hold on…" My tears stopped as I recalled the tugging sensation out in the back yard. "You stopped me back at the house from hurting anyone. That tugging I felt, that was you?"

Rylan hesitated. His expression changed from pleased to grim.

"It was my first attempt to use this new ability to manipulate your power. I was not exactly sure what I was doing or if it could help. I would not have stepped in had I thought you had yourself under control."

My elation popped like a balloon. I hadn't been in control at all. The horror and dread that it would happen again set fire to all the new hope that had just bloomed. My face fell, and I sagged in my seat.

"So, you broke my bracelets *before* you knew you could do this?"

"Yes."

I didn't bother to glare at him. The risk he had taken was too great, and he knew it. What if he had been wrong in his assessment of his connection with my power? Thank goodness he hadn't been mistaken. If he hadn't stepped in to help, I wasn't sure if I would have regained consciousness as quickly as I had, and who knew what I would have done to the three Guardians?

"Why don't you want Arthur and Jasmine to know that you can help me?"

"I will tell them that your power can enhance our abilities. This may help Jasmine with her research. If they find out about your blood, if *anyone* finds out about your blood, Mae, there will be a war," he said with a dark scowl. "Your blood is too dangerous to get into the wrong hands. If someone could resist draining you dry, they would have the ability, like me, to manipulate your power. The fewer people who know about what your blood could do, the safer you are."

The importance of keeping my blood a secret was clear. While I didn't mind Rylan biting me, I absolutely would not allow anyone else to do the same. If the wrong person got a taste of my blood and gained access to my power, the danger could be insurmountable. But now I lived in a house full of bloodsuckers. While they weren't munching on me yet, what if they got hungry? Did Guardians go crazy from the smell of blood like, I assumed, a vampire would?

Then, there was another issue.

What was going to happen to Rylan if he continued to drink my blood? Would this cause him harm in the long run? He said it didn't hurt now, but there had to be side effects. Maybe he wasn't feeling them now, but what would happen in a day, a week, a month or a year from now? Would my power start to destroy him? My heart squeezed painfully in my chest.

"We don't know what my blood is doing to you, Rylan. this isn't safe."

"This is not about me," Rylan said quickly, blowing off my concern for his well-being.

"You're right. It's about both of us," I corrected him with a scowl. "Who knows what's going to happen when you continue to drink my blood? Or what happens if we have sex again and I lose control of my power again? Or—"

"If?" Rylan interrupted with a growl. One of his blond brows rose in surprise. "I was under the impression it was merely a matter of *when* we would have sex again."

Despite the gravity of the situation, I rolled my eyes and chuckled.

"*If,*" I emphasized. "I can't be the reason you get hurt."

"I am willing to risk everything just to feel you cum with my tongue inside you again," he said, his voice deep.

My cheeks burned with a mixture of embarrassment and pleasure. My body came alive at his words, and when I looked at his handsome face, I saw hunger that only fueled my own desire. My nipples hardened, and my heart started beating wildly in my chest.

"Stop, this is serious, Rylan," I said, but my voice came out husky.

"Oh, I am being serious."

And he was. Those red eyes were fixated on me. Out of the corner of my eye, I could see the thick bulge in his pants. I bit my bottom lip, trying to still its quiver. My hand fluttered up to my throat, and his gaze drifted to my neck. I watched as his canines lengthened to become fangs, and I felt myself become instantly damp. Damn, those teeth…

"No, wait, stop," I gasped, trying to rein in the urge to lean forward and let him bite me right then and there. I shuddered and clasped my hands together in my lap. "We were talking about safety…"

"You do not need to worry about me. I am *your* Guardian. *I* will protect *you*." He paused as a frown turned the corner of his lips downward. "And you do not need to fear me. Though your blood is a great temptation, a Guardian cannot kill his own mate. It would be like killing oneself. You do not need to be afraid."

I chuckled darkly and looked away from him as he raised his brow again.

"If I'm going to die, having your fangs in me would be the *best* way to go. Death by orgasm… I don't think there's a better way."

I couldn't say it to his face. I had to say it to my reflection in the window, but I couldn't hide my smile as I thought about dying in his arms in such a perfect manner.

"Do not joke about dying, Mae," Rylan said. His tone caused me to turn to look at him again, and my smile faded. His expression was grave, all teasing set aside. He reached up and cupped my cheek. "Let us go to town and get you something to eat. With my new ability to draw your power to me, I will make sure no harm will come to you, or anyone around you. Let us enjoy our time together."

I stared into his handsome face, wondering how the hell I ended up with him. After two years of a living hell, he was my silver lining. How could this man make me laugh, squirm in my seat with desire, and make me feel protected when I'd only just met him?

Rylan reached forward and slid his hand behind my head. He pulled me forward, and I moved eagerly towards him. Our lips met, and all my fears and concerns temporarily fell away. Oh, how I loved his lips. They pressed against mine and sent electrical waves of pleasure and delight throughout every nerve ending in my body. Then, his tongue slid into my mouth. The contact was delicious. My body grew hotter as I kissed him back passionately. If Rylan was willing to be my rock in this stormy life of mine, then I was going to cling to him while I found my footing. My heart fluttered and a new feeling tickled my senses. It wasn't just his lips I loved…

I pulled away from him as I tried to understand this new feeling. Our eyes met, and we stared at each other, lost in the moment. I reached up and touched my swollen lips, wondering how I had fallen for Rylan so quickly. We had known each other for just a few days… Oh, how things had changed.

Rylan pulled his hand back and smiled at me. The smile was warm and made those teal eyes twinkle. All signs of a Guardian and my power had vanished. I smiled back and then turned to lean back in my seat. I took a shaky breath and squeezed my legs together to give myself some relief. Rylan turned the car back on with a push of a button, and we were off towards town.

To try to get my mind off his body and what I wanted to do with it I asked, "If my blood is as potent as you say, why didn't you notice when you healed my leg?"

Rylan didn't answer right away. Lost in his thoughts, he stared out the windshield. I waited patiently. Time ticked by, and yet Rylan remained silent. Was it that hard of a question, or was he not certain about the answer? Maybe he knew the answer and did not want me to freak out.

"Your leg was sewn up, and I had wiped most of the blood away before administering aid," he said thoughtfully. Hm, maybe a full gulp was needed before the effects of my power occurred.

"Once you tell Jasmine and Arthur what my power can do, they're going to wonder how I was able to direct it straight into you," I chuckled at the thought. "I can't go around having sex with everyone."

A myriad of emotions crossed over Rylan's face. After he was able to control whatever feelings my words had evoked, his lips turned upwards into a smile.

"We will figure it out," he assured me.

We drove in silence for another ten minutes before arriving in Salisbury, Georgia. Unlike the first night, I was awake, alert, and not in pain, so I was able to admire the old buildings. It was like being thrown back into the fifties. The storefronts were adorable with bright colors, signs with large typography, and wonderful displays in the storefront windows. While the stores appeared thrown back in time, everything screamed fresh, fun, and expensive. It was an odd mix that seemed to work. The people out and about were dressed well, smiling, and some even waved at us as we drove by.

Rylan parallel parked outside of an adorable diner and walked around the car to open my door. As I climbed out, I couldn't fail to notice the looks we were receiving. Was it the flashy car or the most ridiculously handsome man towering next to me? Rylan seemed oblivious as he guided me across the street. Curiously, I walked into the small diner and immediately fell in love with its charm. An older woman behind the counter looked up as we entered. She was dressed in a blue dress covered by a white apron.

"Good afternoon, y'all. Just take a seat wherever you want, and I'll be right with you," she said with a warm smile.

Rylan led me over to the far side of the small diner, and we sat down at a booth. He slid in next to me, and we both grabbed the laminated menus that were already on the table waiting for us. I looked around the diner, noting the authentic-looking register, milkshake machine, and behind the counter, the deep fryer and lively waitress who was talking to one of the customers.

I looked at the menu. I don't know why I bothered. At diners, I only ever got the same thing: pancakes and scrambled eggs. How could anyone want anything other than breakfast food when the option was available? Rylan didn't even bother looking at it. He was looking out the window at the people passing by. He had his arm around my shoulders and was playing, absentmindedly, with a stray curl. The waitress took payment from the obvious regular she was talking to and walked him to the door. Once she had said her goodbyes, she hurried over to us.

"How are y'all doin' this afternoon?"

"Well, thank you," Rylan said with a curt nod.

"Good! I haven't seen you two in here before. You just passing through our lovely little town?" she asked putting her hands on her wide hips.

"No, we just moved in on the outskirts of town."

"On the outskirts of town, you say? Are you talkin' about that large plantation?"

"The very same."

"Wow! Well, welcome to Salisbury. My name is Melody Cairns. Who might you two be, so I know what to call you the next time you pop into my restaurant?"

"I am Rylan Wellington, and this here is my beautiful fiancé Mae White. We are here to shop for a ring and to look around," Rylan said, and his lips spread wide into a toothy grin.

All the air in my lungs exhaled. I forced a smiled to hide the surprise and forced myself not to flinch as Rylan's arm withdrew from my shoulders, and he grabbed my hands in an endearing gesture. The waitress squealed in delight. She clapped her hands together and hooted.

"Oh, how wonderful, congratulations you two! If you need any help with planning that wedding, I'm your girl. In the meantime, can I get you somethin' to eat? The fried steak is to die for."

Rylan turned to me, his grin still wide. Was this a joke to him? Engaged? This morning he had mentioned the *wives* there had been before me. Even if we had known each other for years, I was not going to be another wife to him. No matter how I felt about him, marriage was off the table. I tried to fight down my irritation as I realized they were both waiting for me to order something. I had been getting hungry, but my appetite seemed to have vanished.

"I'll just have some orange juice and a bowl of fruit," I said, my voice hoarse.

"That's it? Bless your heart. You are skin and bones. Trust me when I say your man here will appreciate having something to grab in the middle of the night. I'll bring you some grits, butter biscuits and, some fried steak. I promise you won't be disappointed," Melody said. She turned to Rylan. "And you, hon?"

"I will have the same."

"Great, I'll be back with your meal in no time."

Before I could object, Melody turned and walked off. If only she knew why I looked so thin. She wouldn't be so friendly then. I turned my attention to Rylan and glared at him. His grin disappeared, but a smug smile hung around his lips. He let go of my hands and wrapped his arm around my shoulders once more. Oh, so this *was* funny to him. We were so not engaged.

Chapter Fifteen

"Why would you tell her we're engaged!?" I hissed at him.

"Because you are mine. It makes sense to make it official," he told me as he leaned back with a smile.

"I'm not marrying you," I told him, looking him straight in the eye. He had to know I was serious.

His blond brows rose. "Oh? And why not? Most women enjoy the ceremony."

"Maybe your other wives enjoyed their special day, but is it still meaningful to you? How many times does one watch his bride walk down the aisle before he gets bored knowing it will happen again in, what, fifty or sixty years?" I asked him sardonically.

The bemusement on Rylan's face shifted. His brows came together, and he clenched his jaw together.

"Mae, marriage has always been a means to an end. To gain land, money, titles, and respect. How else do you think I have acquired as much as I have?"

I turned my face away from him and stared out the window as I tried to hide my disgust. I understood times were different. Yes, I knew men and women had not always married for love; it was to gain wealth and power, but to knowingly go into a marriage with that mindset... my stomach twisted.

"Mae."

Begrudgingly, I turned my attention back to Rylan who was staring down at me. His anger had disappeared, and concern marred his features.

"None of them meant anything to me. You know I had no emotions before you."

I sighed as guilt overrode my petty attitude. There was no need to cast judgment on him. I was just feeling spiteful for no reason.

"I know, Rylan. That was wrong of me to say that. I'm sorry. I just don't want to be another name on just another marriage license. While I'm still getting used to the idea that souls can be tied to one another, I *am* glad it's your soul that's intertwined with mine. But that doesn't mean we have to get married. I won't make you watch another bride walk down the aisle, okay?"

Rylan took my hand, turned it so my palm was facing upwards and kissed the inside of my wrist. The intimate gesture caused butterflies to flutter in my stomach. I felt my cheeks grow warm. The desire was building again.

"I would move mountains to see you walk towards me down the aisle. I want to *feel* everything one is supposed to feel on the day of one's wedding. While the Joining has just begun, and it is more final than those of the human vows, I wish to promise myself to you in every imaginable way. As my last bride, you are the most meaningful and special."

Rylan's teal eyes were bright with emotion, and the soft smile on his lips spoke promises of devotion. My heart swelled up, and I could feel the joy brimming under my skin. Despite barely knowing him, his words were sweet and comforting. This was clearly important to him, and hearing how much it meant to him caused me to waiver in my decision not to marry him. Before I could say something stupid, like agree to marry a man I had only known a few days, I pulled my hand away to break our physical connection.

"It's a moot point anyway. You haven't even asked me yet," I teased.

Rylan smirked. He leaned down, kissed the top of my head, and said, "You are right. I will have to remedy that soon."

I felt the butterflies flutter around in my stomach again. Honestly, what woman wouldn't accept Rylan's proposal? He was the full package. Maybe that's what each of his previous brides had thought.

"Did any of your wives figure out you weren't, you know, human?" I asked curiously. Suddenly, another question popped into my head. "Usually after marriage, kids follow. Do you have children?"

How had I not thought about Rylan having kids before? He was beyond ancient, and I was sure at least a few of his wives would have complained if they didn't have kids. Especially back in earlier times when having a son was important so the family could pass down their legacy. Rylan frowned thoughtfully. Before he could answer, Melody returned with two large plates in her hand.

Once she dropped off our lunch, she disappeared back into the kitchen. I stared down at the mass of food she left and felt a little lost. Where was I supposed to start? I took the silverware that was rolled up in a napkin and began cutting into the steak.

After a few minutes of silence Rylan said, "I knew several of them had their suspicions. I aged slowly, I rarely ate, and I never became ill. While I spent most of their lives away from them, traveling and working, when I returned, they would notice the lack of change. There were five wives that I did tell my secret to. Women I had grown to respect throughout their years. All five took my secret to their graves."

He unrolled his silverware from his napkin and cut into his fried steak. I watched as he plopped it into his mouth. He grimaced playfully, and I giggled. His arm came around my shoulders again, and I knew the contact was to help me eat this time. I took a bite of the steak. It was delicious.

"To answer your question about kids: no. Guardians cannot conceive children with anyone except with their mate," he said softly. "If you wish to start a family, I am certainly not opposed to the idea."

The piece of steak headed towards my mouth paused. I looked at him, and he was watching my face with amusement. First marriage, and now he wanted to talk about *kids*? I studied his face for a moment. He was obviously waiting for me to object or tout my opinion about the subject. I decided not to entertain the idea.

This was not a conversation I wanted to have. Instead, I asked, "How did you get away with that? Weren't your wives upset when they could never get pregnant?"

"Of course," Rylan said and scooped a bite of grits into his mouth. "Most of my wives went looking for attention in the arms of other men, and I usually ended up having a bastard child here and there." I gaped in surprise. He chuckled and continued, "I was rarely ever around. I was not surprised in the least that my wives would go find love in someone else's arms. Their bastard children would receive a handsome inheritance but would never get the title or the respect after I faked my deaths. It would go to a mysterious uncle, nephew, or stranger no one had ever met, and I would remake my image somewhere else."

I stared at him, all food forgotten. How could he talk about his past so nonchalantly? Did he not realize that what he was saying was not normal? I wondered how many historical events he had witnessed… or caused. What famous politicians, activists, or artists had he met? Did any one event or person stick out to him? I put my fork down as I thought about all the things Rylan could have seen or done. All without the ability to feel anything. Could he feel emotions now when he looked back on everything, or did it remain a bleak, emotionless existence?

"Any more questions?" he asked, amused by my silence.

"Only a thousand or so," I muttered shaking my head. I turned to look at the food on my plate. What *hadn't* Rylan been a part of in his lifetime? I pushed some food around on my plate, my mind whirling with this new information.

"Tell me what you are thinking," Rylan pushed when I stayed silent.

My soft chuckle came out sounding exasperated. "Have you seen that beer commercial where they show you the most interesting man in the world? I think you should be the next spokesperson."

Rylan threw back his head and laughed. Melody looked over at us from where she was standing and smiled. If only she knew what we were talking about… would she still be amused?

"I do not know about that. But I am flattered you think I am interesting."

"I do have one more question for right now," I hedged and looked up at his face curiously. "How old are you?"

Rylan laughed again. His good mood was infectious. I grinned back as I waited.

"Hm… Marcus Aurelius, the emperor of Rome, died the year I was born. That would mean I am around eighteen hundred years old. I do not remember the gods, but my mother and father used to tell me stories of them." I gasped in shock. Rylan laughed at my reaction. "Now that I answered your question, eat, and then we can take a tour of the town. I want to get back to the house as soon as we can."

My mind spun as I tried to follow what he was saying. I was stuck on how old the man next to me claimed to be. He wanted me to eat? Eat what? I looked down at my very full plate. Oh, yeah, the food in front of me. And he wanted to go home? So soon? We had just gotten here.

"What's wrong? Why do we need to go back to the house so soon?" I asked, alarmed that I may have missed something. My sudden apprehension eased as a mischievous grin spread across his handsome face.

Leaning down to whisper in my ear, he breathed, "Each time your mouth pops open, I imagine all the things I want to do to it. I want to take you home to ravish your body."

Oh.

All the air rushed out of my lungs. My body had come alive in the car on our way here, and the burning need for Rylan had only grown since we had entered the diner. My mouth went dry, and my heart tried to explode from my chest and race home, all too eager to take up his invitation. By the time I was done eating, I was sure I had broken some sort of record. My stomach felt bloated with how much food I had inhaled. I guess I had been hungrier than I had originally thought.

After Rylan paid for lunch, we toured Salisbury. It was a charming town. The boutiques we entered were filled with fun knickknacks and trinkets. Every shop owner we met, along with everyone who stopped us on the street to greet us, was warm and friendly. Being greeted by name by so many strangers was disconcerting. How could they possibly know who we were when we had just gotten in two days prior? When I asked Rylan about it, he explained gossip spread fast in a town like this.

During our tour, my body burned. I kept catching myself eyeing up Rylan. The desire pooling in my gut was almost unbearable. A few times I had to force myself to step away from him before I shoved him up against the side of a building and pounced on him. My desire was almost painful. It was a repeat of this morning.

I knew Rylan was aware of my condition. Sometimes our eyes would meet, and the desire I saw on his face was carnal. He didn't try to hide it; he wasn't embarrassed by his desire for me. I saw it burning in those teal eyes. Knowing that he was feeling the same way only made it worse for me. Sometimes his knuckles would caress the side of my cheek. Other times he would swoop down and skim his lips against mine. It didn't matter that there were people around who saw our intimate moments. My world had narrowed to the one man who was making my blood boil. Who whispered in my ear what he wanted to do to me and how much I meant to him.

We stopped for ice cream about two hours later after lunch, and I was relieved. I needed something to cool me down. The ice cream shop was on the edge of a beautiful park where couples were walking around hand in hand, kids were playing frisbee in the open spaces, and there were even a few people in paddleboats out in the small pond. We strolled through the park, talking, as I ate my cold treat. Our conversations stayed on normal, human topics. Rylan asked me about my need to go back to school, questioned me about family traditions I had growing up, and asked me about my views on politics. In return, I questioned him about the different companies he ran and how he managed so much. I asked him about the different places he had lived and where he would like to go again.

We stuck to the shaded areas. Despite the fading light, it was so hot and humid that the shade was the only relief outside. How had it not gotten any cooler now that it was almost September? The humidity made my hair stick to my neck, and sweat dripped down my chest. As we made our way around the park, we found a secluded bench, hidden underneath a willow tree. We ducked under the weeping branches and sat down in the shade. As we sat there and talked, Rylan's phone went off in his pocket. He pulled it out, and I waved him off when he said he had to take it. He stepped out from underneath the thin branches and answered the call.

I finished my cone and sighed as I looked around. It was such a peaceful little town. There was so much charm, and the people were so friendly. The change of pace from Chicago was a relief. Now that I had a moment to myself, I found that my power was still in check. I could feel Rylan, even from the few yards away where he was standing, redirecting my power towards him and back to me. I had been so comfortable all day that I almost forgot I had terrifying magic running through my veins. Rylan had promised a normal afternoon for me, and somehow, he had made that happen.

My heart swelled in my chest as I stared at the Guardian.

As I watched Rylan talk to whoever was on the phone, I heard rustling behind me. I turned towards the sound, expecting a squirrel, only to find a young girl standing directly behind me. I flinched away at her closeness. How had I not heard her approach? She was young, maybe six or seven, with long red hair and a face full of freckles. Her eyes seemed unfocused as she faced me. It took me a moment to realize she was blind. Where were her parents?

"Oh, hello. Are you lost?" I asked. I stood up and walked around the bench to her. I looked around us but didn't see anyone looking for a child.

"No, I'm not lost. I'm right where I'm supposed to be," the child said with a sweet smile.

"Oh, well, I'm sure your parents are probably worried sick about you. Can I help you find them?" I offered, unsure of what to do. I looked around again but still didn't see anyone looking around frantically for a kid. "My name is Mae, what's yours?"

"Hi, Mae," the girl said with a wide grin. "You have a funny aura. You're kind of like us but not really… That's weird. Anyhow, you know she's been looking for you. She'll be so happy to know I found you!"

A chill ran down my spine. What was she talking about? My life had been too weird these past few days to have a little girl say creepy things to me.

"One of us? What do you mean, and who's been looking for me?" I asked slowly, hoping this was some weird game she was playing.

"Darla!" a woman yelled, barreling through the willow branches towards us. "Oh, thank goodness! You can't wander off like that, Darla. I've told you this a thousand times." The woman grabbed her daughter and wrapped her arms around the child in a warm embrace. The woman looked up at me, opened her mouth to say something, but stopped as surprise crossed her face. She shut her mouth. The woman straightened up and pulled her daughter behind her.

"What are *you* doing here?" the woman asked, as her red brows came together in a deep scowl. "And what are you doing with my daughter?"

Who the hell was this woman? What was her problem? Her daughter had come up to me, not the other way around. I opened my mouth to tell her what I thought about her parenting skills, but an arm snaked around my shoulders, sidetracking me.

"Hello, Claire. I see you have met my mate, Mae White. I hope there is no problem here?" Rylan asked pleasantly.

His voice was soft, but I could feel a growl vibrating through him. Claire? Rylan knew this woman? The surprise and fear on Claire's face solidified that she knew exactly who and what Rylan was. What was going on?

"N-n-no, there is no problem, Richard," she said quickly.

"I go by Rylan now," he corrected.

Oh, so she had known him when he lived as someone else? Who was this woman?

"Rylan," she repeated with a nod. "My little girl just wandered off, and Mae helped me find her."

"Hm… Mae and I were just talking about children earlier. She must be more eager than I thought to start a family," Rylan drawled, his expression deadpan. I choked on something between a laugh and a shriek of outrage. "Mae, you really should not steal a witch's child. They frown upon that."

I looked from him to Claire and then back to him. My immediate anger with him joking about children in front of this woman disappeared and was replaced with awe and fear. A witch? A real, honest to God *witch* was standing in front of me? With her witch daughter? Should I be scared? Concerned?

"Oh, Darla just likes to wander off sometimes. Mae did nothing wrong," Claire assured him. "We'll just be going now. It was good to see you again, *Rylan*."

Rylan bowed his head. "Give the coven my regards."

"Will do," she said hastily. She grabbed Darla's hand and pulled her daughter away from us, leaving the privacy of the willow tree.

"A witch?" I hissed at Rylan, shrugging off his arm. "I can't believe I met a real-life witch, oh my God!" I shook my head in disbelief. There had been no green skin, no wart... Claire hadn't even cackled! I turned and pushed at Rylan's chest. He didn't budge. "And what the hell? 'We were just talking about children?'"

Rylan chuckled.

"Are you ready to head home?" he asked, his blue eyes twinkling mischievously. "I would love some of *our* own children to talk about next time."

I pushed at him again, this time unable to stifle my giggle. Rylan grabbed my wrist and pulled me towards him. Knowing what he planned to do, I got to it first. I reached up on my toes and pressed my lips against his. He wrapped his arms around my waist, and he pulled me up against his rock-hard body.

My body's internal temperature spiked to an all-time high. My breathing came in gasps, and my nipples hardened. The witch and her daughter were forgotten; my mind and body were focused on the man standing right before me. Rylan's hands slid from my waist, and he grabbed my butt and squeezed it. I could feel the hard bulge in his pants. My panties became damp, and for a moment, I was afraid it would show through to my shorts.

I broke the kiss but didn't pull away. Keeping my gaze locked on Rylan's, I reached down with one hand and placed my hand on his bulge. I bit my lip to keep it from trembling. A picture of me dropping to my knees flashed in my head, and my mouth watered. But I couldn't. Not here. Instead, I stroked him once, twice, and then reluctantly, I dropped my hand away from him and stepped back.

"Hm… The topic of kids really gets under your skin," Rylan whispered with a devilish smile.

"No, it *really* doesn't," I assured him as I rolled my eyes.

But if I was being honest with myself, the thought of having Rylan's child growing inside me did do something to me. Urgh! No, it was probably just the intense arousal making me think that way. Usually, the idea of kids never appealed to me. Rylan closed the distance between us and leaned down, so his mouth was inches from my ear.

"Liar," he whispered. He gently bit my earlobe and I giggled again. "I want to check in on Charlie at the hospital. Then, we can go home and procreate."

I laughed; it sounded husky.

"I have an IUD. You're not getting any kids from me," I assured him.

He didn't look deterred at all. He grinned, a big white toothy grin.

"A rectifiable situation."

"Let's go to the hospital to see Charlie," I said rolling my eyes and forced myself to turn and walk out from under the willow branches. "Jeez, you barely know me, and you want me to have your kids," I said over my shoulder.

Rylan was right there next to me. He grabbed my hand as we walked out of the park.

"I am getting to know you," he said. The genuinely happy smile on his face caused my desire to spiral wildly out of control. He was so gorgeous…

We talked all the way back to the car. When I climbed into the passenger seat, I felt as if I had known Rylan much longer than a few days. I stared out my window as we drove to the hospital. It was a short ride, but by the time we arrived, I was so uncomfortable, my arousal so intense, that I couldn't stop squirming in my seat. Rylan had barely parked before I was already out of the car. I walked through the sliding glass door and allowed Rylan to walk up to the nurse behind the counter.

We didn't stay at the hospital long. Charlie was sound asleep when we got there, doped up on a lot of pain medication according to Laura who had greeted us warmly. I wasn't sure why I was surprised to hear that Laura and Charlie were both under the impression that he had lost his arm due to a chainsaw accident. Charlie had apparently been cutting down a few low hanging, dead branches when his hold on the cutting instrument had slipped.

When Rylan and I stepped into Charlie's room, the intense desire that had been building up inside of me all day evaporated instantly. Charlie was so deathly pale his face almost blended in with the white linens on his bed. His left shoulder was wrapped in fresh bandages. I stared at the injury as Rylan and Laura spoke softly next to me. A vision of that afternoon, with Charlie lying motionless on the ground, and demons charging at both of us, clouded my mind and fear caused my whole body to shake.

I could feel my power rush outwards, and I panicked. Shit! I couldn't lose control without the bracelets here. I braced myself for the room to shake and Laura's cry of alarm, but the room did not move. Instead, I could feel Rylan tug harder at the surge of power that escaped and drew it into him. My relief that he was able to control the chaos was almost tangible.

I stared down at this man I didn't know and felt the insurmountable guilt begin to build. If I hadn't come to the house, the demons wouldn't have been there to chew off Charlie's arm. This was all my fault. Anytime someone got hurt, whether it was from a demon or my lack of control, I would always be responsible. Guilt made me sick. My stomach twisted, and my throat closed. I looked away from the sleeping man and down at the floor as tears threatened to fall.

After just a few minutes of conversation, Rylan turned to me and took my hand. We said our goodbyes to Laura and left the room. Both of us remained silent all the way to the car.

As we pulled away from the hospital, Rylan said, "The attack was not your fault, Mae."

Despite Rylan's firm assurance, I couldn't look at him. How could he say that when he knew very well it was all my fault? I was a monster, and I had lured more monsters to me. Rylan said nothing else on the way home, and I sat in silence, wondering how I could stop being me.

Chapter Sixteen

Rylan parked the car in the garage, and we walked across the driveway towards the house in silence. Rylan paused just before we started up the steps and turned around. The only indication there was someone behind us was a rush of wind. I turned as Rylan greeted his fellow Guardian,

"Arthur."

"Rylan, Mae," Arthur said with a polite nod of his head. He was in full Guardian mode. He was shirtless, his wings were spread out behind him, and his eyes glowed red. "Rylan, if you have a moment, we need to speak."

"Of course," Rylan turned to me to say something, but I waved him off.

"I'll see you guys inside."

I needed some space anyways. Seeing Charlie laying in that hospital bed because of me… I felt nauseous. I wanted to wash the slimy feeling of guilt and bad luck off me. I took the steps two at a time and walked into the house.

I debated going upstairs and hiding away for a bit but being alone with my thoughts in my room sounded too depressing. Instead, I walked further into the main part of the house. What did I want to do? For a little while that afternoon, I had felt normal. My problems had vanished, I was able to flirt and enjoy my time with the sexiest man ever, and I had even been able to eat a full meal. I wanted to keep that feeling.

I slid open the glass door to the deck and headed out to stare at the destruction I had caused this morning. It was dark, despite the light from inside filtering through the glass into the enclosed deck. It was so dark I didn't notice Jasmine sitting in the far seat until I'd almost sat down on top of her.

"Good evening, Mae," she said, her voice deep, almost hypnotic.

I jumped at the sound of her voice; my heart skipped a beat. I put my hand over my chest. Her chuckle was almost seductive. Were all Guardians alluring?

"Hey, Jasmine, I didn't see you out here. Did you want some privacy?" I asked, wondering if I should head back inside.

"No, I am pleased that you came out. Please, join me."

How could I resist?

I sat down in a fancy wicker loveseat across from her and tried to see her face in the dark. It took me a moment before my eyes adjusted completely. I could see the visible shudder that ran through Jasmine as my presence began to affect her. How odd it must be to feel a rush of emotions run through you so unexpectedly.

"How are you feeling?" Jasmine asked after a long pause between us.

My cheeks warmed in embarrassment even as a cold chill ran down my spine. I wanted normalcy, but I was not normal, and my life would never go back to the way it had been before my power emerged. I frowned at Jasmine; I would have to talk about the monster inside of me. I hated this. I hated how *this* was becoming normal.

"I'm alright. I'm really sorry about this morning. I didn't know that… that I could snap like that."

Jasmine waved off my apology.

"It is my fault for not thinking about the dangers of lurking into the mind of someone as powerful as you are, Mae. Did you know Fae Royalty has a similar type of defense system if someone attempts to enter their mind or bodies?"

"Fae? You mean… fairies?"

"Fae and fairies are different, though there is a common misconception that they are the same. Fairies are, mostly, pure of heart. Faes have darkness in them that they keep in check. There are not many around anymore, but there are a few in Scotland."

Oh.

"I have a darkness in me, maybe I'm part Fae," I whispered as I thought about fairy-like people lurking around Scotland.

Jasmine shook her head.

"There is no darkness within you, Mae. I promise. I would have seen it," she assured me. My heart leaped; that was a good thing, right? "But I did notice something before you kicked me out that I wish to share with you."

Jasmine suddenly stood up, walked over and sat down next to me on the loveseat. She took my hand in hers, and she stared at me through the darkness. Her eyes began to glow red. It was eerie to see the glow of her burning red irises in the darkness.

"Mae, your DNA shifted, changed. Your DNA right now, in this state, is most certainly witch. This is why you can call the spellbook to you and why a pentagram appears on your hand when you chant. The moment I entered your body the second time, your DNA shifted. It was like a chameleon had changed colors. Your witch DNA is a mask to hide what you truly are. What you became… I have never seen DNA structure as intricate as yours. No other species on this planet can manipulate their DNA. I would have said it was impossible to do until I saw it with my own eyes this morning."

Jasmine reached forward and touched my cheek gently, cupping it in her warm palm.

"I believe *you* are forcing this DNA change. By holding back whatever is in you, you are affecting the molecular structure within your body. You must be careful, Mae. I know you are terrified of your power, but I am very concerned that you are doing more damage than good by keeping it at bay."

"I don't understand," I said shaking my head, causing Jasmine's hand to fall away. I knew I could physically hurt myself, but now I was hurting myself on a whole new level? Shit. "I'm not doing anything to change my cells or whatever. And I can't just let it go. You've seen what I can do." I could hear the agitation in my voice.

"I am sure whatever you are doing to cause the change in your body is not intentional," Jasmine said soothingly. "But we must figure out how to let you be who you truly are. You cannot continue to pretend your power does not exist or that you are human any longer. We will figure out how to help you be your true self without hurting yourself or others. I promise."

I looked away from her. My hands shook, and my heart beat wildly in my chest. How was I supposed to be my true self? The thought of being something other than what I was now was terrifying. Was there another way of being me?

"How, I wonder," Jasmine said, after a short silence, "what you must be feeling right now? I see the stress etched around the corners of your eyes, the taut strain around your mouth. Your eyes are haunted… I have studied emotion ever since I was little. We all must, to a degree, so we know how to appropriately react around others. But I cannot fathom what you must be feeling right now."

I shook my head and swallowed down the knot forming in my throat. I didn't want to talk about my emotions. I didn't want to talk about me at all. She took my hand in hers.

"While I may not know what you are feeling, I do know what you are thinking. My exploration into your mind this morning was very informative. There is no monster living inside of you, Mae. I have seen true monsters. They are men and women who lurk among us all. They wander around looking for their next victim, scheming their next bout of disaster. Some come in a shell of outward beauty. Some reflect the ugliness of their souls. I have touched evil, tasted evil upon my tongue. I have heard it whisper in my ear. Whatever you are, Mae, you are no monster.

"I know you are scared. Fear, it is so… irrational and yet, it is a driving factor in one's life," she mused out loud. "I once could say that I had never known fear. I had never experienced the emotion for a single moment in my long life. But I tasted it today for the first time. I know how illogical it is now. How many times had I thought someone a fool for their outrageous fears or concerns?

"When you left on your trip into town with Rylan, I could feel the effects of your power being sucked away with you. I could tell when the curse began to pull the wool over my eyes. The feelings that had been growing and evolving inside of me since I first met you… the feeling of joy, hope, and wonder… they were blanketed and extinguished at your departure. Just as the last ounce of emotions faded, I tasted fear.

"I was scared that you may never return. I know now that my life has been only half lived. Every moment of my life I was only partially experiencing. If something happened to you while you were gone, would I be stuck in this cold shell of a body for the rest of eternity? What if you were the answer to our prayers, only to be taken from us before we could study your potential and help our race?"

Jasmine paused. She stared down at my hand that she still held. She stared at our physical connection for a long time, her expression thoughtful. Her thumb caressed the back of my hand. She closed her eyes and took a deep breath. When she exhaled, her breath came out as a silent rush of warm air. She repeated her hypnotic breathing for a few moments, letting the silence stretch between us. Finally, her shoulders sagged, and when she opened her eyes, they were twinkling. A small smile teased the corner of her lips. Jasmine let go of my hand and I pulled it into my lap.

"When I felt your arrival just a few minutes ago, I was able to feel relief. It was so strong that I fell to my knees and tears sprang to my eyes. Your fears of being a monster are unfounded, irrational, but also completely understandable now. You are good for our people. A monster cannot bring the peace and comfort you hold within you."

Jasmine leaned forward, her face just inches from mine. I almost recoiled; her closeness surprised me. But there was something in her face, even in the darkness, that I could see. There in her beautiful, flawless features was a vulnerability that seemed misplaced within this confident woman. This stunning woman, who looked like she could rule a kingdom, sat before me with tears shining in her eyes as she embraced the emotions that had been taken from her. She scooted closer to me, still leaning forward. She opened her mouth to say something else when she paused and turned her head to the door behind us.

I looked over my shoulder and saw Rylan reach to slide the door open, Arthur was following right behind him. As he stepped out onto the porch, he flicked on the lights. I blinked as my eyes adjusted to the soft lighting. As Rylan approached, he shot Jasmine a dark look. Oh? What was that about? I glanced over at Jasmine, whose tears had cleared up, and she gave Rylan a pointed glare.

Arthur walked over to the chair that Jasmine had occupied originally and sat down. Rylan came and leaned his hip against the love seat beside me. He crossed his arms over his chest and continued to glare at Jasmine. I looked away from my Guardian and turned my attention to Arthur,

"Arthur, I'm really sorry about this morning. I hope you weren't hurt—"

"Nonsense," Arthur said interrupting me with a wave of his hand, just as Jasmine had. "You did nothing wrong, Mae."

"Do not apologize for anything," Rylan scolded me gently.

"Can I at least apologize for destroying your yard?" I asked with a half-smile.

"What is mine is yours so this is *our* yard," Rylan corrected with a scowl. "And no."

I sighed, okay, he wasn't in the mood for jokes. What was going on now?

"Mae, I would like to discuss what you said during the examination this morning," Arthur said.

I looked over at him to see his jaw clench. Uh-oh, this wasn't going to be good. I gulped and braced myself for news I was sure I didn't want to hear. Had Arthur already discussed this with Rylan? Was that the reason for his bad mood? I nodded when I was sure I was ready to handle the news.

"Rylan says you do not recall what happened," Arthur started, his voice calm.

It was like I was back in that room above his fancy bar all over again. Except this time, he was attempting to help me and not assessing my worth amongst humans and supernatural creatures.

I nodded again.

"Let me explain what occurred the moment Jasmine began her second examination. When you threw Jasmine out of your head, you attacked the three of us. As we were pushed back, away from you, you shouted the same phrase three times. The language you used has not been spoken in over four thousand years. I have studied many languages, possibly all of them, and the language you used… It was only ever spoken in a small village a hundred miles from what is now known as the city of Cairo, in Egypt, by religious disciples who worshipped the gods."

Jasmine let out a hiss, and when I glanced over at her she was scowling deeply, her nostrils flared. I let out the shaky breath I'd been holding and turned back to Arthur. The look of disgust and rage on Jasmine's face was alarming.

"'*Only the worthy can wield His sword*' is the direct translation. The only record of this language was written by a High Disciple in the small village. He wrote a book that spoke of the gods as their saviors. I came to possess the book over a thousand years ago, and it is well hidden now. There are only five other Guardians who knew of this language, who have studied language as I have. There is no way you could have ever learned this language on your own.

"I have discussed this with both Jasmine and Rylan; the three of us agree that somehow the gods are involved with your creation. How or why is still unknown, but with the power that surges through you and the fact that you can speak a language that was created by these religious devotees who worshipped the gods, it is certain that you are somehow a weapon created to be wielded by, or *against*, the gods."

I stared at him, my mouth gaping wide open. Holy. Freaking. Shit. I was the focus of interest for gods that I knew nothing about. What the hell did they want with me, and how were they able to affect me when they were supposed to be in another realm? My heart pounded in my chest; it was the only noise in the room.

"How does this information help?" I asked, breaking the brief silence. My voice was a strained whisper.

"It means the gods are paying attention to this realm again," Jasmine said before Arthur could reply. "Any interest from a god is a bad thing; no matter which deity it is."

"It means that your power does not derive from the witch blood that courses through your veins," Rylan said. "So, to reach out to a coven would be useless. We must learn how the gods control their power, and that, in turn, will help us learn how to manage yours."

"I do not know about that," Arthur said, while he stroked his goatee. He frowned. "She is not a goddess. She is a god's weapon. I do not know if learning the inner workings of a god's magic could help Mae. She is designed to do something; we just do not know what yet. In any case, it is time to alert the others."

"*No*," Rylan snarled. His hands came down onto my shoulders, and his grip was almost painful. "No one else finds out about Mae."

"I agree with Rylan, Arthur. We talked about this last night. While initially I believed we should tell the others, you were right in saying that the more people who know about Mae, the more danger she is in. Especially now. Can you imagine what the others will do when they find out that the gods have somehow placed a weapon here on earth? It will be a death sentence for Mae."

Jasmine sat stiffly in her seat. The coldness in her eyes as she gazed upon Arthur sent a shiver down my spine. I looked over at Arthur who scowled at both Guardians.

"You must think clearly. If the gods are somehow manipulating individuals on this earth, it could mean they are trying to come back. What if Mae is a weapon to open the barrier between the realms? We must prepare for—"

"We can prepare without alerting the others about Mae," Rylan interrupted.

"How do we prove that the gods are attempting to assert themselves in this world again if we do not bring up Mae's involvement?" Arthur demanded with a scowl.

"We will figure it out," Rylan told him, "But I will not put Mae in the middle of a witch hunt because the others will be spooked."

"Spooked?" Arthur repeated, his voice colored in disbelief. He rose from his seat, his eyes turning red. "Spooked? They cannot *feel* spooked. They will be able to see things logically; the gods could be coming, and they will need to be stopped. We must band together to stop the gods before they can cause any damage."

"The others will see a threat to this world in the form of a young woman who is somehow connected to the gods. They will kill her at first sight," Jasmine said as she came to her feet.

"They will get close to her and feel her break the curse over them. No one will want to kill her, not once they get the chance to experience the world with emotion again," Arthur said, waving off Jasmine's words. He turned his attention to Rylan. "They will see her as we do. Rylan, you know I will protect Mae with my life. She may be your mate, but she is *our* miracle to treasure. I would not put her life in jeopardy if I did not think this was important. It is our duty to make sure this world remains safe, and the three of us alone cannot stop the gods if they are planning something."

"There will be no more discussion about this!" Rylan roared angrily. He stood protectively in front of me. "The others cannot find out about Mae. Certainly not now."

"Mae, you have to see how important it is for the others to know about you," Arthur said, ignoring Rylan. "If we tell the others about you, we can prepare properly to prevent the gods from coming back. Think about it. With more people knowing about you, someone may have some insight into how your power works."

Before I could answer, Rylan moved so quickly I almost missed it. Suddenly, Arthur went flying across the deck. He landed in a crouch just before the momentum sent him flying through the glass out into the backyard. Arthur's shirt ripped into shreds as his wings grew from his back. The snarl of anger that rippled from his throat was horrifying, and I cringed back in my seat. Arthur leaped forward and swung a fist at Rylan who ducked. As Rylan lunged to attack again, I was finally able to react. I leaped to my feet and took a step forward, but before I got anywhere, Jasmine grabbed me and pulled me back.

"You will get hurt if you intervene."

I shrugged off her hand.

"*Enough!*" I yelled.

The entire room shook. The lightbulbs above us shattered, and several of the remaining glass panels around us cracked. Both men froze but continued to glare at each other. I moved forward, out of reach of Jasmine, and stepped between the two men.

"This is getting us nowhere," I said. "You two need to quit this shit. Since this is about me, I get the final say with what we will or will not do, and right now I'm not deciding anything."

With that, I turned and stormed out of the patio and back into the house. I headed to my room. Once there, I slammed the door shut and stood enveloped in silence. The Guardians were worried about the future and what the gods had in store for this realm. I was worried about what the gods had done to me. With a deep breath, I walked over to my bed and threw myself on top of the comforter. I grabbed my phone and set several alarms. I wasn't sure I wanted Rylan in my bed tonight, so I had to make the necessary precautions. With a sigh, I put my face in one of the many pillows and moaned. Why was my life so crazy now? Luckily, despite the news that I could be a weapon for the gods, the day's events had exhausted me, and I was asleep before I could worry too much.

I opened my eyes slowly, my mind foggy with sleep. It was dark in my room and silent, but something had woken me up. My alarm? No, it would still be going off, and I would have known right away. I blinked a few times and sat up. My gaze swept across the room and landed on the figure sitting in one of the armchairs on the other side of the room. I almost screamed. But at the last moment, I slapped my hand over my mouth. My eyes adjusted, and I realized it was Rylan sitting there, facing the dark fireplace. My heart rate, which had taken off in fear, settled back to a normal pace.

"Rylan?" I called out softly. I saw his head turn towards my voice. "Rylan, are you alright?"

He did not answer right away. His silence made me frown. Something must be wrong. Why didn't he just come to bed? I slipped out of bed, walked over to where he sat, and stopped in front of him.

"Did I wake you?" he asked, his voice rough.

"No, I think my alarms are about to go off any minute, and my body knew," I assured him. "Why don't you come to bed?"

"I will shortly. You should go back to sleep."

"What's wrong?"

"Nothing."

I rolled my eyes. How many times had I answered the same question with the same answer knowing it was a lie? I moved and sat down on his lap, surprising us both. Yes, I was angry with him for overreacting earlier, but I found myself craving his touch. I heard his swift intake of air, and my cheeks warmed at my boldness.

"What's *wrong*, Rylan?"

He leaned his head forward, and his arms came around my waist and pulled me closer.

"I do not want to burden you with more problems."

"If you try to shoulder every problem, you'll be crushed. Let me take some of the load," I offered. Rylan didn't answer right away. Instead, he let the silence stretch and thicken between us. I sat on his lap and patiently waited. Was this about Arthur? About the gods? What was bothering him so much?

Finally, Rylan sighed and said, "We received word that a fellow Guardian has passed on... without his mate."

I gasped as my heart twisted in my chest. Rylan had told me that when a Guardian died without his mate they ceased to exist. What had happened?

"Oh, Rylan, I'm so sorry. Did you know him?"

Rylan didn't answer right away again. I opened my mouth to ask him again, but he sighed again and said, "Yes, and you did, too. It was Zein, the Guardian you met the day Arthur took you."

I gasped in surprise.

"We grew up together," he explained. "He was the child of my parents' best friends. Finding your mate is nearly impossible as a Guardian, but having a child... it is even more difficult.

When my parents gave birth to me and their friends had given birth to Zein, there was great joy amongst the Guardians… the ones with mates at least. Those of us who were born after the time of the gods have emotions from birth until their twentieth year when they begin to fade. I can remember having fun and getting into much trouble with Zein as we grew up. We shared many good times together, and now, thanks to you, I can look back fondly on those moments.

"When our emotions faded, so did our friendship. We respected each other, spoke from time to time, but relationships do not exist without emotions. I confess, it has been quite a while since I have thought of Zein, but now that I have you, that I have emotions, I am… distraught that I let a good friendship slip by. If we still spoke to one another, maybe he would still be here now.

"Long ago, Arthur and I had formed an alliance when we began working with one another. It was important for both of us to build the grand empire we have now and to maintain it. Not only was it to support ourselves, other Guardians, and the other species of this world, but it was also a way to keep an eye on one another. With Guardians taking their lives often now, we ensured neither of us could take our lives, not with so much at stake. I should have done the same with Zein. Instead, I left him to deal with his own demons, and he finally succumbed to them." Rylan ran a hand down his face. "Mae…I am not used to feeling so much, and what I feel now it is… difficult to express."

My heart broke. I wrapped my arms around his neck and pressed my lips gently against his forehead.

"You cannot stop someone from taking their life if that is their decision," I told him, knowing full well the truth behind my words. No one could have stopped me back in my darkest hours. Not a damn soul. "It's not your fault."

"My heart is in disagreement."

I held him tighter. What could I do or say to ease his struggling? Time would have to heal this wound. I planted another soft kiss on his forehead. A few minutes went by without either of us saying a word. When Rylan did speak again, I could hear a different tone in his voice.

"I am glad you are here with me," he said. He turned his head to kiss my jawline. "If it were not for you, I would be unable to grieve for a good man." He kissed me again, and his arms tightened around me. "Zein deserves to have people grieve for him."

I turned my head to meet his lips as he leaned forward. I could feel a difference in this kiss. There was a sense of longing and sadness behind it. My heart crumbled into pieces. This strong, fearless man was quietly suffering. Rylan deepened the kiss, and I opened my mouth to invite him in. My body came to life as his tongue slid into my mouth. I ran my fingers through his hair, and I pressed myself against him. If I could kiss away his pain, I would. If I could take it and make it mine so he would no longer suffer, I would. He moaned and tightened his hold around me. All day my body had ached for his, and now the heat flared back up tenfold.

I broke the kiss and shimmied off his lap. I knew what he needed. He needed me. My body. He needed to lose himself inside me. I offered my hand to help him up, and he took it without hesitation. As he rose, he towered over me and still seemed to climb in height. My mouth watered in anticipation of what was to come. I led him over to the bed and then slipped off my nightshirt and panties. I grabbed the hem of his shirt and tried to peel it off him, but he was much too tall for me to pull it over his head. I giggled as he removed the rest of his shirt. I tugged at the button of his jeans, and when it popped open, I knelt to pull them all the way to his ankles.

From this angle, on my knees, I stared up at him and met his gaze. My gaze traveled to his manhood. His member was thick, pulsating, and ready; I had the strongest desire to taste him just as he had with me this morning. Without pause, I took him in my mouth. It was my first time doing something like this, and it was a heady sensation. I heard his sharp intake of breath, and the moan that followed vibrated throughout his body. His velvety skin felt smooth against my tongue, and as I circled the head of his dick with my tongue, I tasted a salty drop of cum.

The sheer size of him made it impossible for me to take him all the way into my mouth without choking myself. But I took him deep into my throat and suckled, licked, and lapped at him. His hands came down to my head, and his fingers dug into my curls. I could hear his breathing increase, and he leaned his hips forward, wanting more. It was encouraging since I had no idea what I was doing. As I devoured him, I had an idea. I reached forward with one hand and gently cupped his warm balls. Rylan gasped. I looked up at him and found him staring down at me. His glowing red eyes were pinned onto my face.

Emboldened by his response, I sucked harder and moved my head up and down on his cock faster. Another moan, louder this time, escaped passed Rylan's lips. I continued to gently roll his balls in my hand, and I could feel as they began to tighten and rise up to his body.

"Enough," Rylan commanded, his voice strained. I didn't stop; I could feel his body begin to tremble with the first wave of his orgasm. Did he think I would want to miss this moment? "Mae," he choked out.

I smiled as I felt his resolve cave, and he relaxed into his orgasm. I felt the first rope of cum hit the back of my throat, followed by several more. I swallowed it without hesitation. His fingers tightened in my hair, and he leaned into me as he enjoyed the moment. When I was sure he was done, I pulled my mouth away from him.

I rose from the kneeling position. Before I was standing straight, Rylan hooked his hands under my arms, picked me up, and tossed me onto the bed. I gasped and watched as Rylan stood, staring at me from the foot of the bed. His shoulders rose and fell as he tried to catch his breath. I wanted to give him more. My body was hot, my skin felt too tight, and there was a dampness in between my legs. Knowing that I was able to make him fall apart was so hot. I wanted more. I wanted him to bury himself in me and forget his worries.

"Rylan, come here," I said, my voice sounded breathless.

He did not hesitate. He climbed into bed and pinned me under his body. His mouth came down and kissed mine. He didn't seem to care that he could taste himself. His hands slid down my body. He cupped my breasts and teased my nipples with his thumbs. They hardened under his touch. His mouth pulled away from mine, and he leaned down to take one of my nipples into his mouth. He sucked and teased while his other hand continued to play with my other nipple. I bit my bottom lip to keep from crying out, but I couldn't stop the groan that escaped. His mouth moved away from my nipple, and he leaned down to kiss my navel.

His mouth came back up to mine, and we kissed deeply. The one hand still playing with my nipple left my breast and traveled down my stomach and further still. His fingers trailed down between my legs, and I gasped when he caressed my most intimate spot. I moaned when he slowly dipped one finger into me. I shifted my legs wider for him. His finger slowly moved in and out while his tongue penetrated my mouth. He added a second finger, and my body shook. He pressed his thumb on my clit and began a circular motion which caused the world around us to fall away as the pleasure increased. I arched my hips forward and ground against his hand as the sensation began to be too much. I was so close, any moment I would…

Suddenly his hand disappeared, and I cried out in desperation. He positioned himself over me, and his fingers were replaced with his manhood. He was ready again already? Oh, thank goodness! I choked on the pleasure as he stretched me and filled me with his erection. I arched into him, wanting all of him. He filled every inch of me until it felt like we were one. There was no Mae and Rylan, one simply became the other. When he was completely inside of me, he paused, giving me a chance to adjust, but I didn't need it. Pinned under him, I was able to shift my hips forward. I wrapped my legs around his torso and pulled him as close to me as possible. He moved then, in and out. His strokes were much slower than this morning.

He was deliberately prolonging the intimacy between us. I could feel his need to cherish the moment. I kissed his shoulders, his biceps, neck, and chin. Whatever my lips could reach, I planted a kiss in each spot. I gripped him tighter with my legs, wanting him closer. Deeper. I ran my fingers down his back and I grabbed his butt. Oh, God, was it so hard and perfect. My pleasure was building to an all-time high, and I wouldn't last much longer. But I had to fight it; this wasn't for me. I wanted Rylan to know that I was here for him. He needed to lose himself, and I was there for him.

Those longs strokes became faster and harder. I fought the pleasure, but the more I struggled to resist, the more pleasure I felt. I could feel his release was near, and I prayed I could hold on just long enough for him to finish. Then, Rylan's lips planted feathery kisses along the side of my neck. Just knowing those teeth were so close brought me over the edge. Instead of crying out, I bit Rylan's shoulder, trying to muffle my cries. The moment my teeth pressed against his skin, Rylan's body shuddered hard, and he threw back his head and roared. I could feel his orgasm chasing mine, and it set me off again. This time I couldn't help but cry out.

Rylan's body lit up as my power was set free. In the darkness, I could see every vein in his body absorb the foreign power and begin to glow. His eyes changed from glowing red to bright violet. His whole body shuddered again. I reached up and cupped his face, concerned that this time would be different, that he would get hurt, but he leaned down and kissed me passionately. I untangled my legs from around his waist, and he withdrew from me. He collapsed onto the bed next to me, and I turned to look at him.

When our gazes met, I scooted closer to him and reached down to grab his hand, intertwining our fingers. The stark emotion on his face, the awe and wonder as he gazed at me, was overwhelming. I tucked my head against his arm; I didn't deserve that look. Not when I could be a weapon for the gods.

For a while, we lay there in comfortable silence. My heart rate came back down, and my breathing returned to normal. I could feel exhaustion beating at the edges of my consciousness.

"I'm sorry, Rylan, about Zein," I whispered, knowing he could hear me.

"It is not your fault."

I bit my bottom lip and hesitated as I thought about what I was about to say. When I was sure I meant it, that I could commit to what I was about to offer. I propped myself up on my elbow to look at Rylan's face.

"It will be my fault next time. I can't stay hidden from other Guardians if I know that I can help them. From now on, if someone else takes their life, that's on me. We need to let the other Guardians know about me."

Now that my eyes had adjusted to the darkness, I could see the dark scowl on his face. His eyes began to glow again; they appeared more maroon this time than red, thanks to a fresh dose of my power running through him.

"We are not discussing this," he snapped.

I frowned; I didn't want to upset him. That hadn't been my intention at all by offering to meet the other Guardians. Instead of responding, I looked away from him. If he was so against it, I wouldn't fight it. At least not right now. I traced the muscles along his torso with my fingertips, letting my mind wander. Sleep was closing in. When I was too tired to keep my head up, I finally laid it on Rylan's stomach and allowed my eyes to drift shut.

"Mae?"

Rylan's voice pulled me back from the brink of sleep.

"Hm?"

"I did not mean to be sharp with you."

I felt his hand stroke the top of my head. I hummed my understanding, too tired to speak.

"The danger to you far outweighs any benefit you may offer to the other Guardians," he said. "I will not put you in harm's way, even if that means my species goes extinct."

My body stiffened in disgust. Instantly, I was awake. I sat up and glared at him.

"I can't believe you would say that. You'd let me carry the knowledge that I helped kill off an entire race of people because of the possible danger to me?" I shook my head, trying to shake off the feeling of horror as I thought about hundreds of good people dying because I was afraid of what they might do to me. My stomach knotted so painfully that I pressed my hand against it to try to ease the tension. "Rylan, I have tried to take my own life because I am afraid to kill just *one* person with my power. Now you're telling me that I could save people, but you won't let me. I couldn't live in this world knowing that people were dying, and I could have prevented it."

Rylan stared at my face; his jaw clenched tight. His body had tensed, and his eyes began to glow brighter. Neither of us looked away. Finally, Rylan sighed. His body relaxed and his jaw loosened.

"It is not your burden to shoulder."

"Actually, it is," I snapped. "While I may not be consciously doing something, my presence can ease the burden of this curse."

I took a deep breath to rein back my temper. I could feel my power vibrating inside of me. Rylan must be keeping it in check since there was no external evidence I was struggling.

"While our race is bound by honor, if other Guardians found out about you, some would covet you. A few might go as far as to take you from me. We talked about what would happen if another were to drink your blood. It would mean your death or having another control your power. If news of your existence gets to the other Guardians, it would spread to other supernatural creatures. Our enemies would try to get to you, and they would do unspeakable things to you to defeat our race. If word somehow got to the gods about you, the world could end as they try to extinguish your life to keep us Guardians cursed forever. There is too much at stake. I will not let anything happen to you. You have no idea what you mean to me, Mae." His hand came up and cupped my cheek. "Please, do not ask me to put you in harm's way."

The way his voice softened, his vulnerability exposed for me to see, I felt my defenses drop. He was worried about me. His emotions were clouding his better judgment right now. With news of his friend's death and being around his mate, I was sure there were a lot of emotions boiling up under his skin. I'd let it drop, for now.

"I am beginning to understand how much I mean to you," I admitted. With a sigh, I continued, "And you are starting to mean a lot to me, too. I can't see my future without you now." I shook my head at the absurdity. How had this happened so fast? "Look, we don't have to make any decisions tonight. Let's just think about it for a while. I see your side. Please try to see mine, okay?"

Rylan nodded once although his jaw ticked again. At least he was willing to put this aside for the time being. This was obviously going to be a tough sell for him. But seeing the struggle Rylan was having after hearing about the loss of his childhood friend, I knew that I truly had no choice in the matter. Somehow, I was tied to the gods and that was a very bad thing. Jasmine had promised she hadn't seen evil in me, but maybe whatever darkness my power brought hadn't evolved yet? If that was the case, I would do whatever good I could until time ran out. One of those good acts would be to help lift this curse upon the protectors of this world.

I lay back down, and Rylan pulled me close to his body. It took longer this time to drift off to sleep. My mind raced with all the horrible things Rylan had mentioned. I fought my fear with the certainty that by coming out and meeting the others, I would be helping them. With Rylan stroking my hair and with the steady rise and fall of his chest under my cheek, finally, I succumbed to sleep.

Chapter Seventeen

When I awoke, the sunlight was just trickling through the French doors. My heart fluttered, and my body felt restless. I sat up and looked down at Rylan. He was laying on his stomach, the sheet pulled down far enough for me to catch a glimpse of that glorious butt. The urge to lean down and bite it was strong, but I didn't want to wake him. I resisted… for now. Instead, I eased myself out of the bed and headed to the bathroom where I brushed my teeth and washed my face. I felt strung up and tense. I had some pent-up energy that needed to be released, and for once, it didn't have anything to do with my power. While sex might be off the table for a few hours while Rylan slept, there were other ways to burn off some steam.

In the closet, I found workout clothes that were the perfect size. This was insane that Rylan had ordered all these clothes in my size. I shook my head as I changed into my workout gear. To my surprise, there was even a pair of brand new sneakers on one of the shelves full of shoes. I dug into my camping bag and found my Bluetooth speaker. I left the closet, grabbed my phone off the nightstand, and tiptoed out of the room.

Downstairs was empty. I wasn't sure if anyone else was up yet and simply busy doing other things or if they were still asleep. I passed through the kitchen down the hallway and entered the large gym. Carefully, I shut the door behind me, and I looked around the fully equipped gym. Just before my power had emerged, I was in a gym six days a week for at least three hours a day training. After every session, I left deliciously sore and tired, pumped and eager for more. I needed that feeling today. With a grin, I headed over to the treadmill.

An hour later my knuckles were raw and bleeding, my clothes were sweat soaked, and my ears were ringing from the echoing Bluetooth device blaring hardcore rap. I had made my way around the gym. I had started with fifteen minutes on the treadmill to warm up, lifted a few weights and was now on my way to tumbling my imaginary opponent via the punching bag. Even though my lungs were heaving, sweat burned my eyes, and my messy bun was more knot than bun at this point, I felt amazing. I definitely noticed I had been out of the game for a while, but the proper footing, strategic punches, and defensive stances were all slowly coming back to me. A quick adjustment here, a little shift there. If I did this every day like before, I could be unstoppable.

Just as I came into a defensive stance after decking out a right hook, the music came to a sudden stop. I dropped my fists and turned around to see what had happened. Leaning against the door with his arms crossed over his chest, Rylan was smiling warmly at me. He was shirtless, showing off that amazing six-pack, and his pajama pants hung low on his hips so I could see that panty dampening v-line. His blond hair was tousled, and a five o'clock shadow was beginning to show. I used the back of my arm to wipe away the sweat, and I grinned at him.

"Did you come in here for some breakfast?" I teased, tilting my head to one side as an invitation.

My eyes trailed down his body, and I felt desire flare up hard and fast. Rylan's answering grin was spectacular. What little breath I had was stolen from me. He pushed away from the door and sauntered over to me.

"Hm… I am feeling famished."

I could see the answering desire in his gaze, and my mouth watered for him. When he was just a few feet away, I put my hand up to stop him. He paused, raising a brow.

"Well, this morning you have to work for your breakfast."

I raised my fists to a fight stance and shifted my feet. His grin turned into a smirk.

"It would not be a fair fight."

"Oh, I don't know. Why don't you give me a try—?"

Before I knew what happened, my chest was pinned up against the large floor to ceiling mirror hung along one wall of the gym. I stared up at Rylan's reflection, panting in surprise. He had my wrists pinned high above me in one of his hands, and the other in the middle of my back so I couldn't move. His smug smile was devilishly gorgeous. My body went white hot. He leaned down and inhaled my scent.

"Breakfast is my favorite meal of the day. I'm glad that was not too hard," he said. "Keep your hands against the mirror."

He waited until I nodded before letting go of me. Both of his hands trailed down my sides. My sweat didn't seem to bother him. His fingers reached the waistband of my compression shorts, and he gripped it. I thought he might to tear the fabric. Instead, he pulled my shorts down, along with my underwear. He helped me step out of them and then tossed them aside. I watched in the mirror as his face shifted. His eyes, sank in and turned red, his cheeks hollowed, and his fangs lengthened and peeked through his lips. He reached for my sports bra and helped me out of it. When it was off, he pushed me against the mirror again. Our gaze met, and my body quivered with anticipation.

Behind Rylan, his wings grew from his back, and he spread them wide apart. His muscles went taut. He took one step towards me, pressing his pelvis against my lower back. I could feel his hardness. He grabbed my waist with his hands, his fingers digging deep into my skin. My breath caught in my throat.

"Spread your legs," he commanded.

The playfulness had disappeared from his expression. He was all business now. I did as I was told, excited for what was about to come. One hand left my hip, and his finger lightly trailed down my back, over my butt, and made his way in between my legs. I gasped as he caressed my intimate spot. Our gaze never faltered as he sunk his fingers inside of me. I groaned and felt myself dampen even more. My body squeezed his fingers as they sunk deep.

"Hm… breakfast is ready."

His fingers moved, caressing me. I groaned again but refused to look away from the challenge in Rylan's gaze. I leaned into his hand and spread my legs further apart. He leaned down and kissed my shoulders, gently bit my earlobes, all the while stroking me. I began to gasp as my release got closer. I was so close, oh God… The feeling stopped abruptly when Rylan removed his fingers. I cried out in frustration. Staring at his reflection, I watched as he brought his wet fingers up to his mouth and sucked on them. My mouth dropped in surprise. He grinned at my reaction.

"Delicious."

He leaned down and planted a kiss on the back of my neck. Then, he planted one on both sides of my neck. His lips lingered right above my neck, and my heart raced as I watched in the mirror as his fangs lengthened further. My breathing became heavier, my chest rising and falling quickly. I licked my dry lips and waited. He watched my reaction, and I saw his wicked smile. He pulled his fangs away and reached down to release his thick cock from his pajama bottoms. He moved so his tip sat right at my entrance.

I leaned back and impaled myself against him. I finally broke eye contact as I closed my eyes and savored the feel of him filling me. Rylan growled, and I felt the air move around us as his wings shifted. When he was all the way inside me, he stopped. I tried to move my hips forward, and back but he grabbed both of my hips, effectively stopping me.

"Open your eyes," he commanded. I opened them and stared up at his reflection feeling desperate for him to start moving. My body clenched down on him trying to provide its own friction. "I want you to watch yourself cum."

I hesitated. He may find my orgasm attractive, but I knew that my power was close to the surface when we had sex. I had noticed the violet glow under my skin as my veins lit up. I hated in the mirror when my power was near, I hated the monster. I didn't necessarily want to see the monster enjoying herself. I stared at his reflection in the mirror for a moment before reluctantly looking into my own eyes. The monster was there, staring back at me, as I knew she would be.

Rylan moved then. He pulled back until he was almost out and then slammed back into me. I screamed with pleasure. My reservations at seeing the monster vanished as pleasure overrode my insecurities. The veins in my arms began to glow. Rylan didn't pause; he repeated the motion of pulling almost all the way out before thrusting himself back inside me. I cried out again, and the glow continued up my arms and flared out like lightning across my chest and down my stomach. Rylan kept administrating those hard thrusts, picking up speed. I could feel him getting harder inside of me. The sensation I was feeling was becoming too intense. I forced myself to keep my eyes open, but it was a struggle. Over and over he continued, hitting just the right spot. I was about to fall apart.

Rylan moved one hand from my waist, reached around, and his finger circled my clit. My breath caught in my throat as pleasure erupted from between my legs. My world exploded around me. I screamed as I came hard and fast. The pleasure was so intense, and it only intensified as I watched myself come apart in the mirror. I watched as my power flared out, encompassing Rylan. His whole body shuddered as he shouldered the energy that hit him. I could see his veins mimic the same violet glow as mine as I continued to convulse around him.

He continued to pound away, and after a few more strokes his release followed mine. He threw back his head and roared.

I watched in amazement at the sheer ecstasy on his face. Before I knew what was happening, he leaned over me and sank his teeth into my neck. I screamed as another orgasm struck me unexpectedly. My body squeezed his with such force I was afraid I was going to snap his dick off. My orgasm didn't subside right away. Instead, it rippled through me, and I cherished each wave as it washed over me.

A haze distorted my vision, and my mouth began to water. Rylan withdrew from my body, and I turned to him. Rylan brought his hand up, and raked a nail across his chest, causing a thin bloody line to appear. Rylan's other hand came up, gently cradling the back of my head, and pulled me close. There was no struggle. I went willingly. I lapped at the bloody line across his chest. The warm liquid touched my tongue, and I moaned.

I blinked slowly, and when I opened my eyes again, the cut across Rylan's chest was gone. My vision cleared. I blinked again, trying to process what had happened. I looked up into Rylan's face, and he dipped low to kiss my lips. It was a short kiss, but it did the job; I was momentarily distracted.

"I do believe that was the best breakfast I have ever had," he murmured.

I chuckled and stepped away from him. "You should have waited until after I took a shower."

"Hm, I will enjoy you any way I can," he said with a cocky half-smile. "Speaking of food, you need to eat."

I wiggled my brows suggestively as I stared down at his semi-erect package.

Rylan laughed. "Real food."

He stepped away from me and picked up my sweaty gym clothes. I watched as his muscles rippled as he moved. My body warmed again. I grabbed my clothes from his hands and grimaced – putting back on gross clothes did not seem all that appealing.

"The others are engaged elsewhere. We will not be seen," Rylan said as he opened the door with a mischievous smile. He looked so carefree. I returned his grin before rushing out the door and through the house, naked. I felt so naughty, like a teenager sneaking around their parents' house hoping not to get caught.

Thirty minutes later, I stepped out of the shower and got dressed. Rylan had left me to get ready for the morning, so I had time to myself. My body felt well-worn and tired; it was wonderful. Humming to myself, I left my room and headed downstairs where Rylan was busy in the kitchen. He stood over the stove, scrambling up some eggs in one pan and bacon in another. It was so odd to see such a powerful individual doing something so… menial. As I approached him, the smile tugging at the corners of my mouth fell. He had the phone to his ear, and the look on his face was grim.

"They can come here. Tonight," Rylan said. He gazed at me, his eyes red. I could see a slight violet glow in some of the veins in his arms and running up his neck. "I will see you shortly." He hung up the phone.

"What's wrong?"

"I do not want you to worry. The others and I will handle this," Rylan said, blowing off my question. He turned his attention back to my breakfast. I reached over and turned off both burners.

"Rylan." I tried to remain calm. "Something's wrong. Tell me what's going on. Please."

Rylan turned his whole body to me and crossed his arms over his bare chest. His expression gave nothing away. "There is no need to work yourself up, Mae."

"Don't hide things from me. I've told you before: I would rather know what's going on than let my mind go crazy with the possibilities. That's a hundred times worse."

"Do you trust me?"

"Yes."

I didn't hesitate. The answer was the truth and that shook me. I had only known Rylan for a few days, and yet here I was, trusting him. He was the only person I had let get this close to me in years. Rylan's expression softened at my admission. He reached out and put his hands on my shoulders.

"Thank you, Mae. Know that by withholding information from you, I may provide you with some reprieve for a while. I only want you to be safe and happy."

"I don't want to be blindsided by whoever is coming over tonight."

Rylan sighed. The muscle in his jaw twitched, and he studied my face for a long time before he finally answered: "Seven Supremes had the same vision last night and are concerned about what they saw. They want to talk to us about it."

"What are Supremes, and what did they see? Did they tell you?"

"A Supreme is the leader of a witch's coven and is the most powerful witch amongst them," Rylan explained patiently. "The vision was of a witch claiming she was looking for her child."

"Why would they come here to see you?"

"Guardians are the protectors of the supernatural world. The witches feel the vision was ominous, so they are coming to us to help resolve the issue. They are coming here because five of the seven have covens in neighboring states; we are the closest Guardians to voice their concerns to."

"So, why not tell me this from the start? Because I'm not a Guardian?"

"No, it is not that. You are my mate, which allows you to be privy to Guardian knowledge," Rylan said with a shake of his head. He paused, seeming to choose his words carefully. "The vision was of a witch who had been long thought to be dead; this is a red flag. The dead cannot reach out to those living, only the living can make the connection to the dead. Even then, they have to be newly deceased. The second red flag is this morning Darla, the child we met yesterday, and her mother Claire came forth to their Supreme and said that for quite some time a witch had been visiting Darla looking for her child. Last night, the witch had finally given Darla the name of her missing daughter."

His solemn stare told me all I needed to know. I knew it was my name. That had to be the case, or Rylan wouldn't have kept this from me. But I wasn't a missing child. I had been loved by Wilfred and Martha my whole life. There were adoption papers, albeit from a sketchy adoption agency, but still, that had to mean something… right? The conversation with Darla, while brief, floated back to me.

She's looking for you, you know.

A chill ran down my spine. I pulled my gaze from Rylan's face. Why couldn't we have one full day of being worry-free? Trying to give myself a moment to compose myself, I leaned forward and turned both burners back on.

"A vision can be skewed, unreliable, or interpreted wrongly," Rylan said softly. "That is why I agreed for them to come here. We will discuss what they have seen and go from there. It could mean nothing. And Darla is a child; she may misinterpret a dream as a vision."

I didn't say anything. Darla knew who I was, despite being blind, and knew to tell me that someone was looking for me. It wasn't a dream. I knew that deep down in my heart. I didn't know how to feel about the seven Supremes, but my gut was telling me this was all connected. Until we heard from the witches, I would force myself to remain calm. I moved, effectively pushing Rylan out of the way to take over cooking. I needed to do something. Rylan stood behind me and placed his hands on my shoulders.

"Do not fret, Mae."

"No fretting here," I lied.

Rylan leaned down and kissed the side of my temple. He ran his nose through my damp curly hair, and as he did, his hands slid from my shoulders down my sides. His arms snaked around me from behind and wrapped around my waist. I was encased in his strong, powerful arms. My back pressed against a solid, warm chest. Within this intimate embrace, I felt safe, and some of my worries eased. I leaned my head back so I could look up at him. The way he towered over me gave him the advantage to lean his head down and kiss my lips with ease.

I turned my attention back to cooking breakfast, but I savored the feel of being in his arms. When I was done, Rylan grabbed a plate for me to put my breakfast on, and I served myself. I sat down at the island, where Rylan joined me, and I ate in silence. My body grew hot under Rylan's hand that sat high on my thigh as I ate. I tried to push away the growing desire. I had other things to deal with. After I was done eating, I pushed my plate away and propped my elbow on the counter and placed my cheek in my hand. I looked over at Rylan.

"Can I ask you something?"

"Of course."

"I drank your blood for the second time. Why am I not freaking out about that?"

My question was clearly not one he expected. He chuckled in amusement and raised his hand to graze my cheek with his knuckles.

"When mates are going through the Joining, both will go into a trance-like state. I believe this happens so both are more open-minded about what needs to happen for the Joining to be completed. Your mind would recoil from drinking blood since it is not something you would normally do, but it must happen. It takes three blood exchanges to complete the bond that will tie our souls together for eternity."

"Will I always feel the need to drink your blood?"

"You are more than welcome to drink from me," Rylan said with a shrug. "But after our third blood exchange, the Joining will be completed, and you will not fall under the trance or have the desire."

Mentally, I sighed in relief.

"You get a piece of me when you drink my blood," I pointed out. "I can see my power running through you now. What about me? Will I grow, like, fangs or wings soon?"

Rylan chuckled again. It was deep and sultry.

"No, it does not happen like that," he assured me. "But there will be minor changes you should be aware of. We will be able to communicate telepathically with each other. I am told it is a powerful and intimate channel between mates that no one can intercept."

I raised a brow.

"Are you telling me that I'll get to hear all your dirty secrets? You better spill everything now before I start digging around," I teased.

"I hide nothing from you. Whatever you want to know, I will share it with you," Rylan said with a warm smile. "Your senses will become heightened as well. Your hearing will get better; your sense of smell and taste will change. It will be disorienting for a while until you get used to it."

I nodded.

"Then, we will become one," his voice softened. His smile widened as he thought of our future together. Yes, we would be tied together, but for how long? Jasmine had promised a short life with my power being what it was. Something I had already figured out. How much time would we get together before my body couldn't take this anymore? I looked away from Rylan.

"Mae," he said.

I turned my attention back to the Guardian. He surprised me by tugging at my hand, pulling me off my stool, and onto his lap. Without missing a beat, I wrapped my arms around his neck. His arms came around my waist and held me tight against him. I felt so safe in his arms that my worries subsided. Before he could say anything, I kissed him. His answering kiss was passionate and filled with hope for the future. At least one of us had it. Speaking of the future, in just a few days my classes would be starting. I wasn't going to let my fear of my uncertain future get in the way of getting my degree.

"I need to order my textbooks," I murmured against his lips. I pulled my head away so I could look at him. "Do I need to get anything ready for your guests tonight? Put clean sheets on the guest beds? I can make something for dinner."

"They are not going to be staying here. We will make the necessary accommodations for them in town," Rylan said dismissively. I nodded and slid off his lap.

"Since I technically did more of the cooking, you have dish duty," I said with a smirk and skipped out of the kitchen before he could object.

For the next hour, I kept myself busy. I shopped for school textbooks, checked that all my classes were paid for, and then bought a few necessary items online. I had forgotten all about my classes and the excitement for them to start overshadowed the dread that seemed to continuously loom over my head.

Once I received the email that my items were confirmed and getting ready to ship, I put on shoes, slipped out of the house, and headed into the woods. The threat of demons diminished now that I knew witches were having visions of me. Huh, who knew that witches would trump demons in my book of fears?

It took me a while, but I finally found the pond I had discovered my first day here. Before I walked up to the water, I scanned the trees, making sure there was nothing there that could kill me. When I felt sure I was alone, I walked over and sat on the edge of the water. I brought my knees up to my chest and wrapped my arms around them, making myself as small as possible. The silence around me was soothing, the lapping of the water hypnotic. I forced myself to not think of what I would learn tonight from the witches. I simply wanted to enjoy the here and now.

When I finally stood to head back to the house, I felt lighter. I took slow, deep breaths, drinking in the clean air and letting the peace and quiet seep into my soul as I walked back to the house. As I broke through the line of trees and walked around the large crater I had created in the backyard the day before, I caught sight of Arthur. He circled leisurely over the house, once, twice, and on the third circle he landed on the roof, his black feathered wings outstretched behind him. I paused, watching the Guardian as he lifted his head towards the sun, and a smile splayed across his face. He stretched his wings out wider and then he leaped off the roof. He did a backflip and landed in a crouch facing me. He straightened and grinned.

"Pretty cool. Maybe I'll give it a try," I said walking up to him with an answering smile. Arthur's wings retracted into his back as he waited for me to approach.

"That is probably not a smart decision," Arthur said with a grin.

"Rylan said you and Jasmine were out this morning. Did you go shopping or something?"

Arthur chuckled darkly.

"No, we were grabbing breakfast."

I stared at him in surprise as I registered what that meant.

"Who did you gnaw on this morning? A farmer or a townie?"

Arthur threw back his head and laughed. "I enjoy a townie. They are fatter, much tastier than a farmer."

I laughed.

Arthur stepped closer to me, his face suddenly serious. "Mae, I want to apologize for last night. My emotions got the better of me, and I was being thoughtless. You are right; you should decide if or when we tell the other Guardians."

"It's alright, Arthur. Don't sweat it. I know emotions are new to you, and I'm sure that fear and worry about the gods' interest in me is hard to control."

Behind Arthur, Jasmine and Rylan stepped out from the enclosure and walked over to us. I saw the shudder run through Jasmine as she approached, and her mouth curled into a smile.

"Mae, I had wondered where you went. I was just telling Rylan how I wanted to fly," Jasmine said coming up to me with a smile. "I want to enjoy it as I used to as a little girl. I used to race my sister and win every time."

"Want to see if you would still win?" Arthur asked her with a smirk.

Jasmine turned to him and raised a brow. "Careful, old man, I would not want to hurt your pride."

Arthur's wings stretched behind him. Jasmine pulled off her blouse and tossed it to the ground. Her camisole was a beautiful pink that matched her cheeks. Rylan dropped his arm from my shoulders and pulled off his shirt.

"'Old man'?" Arthur repeated incredulously. "I believe I am younger than you."

Jasmine laughed, and as she did thick, black-feathered wings grew from in between her shoulder blades and opened wide. I marveled at the beautiful wings. Would I ever get used to seeing these Guardians in their true form? I hoped not; they were a magical sight. Jasmine was off the ground with a speed I didn't know was possible.

Arthur followed right after her wearing a grin that stretched ear to ear. I watched them speed upwards, towards the blazing sun, with my mouth open in awe. Without warning, Rylan scooped me up and we were airborne. I wrapped my arms around Rylan's neck as we sped towards the other two Guardians who were still ascending. The other times Rylan and I had flown it had been a leisurely pace, drifting here and there. This time, it was completely different. It was like I was holding onto a speeding bullet. The wind whipped passed me, and my eyes watered. The exhilaration of the speed had me grinning like a fool.

And so, we flew. In the sky, the Guardians wove between each other at alarming speeds. I could feel the soft buzz of the telepathic communication between them. There was constant laughter as they ribbed at each other. The heady sensation of flying was contagious. I couldn't stop grinning as I enjoyed the freedom that came with a mate who had wings. At one point, I watched in awe as Jasmine came to a complete stop, her wings straight out on either side. She stretched out her arms above her, and she soaked in the sunlight. She was an angel. Out of nowhere, Arthur rushed her, coming up from underneath. He slammed into her, and they toppled downwards in a spiral.

My gasp was drowned out by Rylan's laughter. I watched in awe as Jasmine disengaged from Arthur only to come up around him and latch onto his back, her teeth against his neck. Arthur's laughter drifted up to us, and I relaxed. We flew for over an hour. Sometimes it was a leisurely pace; sometimes Rylan would shoot upwards or forward as if we were escaping hell.

Eventually, we headed back towards the house. We all drifted lazily through the air. Arthur and Jasmine were just ahead of us, talking out loud with one another. Rylan let them gain some space between us before he descended into the woods, not too far from the house. Carefully, he put me down and immediately took my face in his hands. I saw what he wanted, and I answered his fervent kiss with one of my own. My heart was still flying high above us. My jubilance radiated outwards. He slid his hands from my face into my wild mass of windblown curls, tugging my head further back. Our feverish kisses were not enough for either of us.

My hands slid across his bare chest. His hands went to my breasts and massaged them. His mouth trailed kisses down my neck, and I groaned with desire. Our breathing came in gasps. I fumbled with the button on his pants, but after a moment I got it and finished by unzipping him. I didn't bother pushing them off his waist. Instead, I reached into his fly and grabbed his cock, freeing it from his pants. He seemed to grow even harder in my hand. How was that physically possible?

Rylan pulled off my shirt and pulled down my pants and panties. With ease only a Guardian could have, he lifted me and one fluid motion he impaled himself into me. I cried out in ecstasy. Our mouths met again, and I gyrated my hips back and forth as he held me. He moaned in my mouth, and my body clamped harder around him in response. It didn't take long; my orgasm came hard and fast. I threw my head back and cried out as it washed over me. His whole body lit up as my power rushed through him. Rylan came almost immediately afterward with a deep growl in his throat.

Rylan held me there as we panted, coming down from our highs. I placed my forehead against his and planted a kiss on the tip of his nose. He turned his face up and caught my lips with his. Finally, he set me down, and we quickly got dressed. As I reached up and attempted to run my fingers through the wild curly haystack on top of my head, I glanced over at Rylan. My power was still lighting up most of the veins in his arms and his chest. My mood dipped as concern for Rylan took the forefront. I stopped playing with my hair and grabbed his arm, staring at his glowing skin.

"Maybe we should cool it with the sex for a while," I said with a frown.

"Absolutely not," Rylan said with a grin. I couldn't help it. I smirked.

"We don't know what this is doing to you," I ran my thumb over a particularly bright vein on his arm.

"There are no ill effects," Rylan assured me.

"Right now there aren't," I countered. "But what happens if we just have a day of non-stop sex? What if you just… I don't know, combust or something?"

I was trying to be serious, but Rylan threw his head back and laughed. The sound echoed through the trees and, again, I couldn't stop a smile from playing around my lips.

"If that is how I go, I will not complain. I will boast about my demise to everyone on the other side."

"I'm serious, Rylan," I snapped, annoyed that he could make me giggle in a serious moment. "I can't imagine you getting hurt, especially because of me. I love you too much for—"

The moment the words were out of my mouth I instantly regretted them. I slapped my hand over my mouth to keep from saying more, but I knew it was too late. The cat was out of the bag. I didn't even realize there was a cat in the bag to begin with. But now, saying the words out loud, I realized with instant clarity that I did love him.

Rylan had become my world in a very short amount of time, and somehow, I was okay with that. More than okay. I was happy when I was with him. From the beginning, he had stood by me, unafraid and confident of his ability to guide me through the worst of my problems. I trusted Rylan. I felt safe with him. He made me laugh, and he protected me from myself. He made me feel special, cared for, and I could be myself around him. The barriers I hadn't realized I had erected to keep people at arm's length had crumbled down, and Rylan had stepped forward to capture my heart.

But now that the words were out there, hanging between us, I was instantly vulnerable, and I hated it. Had I not gone through years of heartache as I tried to maneuver through this world with newfound power? Why would I do this to myself? Why would I allow myself to fall so hard for a man I hardly knew? I was an idiot. That was why. I stepped backward and covered my face with my hands; maybe if I hid my face, my humiliation would disappear as well.

I felt Rylan's hand wrap around my wrist. I allowed him to pull my hand away from my face, and I dropped the other. His mouth was twisted upwards in amusement, and his eyes were twinkling. He held my hand in his.

"When you tell me you love me, I would rather not see the look of horror follow suit."

Despite my mortification, I chuckled. "I guess that's not the most romantic way I could have told you."

"I am just happy to know how you feel," he assured me. He pulled me close and looked down at me. Rylan brought my hand up to his chest. Underneath his warm skin, I could feel his steady heartbeat. I stared at my hand against his chest.

"My heart beats only because of you," Rylan told me softly. "My heart races when I lay eyes on you, it skips a beat when you touch me, and it breaks when you are upset or frightened."

Stunned by his candid words, I looked up to meet his gaze.

"I love you, Mae White. I want to spend the rest of my immortal life with you and then follow you through the Golden Gates to Paradise. I will protect you, embolden you, and fight for you. Any obstacles in our way, we will tackle together."

I stopped breathing.

The proclamation of his love stunned me. I don't know why; as I thought back to everything he had done for me up to this point, it was clear that we had a connection. My heart felt like it was swelling painfully in my chest. If Rylan could admit his feelings for me with such confidence, I owed him the same respect. I took a deep breath and mentally braced myself.

"I love you, Rylan Wellington."

Rylan didn't hesitate. He wrapped his arms around me, dipped me backward, and kissed me. I laughed against his lips as all my insecurities evaporated. I was glad we were on the same page.

"Does this mean you will marry me?" he asked, pulling me upwards so I could stand upright.

I rolled my eyes and stepped back away from him. "I told you yesterday. We're not getting married."

"Even if I got down on one knee?" he teased, raising an eyebrow.

"I'd help you back up to your feet. Let's get back to the house, you lovesick fool."

"I will wear you down," he warned with a grin. The joy that radiated from him made me smile.

"We'll see about that."

Rylan laughed and took my hand. We walked back to the house in comfortable silence. My mind reeled at the revelation of my feelings for the Guardian beside me. I savored the feel of his hand holding mine. I stole glances from under my lashes at him and found him smiling as if he had won the lottery. According to the Guardian's story about mates, maybe he *did* win some sort of lottery. Somehow, we had ended up meeting at the right time and right place. In some weird twist of fate, maybe I had won a lottery myself. I could not imagine anyone else by my side.

Chapter Eighteen

The rest of the day passed by in a blur. Rylan and Arthur played several rounds of pool in the billiards room I had missed during my exploration of the house. Jasmine and I watched them play and listened as they joked and taunted one another. Afterward, we moved our small party into the family room where the Guardians regaled me with stories of battles, both victories and the losses. Each Guardian had stories that made us laugh until our stomachs hurt. We cried when the Guardians shared moments in their life that they looked back on with the emotions they should have felt. We were thoughtful when they looked back and wondered how they would have proceeded with certain situations if they had the emotions they did now. Occasionally, the Guardians bickered amongst themselves over trivial details of events in history.

By the time the sun set beyond the trees, I had seen a new side to each of the three Guardians around me. Today had felt more like a reunion than of a gathering of acquaintances. Some stories had been intimate, others shameful, and yet each one had dropped their guard and shared each moment for the rest of us to hear.

We sat in the living room and enjoyed different genres of music to pass the time. It was bizarre; I listened to music all the time, but watching the Guardians truly appreciate music made me feel as if I had taken it for granted all my life. They argued with each other over what to listen to next. With each song, they sat in solemn silence and then dove into a heated discussion about what they liked and what they did not like. I sat back and watched them, laughed with them as they teased each other, and even shared some of my favorites with them.

Time slipped by, and I almost forgot about the witches. During one of Frederic Chopin's musical performances, Rylan stood. He excused himself and left the room. I glanced at the clock on the mantle and realized our guests should be arriving at any moment. Arthur and Jasmine appeared utterly at ease as they continued to listen to the musical performance coming from the speakers. I tried to feel as comfortable as they looked, but my mouth dried, and my palms became sweaty. I tucked my legs under me as I sat there on the couch and tried not to stare in the direction Rylan had vanished.

I didn't hear the front door open, nor did I hear voices, but suddenly Rylan walked back into view with seven other women following behind him. I wasn't sure what I had expected, but the women who strolled in behind Rylan looked normal. I searched for the pentagram symbol tattooed or glowing on any exposed skin as they drew closer.

The first witch who noticed me stopped midstride. Her eyes opened wide, and her mouth dropped open. The second witch who noticed me let out a hiss and gave me a dark scowl. Rylan walked around the couch to stand behind me, seemingly oblivious to their reactions. Arthur straightened from leaning against the mantle, and Jasmine rose gracefully. The rest of the witches filed in.

They stood together in the middle of the room as if corralled. They shifted anxiously where they stood. Their shoulders were tense, and their fugitive glances bounced between me and the Guardians in the room. Whenever I caught the eye of a witch, their curious glance turned dark or disgusted. I squirmed in my seat. Rylan's hands came down on my shoulders, halting my shifting.

"Annabelle, Gabrielle, Sarah, Nora, Amira, Brianna, and Tess, please meet my mate: Mae White," Rylan said with a steely tone. "Gabrielle and Nora are the Supremes who live closest to us." Rylan indicated the two older women who stood in front of the others.

Gabrielle had gray hair and wrinkled skin, but her blue eyes were sharp and looked at me suspiciously. Nora was just starting to gray; her dark hair was twisted in a bun, and her thin lips were pinched together. I gave them a weak smile that no one returned. Gabrielle and Nora, along with the rest of the witches, simply stared at me with mistrust.

Great, this was going well.

"This is the young woman Autumn showed Darla in her dreams," the witch, Nora, said as she leaned close to study me. "Yes, this is most certainly her."

"Please, start from the beginning so we may understand better what is going on and what your concerns are," Arthur said, capturing the witches' attention.

"We will do our best to explain," the Supreme, Gabrielle, said as she came to stand next to Nora. "But first you must know about the witch who came to visit us. A little over three decades ago a young witch came to my coven out in the swamp with a warning that she had seen the gods returning and raining down their wrath upon us. The young witch was Autumn Chester. She was insistent that we prepare ourselves for war. But Autumn was a mutt, so I blew her off. I thought she was there to stir up trouble within my coven. I bound her powers as a reprimand for starting trouble and sent her packing."

"Autumn then came to my coven, in South Carolina," a red-headed woman said; was this Tess? She stepped forward. "Autumn told me the same thing, that the gods were coming, and we had to prepare ourselves. I saw her bindings and called Gabrielle looking for answers. When Gabrielle said she thought Autumn was up to some mischief, I sent the young mutt away."

"She came to Jackie, the Supreme I have taken over for," a brunette witch said. She was so short she was almost hidden in the sea of bodies that surrounded her. "I remember her staying with us for a few weeks. She was frantic, claiming she had seen the end, and we needed to warn the others. Jackie wanted to help the young mutt, but when Autumn became hysterical, causing the other witches to panic, Jackie exiled Autumn from the coven."

"This happened to all of us," Gabrielle said, glancing at the four women who had not spoken. The four of them nodded in agreement. Gabrielle turned her attention back to Rylan. "None of us have seen Autumn since then. We have all scried for her over the years. With someone like that roaming between covens trying to start a problem, you have to keep an eye on them. But none of us ever saw her again."

"That was, until last night. Autumn came to me, came to all of us, with that same warning she had given us years before," Nora said, picking up the story. "In our vision, she appeared much older than when I had first seen her, which is impossible."

"Why is it impossible?" Arthur asked.

"If you cannot find someone through scrying, it means they are dead. Throughout the years we all attempted to scry for Autumn to keep an eye on her, but none of us could find her. She was presumed dead," Gabrielle explained. "It is impossible to receive a vision from someone dead; the dead cannot communicate with the living. She came to us older in our visions, which means she is still alive. How she was able to avoid being found all these years, we have no idea."

Nora nodded and continued, "Autumn told me that the end of the world was near. She said she must find her daughter, and that the deal she struck to save the world lay in the hands of her child. She proceeded by conjuring up an image of her missing daughter."

All seven witches looked down at me with emotions that ranged from curious to disgusted. A deep growl vibrated through

Rylan, which I could feel as it ran through his hands still on my shoulders. The witches looked up, away, or in any direction away from me. What was their problem?

"Once I emerged from the vision, I immediately received calls from my sisters who stand before you, and they said they had all had the same vision. We spoke for hours about what to do. For Autumn to come to us, all seven of us, it must have taken a great deal of power. Power she cannot possibly possess. Something is going on, and we would like help with investigating Autumn. The seven of us have decided to do a joint scry; with our powers combined, we will be able to force her to communicate with us. It takes a lot to do, but I think it is time we take this warning seriously.

"Not long after speaking with my sisters, Claire brought her child Darla to me. Darla had told Claire that Autumn had been visiting her for weeks now, asking Darla to find her child for her and showing her what her child would look like now. I have no doubt that this is true. Darla is a very powerful young witch; her Sight has never been wrong. Alas, Darla is a… strong-willed child and did not tell her mother of these visions until last night when Autumn had thanked her for finding her daughter. When I pressed Darla for more information about what Autumn had shared with her, she told me Autumn called her daughter Mae. Darla then told me that she had met Mae the day before and that she was your mate, Rylan. As you can imagine, I had to contact you right away."

Nora glanced down at me again before immediately looking away. There was silence as we all processed what she had shared with us. My mind whirled; *I* was Autumn's daughter? My stomach tightened painfully. The way these witches were looking at me or avoiding looking at me, I knew that couldn't be a good thing.

Jasmine clasped her hands behind her back, and she strolled over to where Rylan stood. I felt the Guardian's internal communication. Jasmine said nothing out loud.

"You mentioned that Autumn had struck a deal to save the world, but who did she strike a deal with? What is Mae's involvement in the deal that Autumn struck?" Rylan asked.

This time the black-haired witch answered, "We do not know, but we were hoping tonight when we did a joint scry that we would be able to find some answers."

"When were you planning on doing it?" Arthur asked.

"During the witching hour, when our powers are the strongest," Nora told him. "We will call Autumn to us from wherever she is and demand answers."

"The three of us will be there," Rylan assured the witches.

"The four of us," I corrected instantly as I glared up at him.

The seven witches gasped in unison.

"The mutt speaks to you with such disrespect," a younger witch, who had yet to speak, said with a look of revulsion on her face. Rylan's answering snarl was terrifying. I flinched. The witches huddled closer together as he let go of my shoulders and walked around the couch to stand in front of me.

"Do you wish to see dawn tomorrow?" It was Arthur who asked the question, his voice deadpan. He was the closest Guardian to the young witch. She looked at him, her eyes wide and face pale. "Then do not speak about Mae with such contempt."

"Brianna is new in her role as Supreme. Please excuse her insolence," Nora said, quick to jump to the defense of Brianna. I watched another witch grab Brianna's hand in a sign of comradery.

"See to it she learns her place," Rylan hissed. Brianna cringed away from him. "Leave, now. All four of us will be joining you while you search for your answers this evening."

The witches all gave frantic nods and immediately hurried from the room. Jasmine followed the witches out, giving me a wink over her shoulder as she disappeared from the room. Rylan turned around to face me, his scowl deep.

"Do not let their bigotry bother you."

They didn't like me because I was a mutt? Fine, there were other pressing issues to worry about. I shrugged.

"Do you believe that this Autumn witch truly knows the gods are coming?" Arthur asked Rylan.

Rylan turned to meet his friend's gaze. "We should not discount it. With Mae's ability to speak in ancient tongues and her unfamiliar gift... We should be open-minded about the possibility."

There was silence as we all thought about what the consequences could be if Autumn's warning was true. Arthur stroked his goatee thoughtfully before he turned to look at me.

"Unfortunately, I believe we have another issue."

I looked at his solemn expression and felt my stomach drop. There was something I was missing, and he was about to drop a bomb.

"Rylan, Mae's power radiates from her the same way we were taught a god's power radiates from them. Her aura is undeniably strong and unique. If Autumn is Mae's mother that explains her witches blood, but the strength of her power and the ability to speak in a dead language...It could mean that her father could be—"

"A god," Rylan finished grimly.

Both men stared at each other; they didn't have to say anything either out loud or telepathically. They obviously knew what that meant. Me on the other hand, I had no idea what they were talking about.

"I don't understand. I thought the gods were stuck in whatever realm they were forced into. How could Autumn have met a god and had a child with him? And, really guys, don't you think I would know if I was kind of like, I don't know, *godly* or something?"

Neither man said anything. Arthur sighed, and Rylan ran his fingers through his hair. Instead, it was Jasmine who answered. She strolled into the room, her face unreadable.

"Let us hope that all of this is some sort of false vision. Let us not drown in our what-ifs."

"Jasmine—"

"No, Arthur, we will wait to see what happens tonight," she interrupted.

Rylan turned to me slowly and reached out a hand for me to take. His mouth was turned downwards, and his eyes were unfocused. I took his hand, and he led me from the living room into the kitchen without a word. I could feel the telepathy between Jasmine and Arthur. Were they discussing the possibility of my father being a god? Their reluctance to talk out loud about their concerns made me nervous. Rylan pulled out a stool at the island, and I sat down. I didn't pay attention as he walked around to the refrigerator.

My stomach twisted painfully as I tried to think about the reasons why they didn't want to discuss it out loud. Guardians were definitely anti-gods; if other Guardians found out that a spawn of a god was wandering the Earth… that wouldn't be good. So maybe telling the other Guardians about me was now a bad idea. The thought of a whole bunch of vindictive Guardians coming after me because of who my father *might* be was terrifying.

But another thought, more alarming than a bunch of killer Guardians, popped into my head. In high school I had learned about the gods within Greek mythology, and later on in college, I learned about the many gods from the thousands of different cultures all over the world. If it was true, that perhaps a deity was my father… which god could it be? Just a few of the gods I could remember off the top of my head weren't the kindest.

My heart sank as I started to understand why no one wanted to talk about this. The power I had could have come from a very malevolent god. My power was destructive and uncontrollable. Knowing I would be unable to control such a power, perhaps, whoever my father was, he had planned for me to accidentally rip apart the fabric of time and space, allowing the gods to return to start the end of the world. Could that happen? Did I have that much power within me?

I stared at the counter in horror.

The room shook hard as my terror mounted. It immediately stopped; I could feel Rylan's new ability to manipulate my power working as he drew it into himself. My power recycled back to me in a much calmer state, but it wasn't helping the fear I felt. What had Autumn done? What deal could she have struck and with who? This was a nightmare.

I looked up at Rylan. He had preheated the oven, added seasoning to whatever was in the aluminum dish, and pulled out a bottle of water from the refrigerator. His expression was unreadable, but the way he moved around the kitchen did not cause me to think he was distressed.

His calm demeanor cooled the panic I felt. I stood up and walked around the counter to Rylan. He turned towards me with a frown. I wanted to feel as calm as he looked, and I knew I would feel that way in his arms. With a weak smile, I wrapped my arms around his waist. Without hesitation, he wrapped his large arms around me, and I was encased against his solid form. Immediately, I felt better. For now, I was safe. The warmth that radiated off his body relaxed me further, and I buried my head in his chest. I wasn't alone in this. I had Rylan and the other Guardians who would help me deal with whatever came my way.

I turned my head and looked down at what he was warming up.

"I'm not eating all of that," I muttered against him.

I felt his chuckle vibrate through his chest.

"I do not expect you to eat an entire four-person entrée by yourself. Whatever you do not eat we can save for later or toss it."

I stepped back and eyed the chicken pot pie meal my mother used to make. My heart twisted as I thought about her.

"How do you know how to use an oven if you don't eat anything that goes into it?" I asked him curiously.

Rylan chuckled. "I have to appear as human as possible, and that means I have to learn mundane things such as cooking."

"At least one of us knows how to cook."

The tension in the house seemed to ease as dinner warmed in the oven. Jasmine and Arthur disappeared to somewhere else in the house, and Rylan sat quietly next to me, his hand on my thigh, while I ate. When I was full, I saved the rest of the meal and headed upstairs. Rylan left me alone for a bit, and I was grateful. I needed a moment to myself.

Before I knew it, there was a knock at my door. I opened it and found Jasmine waiting for me. Her gaze swept over me; her expression thoughtful. When her dark brown eyes met mine, she gave me a warm smile.

"Are you ready to leave?" she asked.

I nodded silently.

"Good."

I followed her down the hallway, both of us silent, lost in our own thoughts. As we approached the stairs, Jasmine stopped. Confused, I stopped to look at her. She took my hand in hers and tilted her head to one side as she stared at me.

"Tonight, we will be dealing with great magic, Mae," Jasmine said with a sigh, "While I understand your wish to be there, I need you to understand I do not believe that is a good idea. Your power is volatile. I do not know what will happen to you or anyone else when you enter a room full of witches who are casting a powerful spell. By entering that temple, your power could be triggered and innocent lives could be at risk. As a Guardian, it is my duty to protect you *and* the witches. I believe it is in everyone's best interest if you wait somewhere else while the witches work their magic."

Oh. I hadn't thought about that. My stomach dropped as I realized that my presence in the temple could cause some serious problems. What if I accidentally reacted to something I saw or heard? I wanted to know what was going on, but if my being there

could hurt someone or hinder any information being gathered…
I would have to trust Rylan, Jasmine, and Arthur to share what
they learned.

Jasmine looked at me apologetically. She must have seen
the disappointment on my face because she added, "You can still
come and see what a coven is like. Maybe the other witches will
show you around."

From the looks I had received from the other witches, I was
sure a tour of the coven was not in my future.

I grimaced and said, "I'll wait somewhere while you guys go
in, I guess."

Rylan called up from the foyer, "Are you two ready to go?"

"Yes," Jasmine answered as she started down the stairs, I
followed close behind. "Mae has graciously decided to not join us
for the scrying but would still like to come with us."

My gaze met Rylan's. One of his brows rose, and I sighed as
I stepped off the last step and went to him.

"I can't guarantee that I can keep my power in check while
the witches are doing their thing," I said. "I don't need to risk
everyone's life just for the sake of sating my curiosity. You guys
will just have to tell me what happens."

Rylan frowned then glanced at Jasmine with narrowing
pupils.

Jasmine shrugged and said, "*Someone* needed to warn her
of the dangers of her presence in that temple. If she insisted on
being in there, we could protect the witches, but I feel it is best
we avoid danger at all costs."

"It's fine, Rylan," I assured him. "Let's get going. We shouldn't
be late."

Rylan leaned down and kissed the top of my head and said,
"If you change your mind—"

"I won't."

He nodded, took my hand, and we all headed out the front
door. Outside, Arthur was waiting for us. His shirt was gone, and

his wings were stretched out behind him. Just beyond Arthur, in the driveway, was a large beefed up Jeep with large tires, a light bar, a winch system, and a huge metal bumper that stuck way out. I stared at the Jeep in wonder. Where the hell had that come from? Jasmine walked past us down the steps and removed her shirt. I pulled my gaze away from the Jeep to watch black, feathered wings sprout out from her back. Both Jasmine and Arthur looked at each other. I could see the grins they traded before shooting upwards.

"We're not traveling together?"

"No, they will fly ahead to make sure there are no problems along the way," Rylan said as he took my hand and led me down the front steps.

"Are you expecting trouble?"

Rylan opened the door, and I climbed up into the seat. He shut the door and came around to the driver's side.

When he climbed in, he answered, "While Jasmine and Arthur were in town, they found more demons lurking around. We are not taking any chances while we travel tonight."

I turned in my seat to look at him.

"More demons? Rylan, is it because of me?"

"It may be," he said with a sigh as we pulled away from the house. "Or it could be because seven very powerful witches have converged in the same area. The demons have been taken care of, and Jasmine and Arthur scanned the rest of town to make sure there were no more. We should be alright, but we do not want any surprises."

Rylan's jaw was tight; his mouth pressed into a straight line and his eyes were red. I frowned and reached out to touch his leg. He glanced at me.

"Are you alright?" I asked.

"I am well."

His expression did not change, so I pushed, "Are you worried about what the witches are going to find?"

Rylan's jaw ticked, a sign I was beginning to understand. I almost smiled; it was nice being able to read him now.

"I'm worried, too," I said, "but I'm glad you're with me."

Rylan took the hand that I had placed on his leg and brought it up to his mouth. His lips skimmed my knuckles, and my heart fluttered. He turned my hand around and placed a kiss in my palm. Warmth spread throughout my body, and suddenly my worries lessened while desire leaped to the forefront. The look he gave me told me he knew exactly what I was feeling. Briefly, I wondered if I should be embarrassed, but I immediately dismissed the thought.

"I hope this turns out to be some terrible miscommunication, and I have nothing to do with whatever these witches are involved with," I said quietly. "I don't want anything to do with the gods."

Rylan's brows came together, but he said nothing. What was he thinking?

"Do you know anyone that's ever met a god?"

"My mother and father remember them. I remember the stories they told me as I grew up. It was hell on Earth."

I frowned and looked out my window. What would it be like if the gods returned to this realm? Would they be angry because they had been trapped in another realm? What would the wrath of a god look like? Would they bring a plague? Bring a swarm of cicadas? Fires that could not be extinguished? Floods? Then, another thought struck me. I turned back to Rylan.

"Are your parents still alive?"

"Yes."

"Have you told them that you met your… um, other half?"

Rylan looked at me, amused by my question.

Suddenly embarrassed by the topic of conversation, I began to babble, "Are you going to introduce me to your parents? I'd introduce you to my parents if they were still around. I'd probably keep the fact that you suck my blood to myself, though. They wouldn't really be a fan of that, but besides that part, I think they'd like you."

"What makes you think I have not told them that I have found my mate?" Rylan asked with a raised brow.

"Well, did you?"

"I have."

"Did you tell them I blow shit up with my mind?"

Rylan chuckled. "No, I did not tell them about your unique ability. I am sure they will find out eventually."

"Hm… That will be fun for them to learn over a Thanksgiving dinner," I said grimly, and Rylan laughed softly. There was a short pause as we got lost in our thoughts. I stared out the window again and watched the scenery as we sped by.

"I am pleased to hear that you think your parents would have liked me," Rylan said softly.

I turned to him and smiled.

"Oh, they would love you right away, I'm sure of it. After introducing you to them, I would have given it five minutes tops before my dad started regaling you with stories of all the accomplishments of my childhood, all the way back to pre-school, embarrassing me. My mom would have politely interrogated you and then offered you something to eat. Her favorite thing to offer was—"

My throat tightened, and I couldn't speak. I turned my head away and fought back tears. Rylan squeezed my hand but said nothing. He allowed me to compose myself without pushing, and I appreciated it.

When I was sure I could talk without falling to pieces, I continued, "My mom's favorite thing to offer was her homemade biscuits. They were amazing. Then, she would pull out the baby pictures…"

I shook my head.

"I would like to see pictures of you as a child," Rylan said.

I chuckled. "Think of me now but smaller and with a little curly afro."

Rylan laughed loudly. I laughed with him, and my melancholy evaporated. Rylan asked me more about my childhood, and I told him about all the mischief I had gotten into. I was sure he was asking me questions to distract me from what was going to happen at our destination, but honestly, it was nice to talk about something other than the supernatural.

It took about an hour to get to the coven's location. They were on the other side of Salisbury in a thickly wooded area. We turned onto a dirt road, and I immediately understood the need for the Jeep. We bumped and bounced along the dirt road for what felt like an eternity. A loud thump on top of the car caused me to cry out. Rylan tightened his grip around my hand.

"It is Jasmine."

A few minutes later the bumpy dirt path turned into a neatly graveled drive that stopped in front of an ominous wrought iron gate. Behind the gate was a massive brick two-story Georgian style house. The gate opened slowly as we approached, and we drove in. Nora waited for us at the front door. Rylan parked the car, and we both climbed out. Arthur dropped down from the sky right next to me, and Jasmine jumped off the top of the Jeep and came up behind me.

"Nora," Rylan said, his expression hard.

"Rylan, Jasmine, Arthur… Mae," Nora greeted with a nod. She spared me a glance before raising her arm and directing us towards the side of the building. "We will go straight into the temple. We have made the necessary preparations and are ready. The witching hour is almost upon us."

The four of us followed the witch silently through the dark. The gravel under our feet crunched as we followed her around the building towards the back. On the other side of the grand brick house were five miniature versions of the same house built in a circle. In a wonderfully planned garden growing in the middle of the five houses stood a large fountain. Well, it looked like a fountain. Water shot up from a cement basin and twisted and turned into impossible shapes. Under the fountain was a gorgeous mosaic tile design configured into the shape of a pentagram.

We passed these buildings quickly, followed a dark, wooded trail that looked scarcely used, and when the woods cleared there was a circular, stone structure sitting there waiting for us. There were no windows, one slim wooden door, and a thin chimney stack at the tip of the cone roof. On the wood door, I could see a carving of a pentagram. Even from our distance, I could tell it was glowing a deep forest green. I shivered as we grew closer.

Nora walked up to the door, knocked twice, and turned the knob. The door opened, and I expected to see the other witches on the other side waiting for the Guardians. Instead, it was pitch black. The hairs on the back of my neck and arms rose. I came to an abrupt stop as every sane thought in my body said that there was something off about that hut. Rylan put a hand on my shoulder.

"Nora, Mae will not be joining us during the ceremony," he said.

Nora turned to look at Rylan then at me.

"You may wait out here. On the other side of the building is a bench if you would like to sit. The grounds are protected with magic, so there is no danger out here," she told me. Though, she looked at Rylan when she spoke. "The ceremony will not take long. We need to gain answers quickly and then release Autumn. This type of scrying takes a lot of magic, and by forcing her out of hiding, our magic will be connected with hers. The longer we scry, the easier it will be for her to follow the connection back here, and if she wants to, retaliate against us."

"Understood," Rylan said with a nod. He turned and looked down at me, his expression serious. "We will be out shortly. Do not wander too far off."

"Don't worry, I won't," I said glancing at the dark woods surrounding the building. Nope, wandering around these woods didn't seem appealing at all.

Rylan leaned down and planted a kiss on my forehead before he turned back to Nora who was watching us with something close to disgust on her face.

"Lead the way," he told her sharply.

Nora nodded and walked into the darkness. Rylan followed behind her, then Jasmine, and finally Arthur. Arthur glanced back at me and gave me a reassuring smile.

"You have to tell me what happens," I told him.

"I will repeat every word," he assured me and then shut the door.

I was alone in the dark in an unfamiliar setting. The glow from the waning moon provided just enough light for me to see where I was walking as I made my way around the building, but not enough for me to see too far into the woods. I reached up and rubbed my arms as if cold; the raised bumps on my arms hadn't disappeared. On the other side of the building was a pair of cement benches. I walked over and sat down on one but immediately stood up when a large spider crawled up from beneath the seat.

Okay, no sitting. That was okay, I could stand for a bit.

Around me, I could hear the night creatures out in full force. I could hear the croaking frogs, the hum of insects, and even a few hoots from a passing owl. It wasn't long before I began to pace back and forth, feeling restless. This sucked. How incredible would it be to be inside right now watching real, honest to god magic? While I understood why I was out here, it was still annoying.

The pacing helped. I walked around the building and then did it again in the opposite direction. I hummed to myself to pass the time, but every second that passed felt like an hour. I was walking past the front of the building for the tenth time when suddenly I heard rustling coming from the path that led us here.

I turned, wary, only to relax when Darla appeared. Her unfocused gaze was eerie in this lighting.

"Hi Mae," she said with a large, pleased grin.

"Darla? What are you doing here? How did you make it through the woods in the dark?"

"It's always dark to me." She shrugged. "I heard you were here, and I wanted to say hi. Everyone else is acting weird. They don't want to come anywhere near you. They don't like you much."

"Great," I shook my head, annoyed with the stupid witches that lived here. "Where is your mom? Does she know you're out here?"

"No, but she'll find me eventually. She always does," Darla said with a frown. She turned her head towards the temple and said, "They're struggling in there."

What? How did she know that?

"Darla, I don't think you should be out here. I'm sure your mom will curse me or something when she finds out you're hanging out with me again."

Darla laughed.

"She can't curse you. Her powers are in potion-making."

"Great, she'll offer me a cookie or something, and I'll be dumb enough to take it, and I'll be turned into a frog."

Darla laughed again, this time harder.

"You can't be turned into a frog with a cookie!"

"Oh?" I put my hands on my hips, "Then how does it happen?"

"I don't know. Mom doesn't trust me with that stuff yet. I know it's not from a cookie though," Darla said still giggling.

"Well, in any case, it's late. You should head back."

"Wait, listen," Darla said, putting her finger to her lips. I opened my mouth to tell her to go home because this distraction wasn't going to work when I realized what she was saying. The woods had grown silent. The animals had stopped moving and making their usual nightly calls. Darla stepped close to me and whispered, "This isn't good."

She had barely finished talking when a blast of icy cold air hit us from every side. Darla screamed as the wind nearly knocked her over. I reached out to grab her, but a force of wind hit me so hard I was thrown several feet away from her. I landed hard and rolled to a stop. The moment I was able to, I climbed to my feet and started to run towards Darla. As I ran towards her, hoping to protect her from whatever this was, the temple door swung open, and I heard him before I saw him.

"MAE!"

Rylan's roar caused me to turn towards him, but just as I laid eyes on the Guardian, a pair of arms wrapped around my waist and yanked me back into a dark, vast hole. In my head, I heard a deep feminine chuckle as I was sucked downwards.

Chapter Nineteen

It felt like I was freefalling backward into nothingness. Air rushed around me, and I tumbled through the silent, empty darkness. When I tried to scream, only air came out. My arms flailed around, searching for anything to grab or hold onto, but in this black abyss, there was nothing but me and the sound of silence. The falling slowed to a slow-motion descent. I could hardly move now, and what movement I was able to produce felt heavy and awkward. This was almost worse than the speedy descent.

Something broke the silence as I sank downwards. A cry? No, it was a scream. A second scream joined the first and then many more followed. The screams came from every direction, and they proceeded to crescendo until there were screams of hundreds upon thousands of souls deafening my ears. The screams were full of pain and anguish. Broken sobs, pleas for help, and prayers surrounded me. It got so loud that I stopped trying to reach for something to stop my fall in order to cover my ears.

Suddenly, over the deafening sounds of despair, a burst of deep, menacing laughter started. It was so loud and intense it reverberated throughout my body. It enveloped me and drowned out all other noises until it was the only sound I could hear. My descent came to an abrupt halt. While I did not hit the solid floor hard, when I realized I had stopped falling, I gasped. My body shook with fear as I lay there. My hands covered my ears to muffle the deep laughter surrounding me. It was so loud I could have sworn every cell in my body was vibrating.

I thought the laughter was bad but that was before I could feel *them*: Eyes peered at me from somewhere, or maybe from everywhere. I could sense something, someone, close. It was terrifying. My breath came in shaky gasps, and my muscles became paralyzed with fear. I tried reaching for my power, but nothing happened. My power had once been the bane of my existence, but now I desperately wished I had it.

The laughter stopped abruptly; it was followed by silence. I wasn't sure if being dosed with the absence of sound was worse than the maniacal laughter. Before I could dwell on it, a bright light suddenly shone down from nowhere. I blinked repeatedly at the sudden onslaught of light. When my eyes had fully adjusted, I sat up and looked around. I was under some sort of spotlight. Everywhere, except for the space that I took up, was cast in impenetrable blackness. No matter how hard I strained, I could see nothing. I forced my body to move. Getting to my feet was like fighting against a pair of hands trying to keep me down.

Hello, child.

A male voice broke the eerie silence. Or maybe it didn't? Was the voice only in my head?

I am Zyroe, the god of justice, peace, and punishment. I am your father, child. I created you as a weapon for the Guardians to use as the day of doom looms close.

I whirled around, trying to find the owner of the voice, but I could see nothing. There was no movement, no other sound; simple nothingness surrounded me. My heart beat rapidly in my chest; terror bubbled close to the surface, threatening my sanity. I kept silent and tense, waiting for whatever came next.

The blackness shifted around me. A horrible smell wafted through the stillness. At first, it smelled like burnt meat, but as the smell became overpowering, the aroma turned more to rotting meat. Burning, rotting meat. My stomach heaved.

The blackness rippled in front of me, and I saw Jasmine standing before me. She was in Guardian mode; her wings were outstretched behind her, and she stood in a fighting stance. Jasmine stared at me, unmoving. Her image was oddly transparent. I called and reached out towards her, hoping she could hear or see me. But she didn't react. Instead her body jerked forward. A massive hole ripped opened at the base of Jasmine's neck. She opened her mouth as if to scream, but no sound came out. The metallic, coppery smell of blood permeated the air around me. Blood spewed from Jasmine's wound. I cried out for her, my scream echoing around me. The wound continued to grow larger, tearing down her chest, through her stomach and cutting her body completely in half. Jasmine crumbled to the ground.

"Decades ago, I had a vision," a woman's voice said behind me.

I whirled around, but there was no one there. I turned back to where I had seen Jasmine, but she was gone. I was once more surrounded by darkness.

"In my vision," the voice said, "I saw the gods returning to Earth and exacting swift and merciless vengeance."

Suddenly, Arthur's image appeared. He, too, was oddly transparent. He stood with his wings folded behind him. He held a flail in one hand, and the other clenched into a fist. Arthur stared at me, and he frowned and pulled his brows together. His body twitched. His right arm fell off his body. Blood squirted out from the stump left behind. I could hear the blood as it gushed from his body. Arthur's other arm suddenly fell away. His face twisted in agony. I screamed for him as both of his legs were ripped away from his body and tossed behind him. His torso fell to the ground. As it hit, Arthur's head toppled off his shoulders towards me. His gaze never left my face.

I screamed and tears ran down my cheeks.

"I went from coven to coven, hoping someone would heed my warnings," the voice said from behind me.

Autumn. That had to be her! Of course, she was behind this. But what exactly was *this*? I turned, expecting someone to be there, but there was nothing but darkness. I looked over my shoulder, back towards where I had seen Arthur only to find that he had disappeared. I turned to look into the darkness where the woman's voice had come from. I strained to see something, anything. The smell of blood was overpowering. I gagged and gripped my stomach.

"But because I was born outside a coven, grew up without the teaching of a Supreme, I was simply a rogue witch looking to stir up trouble," Autumn's voice said from next to me.

I strained to see into the darkness. Autumn had to be there. She was watching me. I knew it. I also knew she wasn't alone. Zyroe was there, in the darkness, all around me. I could feel his omnipresence bearing down on me. It was terrifying being so vulnerable. I clenched my jaw and fisted my hands. I tried breathing through the panic that was clouding my judgment. Whatever trick or attack this was, I needed to stay focused.

"I called upon a Guardian," Autumn continued.

Beside me, something moved. I turned and found a Guardian staring at me. I had never seen him before. He had long black hair, his skin was pale, and he was on the leaner side. His wings were stretched high above him, his chest was puffed out, and he had his fists pressed against his hips. He stood like a superhero, but the ugly smirk across his face distorted his handsome features and gave him a sinister appearance. The image of the Guardian vanished.

"But he laughed at me and sent me away."

Somewhere in the distance, far into the blackness, I heard a scream. The sound was one of sheer agony twisted with a wail of desperation. At first, the scream was faint, but the sound drifted closer and grew louder. There was a ragged gasp, and the scream continued. Something was burning, I could smell the smoke. I could hear the clang of metal hitting metal. More screams followed. I covered my ears as the noise became deafening.

"I used my powers and sent a cry of help into the universe. I begged for someone to hear me. To help me save the world I loved so much. I promised a lifetime of servitude in return for help."

The screams cut off abruptly. I dropped my hands from my ears and braced myself for whatever was next. The ground beneath my feet trembled once. I stumbled. The ground rumbled again. Then once more. It was rhythmic and deliberate, like the footsteps of something large coming towards me.

"Zyroe heard my cries for help. He knew of the others' intent and knew something needed to be done. We tried to produce a weapon, but each one of the individuals I birthed kept failing at their task. They could not handle the gift Zyroe gave them. The power either killed them, or it drove them into madness."

But then you were born.

That deep male voice penetrated my skull and boomed in my head. I flinched from the force of the omnipresence. His presence bore down on me. My skull felt like it would crack under the weight of his intrusion in my head. He was a force I could not kick out or fight.

The darkness around me shifted in the time it took to blink. Suddenly, there were little glowing pinpoints all around me. I gasped and spun around, trying to figure out what was happening. The pinpoints began to glow brighter before they came into focus. I was seeing stars. Millions upon trillions of stars. My mouth dropped open; I was standing in the middle of the galaxy. I turned slowly, taking in the incredible view. Far above me, I could see the Milky Way.

The scene shifted, and I was traveling through the universe at unimaginable speed. Stars whizzed by; I passed comets, asteroids, and undiscovered planets. My speed slowed, and I was suddenly drifting alongside the moon with a view of the Earth below. From here I could see the blue oceans, mountain ridges, rivers, plains, and lights from the larger cities around the world. The image shifted again, and I was being drawn closer to Earth. All other continents fell away until there was only North America.

The others have been trying to get back to Earth for many millennia. Now, there is someone on Earth with the power to open the gate between the realms. Whoever it is, if not stopped, will succeed in bringing the gods back. This is where the gates of the realm will open.

The image drifted towards the western side of Canada. Was this Alberta? We came close enough for me to see forests, lakes, and rivers, but there was no noticeable landmark of where this was.

The gods seek revenge. Should they step foot on Earth, they will get their chance.

The image of the beautiful scenery shimmered then vanished, leaving me to only see the darkness once again. For a while there was silence. The utter stillness, the lack of anything except the sound of my breathing was terrifying. Being stuck like this, surrounded in nothing, was what I assumed blinking out of existence would feel like. I whirled around looking for something, anything, to assure myself that I wasn't dead.

A drawn-out croaking noise broke the silence. The smell of rotting and burning meat returned. There was a noise, like something wet and heavy sliding across the floor. The croaking noise turned into a sickening gurgle. The smell of urine and feces wafted over me. It mixed with the other smells. I covered my nose, hoping to block out the horrible stench. The sound continued repetitively: croak, slide, gurgle, pause. Whatever was making the noises and causing this horrendous stench was drawing closer. I wasn't sure how I knew, but the hairs on my neck and arms stood on end in warning.

I spun around, looking at the very edges of the spotlight I stood under wondering what was coming at me. Now there was a chorus of croaks and gurgling. Through the gurgles I could hear someone trying, and failing, to draw in a deep breath. I spun around again and almost bumped right into Rylan who, unlike Jasmine and Arthur, stood right under the spotlight with me.

One look at him and I felt instant relief. If Rylan could get here, then he could get us out of here! He was smiling down at me, those teal eyes twinkling with joy. Was that a five o'clock shadow coming in around his face? God, he was so handsome. Despite whatever was coming at us, I felt safe. I reached up to touch those short, spikey, hairs. Just as my hand hovered over his cheek, Rylan's expression changed. One moment he was smiling, the next a look of horror spread across his handsome features.

His eyes glazed over and became unfocused, his usual sun-kissed skin lost its luster and turned a pale grey. His muscles shrank, and his back hunched forward. His cheeks hollowed, and his mouth dropped open. All of Rylan's pearly white teeth tumbled out and landed on the ground. His eyes rolled into the back of his head before they melted out of their sockets and down his cheeks. Rylan's whole body began to shrivel right before my very eyes. A horrible croaking noise passed his lips as he collapsed at my feet.

I screamed and screamed and screamed. Rylan reached out towards me with hands that were just bones, shreds of skin dangled from his fingers. I stumbled away from him as I continued to scream in denial and fear. A maggot wiggled from his empty eye socket, and a worm fell from his mouth. Tears streamed down my face as I stepped away from the creature that was once Rylan. It let out a croak and used its hands to drag itself closer to me. It was the same sound coming from everywhere else around me. The zombie Rylan let out a gurgling noise and a black, shiny slime erupted from its mouth. It took a haggard breath and started its croaking. He dragged himself closer to me, and I continued to scream.

Everyone you have ever known will die when the gods come to Earth. The gods are fueled with hate and that will make them even more dangerous.

Zyroe's words barely registered. I was solely focused on the creature trying to reach for me. I moved left and right, stumbling just out of arms reach of the zombie crawling towards me. I managed to stay under the light that shone down on me, afraid to step into the darkness. As I approached the edge of the light, a rotting hand shot out from the blackness and grabbed my ankle.

I screamed and yanked myself free of the decaying hand. Behind the zombie that had once been Rylan, a centipede crawled along the edge of the light before slinking into the darkness. The other croaks and gurgles were closing in. I could almost feel the warm breath of the other zombies that waited for me just past the light. This was beyond a nightmare.

"You are the only hope to defeat the individual who is attempting to open the gate between realms. By binding your power, you have not allowed it to mature properly and now you have made yourself vulnerable. You *will* give in to your power. It is why you were created."

I ignored Autumn's words. I ignored Zyroe. All I could focus on was the zombie as he slid his body towards me. As I sidestepped him, I could see his intestines were trailing behind him. The zombie crawling towards me abruptly froze mid-croak.

The darkness around me lightened. Instead of more zombie-like creatures surrounding me, as I expected, I found myself on a suburban street. Or at least it used to be a suburban street. I gave the paralyzed zombie a wary glare before I turned to stare at the scene before me. Houses were burned down to the ground, the sky was thick with smoke, trees were on fire or dead, and charred posts were sticking out of the ground. Cars were on fire; bodies littered the street. I turned all the way around, staring at the apocalyptic scene. Something exploded in the distance causing the ground to shake. I quickly glanced over at the Rylan zombie to make sure it hadn't snapped out of its paralysis. To my surprise and horror, it was gone. I was once again alone.

I looked at the disaster around me and frowned. The longer I stared at the scene, the more it became familiar to me. It took me another heartbeat or two to realize I was staring at the street where my childhood house once sat. The entire street had been decimated, hardly recognizable. I stared at the few beams still standing where my house used to be. The mailbox was gone, and the beautiful yard was destroyed. I stared, stunned, at what had once been a tranquil neighborhood. The scene vanished and once more I was alone in the dark.

"Whoever is trying to open the gates has been successful in weakening the magic that keeps them closed. From what information we have been able to gather, the gate will open within two months, Mae," Autumn said.

It will be nearly impossible to shut the gate between realms once they are opened. If the gates open, you must close them before the first god makes its way through. Be warned: The gods will not be the only ones that come through that gate. Be wary of the creatures that serve their masters.

"The witches are calling for you. It is time to return you to the others."

Something brushed up behind me. I whirled around but there was nothing there. As I started to turn back around, a pair of grey, rotting, maggot-infested arms came around from behind me and pinned my arms to my sides. I screamed. A waft of warm, foul-smelling air crossed my face followed by a loud groan in my ear.

I struggled against the zombie's hold on me. Another pair of rotting hands came around and wrapped themselves around my waist. I felt cold, slimy hands shackle my ankles. I screamed and screamed all the while struggling against the incredible strength of the undead. A cockroach ran across my shoulder, and a worm fell from above, hitting me in the face and sliding down my cheek. More hands grabbed me from behind. They grabbed my face, my hair, and legs and began to pull me back into the darkness and away from the light.

While all others have wilted, you will flourish with my gift. Do not fail us, Mae.

The moment I was pulled into the darkness, the light vanished. My screams were wild and desperate as I tried to flail and fight against my undead opponents. Their nails scratched at my skin; jagged bones ripped at my clothes. I could feel small wiggling bodies of bugs crawl over me, and I screamed louder.

Suddenly, I was yanked free of those rotting hands and flung upwards, or at least it felt like upwards. I couldn't tell in the darkness. I tumbled through the endless nothingness. From all around me, I could hear Zyroe's and Autumn's laughter. Just like the first time, there was nothing to grab as I ascended. There was no slowing down.

The journey ended abruptly. My back hit something cold with so much force my breath was knocked out of me. I squeezed my eyes shut as my head hit the hard surface. I thought I might pass out from the impact.

"Mae!" a relieved voice cried out.

A pair of hands grabbed me. My eyes flew open as I screamed in terror and tried to fight off this new foe. The solid surface I was laying on rocked hard, and there was a scream somewhere nearby.

"Mae! Mae, it's me! It's me, Mae, Rylan. Look at me!"

I stopped fighting, but my body remained tense as I opened my eyes. Everything came into focus slowly. I panted, taking quick deep breaths as I tried to steady my nerves. I was inside a dimly lit room, on some sort of ceremonial platform. Rylan's perfect, handsome face came into view as I stared up at the dark ceiling. A strangled cry of relief passed my lips. Rylan cupped my cheek, his angelic features twisted with distress. Tears of relief spilled down my cheeks, and a sob bubbled up, but the sound was cut off as something shifted within me. Deep inside my mind where I kept my barrier erect to ensure my power could not slip, I felt something. A shift… no, a crack. Autumn's chuckle, soft and ominous, echoed in the small room, and I heard someone behind Rylan shriek.

Just as her laughter trailed off, I felt it crumble. The mental wall I had worked so hard to build crumbled and disappeared from my mind. My power didn't come charging out, as it normally would have done. I choked on the warm, oozing power that trickled down my throat and seeped into every vein, cell, and organ. The enormity of the power spilling out into every nook and cranny of my very being paralyzed me. All I could do was stare up into Rylan's horror-stricken face as he stared down at me.

The pressure that built up from my power was indescribable. I couldn't breathe, my heart stuttered, and I was sure my skull was going to crack. My power was filling me, crushing me, and looking for a way out. If it came out now, everyone around me was going to die. I had to warn them. With every ounce of strength that I could muster, through gritted teeth, I rasped:

"Run."

Rylan's jaw ticked, and I watched as the horror in his face shifted to determination. He scooped me up in his arms and yelled something, but as the pressure in my skull increased, my vision blurred and my hearing became muffled. I felt a cool breeze on my face as we emerged outside. The fresh air was the detonator. My power surged forward inside of me. From every single pore of my body, my power expelled outwards. I could tell I was screaming; I could feel the tug in my vocal cords, my mouth was open, but I heard nothing but a soft ringing in my ears as darkness enveloped me.

Chapter Twenty

There was pain. Agony. Liquid lava burning through every fiber of my being. There shouldn't be anything left in its wake except ash. It hurt to breathe; it hurt to think. There were no thoughts of being saved or trying to stop this. I knew it was impossible to stop this raging inferno inside me. What made it worse was knowing that this burning wasn't contained. I felt the raw energy leave my body in every direction with a force that should have burned the entire coven down. I was hurting people. I knew it. But I couldn't stop this.

Just as I thought my heart would give out from the pain and pressure it was enduring, the pain receded. I felt the heat cool in my fingertips and toes first. The sensation continued up my limbs and into my chest. The pressure that threatened to crack my skull lessened, and I was able to breathe again. I gasped as my vision cleared, and the ringing in my ears softened until it was gone. My heart still fluttered rapidly in my chest, and there was pressure under my skin, but it was bearable now. I blinked as my surroundings came into focus. I could hear someone calling my name, but it was like a soft echo in my head.

I was on my hands and knees; my fingers had dug into the soil beneath me. The veins in my hands and arms were glowing brighter than ever before as my power pulsed closed to the surface. Enveloping me were a pair of stunning, jet black wings. I focused my attention on the familiar voice calling to me, quietly reassuring me that I was not alone. Eventually I mustered enough energy to look up into familiar red eyes. There, mixed within those red irises, I could see my violet signature. Evidence of my power did not just sit in the depth of those eyes; his whole body was lit up. The veins in his face and neck were alive with my power running through them. Through his shirt, ripped to shreds, I could see the veins in his chest glowing violet.

Rylan was crouched down in front of me, and we were nearly nose to nose. His chest was heaving, and sweat glistened above his brow, but there was no pain in his face, only determination. Thank God he was alright. My relief mingled with exhaustion. Before I could collapse, Rylan moved. He caught me up under my arms and stood, cradling me against him. His wings pulled back to fold neatly behind him. Now I could see my surroundings.

We were outside the coven's temple. Dazed I looked around, expecting devastation. Instead, the trees around us seemed untouched. Movement caught my eye, I looked over to see Jasmine and Arthur hovering nearby. If I had any energy, I would have been shocked at their present state. They were floating just a few feet off the ground, their wings spread wide like a shield behind them. Their clothes were in tatters, their chests heaved like Rylan's and, like Rylan's, their entire bodies were lit up with my power. Littered around us like confetti were bodies of spider demons.

"Let's go, *now*," Rylan commanded, and suddenly we were sky born.

We weren't in the air for long. Rylan landed next to the Jeep, opened the back door, and with me still in his arms, scooted into the back. Arthur and Jasmine climbed in the front. I lay my head against Rylan's chest. I barely registered the drive home. My body felt leaden, and my eyelids drooped as exhaustion enveloped me.

I couldn't sleep though. Every time my eyelids shut, I found myself back with Autumn and Zyroe in that dark place. I could still see Jasmine's torn body, Arthur's mutilation, and Rylan's decaying body sliding after me. The smell of death lingered on my skin. My heartbeat wouldn't slow down. My body trembled with exhaustion. Sometime during our trip home, I realized I was crying. Tears rolled down my cheeks, blurring my vision, and a sound mixed between a sob and a groan came from my throat.

"—did she do to Mae?" Arthur asked. When had the Guardians started talking?

"I think she forced Mae's power out. I cannot smell any witch's blood in her system, can you?" Jasmine asked.

"No." It was Rylan who replied.

No one spoke after that.

The ride home felt like an eternity. The relief I felt when we pulled up in front of the large plantation manor was almost as great as when I realized I was back from whatever hell I had been in. Fresh tears rolled down my cheeks as Rylan carried me from the car into the house.

Rylan immediately took me upstairs to our bedroom. Once we were in our room, Rylan placed me on the bed and headed to the bathroom. I lowered my head onto my pillow and stared at nothing. My body wouldn't stop shaking. My breathing came in shallow gasps. Was this a nervous breakdown? Was I going crazy? I could hear Rylan moving around, drawing the bath and opening drawers.

A few minutes later he returned. He lifted me off the bed and carried me into the bathroom. It was filled with steam that rose from the clawfoot bathtub. Rylan placed me on my feet and helped remove my clothes. Vaguely, I noted my power still lit up every vein in my body. I was glowing all over. My arms and legs were covered in scratches, some still bleeding. A strangled cry escaped past my lips as I remembered the zombie fingers wrapping themselves around my limbs.

Rylan took my hand and helped me step into the hot water. My whole body shuddered hard at the heat. I lowered myself slowly into the water, barely registering the discomfort as each scratch contacted the hot water. The heat felt good as it soaked my depleted body.

Rylan removed his ruined shirt and pants. Understanding what he wanted, I scooted forward, and he stepped into the tub behind me. Just like mine, his body was glowing violet. Thankfully it was noticeably dimmer now. I hoped it would fade away altogether soon.

As he sat down, his legs came around me. I scooted my back up against his chest. He reached for something, and a flowery aroma floated around me. The smell was refreshing and soothing. A thick loofa rubbed up against my back, and I groaned. Slowly, Rylan lathered my body with the floral soap. Rylan lifted each of my arms and washed each one. He was careful not to rub too hard over the cuts. The loofa came down over my chest, across my stomach, and around my neck. I leaned against him, shifting so he had better access to wherever he wanted. When he was done lathering me up, he grabbed a cloth that he had hung over the edge of the tub and rinsed me off.

As Rylan cared for me, he spoke softly, whispering words of encouragement and reassurance. Sometimes he spoke in English, other times he slipped into languages I had never heard before, but his tone was always soft and sweet. As he rinsed me off, I wept.

We sat in the tub for a while after I was clean. Rylan's thick, muscular arms wrapped around me, holding onto me. I could feel his lips skim over my skin along my neck. He planted kisses on top of my head. Finally, when my tears ran out and the trembling came to a halt, Rylan stood up with me in his arms and stepped out of the tub. He grabbed a towel and gently dried me off. He dried himself off next as I held my towel around me. When he was done, he wrapped his towel around his waist and headed into the closet. He came out holding a t-shirt and sweatpants for me. I was grateful for his thoughtfulness. Rylan helped me into each article of clothing; he did most of the work.

I let out a long sigh as I began to feel human again. The shock was beginning to wear off. While fatigue weighed me down, I wasn't ready to sleep. Instead, I wanted to make sure I was truly present in this world, in this moment, with Rylan. While Rylan pulled on a pair of sweats, I walked over to the mirror and used my towel to dry my hair before twisting up my curls into a bun. When my hair was up, I stared at my reflection.

The woman who stared back didn't look anything like me. She looked haunted. Her eyes were a striking violet, brighter than ever. All the major arteries in her face, neck, chest, and arms were glowing brightly. Any skin not glowing looked ashen, her shoulders sagged in exhaustion, and her hands were trembling. I didn't have enough energy to muster up the appropriate amount of horror at the creature staring back at me. Rylan came up behind me, and I looked up to stare at his reflection. He had decided not to put on a shirt. I almost smiled as my eyes swept over his perfect body. This Rylan was certainly not rotting away.

"My power…" I started, but my voice trailed off when it hurt to talk. My screams had wreaked havoc on my vocal cords.

"Your power runs freely through you now."

"And through you and the others," I rasped. My frown deepened, and my brows scrunched together. I could feel it running through me like an electrical current.

"I redirected the blast into myself and the others," Rylan explained, meeting my eyes in the mirror. Seeing my pained expression, Rylan turned me around to face him and grabbed a hold of my shoulders. "We absorbed your magic, Mae, and it caused us no harm. I can feel it fading from my body, just as it has before. I am sure it will not linger in the others for long."

"You saved everyone from me. Thank you," I attempted to say only to find my voice was gone.

Rylan's brows came crashing together, and his handsome teal eyes changed to red. The disgust that crossed his face worried me. I reached up to caress his cheek, but he pulled away from my touch. Stricken by his rejection, I tried to step back, but he held my shoulders tighter.

"I am sorry, Mae, I have failed you. I have failed as your mate and as a Guardian. Autumn tricked the witches; she wanted to be called forth. The seven Supremes had enough power to pull Autumn from wherever she was waiting, and she broke through the protection circle to get to you. I did not get to you in time, Mae. I will spend forever making it up to you."

My brows came together in confusion. His eyes had cooled, changing back to that heart-stopping teal. His eyes searched my face. How could he feel guilty for something that wasn't his fault? Who could have predicted what Autumn had planned? I wrapped my arms around his waist in a tight hug.

"Not your fault," I rasped.

Rylan held me tight against him for a moment before stepping back, with his hands still on my shoulders.

"I failed you today, but I will never fail you again."

I simply shook my head. I couldn't speak anymore. My voice was gone for the time being. How could he possibly think that he failed me? Everything had happened so quickly. There had been no chance to react. Rylan's hands dropped from my shoulders.

"Come, let me get you into bed, and I will bring you something to eat."

I made a face; food was the last thing I wanted.

Rylan frowned. "You have been gone for over thirty-six hours. You must be starving."

My whole body tensed up in alarm; *thirty-six hours?* The room spun as I tried to comprehend where the time had gone. There was no way I could have been gone that long. I would have been able to tell, right? I couldn't have been gone for over a day.

"Mae. *Mae, breathe!*" Rylan stepped closer, took my face in his hands, and forced me to look up at him. "Breathe, Mae!"

I took a shaky breath and squeezed my eyes shut as I tried to process this information. Okay, so I had lost some time. But it was time that we didn't have to lose. I had to tell Rylan what happened and what I had learned. My eyes flew open, and I looked up at him.

"Gods are coming," I tried to say, but it sounded like a wheeze.

There was so much to tell Rylan and I didn't even know where to start. Even if I knew how to begin, I had no voice to share it. Would they believe me? Even having gone through the entire experience, it all seemed crazy to me. Would they think I was insane once I told them?

"Autumn told you this?" Rylan scowled deeply.

Well, yeah, she did but so did Zyroe. I tried to tell him this, but this time no words came out. I sighed in frustration.

"Mae, will you let me into your memories? I will be able to gather information from your experience that I can share with the others."

"But my power…?" I wheezed, hoping he would understand. With my power coursing through my veins so freely, I was sure a repeat of the other day would occur. I didn't want to blow up his house and start talking in tongues.

"Your power seems to work differently now. The room has not moved since we have been home despite your fragile emotional state. I believe we should give it a try."

"You sure?"

"Yes, but only if you want to."

I nodded. Rylan needed to know what we were up against and maybe he would see more than I did. He took me by the hand and led me into the bedroom where he sat me down on the edge of the bed. I looked up into his eyes, and Rylan took advantage right away. Rylan's gaze became unfocused as he floated through my memories. I stared up into his handsome face, focusing on my Guardian rather than of the discomfort of his intrusion. The silence in the room was not the same as the silence that I had been trapped in. This silence I could handle.

It took a few minutes, but I was aware when Rylan was finished. Rylan's gaze came back into focus. I understood the look of horror that twisted his handsome features. He leaned forward until his nose almost touched mine. Rylan took my chin in his hand, his brows crashed together, and his eyes glowed brightly.

"*No.*" No? Was there a question asked that I missed? Through gritted teeth, Rylan continued, "You are not going to be involved in this. We will not be a pawn in whatever sick game some individual started with the gods." He stepped away from me and ran his fingers through his hair. "I will tell Arthur and Jasmine what is coming so we can prepare for this war, but I refuse to have you involved. You will be as far away from the fight as possible. I will find a place safe for you while we figure this out."

He stepped back, away from me, and let out a roar that shook the room. His wings grew from between his shoulder blades, and they stretched out behind him, casting a long dark shadow around us. His muscles flexed. He turned back to me, his cheeks hollowed, eyes sunken, and irises blazing red. How had I ever been afraid of him like this? In full Guardian mode, he was more stunning than ever before. A fallen angel, just as I had first thought of him.

"The end of the world…" he shook his head in disbelief. "I will pack a bag for you. We are leaving, *now*."

He turned, I assumed, to storm off, but I grabbed his wrist. It wasn't a tight grasp, and he could have easily shaken me off, but he stopped and turned back to me. Good, because I couldn't have yelled after him, and my body felt achy and tired so chasing him was out of the question.

"Can't hide," I wheezed. "Have to help."

"Absolutely not!"

"People will die."

"People die all the time. It is a cycle that cannot be avoided."

"You're trying to have me avoid it." My voice sounded like air coming through a small tube. My shoulders sagged as I stopped trying to talk.

"You are not just anyone, Mae. You are my world," he said. I could see his anger slipping and panic trying to emerge. He scowled deeper. "You are the most important person to me. I will not risk you getting killed in a war that will have many casualties. I will not allow you to be taken from me again. No, absolutely not!"

I frowned. I certainly did not want to fight in a war against a bunch of angry gods. Meeting just one was enough for me. The terror I had felt knowing Zyroe had been everywhere in that darkness with me, controlling what I was experiencing… I never wanted to endure that again. Running away to hide sounded great in theory, but according to Autumn and Zyroe, if I wasn't there to stop whoever was behind this, the world could end. If I was somehow the answer to stopping all of this, I couldn't run or hide.

I tugged at Rylan's wrist, and he stepped closer to me. I patted the bed next to me and looked up at him expectantly. Rylan's jaw clenched tight, and I was sure he was going to object and storm away. Instead, Rylan came and sat down next to me. When he sat down, I leaned my body into him and placed my head on his shoulder. Immediately, his arm snaked around my waist. It felt good having him near.

With a deep breath, I attempted to speak:

"I'm scared, Rylan. I'm scared of the gods. I met one god, and I never want to meet another. I don't want to fight them or have anything to do with them. It also scares me more to think I could be hiding somewhere and suddenly the world blinks out of existence. But…" I paused, swallowing so I could wheeze out just a little more, "I would rather be scared knowing I'm doing the right thing. And that means I need to be there, doing whatever I can to try to stop the gods from coming through whatever gate is being opened."

I winced. My throat was burning.

Rylan scowled and turned away from me, his expression pained. I took his hand and waited. Rylan was a good man, a good Guardian. I knew he would understand what I was saying.

"You are a courageous woman," he said, his voice gruff. "You stood tall as you faced the demands of a god and a very powerful witch." He turned to look at me. "And now you are telling me you would fight alongside me to stop the end of the world. You are an incredible woman, Mae."

Rylan sighed, resigned for the time being. Hopefully, I had gotten through to him. I pulled away from him only so I could turn to face him. Gently, he took my hand. He looked down at it before his eyes traveled up my arms. He paused as he studied the scratches. After seeing the creatures that had created them, was he as disgusted by them as I was? Rylan raised my arm and kissed each little scratch. As he placed those sweet kisses on my arms, he followed the gesture by gently running his tongue over each mark. I tried to pull my arm away in surprise, but he wouldn't let go. I looked down as he worked and watched as each cut healed right before my eyes. I gasped in surprise. I had forgotten about the healing properties of his saliva.

Once he was done with one arm, he started with the other one. As he worked, a familiar warmth began to spread through me. It thawed the numbness and dissipated the shock from my system. The fatigue I was feeling took a backseat as desire gave me a new burst of energy. I needed more than these sweet kisses. Tears rolled down my cheeks as I thought about how much I needed Rylan and his touch. He ran his tongue over the last cut on my shoulder and looked up at me.

I saw the same burning desire in his eyes.

I leaned forward and kissed his lips. Rylan responded instantly by deepening the kiss. I wrapped my arms around his neck and pulled him on top of me as I leaned back onto the bed. Rylan pressed his hips into my pelvis, and I felt his hardness. I moaned. Oh God, I needed him. Now. I needed to know he was alive, safe, and truly here with me. A fresh wave of tears ran down my cheeks as the reality of what happened crashed down on me. I could have been trapped in that hell, never to see him again. I moaned as his hands slid under my shirt and trailed over my body. He squeezed my breasts and tugged at my nipples.

"I was so scared," he muttered into my neck, "that you were gone for good." His concerns echoed my own.

His voice was hoarse. His body trembled as I ran my hands down his chest, caressing his abs and reaching around to pull him closer to me. I pulled away from his mouth and kissed his jawline and trailed kisses down his neck. I nipped at his earlobe before I returned to his mouth.

"Oh Mae… I could not get to you. Ours souls have not Joined, so I was not able to follow you. I was a madman. My world— *you*, Mae—was taken from me." As he spoke, Rylan planted kisses everywhere that he could find skin. As his lips connected with mine, the tension coiled within me relaxed. Any lingering fear that had settled in my bones faded. "Do not ever leave me again." The pain in his voice, the crazed glint in his eyes as he pulled back to look into mine, it spoke volumes of his feelings for me. Feelings that I returned tenfold.

I whispered, "Finish the Joining, Rylan."

Rylan groaned and took my lips with his. This kiss was possessive, harsh, and demanding. I deepened it, needing more. My tongue slipped passed our lips and clashed with his. Rylan's hands gripped my hips, his fingers digging into me, pinning me to the bed.

"I cannot," Rylan said, pulling away ever so slightly. "I want to finish our Joining, I do. But you are too weak right now. Soon, Mae, I promise it."

Rylan yanked down my sweatpants and allowed the towel around his waist to drop. I slipped off my shirt as he placed himself at my entrance. Before he could move, I was already there, impaling myself around him. Rylan gasped as my body clamped down on him. His gasp turned into a growl of pleasure as I started moving. He met my thrusts aggressively. Our mouths clashed, our tongues twisting together. Rylan's hands reached around and squeezed my butt, pulling me closer. I wrapped my legs around Rylan's waist and tilted my hips forward; I needed him deeper.

Rylan's thrusts were ruthless. It should have been painful; instead I loved every second of it. My body arched as the pleasure built inside me. Rylan's mouth moved away from mine. I cried out in protest but moaned as his tongue found a nipple. I grabbed a handful of his blond hair and tugged at it. With my other hand, my nails dug into his back, and I tried to pull him closer to me. My breathing came in gasps as I got closer and closer to the edge of sanity.

Rylan hooked his arms under my thighs and yanked my legs upwards and over his shoulders. When he thrusted inside me again, I cried out as he sunk as far as he could go. It only took a few strokes when my body erupted. I cried out as my orgasm crashed through me. My body gripped Rylan so tightly that it only took him one more thrust before following with his own release.

My power surged forward, and the veins in his chest began to glow again. The glow spread quickly throughout his entire body. He groaned as it flowed through him, his head thrown back in ecstasy. As we came down from our highs, Rylan took my legs off his shoulders and shifted, rolling onto his back and taking me with him so I was suddenly on top.

While he was still hard, I started to ride him again. I wasn't done with him yet. My second orgasm built quickly. Rylan grabbed my hips and leaned into me, his red gaze watching my face. My hands skimmed down his chest. His solid form was reassuring and comforting. He was here with me now. I wasn't alone. He wasn't dead. My body never relaxed its grip on Rylan; instead, I felt it tightened more as my second orgasm rippled through me. I shuddered as pleasure radiated throughout me again. I collapsed against his chest, breathing heavily.

"I love you," I tried to say but it came out softer than a whisper. While barely audible, Rylan heard it with his superior hearing, and he wrapped his arms around me.

"I love you, Mae." He leaned down and kissed my forehead.

We laid there tangled together for a while, listening to each other's breathing. My exhaustion came back with a vengeance. My eyelids drooped, and my bones felt like they had melted. I fought to keep my eyes open. I didn't want to sleep. I reached up and gently traced patterns on Rylan's chest. I didn't want to be anywhere else except here with him. The silence was broken by the doorbell. Surprised at the noise, I flinched violently. Rylan's arms tightened around me, and I slowly relaxed.

"Lunch is here," he said as he withdrew from me. I looked at him confused, and he gave me a megawatt smile. "I told you: You need to eat."

I rolled over and sat up. Food didn't sound any better now than it had back when he had first mentioned it. Rylan stood and grabbed his towel off the floor, but instead of covering himself, he just threw it over his shoulder. I couldn't resist giving him a long, slow look of appreciation. His smirk didn't quite reach his eyes. I could see the worry and fear as he looked down at me.

"You're hot," I mouthed, knowing my voice was gone.

He chuckled as he held out his hand. I grabbed it, and he pulled me off the bed. He scooped down, grabbed my sweatpants off the ground, and handed them to me. I pulled them on and reached for my shirt and pulled it over my head. I briefly wondered if I should grab a bra, but then decided it didn't matter.

"While you eat, I will tell Arthur and Jasmine what we are up against," Rylan said, as we headed to the door of my bedroom.

He opened the door, stark naked, and we strolled down the hall. We didn't go far. We stopped in the first room on the left, and he opened the door. It was a large room, but not nearly as large as the one I slept in. Rylan strolled over to the closet door and opened it. Inside was a walk-in closet filled with his clothes. He grabbed jeans and a plain black shirt. I watched from the doorway as he dressed. When he was done, he walked over to me, and we headed downstairs.

Together we walked into the kitchen where Jasmine was waiting for us. She was sitting on the counter looking at her phone. She placed it down as we approached and gave me an assessing once over. I hurried over to her, and her eyebrows rose as I grabbed her hand. I didn't see any of my power lingering in her eyes or under her skin, but that didn't mean it wasn't there.

"Are you alright?" I rasped.

Her bewildered expression shifted to understanding. She smiled.

"I was a little taken off guard, but I am fine. Rylan failed to mention he could control your gift, but it certainly came in handy." She shot Rylan a look that I couldn't decipher. When she turned her attention back to me, she continued, "Your power magnified ours, and we were able to eliminate the demons that had broken through the coven's defense spells in record time."

I glanced at the pizza box and a foil container on top of it.

"Mae, I have not felt the house shake, but your power is now active. How do you feel?"

"I feel... alright," I said slowly as I did an internal examination. There was pressure under my skin, but it wasn't uncomfortable. My heart rate felt slightly accelerated, but it was nothing alarming.

"Interesting... I would offer to examine you again but..." Jasmine trailed off with a shrug.

"Actually, I was able to access her memories without issue," Rylan said softly, his brows coming together. Jasmine looked over at him in surprise.

I walked over to the pizza box. I felt bad for the delivery guy who drove all this way out of town for just a pizza and… wings? I opened the foil container. Yup, Buffalo wings.

As I reached for a wing, a thought crossed my mind. I paused, frowning, and turned to Rylan. If I had been gone for thirty-six hours, that meant Rylan hadn't eaten for that long either. How could I have forgotten I was his food source? I had been thinking of myself this whole time. How could I be so selfish? Rylan looked down at me curiously, waiting for me to say something.

"You have to be hungry, too." I sighed as it came out as a wheeze.

I raised my wrist to offer him a bite, but the thunderous look on his face had me drop it quickly.

"*Eat*, Mae."

"Let me make you some tea with honey. That will soothe your throat," Jasmine offered quickly, trying to diffuse the fight before it could start. She moved around the counter to find me some tea.

I didn't bother telling her I was fine without it. My voice wouldn't carry that far, and I was sure she was going to do it whether I wanted it or not. I sat down on a stool and grabbed a wing. I stared at it for a moment. Looking at this limb reminded me of the rotting arms and hands that had grabbed me. I shuddered hard and closed my eyes, blocking out the image. I couldn't keep thinking like that. I'd never eat again. They smelled much better than the rotting flesh did. That was good.

Tentatively, I took a bite, and immediately my mouth watered. Oh, I was hungrier than I'd thought. My stomach grumbled, and I took another bite. It wasn't until my second wing that I realized I didn't need any contact from a Guardian to help keep it down. I paused and looked up at Rylan and Jasmine, who were watching me curiously. They must have noticed it, too. Both Guardians exchanged looks but said nothing about this sudden change.

"Where is Arthur?" Rylan asked Jasmine who was boiling water in an electric kettle.

"Here," Arthur answered as he strolled into the room. I stopped eating and looked up at him in concern. I couldn't see any of my power lingering under his skin, and I relaxed. "Ah, Mae, how do you feel?"

"Alright," I told him flippantly. I was sure I had some nightmares coming in my future. "Are *you* okay?"

"I am more than *okay*. I was quite invigorated earlier. Neat trick."

Arthur grinned, but I shivered at the possibility that Rylan's redirection trick could have been fatal for all three Guardians. That had been a lot of power rushing through me. Arthur gave me an appraising look as he came forward, and I could see the concern on his face.

"We have much to discuss," Rylan told the Guardians around us. "Mae, I am going to share with them what you saw and what you heard. Do you mind?"

I shook my head while I kept my eyes on my food. The soft buzzing in my head told me Rylan had started. I focused on the food. I didn't want to relive any of it. I was already struggling to eat these wings without thinking of the undead. In fact, after eating four, I pushed them away from me. The mental strain to not thinking about what they had looked like was too much. I grabbed the roll of paper towels, cleaned my hands, and opened the pizza box. I grabbed a slice of pepperoni pizza and began to chow down.

"Two months?" Jasmine asked, breathless, breaking the silence.

The three Guardians all exchanged looks with each other and then looked towards me, expressions ranging from grim to horrified.

Chapter Twenty-One

The Guardians were silent as they absorbed the information Rylan had given them. They were like statues, frozen from stress. The severity of the situation was great, and the time we had to prepare was almost nonexistent. The only sound in the room was me chowing down on pizza.

Finally, Arthur gave an exasperated sigh before he threw up his hands in frustration. "How is it that Autumn was able to contact a god?"

"How was Zyroe able to answer?" Jasmine asked in return.

No one said anything as they mulled over these questions. As the Guardians contemplated, I rubbed my arms. The pressure under my skin felt like it was humming. It was not uncomfortable, but it was certainly noticeable now. I glanced down at the bright glow that emanated from my hands. How was it that my power wasn't demolishing everything around me? It was evident that it wasn't trapped behind my mental barrier, but it wasn't necessarily *free* either. I sighed. Another thing to puzzle out. Just, not right now. There were other pressing issues.

"My father once spoke of Pockets that the gods used for those who displeased them. He used to threaten to send me to one when I was a child," Rylan broke the silence. He spoke slowly and looked between the three of us. "These Pockets were purgatory of sorts. A space between the realms. Maybe the witches could not find Autumn during a typical scrying session because Autumn managed to find a Pocket and hide there."

"And since it is not on Earth, the gods can convene there. That's how Autumn and Zyroe must have met," Jasmine said, following Rylan's train of thought.

The four of us fell silent once more. I grabbed another slice of pizza, feeling more like myself with every bite. Arthur rubbed his hand over his face.

"Well, in any case, we cannot allow Mae to go anywhere Zyroe deems it necessary for her to be," he said after a beat.

"I have to be there," I objected. Or at least tried to with what was left of my voice.

I wasn't sure why Autumn and Zyroe were sure that I could do something to prevent the gates of the realms from opening, but deep down in my bones, I knew they were right about one thing: Something bad was going to happen. If there was something I could do to prevent the end of the world, then I needed to get to wherever I needed to be to stop it.

"It is a trap," Jasmine said sharply. Arthur nodded in agreement.

"A trap where I make sure the gods *stay* locked in their realm?" I asked, perplexed.

"You could possibly produce enough power to cut through almost any realm if you focused enough, especially now that your power has been unlocked. This could be a trap to get you to that specific location. There could be a weak link between the realms there that you could break through," Arthur answered.

"Zyroe is the god who upholds justice. He would see to it the gods finished out their sentence in their realm. It would make sense that he would answer Autumn's call for help," Rylan mused. "Out of any of the gods, Zyroe would be willing to produce a weapon that would help us even the playing field."

"It is a trick; I am sure of it. Why would he not want to return? Why not come back with the rest of the gods?" Jasmine demanded.

"Zyroe never had a qualm with the Guardians," Rylan said. His expression turned thoughtful. "There were a few gods who did not have Guardians, and he was one of them. He is still worshipped in some of the African countries while most of the other gods have been forgotten. If he helped to wipe out the people on Earth, he would have no followers, which would mean less power."

"It doesn't change anything. Mae cannot be there," Jasmine stated firmly, looking from me to Rylan.

"I'm going," I rasped with a scowl.

She turned her glare to me and bared her teeth. Her eyes went red.

"You will have no choice in the matter, Mae," Jasmine said. "I will tie you up and throw you in a tomb on the other side of the Earth before I allowed you to be anywhere close to danger."

The snarl that erupted from Rylan caused the room to rumble. Something in a nearby room shattered. As surprised as I was by his outburst, I was pleased that it wasn't me that caused something to break this time. He stepped between me and Jasmine, his glare pinned to the female Guardian.

"You have no say in what Mae can or cannot do," he snapped.

"You cannot agree with her, Rylan? To agree with Mae means you agree with Autumn and with *a god*,"Jasmine said with disbelief.

"Of course, she cannot be there!" Rylan snapped.

I turned to look at Rylan, outraged. Didn't we just have this conversation upstairs? I was sure that he had seen reason.

"I'm *going*," I said as I stood up. My hands went to my hips. "I don't *want* to go, but I have to. Autumn and Zyroe said that you guys can use me to help you stop whoever is behind this. Besides, I'm probably safer with you guys around than hogtied somewhere, right?"

I saw Rylan's shoulders stiffen.

He turned to glare at me and said, "You are not going."

I took a deep breath, trying to stay reasonable as anger began to rise.

"Look, let's try to think clearly about this. Why don't we just go to check things out? I don't have to fight; lord knows, I don't have enough control over my power to fight a god or whoever is behind opening this gate. But you guys just saw firsthand today what my power can do now. You felt it. If I can give you a boost or an edge, why not use that to your advantage?"

All three Guardians' red glares pinned me to the spot. If I didn't know them, I would be terrified. To my complete and utter surprise, it was Rylan who caved first. His shoulder sagged, and his eyes shifted back to teal.

"Mae is right. We need to scout the area and look for any indication that Zyroe and Autumn's claims are true. If Mae comes with us, she is safer with us than somewhere else—"

Jasmine's snarl was ear piercing, and I cringed as she grabbed Rylan's arm.

"She could end our curse, Rylan! I will not lose her. I will not be cast back into a bleak world. Do you understand me? This is somehow a trick to lure Mae to her death and to bring about the end of days. No, I will not allow it!" Jasmine snapped as she slammed her free palm against the counter.

Under the force of her palm the entire island cracked, and pieces of it fell to the ground. Rylan leaned forward and bared his teeth, his fangs lengthening.

"*I* am her mate, and I get the last say," he hissed.

Well, that certainly wasn't true, but since he was fighting for me in this situation, I decided to remain silent.

"I will stop you if you try to take her," Jasmine growled back.

Rylan snarled, and Jasmine responded by baring her teeth. She crouched, and Rylan stormed forward, yanking off his shirt. Jasmine's beautifully manicured nails grew into claws. Without thinking, I jumped up and hurried between the Guardians. I put my arms out in front of both Guardians.

"*Stop,*" I wheezed. "It's not for either of you to decide. I need to be there. I can't not go. If I can stop all the death and destruction that could come with the gods returning, I have to try. Isn't it your duty as Guardians to protect this world? Well, you need to use all the weapons at your disposal to stop these assholes, so use me. I will be safe with all three of you there while we figure out how to stop whoever is behind this. Hopefully, it will not come to a war where we could all get hurt. Please stop fighting over—"

My voice disappeared before I could finish. I growled in annoyance.

Jasmine and Rylan stared each other down. Neither appeared interested in backing off.

I sighed in frustration and tried again, "Whoever is behind opening the gates doesn't know about me. Currently, we have the element of surprise."

Arthur stepped forward; his anger turned to resolve.

"As much as I wish it otherwise, Mae is right. If Autumn and Zyroe created Mae with the intent to stop the gods, we should have her there. Our duty is to keep everyone on this Earth safe; it is not about us, Jasmine."

Jasmine shot Arthur a dark glare and hissed at him. Then she turned her attention back to Rylan who had taken the opportunity of her distraction to take a menacing step forward.

"Jazz, I can't sit back knowing the end of the world is just around the corner. I have to help," I said softly. "If a war does break out, and the Guardians can't contain the gods, then it won't matter where I am. The end of the world will be here, and we're all screwed. I would rather be with you guys than by myself if we're all going to die."

She said nothing. Instead, she continued to glare at Rylan. Tension ran high. All I could hear was my heartbeat. With what seemed like an extraordinary amount of effort, she sighed. Her body relaxed, and her eyes went back to the warm brown color

I was used to seeing. Her nails retracted, and her face softened. Rylan growled and took another menacing step towards her, pushing against my hand. Jasmine sighed again and looked away. This seemed to please Rylan because his body language changed. He took my hand off his chest and pulled me to his side.

Arthur cleared his throat and said, "We have to alert the others."

"Tell everyone about the end of the world or of Mae?" Jasmine asked, obviously exasperated.

There was another pause as the Guardians mulled it over. Rylan's jaw clenched, relaxed, then clenched again. I could almost hear his wheels turning. This had been the issue from the beginning, but now we had a new problem. How could we tell the other Guardians there was a threat to the world without explaining how we found out? How could you leave out the part about the half-witch with the blood of a god and a power she couldn't control?

"Before we contact anyone, I believe we should go scour the area for any evidence of wrongdoing," Rylan said thoughtfully. "If there is someone trying to open the gates, we will be able to sense dark magic. Whoever is behind this cannot be completely alone. We will look for lackeys or those under the influence of magic. Should we find *anything* that would indicate what Autumn and Zyroe say is true, we contact only our most trusted warriors first. From there, we will decide how to tell everyone else."

Arthur looked up at the ceiling and shook his head. "A child of a god," he muttered before he turned to look at me. "This will not go over well."

"Even those we trust may try to kill her just because of that," Jasmine said as she wiped a hand down her face. "Or they will try to drink her blood and taste the gifts promised to any who drink the blood of a god."

"Or they will attempt to kill her because she cannot control her power. She is a threat to the supernatural world," Arthur added.

"Actually," Jasmine said with a sour look in my direction, "she is doing quite well right now. Maybe by unlocking her power, it gave her control."

"At the very least, they will covet her in the hopes of maintaining their emotions," Rylan said with a venomous tone. "But I will not allow for any of that to happen."

"I will not allow it either," Jasmine vowed.

"She will be protected by all of us," Arthur added. "There will be some that will see reason and will side with us as well. She will be safe."

The three Guardians shared a look before they all turned their attention to me. Feeling touched by their promise to keep me safe, I looked down at my feet. I had known these three for just over a week now; they should still be strangers to me. Instead, in such a short amount of time, we had become a small family. The thought that we may all die in two months was terrifying. I didn't want to lose anyone. I looked up at Rylan as fear caused my throat to tighten.

To distract myself from my rising fears, I walked over to the pizza box. I closed it and the container the wings had come in. As I turned around, I watched as Jasmine poured the boiling water from the kettle into a mug, dropped a teabag in the water and let it steep. She walked over a cabinet, opened it, and pulled out the honey. Once she had scooped some out and placed it into my tea, she brought the mug over to me. I tried thanking her only to find I was incapable of speech again. Instead, I smiled thankfully at her.

"Who was the Guardian that Autumn showed Mae?" Jasmine asked after another long silence.

"Alfred Woolstead. At least, that was the name he went by when I met him about two centuries ago," Arthur said. "He took his life many years ago."

"He will not be much help to us then," Jasmine said grimly.

I sipped my tea and immediately felt the heat soothe my throat. I closed my eyes and basked in the hot beverage. I took another sip, and I sighed. Rylan came up to me, and he cupped the back of my neck.

"Why would anyone want to open the gate between the realms…?" Arthur asked, more to himself than to us. He stroked his goatee before sighing.

"We have to be careful," Jasmine said. "If whoever is behind this finds out that the Guardians know what they are up to, they may try to open the gates faster. Or if they learn of Mae's involvement, it will make her a target."

"We need to be careful, thorough, and quick. Time is not on our side," Rylan agreed.

"I will make the necessary travel arrangements," Arthur offered. "We will leave tomorrow morning."

Arthur left the kitchen, pausing just before he was out of sight, and looked over his shoulder at me. His face was unreadable. Then he turned and left. Jasmine followed Arthur without another word. Her posture was stiff; she was still upset. There was nothing to be done about it now, though.

I turned my attention back to Rylan and found him frowning. He ran his fingers through his blond hair, and the agonized look that he gave me echoed the feeling in my heart. After what I had gone through with Autumn and Zyroe and what we had to look forward to these next few months, our future together seemed bleak.

Rylan took my hand and pulled me towards him. I wrapped my arms around his waist and closed my eyes. My body was trembling again. I felt utterly spent. Rylan scooped me up in his arms and carried me back upstairs. Gently, he placed me on the bed and slid in next to me.

"You need to rest," he murmured into my hair as I wrapped myself around him.

"No, I'll have nightmares."

My body screamed for sleep, but I knew I would relive everything. I couldn't do it again. I had barely survived it the first time.

"Let me help you," Rylan begged.

I studied his face. He was running on low, and I could see how it was taking a toll on him. I could see white lines of stress around his mouth and eyes that hadn't been there before. There were dark circles under his eyes, his body was tense, and I knew he had to be hungry. We both needed to recover. I squared my shoulders and resolved myself to help us both.

"I can't close my eyes without seeing everything I went through," I told Rylan. He opened his mouth, but I stopped him by putting up my hand. "We're both tired, and you have to be hungry. We both need to be at our best, so I propose a compromise: you eat, and I'll let you use your scary power to compel me to sleep."

He hesitated.

Suspicious of his reluctance, I asked, "Is it because my power is… active? Are you afraid I could hurt you if you drink from me?"

The dark scowl that cast shadows on Rylan's handsome face answered my question before he could say anything.

"I do not fear your power. It has not hurt me before; it will not hurt me now."

His confidence was unwavering. I could see that he truly was not afraid of it or me. I relaxed a little.

Before I could ask why he wouldn't take the offer, he continued, "I do not want to weaken you further."

Now it was my turn to scowl.

"That's not how this works," I told him sharply. "If you and I are… *mates*—" I struggled with the word. "—and depend on each other, then we both need to be at our best. You worry about me, and I worry about you. That's how it's going to be. So, let's work together. Bite me, and I'll sleep. We'll both feel better, okay? Besides, I love it when you bite me."

Rylan inhaled swiftly, and his eyes turned red. He leaned forward and captured my mouth with his. He rolled on top of me and slipped his tongue into my mouth. I moaned as my body came alive. How I had any energy left was beyond me, but my body craved Rylan's touch. I warmed under his hands. I ground my pelvis against him, and my heart skipped a beat as I found him hard. I slipped my hands under his shirt and teased his nipples. Rylan slipped his hand under the band of my sweatpants. When his fingers found my clit, I cried out.

"Say you are my mate again," Rylan growled as he pulled away from my mouth to kiss my jaw.

My chuckle sounded husky. Oh, so he liked hearing that from me, huh? Rylan's fingers slipped further downwards, and he inserted two into me. I cried out again. Jesus, he had slid in so easily.

"Gods, Mae," Rylan muttered. "So wet."

My mind turned to mush as pleasure began to build. With his thumb, he circled my clit, and his two fingers stroked my internal walls. I moaned and tilted my head back into my pillow. Rylan leaned down and trailed kisses down my throat.

"Say it," he hissed, and his hand stopped its ministrations.

"You are my sexy as sin, big, strong Guardian mate," I groaned and spread my legs further apart.

The growl that came from Rylan was so deep and animalistic it brought me closer to the orgasm that was building. His fingers began to work their magic again, and I cried out his name. Suddenly, his teeth sunk into me. The flash of pain turned into such intense pleasure that it radiated throughout every nerve ending in my body, and my orgasm peaked faster than I could imagine. My cry turned into whimpers as my orgasm intensified instead of subsiding.

Rylan drank from me, heavily, and I loved every moment of it. When he finished feeding, he lapped at his teeth marks, effectively closing them. Rylan withdrew his hand from me and looked down into my eyes. The love I saw twinkling in his eyes caused my heart to beat wildly in my chest.

"Mae, you will sleep until tomorrow morning. You will not have nightmares, and if at any time you may wake, you should not become alarmed. Sleep, now."

I didn't have time to balk in alarm when I realized what he was doing. I could feel the mental *push* as if he had thrown a blanket over my consciousness. My eyelids shut of their own accord, and I felt myself slip into unconsciousness.

When I awoke in the morning, light was flooding into the room from the French doors. There was a strong pressure pushing outwards under my overly warm skin, and my heartbeat felt uncomfortably fast in my chest. Blinking the sleep out of my eyes, I glanced down and saw the glowing under my skin was brighter than ever. With a peek under my shirt, I could see my whole body continued to glow.

I rubbed my arms hoping to lessen the pressure. Is this what a balloon with too much air felt like? As my mind began to wake up, I looked around the room. What time was it? When had I gone to sleep? Rylan's glowing red eyes came to mind, and suddenly, I remembered.

I gasped and looked over to where Rylan usually lay but found the bed empty. He had hypnotized me! Part of me was scared. I mean, who wanted to have no control over themselves? But that fear wasn't as great as I thought it would be. I trusted Rylan, and I had asked him to do it. With a sigh, I threw the covers off me and swung my legs out of bed.

As my feet touched the floor, the door opened, and Rylan strolled in. He was wearing fresh clothes, and his hair was wet from a shower. The warm grin that spread across his face sent my already racing heart into overdrive. He came over to the bed and kissed me.

"Good morning. How do you feel?" he asked.

His eyes trailed over my face and then down my body. A flash of worry clouded his gaze, but he blinked and the concern disappeared.

"Refreshed, thank you," I said with a smile.

"Good." He took my hand and pulled me onto my feet. "We leave in an hour. Arthur has made transportation and lodging arrangements."

"Where exactly are we going?"

"According to the location Zyroe showed you, it looks like whoever is behind this will be trying to open the gates around Jasper National Park in Alberta, Canada. We have found lodging nearby where we will take shelter while we investigate the area."

"I don't have my passport or the proper clothes, and I…" I looked down at my arms. "I can't go out in public looking like this."

I couldn't imagine what my face looked like.

"Do not worry about your passport or clothes. Everything has been taken care of." He ran his hands down my arms. "Before we leave, Jasmine would like to examine you. It will not be like before. She will use modern technology," he added when I frowned.

I nodded. "Give me twenty minutes, and then I'll go find Jasmine."

"I will make you breakfast as you get ready."

With that, he kissed my forehead and left the room. My shower was quick, and I dressed even faster. I donned a light t-shirt and jeans but grabbed a brand-new pullover and put it on to cover my arms. I couldn't stare at the glowing veins all day, and

I was sure the Guardians needed me to be as discreet as possible once we left here. A glance in the mirror let me know that the veins around my eyes and mouth were glowing, and my irises were still violet. I'd need to get a hat and sunglasses somewhere.

As I got ready, I found myself having to pause to take a steadying breath. My heartbeat grew uncomfortable as it continued to flutter unusually fast. I felt like I had gone for a jog even though I was moving at a snail's pace. Trying to push down the rising concern, I left the room and headed downstairs.

Waiting for me was a plate of hot pancakes, hard-boiled eggs, and a bowl of fruit. My mouth watered, and my stomached growled. I kissed Rylan on the cheek before I devoured the meal without assistance. I hadn't needed help eating the wings and pizza last night either. I guessed I had to take the little victories as they came. Just as I finished up, Arthur walked into the room with a duffle bag over his shoulder. Jasmine came up behind him, her expression unreadable.

"Good morning, Mae," Arthur greeted with a nod. His gaze trailed over my face and my body. "How are you feeling?"

"Alright, considering everything," I said, shifting uncomfortably under his gaze.

"Good," Arthur turned to Rylan and said, "We are nearly ready to go."

Jasmine walked over to stand next to me and asked, "If you are done, would you come downstairs with me? The way your power is now freely moving through your body is concerning to me. I would like to make sure your vitals are stable and your health is not being affected by this new energy running through it."

I nodded. I got up and followed her out of the kitchen to the secret door down the hallway. She scanned her eye, the door opened, and I followed her down the stairs. We walked into the room where Rylan had once stitched me up. That moment together seemed so far away now. Jasmine patted the hospital bed, indicating for me to come over and sit. I did as I was instructed.

"Mae, this room is magicked to keep power suppressed. How do you feel?" Jasmine asked, her voice soft.

Ah, that was why when Rylan had cleaned my wound with fairy tears the room hadn't collapsed on us. My power had been stifled. Jasmine looked over my body, taking in the glow. I realized she was waiting for an answer, and I cleared my throat.

"Uncomfortable."

The pressure had increased the moment I walked into the room. My heart was fluttering harder now than before, and it was causing me to sweat. Jasmine nodded as if she had known the answer already. She took my hand, and I looked into her eyes.

"I am going to try to enter your body again," she said. When I opened my mouth to protest, she held up her other hand to stop me. "I know that I promised Rylan that I would use human methods to monitor your vitals, but Rylan was able to get to your memories. If he can enter safely, so can I. Your body and power are reacting much differently now."

It would be faster, and I needed to know what was going on inside me. Maybe now she could see how I could pull my power back or control it. I nodded, and she gave me a half-smile that didn't reach her eyes. Her brown eyes shifted, turning red, and then I felt her. I braced myself for my body to rebel against the new presence like it had before, but Jasmine had been right. Nothing happened.

I relaxed once I realized everything was going well and let Jasmine do her examination. It took less time than before; she was back in her body in under ten minutes. She blinked as she came to. Her red eyes shifted back to brown as she turned to pace away from me. She ran her fingers through her dark hair.

"Is everything alright?" I asked.

Jasmine didn't stop pacing nor did she answer me right away. She did four laps around the small room before finally coming to a stop in front of me. She reached up and touched my cheek softly.

"Your power, as we assumed, has overridden any traces of witch blood in your system. You are certainly a child of a god…" Her voice trailed off, and she looked away, appearing dazed. She shook her head and looked back at me. "Your power seems much more stable now that it is free to move throughout you. It is coursing through your veins burning energy that your body does not have, Mae. Your heart and your other organs are trying to compensate, but this state your body is in… It will not last."

My breakfast suddenly felt too heavy in my stomach.

"Mae, your body… It could give out much sooner than I had originally thought if we do not figure out how to help you. Have you tried to use your power since we have been home?"

I shook my head.

"I think if we give your power somewhere to go other than through you, it may help slow down the breakdown happening in your system. We leave soon, but when we arrive at our new location, we need to try to let you blow off some of that steam."

My head bobbed up and down. The movement felt jerky, but I was too busy struggling to wrap my head around what she was saying. Jasmine had told me before that I was dying; at the time, it was nothing new. But now? Now I had someone worth living for. Rylan's face appeared in my head. My fluttering heart twisted painfully. With the threat of gods returning and my body giving out on me, it did not appear we were going to have much of a future together. I looked up at Jasmine.

"We should get ready to leave," I muttered

Jasmine gazed at my expression, searching for something in my face.

"We need to get you a hat and some sunglasses," she muttered, echoing my thoughts from earlier. She stepped away from me.

"Jasmine," I said, sliding off the hospital bed. "I know we have a lot on our plates, but now that I have *some* control over this power, maybe I can find a way to break the spell before… Well, before everything happens. I'll work as hard as I can to help you."

Jasmine smiled half-heartedly. She gave me a short hug before we left the room and headed back upstairs. I headed back to my room where I grabbed the duffle bag that I had brought to Salisbury and shoved a few of the brand-new clothes that Rylan had ordered for me into it. I grabbed my purse but hesitated when I reached for my laptop.

Today was the first day of classes.

They were online, so I could probably just pull up the video lectures wherever we were headed, but my desire to go back to school had been pushed far down on my list of things to do. I tried not to feel disappointed; obviously trying to save the world before I died was the most important thing to worry about. But going back to school had meant I was gaining some type of control in my life. Now, any sense of control I felt about my future was gone. I pushed down the emotions that tightened my throat and grabbed my laptop.

Downstairs, Rylan was waiting for me. He had a plain black baseball cap and a pair of sunglasses in his hands. When I came to stand next to him, he took the duffle bag from me, and I took the accessories out of his hands. With a grimace, I pulled the cap on but hung the sunglasses on the collar of my hoodie. I didn't want to wear them now. I'd hide the monster when we were around others.

"Do you need to grab anything else?" Rylan asked.

I didn't look directly at him; Jasmine's revelation was too fresh. While I worked hard to keep my expression neutral, I knew he would see the fear in my eyes.

"No, I'm good. Where is everyone else?"

"Jasmine is gathering the rest of her things and will be out momentarily. Arthur is waiting outside."

With a nod, I followed Rylan out of the front door and down the front steps. Arthur strolled up to us, his face twisted in anger, his cell phone curled in his fist. His blazing red eyes bore into Rylan as he approached.

"Rylan, we have a situation. It appears Zein's death was not a suicide."

Rylan froze mid-step. Being slightly behind him, I bumped into his solid frame.

"Gabriel Newton called; he went to investigate Zein's death. He said the suicide note had a faint trace of someone else's blood on it. When he got to the house, he said it looked like a massacre. Whoever did this was sloppy. Gabriel said there's more, and he's sending pictures as we speak."

I grabbed Rylan's arm and looked up at him. His red eyes were glowing, his fangs had lengthened, and the tension in his body told me his wings were near. Before I could say anything, Arthur's cell phone vibrated. He pulled up whatever message Gabriel had sent and stiffened. Arthur looked up, his face grave, and looked from me to Rylan.

"What is it?" Rylan asked through gritted teeth.

Instead of telling us, Arthur closed the distance between the three of us and showed us the picture Gabriel sent. The picture had been taken inside of a study. A bookshelf was pushed over, and there was a large pool of blood on the hardwood floor. But in the center of the picture was something written in blood on the wallpaper. The letters were large, but the writing was in a language I had never seen before. Above the writing was a pair of black feathered wings that had been ripped from the back of a Guardian.

I gasped and recoiled from the phone, dropping my hand from Rylan's arm and took a step back.

"What does the writing say?" I asked, my voice a strained whisper.

After a moment of shocked silence, Arthur answered, "*We shall serve Them again.*"

Arthur and Rylan exchanged glances; the tension rising between them was stifling. My heart slammed against my chest. Rylan's friend had been *murdered*. It was evident from the bloody crime scene that the pain Zein had suffered must have been nothing short of torture. My stomach tightened. I thought I was going to hurl. I took another step away, hoping I wouldn't throw up on anyone.

Behind me, I heard Jasmine's soft footsteps descending the stairs. She paused to stand next to me and glanced at the phone. Her eyes bulged, and she glanced at Arthur. There was a soft buzzing in my head and then Jasmine snarled.

"Who could have done this?" she demanded, her voice a shriek of anger. "Zein was a great warrior!"

"Gabriel Newton is gathering information from the scene as we speak. He said he will contact me once he has taken care of the mess," Arthur told her.

"We need to leave, now," Rylan snapped.

He grabbed my arm and almost dragged me to the SUV. He opened the door, and I climbed into the backseat. He threw my stuff in the trunk and did the same with Jasmine's belongings as she came over to the car. This time Jasmine sat in the driver's seat, and Arthur climbed into the passenger side. Rylan joined me in the back, and when we were all settled, Jasmine floored it. I glanced over my shoulder at the beautiful plantation manor that had briefly been my home and wondered if I would ever see it again.

I turned back in my seat, and my gaze shifted between the three Guardians. The anxiety in the car was at an all-time high. There was buzzing in my head, and it lasted a few minutes before stopping. Rylan took my hand, brought it to his mouth, and kissed the inside of my wrist. I looked over at him and met his gaze. I was sure he wanted me to see the reassurance that he was projecting. I could almost hear his promise that he would keep me safe and everything was okay.

But behind those red eyes, I saw the panic. Jasmine must have told him about her findings. We all had so much more to deal with now than worrying about my own timeline. First, we had to find out if someone was trying to open the gate between realms. Second, if there was a threat, we had to figure out who was behind it and how to stop them. All while trying to convince all the other Guardians that I was not a threat when we called them in for backup. And now, there was a Guardian murderer on the loose who we needed to stop.

My death was at the bottom of the list of things to worry about. I squeezed Rylan's hand, leaned forward, and kissed his cheek.

When I pulled away, I said loudly enough for everyone to hear, "We'll figure out what the hell is going on in Canada, and then when we're done, we'll get revenge for your friend. In the meantime, we're all going to be alright. We're family now, and we'll keep an eye on each other, okay?"

Each family member nodded in agreement. With that, I leaned back in my seat and braced myself for what was in store for us when we arrived in Alberta, Canada.

To Be Continued...

Dear Readers

I sincerely hope you all have enjoyed Song of Desolation, book one in the Ballads of Mae series. I love to hear from readers so let me know what you think of this book by going online and leaving a review.

While you're at it sign up for my monthly newsletter where you will be the first to hear about current works in progress, release dates for new books and series, and get exclusive sneak peeks and enjoy deleted scenes. You will also be privy to discounts, promotional giveaways, and more. Go to my website at: www.salemcrossauthor.com and sign up today.

Turn the page for an exclusive sneak peek into book two in the Ballads of Mae series: *Song of Resurgence*

SONG OF RESURGENCE

BALLADS OF MAE
BOOK TWO

SALEM CROSS

Chapter One

RYLAN

Distressed moans broke the silence that blanketed the room. They were expected. It had been two hours since Mae had fallen asleep, which meant that at any moment, she would wake again. Her body tensed in my arms and she began to shake. I pulled her tight against my chest. Blazing heat flared through my veins, and the darkness of our bedroom turned to red.

I wanted the blood of the witch and the god who had done this to my mate. I had no idea how to kill a god, but I certainly had a few ideas of how to rid this world of Autumn; Mae's mother. The witch had made a deal with the enemy, and she would pay. It would be a joy to watch the life drain from Autumn's eyes after I ripped her head off with my bare hands, or I could use my fangs to behead the witch. . . it would be a clean cut that way. Alternatively, I could rip each limb from her body. If I did that, it would prolong her death. I could almost hear her screams of agony as I imagined removing each appendage. A cruel smile tugged at the corner of my lips as I thought about those agonizing screams.

It was Mae's screams, though, that paused my murderous thoughts. My heart twisted in agony at my mate's distress, and red hate that had filled room vanished.

"Shh, you are safe Mae," I whispered into her wild curls. I could hear her heartbeat drumming rapidly in her chest.

"Rylan." My name on her lips sounded reverent.

The half of my soul I still carried reached out for her. I closed my eyes and breathed in her sweet scent: a mix of vanilla and honey.

"I am here, Mae," I assured her.

I pressed my lips against her forehead. *I will always be here for you.*

The power coursing just underneath her skin surged forward, and light shot through her veins in a random display of power. It flashed like lightning across her arms, legs, and chest. I ran my hand over her arm, trying to soothe her.

I waited for her power to leak.

Before her trip to the Pocket, her power would have come crashing out. I braced myself, ready to capture it, ready to take it within me and pull more away from her. It needed to happen. It would give her some peace before it began to build again.

But the leak did not happen.

She hadn't expelled any of her power since she had returned two days ago. Instead, it festered within her. That power was building in strength as it drew energy from her body, and it was slowly killing her. My mate thought she was sparing me by hiding her pain as if I wouldn't notice the way her thumbs absentmindedly caressed the thick scars around her wrists where her cursed bracelets had once sat. How could she believe I wouldn't notice the shallowness of her breath or her ever-increasing heart rate?

Mae relaxed and let out a long sigh. Her hand slid down my chest before stopping right below my navel. Her fingers teased the trail of hair there. Instantly, my dick stiffened. We had made love three times this night, but the desire to bury myself in my mate again was overpowering. My arousal was so intense that I almost rolled Mae onto her back to devour her right then and there.

But that was not what she needed right now.

Mae's body was struggling to keep up with the power her father had given her. It was eating away at her. She needed to sleep. Most importantly, she needed to let some of this power go.

Hopefully, we would be able to do that later today when we got to our destination. Her health and wellbeing were my upmost concern. My need to be buried inside Mae could be put on the backburner.

Mae's breathing slowed, and her hand went limp on my stomach as she drifted back to sleep. I took it and held it in my own. Her heart continued to flutter far too fast. My own heart squeezed painfully in my chest. *Don't give up.* My throat tightened as did my grip on Mae's hand. She shifted uncomfortably in her sleep, and I relaxed my hold on her, afraid she would awaken.

I squeezed my eyes shut tight. How was I going to help her? I wanted to whisk Mae away to hide her from everyone. I could easily buy a private island where it would only be the two of us and the sun. I wished I could do that. If I could, I would rip this toxic power out of her, stripping her down until she was only a half-witch. I would satisfy her every need and want, keeping her all to myself. . . and safe. I couldn't lose her.

Rage. Desire. Fear.

Each emotion was so new, so raw, that they consumed me, twisting my thoughts into irrational playthings. Before Mae, I had no emotions. Every thought I had was logical, precise, and had a point. The only reason that I would have ever second-guessed myself was the event of a superior idea. Now, I questioned every move I made.

We were on our way to a small, remote area just north of Jasper National Park in Alberta, Canada. We would station ourselves there for the next two weeks while Arthur House, Jasmine Sing, and I patrolled the south end of the park. That was where Zyroe and Autumn had shown Mae the gates would open that would allow the demi-gods to return to this realm. The place we were staying was remote enough to keep Mae away from any danger that might be present in the south end of the park. She would be safe.

Well. . . relatively safe.

If there was someone out there trying to open the gates to bring back the gods, they would not be alone. They would have minions to help them. If our foe somehow found out we were there to stop them, they might be able to outnumber and overwhelm us. There would be traps set all around to make sure no one got close to their lair. It could be assumed that someone so dastardly was probably also tampering with dark magic, which was unpredictable and deadly. Worst case scenario, our foe could find out about Mae and her connection to the gods, making her a target.

It was a risk bringing Mae here. I knew it, Arthur and Jasmine knew it, and I knew deep down that despite her insistence of coming, Mae knew it too. But what was the alternative? I couldn't leave her behind. Knowing how stubborn Mae White was, she would have just found a way here herself. Her experience with Autumn and Zyroe had shaken her enough that she needed to confirm for herself that nothing was going on here.

With her growing power, she was a beacon for spider demons. They had already risked attacking her twice while in my care. Other supernatural creatures were bound to find her eventually, and it would pull her into a spotlight none of us wanted for her. Worse yet, another Guardian would inevitably stumble upon Mae. The thought sent a chill down my spine.

I could not be apart from my mate. She was the air I breathed and the reason my heart kept beating. She was the only reason I cared about what happened to the world. If she ceased to exist, then the world would burn.

I hated putting her safety at risk. If we stumbled upon any evidence that Autumn and Zyroe were right about their prediction, we would have to call in other Guardians. More Guardians meant there would be more wings in the air to help find our culprit, but it also meant that we would be placing Mae in even more danger. They would see her as a child of a god, making her one of our mortal enemies. They would try to kill her. Or worse, they would covet her. With her ability to temporarily lift our curse, some of them would see her as the ultimate prize. Some would try to take her from me. My vision went red at the very thought of it.

I took a deep breath and stared up at the ceiling. Emotions. They made things much more complicated. I stayed like that for the rest of the night, staring up at the ceiling, adrift in the waves of these new feelings inside of me.

Sunrays from the early morning light broke through the curtains just as Mae's screams began again. I held her until her fear subsided. She sat up. Her curly hair tumbled around her face, falling down past her shoulders. She turned her violet gaze upon me, and my dick stiffened. Before she had been kidnapped, her power had only lit up under her skin when it was ready to emerge. But for the past two days now, the glow had remained. I knew she hated and feared it. Violet light streaked through her face, down her neck, and throughout her body. She thought she was a monster. I didn't think anyone could be more wrong about themselves.

I had lived thousands of lives, and seen hundreds upon thousands of women across the world. I had seen the richest of women in the finest of clothes. I had witnessed the poorest of women in rags covered in filth. There had been obese, skinny, fragile, old, and young women in my life. I had met what most had called beautiful, and maybe they had been. But none compared to the woman sitting next to me now. Even tired and underweight, she was gorgeous.

"I'm sorry, I probably kept you up all night," she said softly as her mouth turned downwards.

I sighed. Of course she was upset that she thought she had disturbed me. Her wellbeing was never her first thought. She didn't know that I could go weeks without sleep.

"You should have let me help you."

Mae's frown deepened. She hated the idea. She was scared that Guardians had the ability to compel someone against their will. Mae had ultimately allowed me to compel her to sleep when she had returned from the Pocket, but that was only if I agreed to eat. She was always putting others before herself. Yesterday, we had traveled from Salisbury, Georgia to Toronto, Ontario, and then to Edmonton, Alberta. From there, we drove to just outside Edmonton. Arthur and Jasmine had continued to the final destination to scan the area, while Mae and I had stayed in a house I was renting. Mae had been quiet for most of the trip. We all had. But I saw her pain, I saw the fatigue. When I had brought up the idea to compel her to sleep, she had rebelled. She wanted to overcome the nightmares on her own. But she didn't have to do this on her own.

Suddenly, Mae's frown flipped upwards. Her salacious smile and bright violet eyes made my erection grow harder.

"How about I make it up to you?" she offered.

She reached down and tugged the shirt she was wearing, one of mine, over her head. She was a petite woman, and her frame was too thin from not being able to eat often, but even underweight she maintained full breasts and a fantastic ass. Her flawless skin was naturally sun-kissed and soft, and her lips. . . they were perfect, just like the rest of her.

How did I get so lucky?

<u>*Ballads of Mae Series*</u>
Song of Desolation
Song of Resurgence (Release Date: Fall 2020)
Song of Transcendence (Release Date: Spring 2021)

About the Author

Salem Cross is an avid writer who finds inspiration for her stories in even the smallest details in her life. She lives on the coast of North Carolina where you will either find her lounging on the beach or curled up with her three dogs on the couch while she reads a good book. She enjoys travelling, running, and woodworking. Visit her website at www.salemcrossauthor.com to find out more about Salem Cross.